A

NATURAL
HISTORY
OF
HELL

Also by Jeffrey Ford

Vanitas
The Physiognomy
Memoranda
The Beyond
The Fantasy Writer's Assistant
The Portrait of Mrs. Charbuque
The Girl in the Glass
The Cosmology of the Wider World
The Empire of Ice Cream
The Shadow Year
The Drowned Life
Crackpot Palace

A NATURAL HISTORY OF HELL

STORIES

JEFFREY FORD

Small Beer Press
Easthampton, MA

A Natural History of Hell: Stories copyright © 2016 by Jeffrey Ford (well-builtcity.com). All rights reserved. Page 282 is an extension of the copyright page.

Small Beer Press
150 Pleasant Street #306
Easthampton, MA 01027
smallbeerpress.com
weightlessbooks.com
info@smallbeerpress.com

Distributed to the trade by Consortium.

Library of Congress Cataloging-in-Publication Data

Names: Ford, Jeffrey, 1955- author.
Title: A natural history of hell : stories / Jeffrey Ford.
Description: First edition. | Easthampton, MA : Small Beer Press, [2016]
Identifiers: LCCN 2015046490 (print) | LCCN 2015050550 (ebook) | ISBN
  9781618731180 (softcover) | ISBN 9781618731197 (ebook) | ISBN
  9781618731197 ()
Subjects: | BISAC: FICTION / Fantasy / Short Stories. | FICTION / Short
  Stories (single author). | FICTION / Literary. | FICTION / Fantasy /
  Contemporary. | GSAFD: Fantasy fiction. | Occult fiction.
Classification: LCC PS3556.O6997 A6 2016 (print) | LCC PS3556.O6997 (ebook) |
  DDC 813/.54--dc23
LC record available at http://lccn.loc.gov/2015046490

First edition 1 2 3 4 5 6 7 8 9

Set in Minion 12 pt.
Cover illustration © 2015 by Jeffrey Alan Love (jeffreyalanlove.com).

Printed on 50# Natures Natural 30% PCR recycled paper by the Maple Press in York, PA.

Natural Histories

For Lynn, Derek, Jack & Brianna with all my love.

The Blameless

They were sitting at their respective ends of the couch, drinking coffee. He was telling her about a cucumber salad he'd made a few days earlier, and she was going through the day's mail, half listening. In the midst of him reeling off his newly invented recipe, she held up a square envelope and set her coffee down on the table next to her.

"A wedding invitation?" she said, cutting him off.

"Who's it from?"

"The people up the street."

"Which ones?"

"The Crorys."

"I have no idea," he said.

"Three doors down and on the other side. Remember, we met them at Canoe Carnival. Ina's a secretary at the high school and he's some kind of engineer." She opened the envelope and took out a card.

"Who's getting married?"

"It's for their daughter, Grace."

"She's not even out of high school, I don't think."

"It's not a wedding. It's an invitation to her exorcism."

He laughed. "Get outa here."

"'Dear Tom and Helen, we hope that you will be able to attend our daughter Grace's Spring Exorcism' . . . It's at their

1

house on Sunday, May 7th at 7:00 p.m. Two weeks from tomorrow."

"What?"

"This is big now, exorcism," she said. "Haven't you heard about it?"

"No."

"Yeah, people are getting their kids exorcised for whatever ails them."

"What do you mean?" he said.

"You know, if your kid doesn't listen, is screwing up in school, hanging with knuckleheads."

"You mean sex, drugs, and rock and roll?"

"Basically. I heard it on NPR. A few evangelical groups started and then it spread. Now people who aren't even religious are getting it done. It costs like a grand to have your kid spring-cleaned."

"That's crazy."

"Which is why we should go. I want to check it out."

"Are you serious?"

"It'll be interesting and we can meet some people."

"I have zero interest."

"You're going," she said. "You were just sitting here five minutes ago carrying on about some fuckin' cucumber salad. You need to get out of the house."

At 6:30 on May 7th, she put on a turquoise dress, matching shoes, and jewelry. She told Tom that she tried to pick a spring color. He dressed in a black T-shirt and jeans, and she said, "It's not a funeral, you know." He said, "We'll represent cosmic light and darkness." She shook her head, sighed, and left the room. He changed his shirt.

It was raining, so they took the umbrella. Helen held it over both of them. As they made their way up the street, she pointed out through the dusk that the daffodils and lilacs were budding. Tom noticed that the lawns were going green. There was a softness to the breeze. The streetlight reflected a sheen off the wet asphalt, and the scent of worms was everywhere.

There were cars parked in front of the Crory's house, on both sides of the street. As they approached, they saw a man and a woman on the doorstep. He was ringing the bell.

"That's Jake and Alice," said Helen.

"It's not too late to go home," Tom said.

"Go ahead," she told him. "I'll go by myself."

"Say the devil shows up?"

"The invitation says there'll be punch and finger sandwiches."

"I hope they appreciate that I wore my pink, button shirt."

"How could they not?"

A middle-aged blonde woman answered the door. "So glad you could make it," she said in a high-pitched voice laced with gin. Her dress was the same color pink as Tom's shirt.

"Hi, Ina," said Helen. "You must be pretty excited."

"Well," she said, "yes, but we need to keep a lid on it. You know, to retain the religious dignity of things."

"Absolutely," said Tom.

When they entered the living room, everyone turned and stared. After eyeing Tom and Helen up and down, a few neighbors nodded and waved and turned back to their conversations. Helen's friend, Alice, who was also a nursing administrator, came over and said hello. They worked at different local hospitals, but they knew all the same people. In an instant they were off on a conversation about work. Tom spotted a guy holding a beer, and went in search of.

In the kitchen, he found a cooler and his ex-assistant soccer coach, Bill Stewart. The two had bonded years earlier through losing seasons over the fact that neither of them had ever played or knew anything about soccer. Tom chose a can of Rolling Rock from the cooler, opened it, and looked quickly over his shoulder to make sure they were alone. "Ready for the exorcism?" he asked.

Bill leaned against the sink, arms folded across his chest, beer in his right hand. "I can deal with religion, but this is like some kind of *Children of the Corn* shit," he said.

Tom laughed.

Bill took a drink of beer and said, "You know, with these people, everything's an infraction. If you sneeze and fart at the same time, you're cut out of the Rapture."

Tom milled around, had a few beers, and checked in with Helen, who was talking baseball with Oshea, the owner of the service station. Nothing seemed pressing, so he sat down in a chair at the end of the food table and watched the goings on. Right next to him he was surprised to find a bowl of cucumber salad. He had a small plate. "Better than mine," he thought. While he ate, snatches of conversation popped out of the surrounding storm of voices. From one of them, he learned that when the cashier at the pizza place had her kid exorcised there was shotgun vomiting and bed-shaking to beat the band. From another he overheard that there was now a 24-hour exorcist service in the tri-state area.

"The devil's busy," thought Tom. And then Grace made her entrance. She was wearing what looked like a young girl's communion dress, all white, sleeveless, satin and crinoline, with a pair of white, patent-leather shoes. Her brown hair was twisted into an intricate single braid down her back, and on top of her head rested a wreath of tiny white and violet flowers. How different she looked to Tom compared to the last he'd seen her.

He'd been driving by the recycle center downtown around Christmas time and noticed a tall, lanky kid jumping up and down and flapping his arms. He realized it was the Zecks' son, from around the corner. Morrison was his name. As Tom passed, he saw the reason for the goofball antics. The Crory girl was sitting on a low wall, rocking back and forth, laughing. She had a cigarette going; her hair hung loose. Her eyeliner and mascara were copious and black. Tom remembered that the sight of them had made him smile.

Unlike that winter day, she now seemed embarrassed, and her face was scrubbed clean and shone like a polished apple. He hardly recognized her. She was pretending to be calm like a bride on her wedding day. In less than a second, a crowd drew around her. Tom heard Helen whispering in his ear, "Slow down on the beer." He turned and she was standing next to his chair. "I'm just trying to retain the religious dignity of things," he told her.

"Grace looks beautiful, doesn't she?"

"Almost as lovely as you."

She lightly smacked him in the back of the head.

He pointed to the cucumber salad and they laughed.

"You know," Tom said. "I see people giving her cards. Do they actually have, like, cards for this now?"

"I have one in my purse for her."

"What's it say?"

"*Congratulations On Your Exorcism.* I didn't go for the funny ones. It's very tasteful."

"How much are we giving her?"

"Fifty."

"Jeez, she'll clean up."

Helen went and got the card, and Tom stood. They slowly made their way toward the crowd of well-wishers. Before they could get anywhere close to Grace, though, Mr. Crory appeared. It was the first they'd seen of him. He stood stiff and smiling, dressed in a powder-blue pajama suit with bow tie.

"Escape from Hugh Hefner's closet," Helen said from the corner of her mouth.

"Dig the smoke-tinted circular lenses," said Tom.

There were visible beads of sweat on Crory's forehead. He said, "Ladies and gentlemen, friends and neighbors, the exorcist will be here any second. I ask that when he arrives you all back off to that side of the room, in front of the window. You must remain as quiet as possible throughout the exorcism. If you need to leave, please use the back door, which is through the kitchen. Ina and Grace and I want to thank you for joining us." Everybody applauded. When he was finished, he went down the hallway and returned with a cot, which he set up in front of the fireplace. The final touch was a puffy pillow the size of a cloud in a cream-colored pillowcase.

There was a loud knock at the door. Ina said, "It's him," and finished off the remainder of a martini. A rumble went through those assembled. Some smiled vaguely and the rest wore expressions of guilt.

"I wonder if I can take pictures?" said Helen, holding up her phone.

"Just leave the flash off. Who'll know?"

Ina led the exorcist into the living room. He was a short, heavy-set guy in a baggy black suit. Dark beard and hair going gray. Mr. Crory shook hands with him, and Ina gave him a hug and a kiss on the cheek. She then turned to the neighbors and said, "This is the Reverend Emanuel Kan. He's the High Holy Blameless from the local chapter of God's Church Before the Flood of Mankind." During the crowd's applause, Helen whispered, "Check those brows." Tom did. It was as if the reverend had half a handlebar mustache over each eye.

The Crorys backed away to join the crowd, and it was just Grace and Emanuel Kan. That name made Tom giddy and brought him to the very edge of laughing out loud. The reverend set his black bag down on the floor and took the girl's extended fingers in his hands. He looked into her eyes and said, "Are you ready now?" in a regional dialect, neither south nor north. She put on a very slight smile, and a tear ran down her cheek.

"Aww," said voices in the crowd. They were promptly shushed by Mr. Crory. Grace nodded to the reverend, and he released her hands. "I'm going to remove some evil spirits from you today employing Serenithy, the language in which angels dream, and then I'll bring to bear the righteous weapons of the Almighty, who has whispered to me through my eyes the number four. And so I will take a demon from your left eye, one from your right ear, one from your mouth, and then one from lower down. The last will be the most difficult, but you'll get through it. You're young and strong." Grace smiled and nodded, and then he took her fingertips again and led her to the cot.

"Starting to get creepy," said Helen.

Out of his black bag the Blameless one took a plastic bottle of water, a cigarette lighter, a pack of Marlboros, and an eight-inch hatpin. He set these items down on the seat of an empty chair, and then turned back to the cot. "Comfortable?" he asked Grace. She nodded. "You will soon be in a trance," he said. "Don't try to listen to what I'm saying. Instead, think of the sound of my voice as water, flowing upward into the land without worry." He turned to face the gathering, opened his mouth, and out came a string of gibberish, startling in its speed. More followed like blasts from an uzi. Tom heard somebody behind him ask quietly, "Is that Latin?"

He knew enough Latin to know it was instead just nonsense. Like bad scat singing. Phrases like "dippy doop" and "fa fa fa fa fa fa fa" were a giveaway. The reverend trod in tight circles, always turning his head so as to keep his imperious gaze trained on the crowd. Just when Tom was ready to slip out into the kitchen for a beer, Kan suddenly broke from his little circle with a move that became a slow, loopy dance. He was all over the place, back and forth, side to side, movement minus style and rhythm. At one point he bent his forearms in toward his chest and waved his elbows like a chicken. Through all of it, the gibberish poured forth.

"Ridiculous," said Helen.

"I've had enough, but you gotta get a shot of this guy before we go."

"I've got like a dozen of him already."

"Let's blow."

"OK," Helen said, but Grace opened her mouth and groaned in an echoing underground voice that was chilling. Tom moved closer to Helen and took her hand. The place was dead quiet. Even the reverend went silent. Another groan came. Her entire body was trembling, and one steel leg of the cot tapped a code on the hardwood floor.

Emanuel Kan lit a cigarette, picked up the hat pin, and addressed the crowd. "Watch closely," he said. "I am now going to evict from Grace's left eye a demon known as the Skitterby, Prince of Illicit Visions. This should go quickly now." He took a drag of the cigarette and held it in the corner of his mouth while walking backward toward the cot. He turned, leaned over the girl, and blew a stream of smoke into her face. Quick as a snake, his free hand shot out and it appeared he was pinching Grace's vacant left eye. As he slowly withdrew his pincered fingers, Tom and Helen and the rest noticed a bright blue blob, an amoebic form the size of a plum with wriggling almost-limbs and a pointy head trapped between the nails of his index finger and thumb. The Blameless let it squirm for a moment before stabbing it with the hatpin. The instant it was impaled, it shattered like a blue glass bubble.

"That was a trick, right?" said Tom.

"I think he's like a magician," said Helen.

"Looked pretty real for whatever it was."

A few people applauded, and Mr. Crory angrily shushed them. Emanuel Kan removed the cigarette from his lips and took a slight bow. "That was easy enough," he said. "Next I will extract the mouth demon, Verbopolis, and the ear demon, Waxion. In one swift eviction. I will take them both out through the mouth. Not too many exorcists can perform this double demon pull. Look for a red figure and a green figure." He put the cigarette back in his mouth and took a deep drag. As he approached Grace, she gave a pitiful groan and belched. He swept low and blew smoke down her throat.

His arm shot out, and those pinching fingers entered her open mouth. His wrist twitched once, and he withdrew two more writhing blobs. Their colors were brilliant. The red one growled and the green wore a jellified smile. "Verbopolis and Waxion, ladies and gentleman," said the reverend. He jabbed the needle through both at once, and they burst into Christmas glitter. "We will now have a fifteen-minute intermission before we descend into the lair of Moxioton."

Everyone in the living room headed for the kitchen. Ina was already there, dashing off a martini. Tom and Helen got beers and then stepped outside on the patio, where there was an awning and two chairs. The light rain tapped above them.

"Psyched for the lair of Moxioton?" said Tom.

"The whole thing's disturbing."

"You wanna split?"

Helen took a drink and shook her head. "No. I'm going to go back in there and watch, and if something crosses the line, I'm going to call the cops."

"What line?"

"My line," she said.

"How's he doing those little creatures?"

"I don't know. Instantly inflating balloons?"

"Is that a real thing, instantly inflating balloons?"

"I don't know," said Helen. "I'm a product of the Age of Reason, though," she said.

"I'm with you."

"All I know is we're getting old and the world is weird," said Helen.

"Fucked up," said Tom and put his arm around her.

Tom and Helen maneuvered their way back through the crowded kitchen. Words of bewilderment and awe were in the air. Ina was dashing off a martini. Jake was darting his pinched fingers at Alice's mouth. She was giving him a look of disgust. In the shadowy corner of the dining room, Bill Stewart was asleep in a chair, his arms folded across his chest. They made it back to the living room and took a spot a little closer to the fireplace. Grace was still intermittently groaning, her stare still blank. The crowd soon came in from the kitchen. Crory lectured about silence, and the room quieted down. Everybody heard a toilet flush, and, after, the footsteps of the Blameless approaching from the hall.

His first order of business was to check on Grace's condition. He spoke his gibberish to her for a few seconds, and she panted. "She needs to get heated up," the reverend said over his shoulder to the crowd. He danced erratic for a dozen steps, stopped only a few feet from Tom and Helen, and spoke. "Moxioton, The Granee Champio of negative entities," he said. "This spirit of destruction, spirit of grief, is an aggregate of Grace's sins, both real and imagined by herself and others. A powerful demon that once removed will leave her feeling five pounds lighter."

"My mind's reeling with scenarios of what's about to happen. None of them good," said Tom, leaning down over Helen. He looked up and saw Crory glaring at him. Tom gave him a wave and put his finger to his lips. Crory shook his head in disappointment. Helen caught sight of the exchange and said, "What a Nazi." Meanwhile, the reverend again took to dancing and spitting out gibberish. Grace suddenly shrieked, and the crowd jumped and murmured. She shuddered, and the cot banged against the floor.

"OK, OK," said Emanuel Kan, and stood still, breathing heavily from the exertion of his pathetic waltz. "What's about to happen is somewhat dangerous. So please remain calm and still. The creature I'm about to expose is frightening, but do not cry out or he could possibly be drawn to you." He walked over to his black bag, leaned down, and retrieved a gleaming 9mm pistol from it. "I've found a hatpin doesn't quite do it."

"Whoa," somebody said in the crowd, and a half-dozen people headed for the back door. "Yes, that's it," said the reverend. "Let those without faith in the Almighty flee his judgment." Tom looked down at Helen. She looked up at him. Without speaking, they decided to stay. Kan stood and walked in front of Grace, facing the crowd. She was having a pitiful time of it, bouncing against the cot, crying out. "The demon knows I'm coming for him. And now I will invite the young woman's father to join me and read off a list of her sins. And the mother will step forward and remove an article of her clothing so that I might proceed." He waved the parents out of the crowd with the muzzle of the gun and then put the weapon on the chair with his other tools.

Crory and Ina stepped forward. He reached into the pocket of his jacket and brought out a pink 3X5 index card. She had tears streaming down her face, smearing her makeup, and held onto his right arm with a trembling hand. She wove to and fro, obviously drunk. Her husband adjusted his glasses, cocked his big head forward, and read in a strained voice.

"Our daughter, Grace, has lost her way, fallen into temptation under the influence of evil. Here are the sins we are conscious of. 1) Pleasuring herself. 2) Partaking of the pernicious weed. 3) Drinking alcohol. 4) Consorting with atheists. 5) She is ten pounds overweight. 6) Painting her face and wearing suggestive clothing." When he was finished, he assumed a solemn air, folded the paper twice, and returned it to his pocket.

"With the exception of the last one," Tom whispered, "that's like a normal day for me." Helen stuck her index finger into his belly. "Try twenty pounds overweight," she said.

"I just want my baby back," cried Ina. She looked wrung out, ready to drop over.

"Poor thing," said Helen.

Crory returned to his spot in the crowd. The reverend ushered Ina to the cot. He leaned over the writhing girl, put his open palms less than an inch from her forehead, and moved them slowly around like he was polishing a car. He continued with this motion down the length of her body, very nearly but not touching her throat, her breasts, her stomach. He spent a long time conjuring above her crotch, and then swept the rest of the way to her feet. Ina stepped over then and removed Grace's right shoe. In the act of pulling it off, she staggered, and the reverend caught her. He motioned to Crory and said, "Please, take care of this." Crory emerged from the crowd to lead his wife away.

"That's right, ladies and gentlemen, the big toe," said the Blameless. "The seat of Moxioton's rule. You can't walk straight without a big toe, and the Almighty wants this young woman to walk straight." He went quickly to the chair, took up his cigarettes and lit one, keeping it in the corner of his mouth. He threw the pack down and grabbed the gun, holding it at the ready in his right hand. Back at the cot, he blew smoke rings onto Grace's big toe. He wiggled the fingers of his left hand all around Moxioton's lair. "Stand back now," he yelled. The girl was fish flopping on the cot, sweating, groaning, shrieking, letting off snatches of her own gibberish.

The reverend's pinching fingers shot out and pincered something just beneath the curve of the toe nail. He planted his feet and pulled back, and his pose made it obvious there was a struggle going on. Slowly, he extracted what looked like a khaki-colored blob. He backed up and drew it out a little farther. It was immensely bigger than all the other demons put together, and it kept emerging from her toe. As it grew it took on the features of a face, and it became clear he had it by its pointed nose. Its mouth opened to show sharp teeth, and it growled and barked. One of its big yellow eyes stared hard at the exorcist and the other scanned the crowd. A string of curse words came from Kan, followed by a loud, "Get the fuck out here." There was a snapping noise, and it retracted back into her toe. A wave of gasps erupted from the crowd.

"What the F?" said Tom.

"Satan's bubble gum," said Helen.

The reverend wiped his forehead with his sleeve, and then his fingers dove in for a second try. He caught hold of it, pinched hard, and pulled. Moxioton appeared again, growing like an angry tan thought. Kan lifted the gun, stuck it into the side of the demon, and pulled the trigger twice. The crowd ducked at the report of the 9mm. The demon seemed insubstantial enough for the bullets to pass through easily, but they didn't. Gun smoke misted the weird tableau. Grace, the reverend, and

Moxioton reached a fever-pitch chorus of agonizing grunts and squeals. "I've got to pull it free from her to destroy it," yelled the exorcist. The struggle continued. People fled for the back door. Then that sharp-toothed maw opened wide, and a burst of fire shot out as if it were a flamethrower.

The reverend's baggy black suit, beard, and eyebrows were instantly aflame. He stumbled backward, firing off shots into the ceiling. His arms waved up and down, but this time he wasn't dancing. He lurched toward what was left of the crowd. Helen grabbed Tom by the arm and pulled him out of the way. Emanuel Kan, all smoldering hair and a stink of singed meat, swept past them into the drapes of the living room's front window. The gun went off and shot out one of the panes as he fell to the floor. Fire swept up the fabric and leaped onto the couch. The place was in an uproar.

Tom and Helen made for the back door through the smoke and commotion. He looked over his shoulder and saw three things happen almost simultaneously. Somehow Crory had come up with a fire extinguisher and was dousing the Blameless, the drapes and furniture. Ina had made it to the cot and was helping Grace up. The last was the most spectacular. Morrison Zeck, that lanky kid, who'd not shown himself all night, appeared. He pushed Ina onto the floor and helped the bleary Grace stand by putting her arm over his shoulders. The two of them headed for the front door. That was the last Tom saw before he and Helen passed into the dining room and on to the kitchen.

Outside, it was still drizzling. They ran into Bill Stewart, standing amid a clutch of neighbors on the front lawn. "Did you see it?" he asked Tom.

"I thought you were asleep in the dining room."

"No, I woke up when the second act got under way. I caught most of it, but once he started shooting I took off."

"Remind me never to doubt the existence of demons again," said Tom.

"Unbelievable," said Bill.

"I don't buy it," said Helen.

"Well, you may not, but Emanuel Kan did," said Tom.

Twenty minutes passed, and yet the neighbors remained on the lawn in the fine drizzle, waiting for a sign that all was well. Eventually the front door opened and the reverend appeared in the porch light somewhat blackened and frayed, but on his feet. He carried his black bag in one hand and his pistol in the other. Crory and Ina appeared behind him in the doorway. Kan turned and yelled back at them, "You'll be hearing from my lawyer." As he passed toward the road and his car, he glowered at the crowd. "Ignorant sinners," he shouted.

"If that's an act," said Bill, "he should be on *America's Got Talent.*"

"He's a menace," said Helen.

Tom looked to the house and saw Ina weaving across the lawn toward the neighbors. He barely heard her voice as she thanked Jake and Alice and Oshea. Behind her, Mr. Crory sat on the porch, his powder-blue jacket and bowtie gone, his face in his hands, elbows resting on knees. It looked like he was sobbing.

"Check it out," Tom said to Helen and nudged her.

She turned and looked. "What a mess," she said.

"I've been exactly there more than once," said Tom.

Ina staggered over to them in her rounds. "I'm so sorry about tonight," she said. "Please forgive us. The last thing we wanted was to put you in harm's way. The exorcist came highly recommended."

"Recommended by who?" asked Bill.

"He had four five-star reviews out of six on Yahoo," she said.

"No sweat," said Tom.

Ina said to Helen, "Can I talk to you for a second," and took her wrist. They moved away from Tom and Bill.

Fifteen minutes later, Tom and Helen were in their CRV, moving slowly along the twisting suburban night streets. Helen drove. Tom squinted and scanned the hedge-lined properties, the oak thickets and trim lawns.

"Why didn't they just call the cops?" Tom asked.

"You know what that's like from our own kids."

"Yeah, I remember."

"They can't have gone far on foot."

"That Zeck kid rescuing Grace reminded me of the end of *The Graduate*."

"Well, she's got to get home now. Ina's distraught."

"Even the weird old man looked on the verge."

"What are you doing on your phone? You're supposed to be keeping an eye out."

"How are we going to miss her? She's dressed like the fucking Snow Queen. I'm looking up if there's such a thing as self-inflating balloons."

"I'm telling you, it was all tricks gone wrong," she said.

"Here it is. There is such a thing as self-inflating balloons, but they don't look anything like that stuff the Blameless was pulling out of Grace. That shit seemed alive."

"Remember *Jurassic Park*, the dinosaurs? Did they look real?"

"Yeah."

"Case closed."

"Why don't you check over by the lake? That's where our guys always went to get in trouble."

They drove slowly, in silence, till they arrived at the dirt parking lot near the playground at Halloway Lake. The rain had stopped and the moon played peek-a-boo from behind the clouds. Helen put the car in park and reached to turn the lights off. She didn't, though. "You see out to the left, near the shore, over by where the cat tails start. I think there's somebody sitting on that bench."

He squinted. "I can't see shit."

"Come on, we'll go check it out," she said and killed the headlights.

"What if it's Moxioton?"

She opened the door and got out. He followed her. They walked across the sand beyond the swing set. The lake smelled of spring and stirred in the breeze.

"Tell me honestly," he said. "When the Blameless first spoke of Moxioton, did you ever think he was gonna pull that demon from her big toe?"

"That one will come from lower down," she said in the reverend's voice and laughed.

"If you're right, and it's an act, it's genius."

"The gun was a surprise."

"Next time we get an invitation to one of these, say no."

Helen raised her arm and motioned for him to be quiet. They were getting closer to the bench. "Walk soft," she whispered. They drew within twenty feet, and the moon came through the clouds. The girl's dress shone like a beacon in the sudden light. Grace and Morrison Zeck, slumped shoulder to shoulder, both asleep. Tom and Helen quietly moved a few feet closer. She took his wrist when she wanted him to stop. They stood in silence for a moment. Tom leaned down and whispered in her ear, "That Zeck kid is a goofball."

Helen shook her head.

"Do I call Ina?" he asked, taking out his cell phone.

It took her a while to answer. "No," she said. "I don't think so."

"Why not?"

"They're too young to be lovers. They must be friends."

When the moon went away, they walked back to the CRV and drove home. Later, the rain started in again. The sound and smell of spring came through the screen of their bedroom window while he dreamt in the language the angels dream in, and she, of the land without worry.

Word Doll

Every morning I take the back way to town, a fifteen-mile drive on narrow two-lane roads that cut through oceans of corn. The cracked and patched asphalt is lined on either side by telephone poles shrinking into the distance. Sometimes I pass a hawk on a line. Every few miles there's a farm house, mostly old, like ours. In the winter, the wind is fierce, whipping across the barren fields, and I have to work to keep the car in its lane, but in summer, after I get my cigarettes in town and stop at the diner for a cup of coffee and a glance at the newspaper, I drive home and go out back under the apple trees, sit at a little table, and write stories. Sunlight filters down through the branches, and there's always a breeze blowing across the fields that finds me there. Sometimes the stories flow and I don't notice the birds at the feeders, the jingle of the dog's collar or the bees in the garden just beyond the orchard, and when they don't, I stare out into the sea of green and daydream into its depths.

In late September, on a Monday's journey to town, I passed this old place at a bend in the road like I'd passed it every morning. It was a Queen Anne Victorian with a wraparound screened-in porch, painted blue and white. The house was in good shape, but the barn out back was shedding shingles, and the paint had weathered off its splintered boards. I'd often seen chickens bobbing around on the property, and a rooster at times dangerously close to the road. There were blackberry bushes tangled in a low wall on either side of the entrance to its gravel drive. As I rolled past, I noticed something partially covered by those bushes. It looked like a sign of some kind, but it was faded and I was going too fast to catch a good glance.

On the way back from town I forgot to slow down and look, but the following day I woke up with the thought that I should stop and investigate that sign. Nine times out of ten, I could drive to town and back and never pass another car, and that day was no exception. I slowed as I got close to the place, and right across from the sign, I stopped and studied it—about two by three foot, made of tin, fading white with black letters. It was attached to a short rusted post. The berry bushes had grown up and partially over it, but now that I'd stopped I could make out its message. It said—WORD DOLL MUSEUM—and beneath that—Open 10 to 5 Monday thru Friday.

The next morning I got up, and, instead of driving to town, I took a shower and put on a white shirt and dress pants. I took a cup of coffee out under the apple trees. Instead of writing, I sat there, smoking and wondering into the heart of the corn-field what the hell a *word doll* was. At 10:30, I got in the car and drove toward town. The sun was strong and the sky was clear blue. The corn had begun to brown, it being summer's end. At the bend in the road, without hesitating, I pulled into the driveway of the Victorian. The chickens were in a clutch over by the corner of the house. The place was still. I didn't hear any television or radio playing. I walked slowly to the porch door, scuffing the gravel in the drive in order to let anybody listening know I was there. The screen door on the porch was unlatched. I opened it and called in, "Hello?"

There was no reply, so I entered, the screen door banging shut behind me, and walked to the main door of the house. I knuckle-rapped the glass three times and then folded my arms and waited. The lilacs bordering the porch gave off a strong scent, and a wind chime in the corner over an old rocker pinged in the breeze sifting through the screen. I was about to give up and leave, when the door pulled back. There was a thin old woman, a little bent, with a cloud of white hair and big glasses. She wore a loose, button-up dress, yellow with white flowers.

"What do ya want?" she asked.

"I'm here for the Word Doll Museum," I said.

My pronouncement seemed to momentarily stun her. She reached up and gently grabbed the door jamb. "Are you kidding?" she asked and smiled.

"Should I be?" I said.

Her demeanor instantly changed. I could see her relax. "Hold on," she said, "I have to get the keys. Meet me over by the barn."

I left the porch, and the chickens followed me. The entire gray structure of the barn, like some weary pachyderm, was actually listing more than a few degrees to the south, something I'd not noticed from the road. The door was hanging on by only the top hinge. The lady came out the back of the house and walked with the help of a three-pronged cane over the lumpy ground of the yard. As she drew closer, she said, "Where you from?"

"Not far. I pass your place on the way to town every morning, and I saw the sign the other day."

"My name is Beverly Gearing," she said and held out her hand.

I took it in mine and we shook. "I'm Jeff Ford," I told her.

As she passed by me toward the ramshackle barn, she said, "So, Mr. Ford, what's your interest in word dolls?"

"I don't know anything about them."

"Well, that's OK," she said, and opened the broken door.

I followed her inside. She shuffled over the hay-strewn floor. Swifts flew back and forth in the rafters, and the holes in the roof allowed sunbeams to cut the shadows. On one side of the barn were animal stalls, all empty, and on the other there was a wall of implements and tools and a small room built within the greater structure. Over the door to it was a wooden sign with the words *Word Doll Museum* burned in script and shellacked. She fished in the pocket of her dress and eventually came out with the key. Opening the door, she flipped on a light switch, and then stepped aside, allowing me to enter first. The room was painted a light blue. There was a window on each wall that looked out at nothing but bare plywood, and inside, window boxes fixed up with plastic flowers.

"Have a seat," she said, and I sat in a chair at the card table at the center of the room. She worked her way to the other chair at the table and half-sat/ half-fell backward into it. Once she was settled, she took a pack of Marlboros out of her pocket and a black lighter. She leaned forward on the table with one arm. "Word dolls," she said.

I nodded.

"You're the first person to ask about the museum in about twenty years." She laughed, and I saw she was missing a tooth on the upper right side.

"You can hardly see your sign from the road," I said.

"The sign's a last resort," she said. "I have a permanent spot in the *What's Happening* section of three of the local papers. In January, I send them enough to run the ads for a year. Still, no one pays attention."

"I'm guessing most people don't know what a word doll is."

"I know," she said and lit the cigarette she held. She took a drag and then pointed with it at the left wall, where there were three beige file cabinets. The middle one had a golden laughing Buddha statue on it. "What's in those nine drawers over there is all that remains of the history of word dolls. This is the largest repository of material evidence of the existence of the tradition. When I'm gone, knowledge of it will have been pretty much erased from history. You live long enough, Mr. Ford, you might be the last person on earth to ever think of word dolls."

"I might be," I said, "but I don't know what they are."

Beverly put her cig out in a half cup of coffee that looked like it had been on the table for a week. "I want you to know something before I start," she said. "This is serious to me. I have a doctorate in anthropology from OSU, class of '63."

"Yes, ma'am," I said. "I seriously want to know."

She sat quiet for a moment, eyes half shut, before taking a deep breath. "A 'word doll' is the same thing as a 'field friend,' they're interchangeable. Their existence is very brief measured in anthropological time and also very localized. Only in the area that's now roughly defined by our county border was this ritual observed. It sprang up in the mid-19th century and for the time in which it ran its course affected no more than fifty or sixty families at the most. No one's certain of its origin. Some women I interviewed back when I was in graduate school, they were all in their 80s and 90s then, swore the phenomenon was something brought over from Europe. So I asked, where in Europe? But none could say. Others told me it originated with a woman named Mary Elder, back in the 1830s. She was also known as The Widow, and I have a picture of her in the cabinet, but her candidacy for the creation of the tradition is called into question by a number of factors.

"Anyway, back in the day, I'm talking the mid-1800s on, in rural areas like this, kids, when they reached a certain age were sent out to participate in the fall harvest. By about age six or seven, they were initiated into the hard work of the fields during that season of long hours well into the night. It was a difficult adjustment for them. There are a lot of writings from the time where farmers or their wives complain about the wayward nature of their children, their inability to focus through the hours of toil. Training a kid to endure a harvest season with no real prior experience appears to have been a common problem. So, to offset that, someone came up with the idea of the word dolls. The idea in a nutshell is to allow the child to escape into her imagination while her physical body stays on the task at hand.

"Whoever came up with it really could have been a psychologist. They attached a ritual to it, which was a smart way to embed the thing into the local culture. So, in September, usually around the equinox, if you were one of those kids who was to be sent out in the fields for the first time come harvest, you could expect a visit from the doll maker. The doll maker came at night, right after everyone was in bed, carrying a lantern and wearing a mask. As far as I can tell, the doll makers were usually women in disguise. There'd be a knock at the door, three times and then three times again. The parents would get up and answer the call. When the child was finally ushered into the dark room and seated next to the fireplace, the doll maker was already there in her own seat that faced his. Her hands were reportedly blue, and bejeweled with chains and a large ring, its carnelian etched to show an angel in flight. She was wrapped in black velvet with a hood sewn into it to cover her head. And the mask, the mask was a story unto itself.

"By all accounts that mask was dug up on one of the local farms. It had deep-set eyes, a crooked nose, and a large oval mouth opening bordered by sharp teeth. It was an old Iroquois False Face mask, and could have been in the ground a hundred years before it was plowed up. It was made of basswood and had rotted at the edges. One of the farmers painted it white. I suppose you're starting to see that the whole community was in on this?"

"Everybody but the kids," I said.

"Oh, the tenacity with which the secrets of the doll maker were kept from the young ones then far exceeds what's now done in the name of Santa Claus."

"So they wanted to scare the kids?"

"Not so much scare them as put them in a state of awe. Remember, the promise was that the doll maker was coming to them with a gift. The competing qualities of her aspect and her purpose no doubt caused a heightened sense of tension."

"Do you know anything about the False Face mask?"

"The False Face was a society of the Iroquois tribes. Their rituals dealt with healing. There were two ways to join the society—if you were cured by them or if you dreamed you should join them. It doesn't really have any bearing on the word-doll tradition. Just an artifact that was appropriated by another culture and put to another purpose."

"OK, the kid is sitting there next to the fireplace with the doll maker . . ."

"Well, the parents leave the room. Then, as I was told by those surviving members of the ritual back in my graduate days, the doll maker tells the child not to be afraid. She's going to make the child a doll to take into the fields with him or her, a companion to play with in the imagination while the hard work goes on. The doll maker cups her hands in front of her like this." Beverly demonstrated. "And then leans over so the mouth of the mask is right over her palms. You see?" she said and showed me.

"The voice was a kind of harsh whisper that none of my interview subjects could hear well or follow completely. The words poured out of the doll maker's mouth into the cupped hands. One woman told me a string of words she remembered her whole long life that came from behind the mask. Hold on, let me see if I can get this right."

While Beverly thought, I took out my cigarettes and held them up for her to see. "OK?" I asked. She nodded. I lit up and drew the coffee cup closer to use as an ashtray. She held her hands up and snapped her fingers. "Oh, yes. I used to have this memorized so good. It's like a poem. My mind is scattered by age," she said and smiled.

She was still for a second. Her eyes shifted and she stared hard at me. "*The green sea, the deep down below the sweep of rolling waves, whales and long eight-legged pudding heads with eye over which the great ship glides, and Captain Moss spinning the wheel . . .* That's the part she remembered, but she said the whole, what was called, 'talking out of the doll,' went on for some time. The average I got was about fifteen minutes. When the doll maker spoke the last word, she rubbed her hands together vigorously and then reached over and covered the child's ears with them."

"You mean as if the words were going inside the kid's head?" I asked.

"I suppose, but from that night on, the child had, in his or her imagination, this word doll that had a name and a form and a little bit of history. The more the child played with it during work, the clearer it became till it had the same detail as dreams or memories. Word dolls all had a one-syllable name attached to whatever its profession was. So you had like, Captain Moss, Hunter Brot, Milker May, Teacher Poll. The woman who was given the Captain told me she'd never seen the ocean but had only heard about it from elders and travelers passing through the area. She said the Captain turned out to be a man of high adventure. She followed him on his voyages through her child-hood into adulthood and then old age. Another interviewee said he'd been gifted Clerk Fick, but that as he followed the days of Clerk Fick while toiling in the fields, the doll slowly became a glamorous woman, Dancer Hence. He hadn't thought of her in years, he said. 'She's still with me, but I put her away when I left the farm.'"

Beverly got her cane under her and slowly stood. She walked to the files, bent over, and opened the second drawer down on the left hand. Reaching in, she drew out an armful of stuff. I asked her if she needed help. "Please," she said. I went to her side, and the first thing she handed me was the white False Face mask. After that she gave me a rusted sickle with a wooden handle. "OK," she said, closed the drawer with her cane, and we started back.

"I can't believe you've got the mask," I said, laying it down. I put the sickle next to it.

She sat and shoved her pile onto the table. "The mask came easy. A lot of this stuff I really had to dig for." Pulling an old book out of the pile, she opened it, turned a few pages, and took out a large rectangle of cardboard. She turned it over and laid it in front of me. It was the picture of a woman in a high-collar black dress. Her hair was parted in the middle and pulled severely back. Her glasses were circular. She wore a righteous expression.

"The Widow?" I asked.

Beverly nodded and said, "That's a daguerreotype, not a photograph. From the 1850s. She looks like a pill, doesn't she? I used to have it in plastic, but I've slacked off over the years as far as preserving all this. I resigned myself to its eventual demise when I did my own."

"It's a remarkable story and archive," I said.

"My husband built me this place to house it. He was very supportive, and as long as he lived that kept me going with it. His family farmed all this acreage around here at one point."

"You got a PhD in Anthropology at OSU and then married a farmer?"

"I know," she said and laughed wistfully. "It was true love, but I still had it in my mind to be the next Margaret Meade. I knew I wasn't going to make it to Samoa any time soon, so I looked closer to home and found this." She moved her shaking hands over the things on the table.

We passed an hour with her reading me parts of her interviews, journal entries from dirty old leather-bound diaries, all of which attested to the strength of the image of the word doll, a doll that grew as you did, could speak to you in your mind, lead you to places you'd never been. The strangest particulars surfaced. One woman, thirty years old at the time, wrote in her diary that in all the years she'd played with Cook Gray, she'd never seen him naked, but she knew without looking that he only had one testicle. His best dish was roasted possum with cabbage, and she often used his recipes in cooking for her family. One interviewee said that her word doll was Deacon Tru, and that her husband's had begun as Builder Cy but somehow transformed into Barkeep Jon and was subsequently the ruination of their love. Among the papers was a letter detailing a farmer's thirty-year argument with his field friend. After he retired, he said he realized that fight had been the one thing that kept him going through thick and thin.

Eventually Beverly ran out of steam. She lit a cigarette and eased back in her chair. "It's completely mad," she said, flicked her ash on the floor, and smiled.

"What about this?" I said and lifted the sickle off the table.

She blinked, pursed her lips, and said, "Mower Manc. That was the end of the whole shebang."

"The end of the ritual?"

She nodded. "In the early 1880s, word dolls were still part of the local culture. Who knows how much longer they would have carried on with the 20th century coming full speed ahead. But in that last year, somewhere around midsummer, a fire started in the minister's barn one night. The place burned to the ground and the minister's wife's buggy horse died in the flames. Every one suspected this boy, Evron Simms, who'd been caught lighting fires before. The minister, knowing the boy's parents well, decided not to pursue punishment for the crime. Come the equinox, only a week later, Evron was due a visit from the doll maker, and the doll maker came.

"Some of the folks I interviewed in the '60s knew this boy, grew up with him. He'd told more than one of them that his field friend was Mower Manc, a straw hat brim covering his eyes, a laborer's shirt and suspenders, calloused hands, and a large sickle. In other words, the doll maker made Evron a word doll whose very job was to toil in the fields. That doll maker, I discovered, was none other than the minister's wife. You can't be sure that her choice for him was malicious or that he didn't change the aspect of what was initially given to him, but if she did knowingly make his only plaything in the fields *work itself*, that would be hard-hearted."

I looked down at the sickle and said, "This doesn't sound like it's gonna end well."

"Hold on," she said and put her hand out like a traffic cop to stop me. "Harvest starts, and Evron's sent out into the fields with that sickle you see there and is given a huge plot of hay to cut. By many accounts he immediately set to work and worked with a kind of ferocity that made him seem possessed. By sunset the field was mown, and the boy had a violet pallor, froth at the corners of his mouth. Even his father, a severe man, worried about what he'd witnessed. He wrote, 'I never thought I'd see an instance where a boy could work too hard, but today I seen it. My own Evron. I should be proud, but the sight of it wasn't a prideful thing. I'd describe it more as frightful.'"

"People passed by the farm frequently after that first harvest to catch a glimpse of the boy mowing hay. They noticed that he had taken to wearing a broad-brimmed straw hat to block the sun. When the minister passed away, among his papers was a sermon he'd written about the boy's mowing. It's a very elegant document for what's there, predictably linking Evron's sickle with the scythe of Death, but half way down the page the minister runs out of words. There are marks on the paper then, circles and crosses and a simple sun. At the bottom he writes—*Elegast*."

"What was that?" I asked, unsure I'd heard correctly.

"Elegast, an entity from the folklore of the Dutch Low Countries. A supernatural creature, like the field and forest in human form. Only the minister made that connection, though, whereas most of the local folks were convinced Evron was just touched in the head. Three years at the harvest and his look became more distant, his words fewer and fewer. When not working he'd sit perfectly still, eyes closed, and sniff at the wind. During the following winter, he was working on a hay wagon, changing one of the tin-covered wooden wheels, when the axle splintered and the cart fell and broke his left leg. That's when the real trouble started."

"Because he couldn't work?" I asked.

"Exactly. They had to tie him down to keep him from tending to the horses and cows, or shoveling the snow off the path, or keeping a low fire going in the barn during the frozen nights. He struggled to get free. The local doctor prescribed laudanum and told him if he didn't stay put and let the break mend, he'd never make it back out into the field. So they kept him in a stupor for months. Meanwhile, that winter of 1883, a stranger was spotted by more than a few folks, usually off at a distance, limping across the stubbled, misty fields, carrying a sickle and wearing a broad-brimmed straw hat. They swore it was Evron, but on the few occasions someone got close to this mysterious figure, it proved to be that of a wasted and grisly old man.

"One day Evron's father saw the old man moving across the distant landscape, and he saddled a horse and rode out to meet him. In his diary he reports, 'I confronted the grim old fellow and told him he trod upon my field. He wore no coat, though the wind was bitter, but only the summer clothes of a day laborer. I asked what it was he was looking for. He yelled at me in a harsh voice, "Work. I want work." I reminded him it was the dead of winter. He stalked away, dragging his bad leg. By then a fierce snow had begun to fall and in a moment I lost sight of him.'"

"You've got an incredible memory," I told her.

"I've been waiting to tell somebody all of this for forty years," she said. "I'll jump ahead. I know I've kept you too long already."

"Take your time."

"To make a long story shorter, the minister's wife was found one afternoon, not but a few days later, hacked to pieces in a church pew. Nobody had a doubt but that it was the stranger. A posse was formed and the men went out into the fields on horseback searching for him. At night they carried torches. Always they would glimpse him in the distance across the vast acreage of a barren field, but when they arrived at that spot, he'd be gone. Still, he struck twice more. A fifteen-year-old girl, who lived two miles down the road from the Simms' place. Her body was found in a horse trough, neck cut so bad that when they lifted her out of her frozen blood, her head fell off. Then a farmer slashed to ribbons, his body still upright in the seat of his buckboard, leaving a long trail of red in his wake as the horses stepped smartly through the snow.

"The younger boys called the killer Mower Manc after Evron's field friend. Everyone saw the connection, but it was impossible to blame the killings on the boy who was in a perpetual daze at home, fastened to his bed. All through the rest of that winter and into the spring, they chased the illusive figure. Sometimes he'd disappear for months and then there'd be a sighting of him. Once the crops were put in and the corn and wheat came up at the end of the spring, it got still more difficult to track him. Someone would see him cross the dirt road and then he'd plunge into a cornfield and vanish.

"Harvest time finally came, and Evron was allowed to return to the fields to mow. His leg was still tender, and there was a slight but noticeable limp, but the boy, sickle in hand, went out into the fields to cut wheat. His father, his mother, his sister, the doctor, and a neighboring farmer watched Evron walk into the wind-rippled amber expanse, and that was the last anyone ever saw of him. All they found was that sickle." Beverly clasped her hands, set them in her lap, and sighed.

"He ran away," I said.

"I suppose," she said. "But all through the end of the 19th century, through the 20th, and into the 21st up to today, folks have continued to farm this land. Geologists call it the Ohio Till Plain, one of the most fertile spots in the country. In all that time, every so often someone peering from a second-floor window of a farm house spots a strange figure in a distant field moving through the corn. A shadow with a hat. A loping scarecrow with a sickle. People nowadays refer to this phantom simply as *The Mower*. If you live here long enough, Mr.

Ford, and you get to know the farmers well enough, you'll hear someone speak of it. It's said that certain nights in deep winter, below the howl of the wind, you can hear him weeping for want of work. If you wake on a cold morning and find your garage door open when it wasn't the night before, it means The Mower has taken refuge from the cold in there."

Beverly got up and took her papers and old diaries and daguerreotypes to the filing cabinet and put them away. I carried the false face and the sickle. She took the mask from me and stored it, but when I handed her the tool, she said, "No, you keep that."

After all she'd told me, I wasn't sure I wanted it, but eventually my sense of politeness kicked in and I thanked her. She walked with me to my car, and before I got in, we shook hands. "You're the last one," she said before I drove off. When I got home, I immediately looked around for a place to stow the sickle. Crazy as it was, I shoved it down into the big freezer in the garage underneath the layers of frozen vegetables from the garden. I figured I'd freeze the creep out of it.

The Word Doll Museum and old Doctor Geary stuck with me for a week or so, and I'd sit out under the apple trees and stare off into the corn to see if I could spot a shadowy figure passing amid the rows. Nothing. Just as it started to get too cold to sit out there, and Farmer Frank had the combine out harvesting corn, I got an idea for a story about a religious painter who's sent out by a prelate on a journey to find and paint a true portrait of the devil. It was a relatively long piece and it consumed my imagination. By the time I finished a first draft the fields were barren, and I was forced to move inside. The revisions on that story turned out to be extensive, and I didn't finish it until the middle of winter.

The very night I was finally satisfied that the piece was ready to send out, the coldest night of the year, I had a dream of Mower Manc. In it I got out of bed and went to the window. It was night and the light in the room was off. There was a full moon, though, and I saw, out in the barren field past the orchard and the garden, a figure moving through the snow, curved blade glinting as it swung like the pendulum of an old clock. Across that distance, I heard the weeping clear as a bell, and its anguish woke me.

When I went out to get my cigarettes the next morning, I came around that bend and saw that the gray barn and home of the Word Doll Museum had at some point since the day before collapsed into a smoldering pile of rubble. Orange flames still darted from the charred wreckage and smoke rolled across the yard and fields like a storm cloud come down to earth. I thought instantly of Beverly's habit of flicking her cigarette ash on the floor of the place and just as quickly of Evron's penchant for lighting fires. Then I saw her, on the snow-covered lawn in front of the house, cane nowhere in sight, in a long blue nightgown and dirty pink slippers, white hair lurid in the wind. There was a cop car in the driveway, and the officer stood next to her with a pen and pad as if waiting to take down her statement. She was just staring into the distance, though, her grief-stricken expression pale and distorted like the False Face mask, and as I passed I realized that what I was seeing was the end of it—a doll maker, all out of words.

The Angel Seems

In late autumn, after the harvest had been brought in and the first real snow had fallen, he came from the forest on a stagbone sled drawn by enormous twin mastiffs. He was slight and trim, with white hair and beard, and he wore a snug black suit with slits in the back of the jacket for his wings to fit through. They were small, violet, and made of scales instead of feathers. It was a wonder how they could lift him, but a number of folk had spotted the angel Seems across the field, flying above the tree tops, wings fluttering like a moth's.

On his first journey to the village, he glided in on his sled, requested that the people gather, and then announced that his name was Alfrod Seems and that he was an angel. "I'm here to prepare you for the coming of God," he shouted, lifting his ivory walking stick into the air, and, convinced by his wings, they listened. He promised to protect the villagers from their enemies, their crops from blight or drought, and their homes from storms and floods and fires. They cheered. There was, though, one stipulation, and it was that each year he be allowed to pick from among the people a servant to help him in his sacred duties at his den in the forest.

It seemed like a fair trade until it came time for the angel to make his first choice. When he arrived, they stared in disbelief, as if they'd never seen him before outside of a dream, and yet they knew full well what they'd promised. He strode the snow-filled streets and saw a woman by the name of Elshin Marsh carrying a load of laundry from the river. He approached her, bowed, and grasped her forearm. Upon realizing who it was that had stopped her, she froze. "You must put down your load here and this minute come with me to my den." Elshin screamed, and, since she was close to home, her husband heard her.

He came running, carrying an old chair leg. Elshin tried to flee, but Seems held her fast. Mr. Marsh rushed the angel, holding up the crude club. Fast as a snake striking, Seems lifted his hand and, with his fingers curled but for the first two, aimed for the man's eyes. A moment later, Marsh was on his knees, crying blood into his hands.

When Elshin was returned to the village the following year, her husband was dead and a set of antlers grew from the temples of her forehead. She'd lost the power of speech and only grunted. In her possession was a thin glass tube that contained a yellow liquor, which the angel had promised could bestow a very minor miracle upon the drinker.

Months later, it was discovered she was pregnant. The village was in an uproar, frantic with outrage and fear. After seeing what Seems had done to Elshin and her husband, though, they wondered what else he was capable of. The leader of the village council proposed that they tell the angel they no longer desired his protection. Because no one knew where Seems lived, they were forced to wait until he appeared, which no one minded.

When the poor woman went into labor, she drank from the glass tube and wished for death. Elshin Marsh gave birth not to a baby but a manikin—a miniature Alfrod Seems with white hair and beard and fluttering violet wings. The poor mother's heart stopped during the delivery, and not an hour after the strange homunculus came into the world, there was heard from across the fields, from somewhere deep in the forest, the baying of the angel's mastiffs. They came, galloping out of the trees, dashing through the fields. Their call was piercing, and people hid beneath their covers with their hands over their ears. The dogs' approach seemed both an instant and a year, but they came to the door of healer Struth's home, where Elshin lay dead upon the table and the little Alfrod Seems was just learning to stand.

Hearing the beasts panting outside his home, the healer went for a pistol he kept in his desk, but before he could open the drawer, the dogs smashed into the room, boards and splinters flying. One of the monsters held him at bay, growling, while the other caught the miniature Seems and devoured it. Struth would later take his own life. He'd told more than one that the screams of the miniature angel as the creature's fangs turned it to gore never left his head. That night, the mastiffs made one more stop.

The leader of the village council, Matten Gersha, was in bed with his wife, cowering beneath the covers, when the dogs let themselves into his home. One tore the blankets off the frightened couple. The other took off Mrs. Gersha's left foot at the ankle and swallowed it without chewing. Then they pulled the leader of the council out into the street, and as the shrouded faces behind window curtains looked on, the beast who'd torn away the blankets tore away Gersha's face in one piece and left it on the snow like a mask in the moonlight.

Through the care of Struth, the Mrs. survived the amputation but contracted an unheard-of disease which caused her to vomit billowing clouds of dirt. She was shunned for fear of infection and died soon after the doctor killed himself. After the mastiffs' visit, the topic of giving Alfrod Seems a piece of their mind was never raised by the villagers in any tone louder than a whisper.

Year followed year, and when the snow fell the angel made his visits, taking one and sometimes leaving one. When asked by the trembling baker, whose wife never returned, where she was, Seems smiled and told him, "It didn't work out." The baker only barely thought of murder and found the sharp tip of the angel's ivory cane resting against his throat. The women who were returned were always pregnant with miniature Alfrods. The copies who survived birth were taken each time by the mastiffs; the ones who didn't remained within till the end of their mothers' days. Those servants who returned were all in some way physically deformed—extra appendages, third eyes, animal traits—and spoke a language of moans and grunts that meant nothing.

Pella Thilem, who had served the angel and returned with fur and snout, was unusual. Most of the servants who came back to the village passed away soon after. Pella lived on, and in her later years she regained, to a very limited degree, her human language. In her own way, she told the villagers what had happened at the angel's den. "Like a glory," she said. "Lights and ice. Trees fingers. Dogs. Work at fire. Angel hand. Face. Scream every day. A fountain."

Some passed off Pella's words as nonsense, and others studied them carefully, letting the imagination unfold the possibilities of their message. Theories about the origin and nature of Alfrod Seems abounded. He was thought to be a demon, but there were those who believed he actually was an angel sent by a jealous God. Alfrod Seems, himself, claimed to have been grown in a pale woman's garden, pulled up by the roots, and left to play in the forest at night.

One thing that was true about the angel, he was good to his word, for even though disasters befell neighboring villages, they never troubled the land of his servants. When the river flooded, the water should have swamped the fields, but it miraculously stopped at the edge of the village and built up to six feet high, not one drop of it falling past the invisible boundary. It was said you could walk along beside it, a blue wall, and watch the fish swimming.

After the highwayman, Jado, robbed the village merchants on their way to market, he was found hanging in a tree at the crossroad, naked and skewered like a sausage, ass to mouth, on a long oak branch. And the plague came only for a day, blown off by a magical breeze. No one died from it, whereas only two miles away at Cleneth, the bodies were stacked three high and burning.

Whatever solace was gained from Alfrod's protection, it was lost in the dog days, the height of the summer heat, when the mastiffs went mad and roved the wheat fields and corn-fields in search of prey, rushing through the tunnels of green shade. Farmers went missing. Sometimes a scrap of clothing and a shattered bone would be found, once a half a skull, but most often nothing, as if they'd never lived. From the safety of a tree, one could watch the beasts moving through the wheat, a furious rippling, heading directly for an unsuspecting man whistling at his work. He was there and never there in the blink of an eye.

On the fifth of his yearly visits, the angel told the people that on his next he expected a feast in his honor at which he and they would all sit down and celebrate him. "Make it lavish," he said. They didn't know what lavish meant, but after gather-ing the harvest that sixth year, they set about creating a banquet for Alfrod Seems that they hoped he would find satisfactory. Even the baker, whose wife never returned, gave in and joined the effort.

When a distant curl of red smoke was sighted above the treetops of the forest, his signal to them that he was coming, the village readied itself. Pine garland fringed windows and door-ways, and every dark space had a candle burning in it. In the village square there were two enormous black cauldrons, sim-mering mucine and glifero, spices from the Far Islands. The feast was laid on long tables in the street as there was no build-ing that could contain it. When his sleigh came to a halt, all were seated but for the new leader of the council, who went to serve as escort to the angel.

In the back of the sled sat a figure wrapped in black. The council leader barely recognized her as Anamita Beruk, who'd left the previous year. Set into her forehead was a window with a glass pane. Through it he could see the stars. The woman was haggard, her complexion a pale gray. Pitiful whimpers escaped her, and the angel nodded and said to the council leader, "She's had a little too much of the Holy Ghost. You know how it is."

"What shall I do with her?" asked the leader.

Seems shrugged. "I'd drop her in an old well."

The angel smiled and nodded at the sight of the table and all gathered at it. He sat at the head and gazed up and down each side. No one returned his look for fear he might be deciding on his next servant. Then he clapped his hands, making some jump in their seats, and said, "Eat and talk." He lifted the top loaf from a basket next to his arm and added, "Let me hear laughter." There was a round of pathetic laughter, but it pleased him greatly. He broke the loaf in two and took a bite.

A moment later, he was on his feet, leaning over the table, choking. Something brown fell from his mouth onto his plate. The angel spit profusely and seized up the wine goblet of the frightened woman next to him. "Shit in the bread?" he screamed. The baker was lifted by invisible means out of his seat and floated down the length of the table in a sitting position toward Alford Seems. The angel lifted his walking stick and, with a distinct crack, thrust it through the baker's forehead. The poor man remained floating above the table. People pushed away from the blood that rained down. Seems twisted the end of the cane, as if tuning the man's skull, and the baker let out a scream that split the sky.

A heartbeat, and then the air was filled with the screech and flap of starlings, pecking and clawing at the assembled. The dark birds were so thick, each breath was a breath through feathers, impossible to see or even scream. A few moments later, when the flock suddenly vanished in a flutter of smoke, three eyes and three tongues were missing, as was Alford Seems and his sled. Also gone was the Kremply girl.

Needless to say, the loaves held no surprises the following year. Still, the tale of the baker's turd was told and retold, whispered into the ears of tired children as they lay in bed, the candle out. There were disagreements as to what message it taught, but it was dangerous to discuss the theories aloud. And the days passed. The crops grew. Occasionally a child's head would burst into flame.

In the twelfth year of the angel's protection, during the harvest time, a young woman, Mira Doune, had a dream. The next day she pulled her husband, Jon, into the closet and shut the door behind them. She whispered her dream to him in the dark. When she finished, he promised to help her. No more was said. He went to slaughter a lamb while she got the fire ready. Hours later, when the animal was roasted, Jon cut a huge slab of meat off it and set it on a plate for his wife. Working in silence, by candlelight, Mira used a knife and a cleaver to shape the mutton into a small hand. When it was complete it was put into a clay jar sealed tight with bees wax and sunk on a line into the cool underground stream of the south cave.

The angel arrived for his harvest dinner, delivered old lady Sharett, who in her service had grown a face on the back of her head exactly like the one on the front, and whisked away the Childs lad to serve in his den. Mira and Jon wondered if it was possible, but a few months after her return old lady Sharett began to show. They were as excited as if they themselves were to be parents. Late that night, they ran across the field to healer Mulithot's home and whispered to him in his closet.

Mulithot was not so brave as his mentor, Struth, nor was he as smart. When the plot against the angel was put forward, he became frightened that he was being tested. When he finally agreed, he could not say the words, even in a whisper, but simply gave a subtle nod.

While they waited for old lady Sharett to come to term, Mira and Jon were torn between the fear that something might happen to her before she could give birth, and the fear that nothing would happen to her, and they would have no choice but to carry out their plan. They and the healer kept the secret for months, like holding in a scream, and Mulithot, in the meantime, though keeping mum, took to strong drink. At night Mira slept on top of Jon to protect him from the doubts she knew tried to invade him in his sleep.

The hard months staggered by and then . . . the old lady grunted from both sides of her head as the sleek, winged, Alfrod was pulled from her womb by Mulithot's forceps. Mira and Jon held the creature down by its neck and wrists, while the healer fetched the cleaver. The little Alfrod's struggle was great, and it was difficult to keep him still what with the desperate action of the violet wings and the fact that he was growing by the minute.

The cleaver struck through the tiny arm on the second blow, and Alfrod luckily screamed precisely when the mastiffs charged out of the shadow of the forest and onto the open fields. Mira nervously opened the clay jar and withdrew the mutton hand. She then placed the real hand inside and fitted the lid on tight. The healer and Jon held the baby down, and she sewed the false hand onto his stump with a coarse thread woven from vines of the herb dognip.

Mira and Jon were just closing the closet door when the front door to Mulithot's home burst in. The healer backed away and slouched against the wall. One dog sniffed at his crotch while the other caught up the newborn and devoured it in three bites. They left as quickly as they'd arrived, and when they were gone the healer passed out. Mira went to the clay jar, looked inside, and gave the barest smile.

The hand simmered in a stew with carrots and onions. Jon opened the lid to get a whiff of dinner, saw the pale hand bobbing, and shivered, picturing himself picking his teeth with its sharp nails. After many hours, Mira lifted the shriveled mass out of the pot with a fork and called her husband to come eat. Using her sharpest knife, she sliced the meat off the palm and fingers and served it with carrots and onions and gravy . It was so sweet it made them gag, but they hoped it would confer a shred of the angel's power, or offer some kind of protection.

They buried the diminutive skeleton hand in a metal box by the side of the road.

That night, while the village slept, Mira and Jon left home and carefully made their way across the fields to the forest. They carried no torch or lantern and said nothing. When they reached the tree line and passed into perfect night, where neither the stars nor moon were visible, they tied one end of a length of twine around his waist and the other end around hers. Groping blindly forward, they went in search of the sacred den.

They bruised their shins and cut their arms and faces on the grasping branches. Although she was frightened and exhausted, Mira took heart in the fact that they'd been in the forest so long without a sign or sound from the dogs. She wanted to trust the recipe given to her in the dream. Jon, on the other hand, doubted everything and was certain they'd end the night being devoured. He tugged gently on the rope attaching him to his wife. She drew close and put her hands on his shoulders. She traced the direction his arm was pointing. Mira turned and squinted into the dark. Off in the far distance, she detected a smudge of light.

As they approached, the glow of the den allowed them to first distinguish the movement of shadows and eventually to see each other's faces as if by candle from another room. The light poured forth from a wide hole in the ground. On either side of the opening lay the sleeping mastiffs. The desperate squeals of animals issued up from the tunnel that led to the angel's den. Jon and Mira held their breath and hesitated only yards from the snoring beasts. They looked at each other. Finally she tugged the twine and moved them toward the bright underground. He shook his head but followed.

At the same moment, both dogs scratched a dream itch with a back leg as the couple passed. Mira nearly cried out, for it was precisely at this point that her dream ended. She put her arm around Jon, and they both closed their eyes and continued, descending into a tunnel of light. The walls around them were coated with a thick wax that glowed of its own accord. As they inched forward, expecting Seems to appear around every turn of the snake-like passage, a strong, hot wind pushed up toward the surface, lifting their hair behind them, causing them to sweat.

The den was deep and at its center was a crystal fountain like a tree growing, dripping water from every glistening branch into a surrounding pond. The thing reached nearly to the ceiling of the enormous cavern. From where Mira and Jon hid behind a heap of firewood, they could see an old man on a floating couch drifting through the rain in the fountain pond. He had a long white beard, a mere ring of hair, his head resting on blue pillows. Even from the distance of their hiding place, they could see he was in torment.

Twenty yards away from the fountain, Alfrod Seems was sitting in an ornate chair at the edge of a pit, slaughtering deer with a long knife. More than a dozen of the creatures stood in line, dazed, with the eyes of sleepwalkers. Each stepped forward to have its throat cut, lose its blood into the pit, sway, and then fall, making a place for the next. The angel moved with grace and expert precision in his work. Only once did he hesitate. He turned, sniffed the air, rested his free hand briefly on the head of his walking stick, which leaned against the arm of the throne, and with a brief ruffle of his wings went back to his work.

Mira tugged on the twine, and Jon looked at her. She waved her hand, signaling that he should follow. He shook his head. She waved her hand. He couldn't move. She slipped a knife out of her apron and cut the twine. He reached for her, but she was already gone out from behind the woodpile. With fingers covering one eye, he watched as Mira crept closer to the angel, hiding herself amid the line of deer. As each of the beasts gave their gurgling death cry, she used the noise to cover her next move forward.

When she was no more than two from the angel's throne, a small beast, Jon at first thought it a pig, appeared from behind the fountain. He could tell it had noticed Mira and was hobbling awkwardly toward her. It's bird calls alerted Alfrod, who halted his infernal work in mid-slice. Without thinking, Jon rushed from behind the woodpile, screaming, swinging a stick of kindling. He saw Alfrod notice him, and he remembered the sight of Marsh on the ground crying blood, which stopped him dead in his tracks. The angel rose from the chair and reached for his stick. As he did, it vanished.

Mira was upon him with the ivory spike. She drove it with all her might through his chest, which cracked like the shell of an insect. He gasped, his wings buzzing frantically. Then she turned it as he had done to the baker, tuning his heart. He stumbled forward to grab her, but the strange beast that had given her away, leaped, chirping, off the ground and tore at the angel's stomach. Mira recognized the freckled face of the Childs lad. Alfrod sliced its throat with the knife, and then the two of them, angel and beast fell back into the pit.

Mira staggered away and turned. Jon moved again, running to hold her, and just before they embraced, a fierce wind rose up from nowhere and swallowed them in its fury. They spun apart as the shrieking gale echoed through the cavern. And the next thing they knew, they were back in the village, standing side by side, clasping hands, and the old man from the couch in the fountain stood beside them. The sun was rising and the birds were singing. The couple shook their heads as if waking from an unexpected nap.

"I'm God," said the stranger in a tired voice. Only then did they notice his sky blue wings, composed of feathers. The ends of his beard seemed to fizz in the air. His eyes shone.

The first question the villagers had, once they heard that the angel had been done away with, was, "What about those two damn mastiffs?"

"I've destroyed one," said God. "The other is left to roam the woods. Be wary of him."

They were confused by his response. Some scratched their heads, others rubbed their chins. They then wanted to know what Mira's dream had been. She spoke about a woman with a window in her head, through which the stars were visible. "I saw the plan in her head. The stars and planets told me what to do."

They shrugged and asked God if Alfrod Seems was an angel.

"I met him some centuries ago in the Far Islands," said the old man. "He was an explorer, and I was there convalescing. We spent many nights drinking grog on the beach, pondering the workings of the universe. We became fast friends, and I thought I knew him. To prove to myself that he was true, I tested him. "I will grant you a wish," I told him, and to my astonishment he accepted.

"You made him an angel?" asked Relst, the carpenter.

"Well, I'm God," said the old man. "Still, Seems turned on me in the moment the wish was granted, and I've been his servant ever since."

A mumble ran through the crowd.

"In the end, did the lion not lie down with the lamb?" said God, trying to catch sight of the few who were snickering.

"Why was the angel slaughtering deer?" asked Jon.

"Forgive me," he said. "I'm so weary. I need to lie down." His couch appeared beneath him, and he lay upon it, resting his head against the blue pillows. "Tomorrow, I will give you my ten commandments." With this, he closed his shining eyes, his wings went still, and a light snoring could be heard.

The villagers exchanged no words, but all shared a look. They went back to their homes and readied their weapons. That night they moved against God. As frail as he appeared, he still put up a fierce battle. But the sheer number of villagers and the force of their determination was a weapon the old man could not withstand. He was beaten down to nothing, and all that remained of him come sunrise was his long, fizzing beard, which was hung from a pole like a flag. From that night forward the savage incident would forever be referred to in the village as the Eleventh Commandment, and its memory sustained them through floods and fires.

As for the remaining mastiff, he roamed the remote places, and every so many years a report of him would find its way to the village. It seems the dog no longer had a taste for human flesh and gave up killing for the joy of it, with the exception of the time those in Cleneth sent a hunting party to trap him. The last he was seen was on the day of Mira's funeral. Jon lost her to the plague one spring, and the snapping of the twine that joined them was heard far off in the heart of the forest. The beast appeared at the tree line of the last field and bayed as the corpse was set aflame. By the time the smoke cleared, the dog had vanished.

Mount Chary Galore

Mrs. Oftshaw was best known for a liniment of her own concoction, *Mount Chary Galore*, that had no other curative property than to make you feel generally *right* and was suspected of being some part of the black lace mushrooms she gathered by the light of an orange moon. She was a strange, solitary old bat, who'd been around so long she was part of the landscape. She'd swoop into town out of the deep woods at the base of the looming mountain, swerving all over the asphalt in her rusted Pontiac. Even the young boys with new driver's licenses and stupid with courage cleared the road when they saw her coming. Sheriff Bedlow wrote her a stack of tickets through the years, but he was not particularly fearless and would only stick them under the busted windshield wiper when the car was parked and empty. She'd just crumple them in her boney hands and toss them in the dirt.

When she arrived in town, nobody ever came out to greet her, but eyes gazed from behind curtains or betwixt blinds. Those who relied on the Galore were watching, silently counting their nickels and dimes. She eased out of the front seat of that jalopy and gave a little hop down to the ground. She was short and bent with age, but she had a quickness to her—birdlike. Her outfits were layered, mostly the same for either winter or summer, except in the snowy part of the year, when she'd add an oversized sailor's peacoat to the getup—blue leggings, a loose billowing dress, wooden shoes, and a voluminous kerchief draped around her head, a tunnel of fabric you had to peer into to see her pale, wrinkled face like some critter living in a hollow log.

If you got close enough, as I did when she came to deliver a jar of Galore to my poor ma, you could catch a whiff of her scent, which was not old or ugly or rotten, but beautiful, like the smell of wisteria. Ma always served lavender tea with honey at the parlor table. Mrs. Oftshaw was partial to a jigger of Old Overholt in hers, and she kept a pint in the pocket of that peacoat when the weather got raw. They whispered back and forth for a time. When I asked my ma what they talked about, she'd smile and say, "Men." "Like Pa?" I asked. She sighed, shook her head and laughed. Just before leaving, the old lady always slipped a jar of Galore from her pocket and placed it next to the tea cup, never asking for a cent.

On the 27th of every month, she came to town, the Pontiac's trunk full of cardboard boxes, each holding six Ball jars of a bright green paste that smelled like, as Lardner Scott, Charyville's postmaster, had described it, "A home permanent on the Devil's ass hair." Once liberally applied to the chest or the back of the neck, the Galore had a way of easing you down, as if taking your hand and whispering, helping you to sit back into the comfy chair that, amazingly enough, at that moment, you would just be realizing was your life. For a woman who was much feared and much gossiped about, Lillian Oftshaw had a lot of customers—some steady as sunrise, some seasonal, some just passing through. The fact is, she never left town at the end of the month that those boxes in her trunk weren't entirely empty.

On the other hand, during those liniment runs, her passenger seat was never empty, for she was accompanied each time by a large gray hog, nearly three hundred pounds, named Jundle, who sat upright, resting his spine against the seat back, crossing his short hind legs, the right over the left, and leaning his right front leg out the open window. I saw it with my own eyes. That remarkable creature sometimes smoked a fat roll-up of a cheroot, holding it in the split of his cloven hoof and every now and then bringing it up to his snout to take a long drag. Jundle got out of the car and accompanied her to each doorstep as she delivered the Galore and collected her cash. Once a couple of smart-alec kids thought they'd have some fun with the old lady and then make off with her velvet sack of quarters and dimes. Legs were swiftly broken, and, as it's told, those boys were lucky it wasn't necks. Jundle was a jolly creature, but he had a serious side when it came to the well-being of Mrs. Oftshaw.

A jar of the Galore cost fifty cents, which, at the time, was a dear price. There were folks with steady income who went for a jar of the green mystery every month, and there were others who had to use it sparingly, skimping on the application to achieve at least half-rightness half the time. Mote Kimber, a veteran of the Great War, who had seen the fellows of his regiment mowed down like summer wheat at the Belleau Wood in France and when captured was tortured—a thin, white hot iron inserted into the opening of his pecker—slathered the Galore onto his bald noggin like he was painting a fence post. After a while the crown of his head had turned jade green, and he could be counted on at any hour after that of breakfast to usually be way past *right*. He was a bona-fide war hero, though, and drew a nice pension for his courage. Before being taken by the enemy, he'd rescued three men who'd been wounded and pinned down. Mote would tell you himself that he bought two jars of Galore a month from Lillian. "Either that or kill myself," he said, and everybody knew he meant it.

There were a number of folks in town who used the liniment for medical purposes—gout, heartburn, bad back, aches and pains of the joints, the head, the heart. Even Dr. Shevin used it. When asked about its unscientific nature and reliance on backwoods hoodoo, he smiled as if realizing his guilt, shrugged, and said, "When I get a crick in my neck, which I do often enough from a bad sleeping posture, just a dab of that Galore on the stiff patch and all's well and then some. Now, if you're asking me if I prescribe it for my patients, I'd have to give you an unequivocal 'No.' I'm a man of Science. I don't suggest anyone else use it, but if they do . . . ?" The discussion never went any further. There was no point. If the doctor had been laying it on like old Mote Kimber and was too *right* all the time, now that would have been a problem, but as it was, he used it like most everyone else—"Pro re nata," as he said, which Postmaster Scott translated for us as, "When the bullshit gets too thick."

Old lady Oftshaw was mysterious, that's for certain, but I wouldn't say she was evil. There were a lot of folks who just couldn't afford the Galore, and some of them were the ones that needed it most. My ma was one of them. Ever since my daddy ran off on us, she had to work double shifts over at the chicken-packing plant in Hartmere just to keep the house, put food on the table, and gas in the Chevy. And it wasn't just me and her. There was Alice Jane and Pretty Please who also lived under our roof. They were the kids of the woman who Daddy ran off with. Their mother simply abandoned them— something no wild animal would do. Instead of letting Sheriff Bedlow cart the kids away to an orphanage in Johnston, the county seat, my ma asked him to leave them with her. I was there when she made her case. "No sense in having everybody suffer," she said. "They're just kids, and they need to know a little love before they get too old." The sheriff, though short on courage, was long on heart, and he trusted her. He closed his eyes to the law, something that could never happen today, letting Alice Jane become my sort of sister and Pretty Please become my sort of brother.

I suspect you want to know something else about my daddy and why he left Ma, but I truly don't know anything to tell. I was happy to see him go. He was a moody fellow. Quiet. Never did anything father-like with me that I can remember. Although I will say he did buy me a 22 rifle and taught me to shoot out in the prairie over by the creek on the way to Mount Chary. But it wasn't like he did it to get closer to me, more like he was teaching me to take the garbage out to the curb or how to make coffee so he didn't have to get up quite as early in the morning. Although she never said anything about him, I remember Ma's eyes being red a lot and more than once a big yellow-blue bruise on her neck.

Mrs. Adler had no man at the time Daddy ran off with her, and Alice never had any stories about her pa or photographs for that matter. The whole thing was a mystery I never got to the bottom of. If I'd asked my ma, I know she'd have told me, but I came to avoid that question, afraid it might leave a wound, like a bullet from the 22.

I was fourteen the year our family declined by one and then grew by two. Alice Jane was the same age as me, but born in summer while I was born in winter. She had long hair braided into pigtails and a freckled face with sleepy green eyes. I thought she was nice, but I didn't let on. She could throw a hard punch or climb a tree, beat me in a race. Her brother, Pretty Please, was "something of a enigma," or at least that's what I heard Postmaster Scott whisper to Ma when she told him she'd taken on responsibility for the Adler children. We were at the counter and I was standing next to her while Alice and Pretty were standing over by the private mailboxes. Men of all kinds seemed to make my sort-of-siblings both shy and scared. "The girl's cute enough, but that boy is . . . *pe-culiar,*" said Scott. "He just looks a sight," said my mother, "inside he's true."

I turned and looked at Pretty Please. He was fifteen, and not but an inch or two taller than me, but he had a big old head, full-moon pale and shorn close, looking like a peeled potato with beady eyes. He wore a pair of overalls with no shirt in summer. He seemed always busy, looking around, up and down and all over, rarely fixing on any one sight. Whenever somebody said anything to Ma about him, she'd nod and say, "He's OK," as if trying to convince herself. The only words he ever said were "Pretty please" in a kind of parrot voice. We didn't know where he learned it from, but he seemed to have a vague sense of how to make use of it. Ma asked Alice Jane if he'd always been simple, and she just nodded and confided that their mother used to beat him with a hair brush. His real name, Alice told us, was Jelibai, and Ma asked us to call him that but we didn't.

The fact that my ma took in the kids of the woman who ran off with my pa was, even to me, downright odd, and to the rest of the town she was either touched by God or touched in the head. I think some thought she had nefarious purposes in mind, maybe to torture them in the place of the woman who stole her man? But in Charyville the rule was to keep your mouth shut and mind your own business. Things had to get really out of hand for someone to pipe up.

The first summer of our new family came, and Alice Jane and I were out of school, on the loose. Pretty Please didn't go to school. The reason Principal Otis gave Ma for not letting him in was, "That poor boy is gone over the hill." Pretty was delighted for us to be home every day, 'cause usually, when school was in session, he'd have to be by himself, locked up in the basement with my dog, Ghost, a mop head with legs and a bark. Ma would make Pretty peanut butter sandwiches and he could listen to the radio or look at books or say Pretty Please to the dog a hundred times. He liked to draw, and you shoulda seen his pictures—yow—people with scribbledy heads and no eyes.

There was a bathroom in the basement, and it was cozy enough and lonely enough. Ma just didn't want him getting to the burner of the stove, where he could leave the gas on and blow the place up or set himself on fire. But when *we* were on the loose, Pretty was on the loose. We all liked to be free and always had something to do from the time Ma left in the morning for work to when she came back at night and Alice Jane and me cooked her dinner. I could tell she was worried about us on our own, but I told her, "We're not babies anymore. We can watch out for each other." Her hand that held the cigarette shook a little, and Alice patted her back soft like Ma did for us at night as we went to sleep.

The summers were fine for fishing, fist fights, shooting guns, drinking pop, catching snakes, swimming the creek, riding bikes, playing baseball, bottling lightning bugs, and watching the big moon rise. When on Sundays the minister spoke of Paradise, all I had to compare it to was summer vacation.

Then on a bright morning in late July, the three of us were out early, and Alice Jane and I decided we would find the day's adventure by just letting Pretty Please run up ahead of our bikes. We followed him wherever he went. It didn't make any sense, and we all laughed, even Pretty, when he ran ten times in the same tight circle. We wound up traveling all the way to the edge of town to the red brick arches of the entrance to the church's side garden. We went there a couple times a week in the early morning. There was a fountain and a bench within those walls. Tears issued from the eyes of a sculpted woman. The water trickled down, plashing from level to level quieter than a whisper. The aroma of the roses was almost too much.

One bright morning, following that scent without hesitation, Pretty walked right in there. Alice Jane and I left our bikes on the sidewalk and followed. We found him standing still as a store manikin, staring up at Minister Sauter, who stood over him looking annoyed. When the preacher saw us enter the garden, his expression quickly changed to a smile. He took a seat on a bench by the fountain and motioned for us to sit down as well. We did. Alice and I were on either side of the minister, and Pretty, watching ripples in the water, slumped on the bench next to his sister.

Sauter said, "How'd you kids like to make some money?"

"Whata we gotta do?" asked Alice.

"Well, I want you to ride out to the woods beneath the mountain and find that old woman Oftshaw's house."

"Pardon," I said, "but she's an old witch, ain't she? My ma says she's got spells."

Alice smacked herself in the forehead for my ignorance.

The minister laughed. "The old lady's a Christian, I think," he said.

"How much money?" asked Alice.

"Let's see," said Sauter. "I want you to go out there and I want you to watch what she does. I want you to remember it and then come back and tell me."

"Easy," said Alice Jane. I nodded. Pretty Please said, "Pretty please."

"One thing, though," said the minister. "You can't let her see you watchin' her."

"That's spying," said Alice.

"It would be," said Sauter, "but I'm gonna make you all deputy angels before you go. As a deputy angel, you can do my bidding and not get in trouble with the law or God. The Lord has put his trust in me, and so must you."

"I don't want to go to heaven," I said.

"Do you want to make twenty cents?" asked Alice.

We took the oath, and then Alice Jane took it again once for Pretty. I kept messing up the words, and at one point the minister put his hand at the base of my throat to steady me, but in the moment I wasn't sure he didn't intend to strangle me. As soon as we were deputy angels, he shooed us out of the garden. As we mounted our bikes, he whispered to us from the entrance, "Report to me tomorrow at this time. Tell no one. The devil is listening."

Mention of the devil scared us, and we rode silently and with great determination straight north toward Chary Mountain. Pretty Please ran ahead along the side of the empty road, never tiring. That morning the dew had covered everything, made everything glimmer. The sky was deep blue, and there were just white wisps but no real clouds. It was a good couple of miles out to Chary, and so eventually we slowed down and Alice told Pretty to also.

"Why's this lady live all the way out here by herself?" asked Alice, slow pedaling beside me.

"I don't know too much about her, but she had a husband who either died or ran off."

"Probably ran off," said Alice.

"Ma says Mrs. Oftshaw's from some other country."

"Which one?"

"From across an ocean."

I didn't say anything for a while, and Alice asked me, "Is that all you know?"

"Oh, you must've seen her. She's got a smoking hog name of Jundle."

We laughed, and when I focused back on the road, I spotted Pretty Please, way up ahead, making for the tree line.

Alice no doubt saw it before I did and had taken off, pumping her legs furiously. I worked to catch up with her. Every once in a while, Pretty would get what we called "the urge." Sometimes he just bolted away. It didn't happen often, maybe once every couple weeks. This time he was really moving at a clip, and we both saw him reach the boundary of the woods and slip inside. We left the road and cut across the short field that bordered the tree line. Riding our bikes amidst the trees was slowing us down, so we dropped them and went forward on foot. Alice's voice could be ear-splitting, and she used it every few steps. "Pretty, Pretty, Pretty, Please," she called.

She grew more frantic the farther we went. "I can't lose him," she said to me.

I tried to tell her he'd turn up, but every time I spoke those words, she shook her head and walked faster. By the time I had to take her hand to calm her down, we'd come to the top of a rise. We stood at the crown of the hill and looked down through the trunks of cedar pine and birch trees at a glittering pond. Sitting at the water's edge was Pretty Please, investigating something in the sand. At the sight of him, Alice sighed and turned in toward me. I put my arm around her and froze. She shrugged me off and took a seat a few feet down the incline. I followed and sat next to her.

"I want to ask that brother of yours, pretty please to not run off like that anymore."

"My old ma, not your ma, told me once that Pretty was a bag of flesh filled with wind." She took a couple breaths, staring down at her brother. "My Ma was a mean bitch."

When she said that, we both broke out laughing. That one knocked me over. When I sat back up I took her hand in mine again. She didn't make like she noticed. We sat there quiet, taking in the smell of the cedar pines and the sound of goldfinches. The glitter on the water was diamonds and stars. She turned to look into my eyes and said, "We should kiss."

At the moment, I couldn't think of one good reason not to. So we did. And before long she stuck her tongue in my mouth and then we were rolling on the ground rubbing each other up. So much rubbing—we had "the urge"—I thought the two of us would be erased. We reached a point where I had my hand up her shirt, and she had just grabbed my pecker down my pants, when out of the blue, she gets suddenly still, turns her head, and yells, "Pretty Please." In a heartbeat she was off the ground, fixing her clothes. Pretty was gone, and it was the only time I ever wished him ill.

We ran through the woods, toward the base of the mountain, and the undergrowth grew more tangled and difficult to manage. We'd follow a natural path through the trees and then eventually be stopped by a wall of thorn bushes and turn back to find another way forward. Alice was frantic again, and I had to keep her a few times from trying to find passage through the heart of one of those bushes that would rip her to shreds. Eventually we came to a clearing in the shade of the mountain.

It was, by then, late afternoon, but dark as twilight where we stood. I was happy just to have some open ground before us.

Alice noticed it first. The place was so covered in ivy and some other trailing vine I didn't recognize it as a house. Only when she pointed to where lamplight glowed through a small window, one mere corner of its glass not covered by leaves, did I see it. Then I noticed that there was smoke issuing from inside through the metal chimney of a stove. The house wasn't huge but it had two floors and seemed out of place in the woods—more like a home you might find in a big town. It had a slate roof, and you could make out the fancy wood carvings they call gingerbread beneath the ivy.

"Should we do some spying?" I asked Alice in a whisper.

I know she was thinking about Pretty 'cause she hesitated for a second. "Twenty cents is twenty cents," she said. "We'll just peek in the window and see what we see. Then we gotta get. Whatever we see, we'll tell the minister."

"What if it ain't much?"

"We'll make something up like good deputy angels."

"Stay quiet," I said to her and tried to take her hand. She pushed me away.

"I can do this myself," she said, and we proceeded side by side.

As we approached the back of the house we heard noises coming out from inside. I realized the back door was slightly ajar. The closer we got, the smaller the steps we took until we were only inching along a little at a time. I felt cold in my gut, slightly dizzy, and my legs felt weighed down like in those dreams where you need to run but can't. Alice was breathing quickly, her eyes focused on the light coming through the sliver of an entrance.

Sitting on a tree stump, right outside the back door, there was a little painted box with a design like fancy wallpaper. Alice lifted it quickly, tipped the lid up, and peered inside. She slipped it into her pocket. "That's thievery," I whispered. She shhh'd me and showed me the back of her hand as if getting ready to smack me.

No less than a breath later, the door suddenly flew open and there stood old lady Oftshaw without her tunnel scarf, her pale face and wild hair unhidden. She was lit from behind, and the glow made her seem some kind of spirit. I stopped dead in my tracks and froze. Alice grabbed my hand and spun us around. She started to yell "Run," I think, but whatever the word was it vanished, 'cause standing right in our path was Jundle. Alice took a step, and the hog made a noise from deep inside his huge body that sounded like the earth grunting. He came at us, plodding slowly, and we turned and walked toward Mrs. Oftshaw. I couldn't get any spit in my mouth, and my legs were like two dead fish.

"Come in, children," said the old lady, and she stepped back and held open the door for us. We stepped into her kitchen, first Alice and then me. We stood right next to each other and kept some distance between us and Mrs. Oftshaw. She let the door go, and it slammed shut, making us start. I don't know how, but I was able to look up at her face. I'd never seen it clearly before. In that moment, I saw that she wasn't a homely old woman but just an old woman.

"You kids here to spy on me?" she asked and smiled in a way that made me scared.

I was all set to spill the beans, but before I could open my mouth, Alice stepped forward and said, "We brought my brother out to the pond in the woods, but we lost him. Can you help us find him?"

The old lady said, "He's not lost."

"We really don't know where he is, and I have to find him." Alice said.

"He's not lost, child. He's on an expedition."

"Where is he?" I asked.

"He's travelling far," she said. "But I can help you. I'll send Cynara, the world's oldest heifer, after him. She'll bring him home." She went to the door, opened it, and whistled. With her hand, she motioned for us to come and join her by the entrance. In a few moments, Jundle slowly came waddling into sight. He stood in front of us, a cigarette in the corner of his mouth, smoke issuing in pigtails.

"Take Cynara and go and fetch the Pretty boy."

Jundle dropped a little pile of turds, grumbled, and trotted off.

"Done and done," said the old lady. "Now let me make you kids a snack."

She led us into her house, through the kitchen and into the parlor, all lace doilies and puffy furniture in pea green. There was a small chandelier above, its pendants glinting, and below a braided rug in blue and silver.

"You can sit on the love seat," she said and pointed at a small couch. "I'll be right back. Gon fetch you some of my special cookies."

When she left the room, we saw it. It had been sitting behind her on a shiny wooden pedestal. No, not a radio, but a big clear glass ball with a man's head floating in it. I jumped at the sight and Alice whispered, "What?" And "what" was right— a head with wavy black hair, waving in the water, a black beard and mustache, eyes shut and mouth part way open to show a few teeth. At the bottom of the glass ball there was sand and a little hermit crab scuttling around in it. Tiny starfish were suspended around the head.

Mrs. Oftshaw suddenly appeared with a tray full of cookies and two glasses of what looked like yellow milk. "Have a treat," she said and laid it down on the little table in front of us. She backed away, and said, "Go ahead."

The cookies were fat and misshapen, the color of eggplant, with shreds of something sticking out all over. Neither of us made a move for them. She sat down in the armchair next to the pedestal. "I see you've met Captain Gruthwal," she said and pointed to the floating head.

We nodded.

"Have a cookie, and we'll wake him up."

Alice leaned over first and took one of the lumpy "treats." I followed her lead. The thing was soggy as a turd and smelled like what Pa used to pull out of the gutters in spring. We bit into them at the same time, like biting into a clod of dirt, but the taste was better than sweet and made me shiver. One bite and you wanted another till the thing was gone. We each ate two more, and every time one of us would slip one off the tray, the old lady nodded and said, "That's right. That's right."

After the third, we sat back. I don't know about Alice but my head was spinning a little and I felt kind of good all over. I looked at her and she smiled at me, lids half closed. "Drink your peach milk," said Mrs. Oftshaw. It seemed like a good idea, so I did and so did Alice. I can't recall what the peach milk tasted like, whether peaches or something else. We put the empty glasses on the tray, and the old lady turned to face the glass globe beside her.

"Wake up, Captain Gruthwal," she said. "Wake up."

I swear, Alice screamed louder than me when the eyes of the floating head opened and stared at us. "Captain," said Mrs. Oftshaw. "These children want to know about the big-headed boy."

The floating face grimaced, as if annoyed at being awoken. Its eyes shifted toward the old lady and then rolled up, showing only white. The captain's mouth opened wider and then wider, and I thought he would scream in the water. We waited for a torrent of bubbles and the muffled sound, but instead something showed itself from within the dark cavern. It was a pale knob, like a diseased tongue but much larger. It filled the rim of his lips and continued to squeeze itself out from inside him. Two tentacles emerged and then more. "An octopus," I said and gagged.

"Ugghh," said Alice and turned her face from the sight.

"Watch it, child," said Mrs. Oftshaw. "Watch it good. The captain's gonna show us something."

I felt Alice's hand on my shoulder, as the octopus, now free, swam, pulsing its tentacles in circles around the floating head. As the pale sac of life swept in orbit around the captain, its ink oozed out of it in black plumes. Alice's grip tightened as the face and everything else inside the globe was slowly obscured.

"Like a dream," said Mrs. Oftshaw, and out of the murk came an image of Pretty Please walking along the side of the road in the moonlight.

"Pretty," yelled Alice, and her brother turned his potato head and glanced over his shoulder. She yelled again, "Come back," but the ink was already swirling the image away to reveal a different scene of Jundle riding atop a sorry old cow all skin and bones, the way a person might, straddling its back. They moved along at a snail's pace, the hog strumming the steel strings of a little guitar and grunting softly.

More swirling of the ink and image and then we were back to Pretty and saw him standing next to a one-story house, not much more than a shack. He was peering in a window with the moonlight shining over his shoulder. Through the dirty glass and the shadows, I saw two people sleeping in a bed: a man and a woman.

"That's my ma," said Alice and stood up.

"Very good, child," said Mrs. Oftshaw.

"What's that in Pretty's hand?" I asked, noticing something glint in the moonlight. I squinted and saw it was an open straight razor, the one Pa had left behind in the bathroom cabinet. "Either Pretty's 'bout to do some shavin' or he's possessed by a bad idea," I said.

Alice noticed the razor and stepped toward the globe. "No, Pretty," she said. Her hands, fingers spread wide, reached for the glass.

Just then he lifted the blade and the man in the bed next to Alice's ma, my pa, opened his eyes and witnessed the scene at the window. We saw him shake his head, look again, and heard, muffled by the window glass, him yell, "Mattie, your nitwit kid's outside and he's totin' a cutthroat."

"What?" said Mrs. Adler, and she woke and looked and shook her head too. "Christ, it's him. How can it be?"

"It's bewitchment," said Pa. "I'm gonna take care of this right now." He stood up, naked, in the further shadows behind the bed. I lost sight of him for a moment, and then he appeared again in the moonlight, holding his 22 rifle. He left the room.

"Ya can't shoot him," called Mrs. Adler.

As the front door to the little house creaked open, we could hear Pa yell back, "Self-defense."

Alice screamed, "No!" and lunged at the globe. She tripped, hit the pedestal, and although Mrs. Oftshaw moved to catch either her or Captain Gruthwal, she caught neither. The globe hit the floor and exploded into stars of glass as the ink seeped into the parlor. There was more blackness in that glass bubble than you could have guessed. Darkness filled the room by the time I'd grabbed Alice's hand and was helping her off the floor. I couldn't see a damn thing, but I held on tight to my sort of sister and she held on to me until the moonlight shone.

We were standing in the clearing of pines where the shack was. Pretty was walking around the side of the place, obviously heading for the front door, while Pa, naked as a jaybird, his pecker flopping, the 22 raised and aimed, was heading for the side. At the corner they met face-to-face.

"Say yer prayers, tater face," said Pa, and I yelled out for him not to shoot.

He turned quick and saw me and Alice standing there, and his eyes bugged. "Oh," he said, and it was like he lost his breath for a second. It was the first time I seen him scared.

"The whole fuckin' family," he said. "No problem, I'll plug all you crumb snatchers at once." Mrs. Adler was at the window just plain screaming, not even saying anything.

Pretty swept the razor in front of him and slashed Pa's forearm. The gun dipped down for a moment, but Pa groaned a little and raised it again. I couldn't look and I couldn't not look, expecting any second for Pretty's head to be shattered like the glass globe. He brought the razor up as if he meant to split Pa down the middle, and Pa froze in his usual stance when he was about to pull the trigger. Before he could fire, though, we saw some shadow, moving low through the night.

Jundle hit Pa behind the knees and my old man crumpled up and whimpered, the gun flying out of his hands. I dove for it and grabbed it away, but backing up I fell onto my ass. Pa kicked the hog in the head and scrabbled after me on his knees. "Give me that gun, Jr. That's an order."

He got up and stood over me with burning eyes and a hideous expression. In my fear, I pulled the trigger, and the bullet went through his left eye and come straight out the back with the crack of bone and a splurt of blood and brain. He stood there for a second, that eye hole smoking like the ash on one of Jundle's cheroots, and then he fell forward like a cut tree. I rolled out of the way. He was so heavy with death that he would have made a pancake of me.

I wanted to think about the fact that I'd just killed my pa, but there wasn't a second. Alice was standing at the window staring out like she was hypnotized. By the time I reached her, Pretty had already commenced slicing up Mrs. Adler. She was slit open from the chin to belly button and blood was everywhere, soaking her night gown, pooling on the floor in the moonlight. I saw her heart beating inside her. She moved her mouth to make a blood-bubble whisper, and I could tell by reading her lips that her last words were "Pretty Please."

I pulled Alice away and put my arms around her. She didn't move a muscle and was cold as stone. When I drew away, I found a huge grin on her face. Next I knew, Pretty was beside us, drenched in blood, laughing, with an arm around each of our shoulders. "How'd we get here?" I asked Alice when the hug broke up.

"I don't know," she said, "but let's get."

I looked around and saw Jundle, recovered from his foot to the face, taking a piss against the side of the house. When he was done, he took the burning cheroot from his mouth and touched its red-hot tip to the planks where he'd relieved himself. Fire sprang up as if from gasoline, and in a blink the flames were creeping up the side of the shack.

The hog trotted over to us and made a motion with his head that we were to climb on his back. Somehow, though it didn't seem possible, we all fit. He grunted, squealed, farted, took three enormous jumps, and lit into the sky. We were flying upward on the back of a hog. I was petrified, and could feel Alice's arms wrapped around my chest and her face pressing into my back. I couldn't see Pretty, and didn't know how he was managing to hang on, but I still heard his laughter, which hadn't ceased since he sliced up his ma.

At one point Jundle swept down low over a dirt path through a wood, and we saw the shot and butchered bodies of our parents riding the back of Cynara the old heifer, heading off to, I guessed, hell. By the time Jundle reached an altitude where we were soaring through white clouds and stars, I was exhausted. It was peaceful way up there. I wrapped my arms around the enchanted animal's thick bristly neck as I fell forward into sleep.

I woke, confused, in my own bed the next morning, and so did Alice and Pretty Please. Ma, who had our breakfast ready as always before leaving for work, seemed never to suspect a thing. We couldn't wait for her to leave for work. When she finally did, Alice said to me. "What do you make of it?"

"Did we kill your ma and my pa?"

"I guess we did," she said.

Pretty actually nodded.

"It ain't possible," I said. I ran to the bathroom and checked for the razor in the cabinet. It was gone. I ran back to report to Alice.

"We gotta act like nothing happened," she said. "Deny everything."

"Its gonna be hard to forget. How'd we get back from Mrs. Oftshaw's?"

"Jundle," said Pretty Please, and me and Alice almost fell over. It was the first time her brother had said anything but that which had become his name.

Later that morning, we were back at the rose garden of the church in order to keep our deal. We sat on the bench, looking at the fountain, all of us still tired from the doings of the night. Eventually the minister came out to see us. We gave him a seat on the bench between me and Alice. Pretty didn't budge for him.

"Did you go and look in on Mrs. Oftshaw?" he asked.

I nodded, and Alice said, "We did."

"She's got a magic hog," I told him.

"She's got a man's head floatin' in water," said Alice.

"We shaved," said Pretty Please, another surprise.

The minister looked quizzically at us. "You must tell me the truth," he said.

"Us deputy angels got inside her place, and I took this little box," said Alice. "I spied on her whispering into it. Then she shut the lid down tight. Must have been a curse or something."

I looked at Alice, but she wouldn't look at me.

"Give me that," said the minister and took the fancy box from her hand. "There's no such thing as curses, dear." He pulled the lid off and held it up to look inside. We saw it there, a shiny red wasp with a long stinger that looked like a piece of jewelry cut from ruby. Only thing is, its wings started to flutter, and then all of a sudden it took off. It flew straight up into the minister's face and sunk that long stinger into the white jelly of his left eye. The box hit the paving stones, and the poor man screamed, bringing his hands up to cover his face.

We never got paid for spying that day 'cause we ran for our bikes with Pretty hot behind us. We pedaled like mad back home and hid with the curtains pulled over, expecting Sheriff Bedlow any minute for hours on end. But he never did come, and the minister never told on us. Maybe he was afraid that people would find out he'd promised to pay us for spying on Mrs. Oftshaw. As it was, he had to start using the Mount Chary Galore on that eye, the only thing he claimed would stop the burning.

The summer ended and it was time to return to school for me and Alice, and Pretty had to go back to the basement. We thought that he'd start using more words now that he'd said a few, but that petered out soon enough. A few weeks had gone by, and I still didn't know what to make of that crazy night. Then one day my ma called all us kids together when she returned home from work. Before we ate dinner, she sat us down on the couch, herself in a chair across from us.

"I hate to have to tell you this," she said, and I could see her grow weak. She lowered her head slightly so we couldn't see her eyes. "Your ma," she said, nodding toward Alice, "and your pa," she said to me, "are dead. I don't know how else to put it."

Neither Alice or me said a peep. If my sort of sister was half as surprised as I was, her tongue felt turned to stone.

My mother cried, and we moved closer and put our arms around her. Finally Alice said, "What happened?"

My ma just shook her head.

"How'd they die?" I asked.

She was silent for a time, drying her eyes, and eventually said, "Car crash out in California."

"That ain't really what happened, is it?" asked Alice, softly, stroking the back of Ma's neck.

Ma shook her head. In a whisper she said, "No."

"What then?" I asked.

"It's too terrible. Far too terrible to describe."

A few days later, the summer ended. Me and Alice had to go back to school and Pretty was sent to the basement. He'd slowly lost all his new power of speech, but not before my ma got to hear him say the word "Love," which managed to lift her out of the funk caused by finding out about Pa's death. From then on, when Mrs. Oftshaw was coming to the house, me and Alice made sure we were out. We'd had enough of her magic, but it was our secret and we talked about it when we'd slip out into the woods to kiss. Late one afternoon that fall, after the weather had gone cold, I spied Mount Chary bathed in the last golden light of day, like an ancient, gilded pyramid, looming in the distance down the end of the one road out of town, and I got a feeling for the first time in my life that everything was finally *right.*

A Natural History of Autumn

On a blue afternoon in autumn, Riku and Michi drove south from Numazu in his silver convertible along the coast of the Izu Peninsula. The temperature was mild for the end of October, and the air was clear, the sun glinting off Suruga Bay. She wore sunglasses and, to protect her hair, a yellow scarf with a design of orange butterflies. He wore driving gloves, a black dress shirt, a loosened white tie. The car, the open road, the rush of the wind made it impossible to converse, and so for miles she watched the bay to their right and he the rising slopes of maple and pine to their left. Just outside the town of Dogashima, a song came on the radio, "Just You, Just Me," and they turned to look at each other. She waited for him to smile. He did. She smiled back, and then he headed inland to search for the hidden onsen, Inugami.

They'd met the previous night at the Limit, an upscale hostess bar. Riku's employer had a tab there and he was free to use it when in Numazu. He'd been once before, drunk, and spent time with a hostess. Her conversation had sounded rote, like a script; her flattery grotesquely opulent and therefore flat. The instant he saw Michi, though, in her short black dress with a look of uncertainty in her eyes, he knew it would be a different experience. He ordered a bottle of Nikka Yoichi and two glasses. She introduced herself. He stood and bowed. They were in a private room at a polished table of blond wood. The chairs were high-backed and upholstered like thrones. To their right was an open-air view of pines and the coast. She waited for him to smile and eventually he did. She smiled back and told him, "I'm writing a book."

Riku said, "Aren't you supposed to tell me how handsome I am?"

"Your hair is perfect," she said.

He laughed. "I see."

"I'm writing a book," she said again. "I decided to make a study of something."

"You're a scientist?" he said.

"We're all scientists," she said. "We watch and listen, take in information, process it. We spin theories by which we live."

"What if they're false?"

"What if they're not?" she said.

He shook his head and took a drink.

They sat in silence for a time. She stared out past the pines, sipping her whisky. He stared at her.

"Tell me about your family," said Riku.

She told him about her dead father, her ill mother, her younger sister and brother, but when she inquired about his parents, he said, "Okay, tell me about your book."

"I decided to study a season, and since autumn is the season I'm in, it would be autumn. It's a natural history of autumn."

"You've obviously been to the university," he said.

She shook her head. "No, I read a lot to pass the time between clients."

"How much have you written?"

"Nothing yet. I'm researching now, taking notes."

"Do you go out to Thousand Tree Beach and stare at Fuji in the morning?"

"Your sarcasm is intoxicating," she said.

He filled her glass.

"No, I do my research here. I ask each client what autumn means to him."

"And they tell you?"

She nodded. "Some just want me to say how big their biceps are but most sit back and really think about it. The thought of it makes all the white-haired ojiisans smile, the businessmen cry, the young men a little scared. A lot of it is the same. Just images—the colorful leaves, the clear cold mornings by the bay, a certain pet dog, a childhood friend, a drunken night. But sometimes they tell me whole stories."

"What kind of stories?"

"A very powerful businessman—one of the other hostesses swore he was a master of the five elements—once told me his own love story, about a young woman he had an affair with. It began on the final day of summer, lasted only as long as the following season, and ended in the snow."

"What did you learn from that story? What did you put in your notes?"

"I recorded his story as he'd told it, and afterward wrote, 'The Story of a Ghost.'"

"Why a ghost?" he asked.

"I forget," she said. "And I lied—I attended Waseda University for two years before my father died."

"You didn't have to tell me," he said. "I knew when you told me you called the businessman's story 'The Story of a Ghost.'"

"Pretentious?" she asked.

He shrugged.

"Maybe," she said and smiled.

"Forget about that," said Riku. "I will top that make-inu businessman's exquisite melancholy by proposing a field trip." He sat forward in his chair and touched the tabletop with his index finger. "My employer recently rewarded me for a job well done and suggested I use, whenever I like, a private onsen he has an arrangement with down in Izu. I need only call a few hours in advance."

"A field trip?" she said. "What will we be researching?"

"Autumn. The red and yellow leaves. The place is out in the woods on a mountainside, hidden and very old-fashioned, no frills. I propose a dohan, an overnight journey to the onsen, Inugami."

"A date," she said. "And our attentions will only be on autumn, nothing else?"

"You can trust me when I say, that is entirely up to you."

"Your hair inspires confidence," she said. "You can arrange things with the house on the way out."

"I intend to be in your book," he said and prevented himself from smiling.

After hours of winding along the rims of steep cliffs and bumping down tight dirt paths through the woods, the silver car pulled to a stop in a clearing, in front of a large, slightly sagging farmhouse—minka style, built of logs with a thatched roof. Twenty yards to the left of the place there was a sizeable garden filled with dying sunflowers, ten-foot stalks, their heads bowed. To the right of the house there was a slate path that led away into the pines. The golden late-afternoon light slanted down on the clearing, shadows beginning to form at the tree line.

"We're losing the day," said Riku. "We'll have to hurry."

Michi got out of the car and stretched. She removed her sunglasses and stood still for a moment, taking in the cool air.

"I have your bag," said Riku and shut the trunk.

As they headed for the house, two figures appeared on the porch. One was a small old woman with white hair, wearing monpe pants and an indigo Katazome jacket with a design of white flames. Next to her stood what Michi at first mistook for a pony. The sight of the animal surprised her and she stopped walking. Riku went on ahead. "Grandmother Chinatsu," he said and bowed.

"Your employer has arranged everything with me. Welcome," she said. A small, wrinkled hand with dirty nails appeared from within the sleeve of the jacket. She beckoned to Michi. "Come, my dear, don't be afraid of my pet, Ono. He doesn't bite." She smiled and waved her arm.

As Michi approached, she bowed to Grandmother Chinatsu, who only offered a nod. The instant the young woman's foot touched the first step of the porch, the dog gave a low growl. The old lady wagged a finger at the creature and snapped, "Yemeti!" Then she laughed, low and gruff, the sound at odds with her diminutive size. She extended her hand and helped Michi up onto the porch. "Come in," she said and led them into the farmhouse.

Michi was last in line. She turned to look at the dog. Its coat was more like curly human hair than fur. She winced in disgust. A large flattened pug face, no snout to speak of, black eyes, sharp ears, and a thick bottom lip bubbling with drool. "Ono," she said and bowed slightly in passing. As she stepped into the shadow beyond the doorway, she felt the dog's nose press momentarily against the back of her dress.

In the main room there was a rock fireplace within which a low flame licked two maple logs. Above hung a large paper lantern, orange with white blossoms, shedding a soft light in the center of the room. The place was rustic, wonderfully simple. All was wood: the walls, the ceiling, the floor. There were three ancient carved wooden chairs gathered around a low table off in an alcove at one side of the room. Grandmother led them down a hallway to the back of the place. They passed a room on the left, its screen shut. At the next room, the old lady slid open the panel and said, "The toilet." Farther on, they came to two rooms, one on either side of the hallway. She let them know who was to occupy which by mere nods of her head. "The bath is at the end of the hall," she said.

Their rooms were tatami style, straw mats and a platform bed with a futon mattress in the far corner. They undressed, put on robes and sandals, and met in the hallway. As they passed through the main room of the house, Ono stirred from his spot by the fireplace, looked up at them, and snorted.

"Easy, easy," said Riku to the creature. He stepped aside and let Michi get in front of him. Once out on the porch, she said, "Ono is a little scary."

"Only a little?" he asked.

Grandmother appeared from within the plot of dying sunflowers and called that there were towels in the shed out by the spring. Riku waved to her as he and Michi took the slate path into the pines. Shadows were rising beneath the trees and the sky was losing its last blue to an orange glow. Leaves littered the path and the temperature had dropped. The scent of pine was everywhere. Curlews whistled from the branches above.

"Are you taking notes?" he called ahead to her.

She stopped and waited for him. "Which do you think is more autumnal—the leaves, the dying sunflowers, or Grandmother Chinatsu?"

"Too early to tell," he said. "I'm withholding judgment."

Another hundred yards down the winding path they came upon the spring, nearly surrounded by pines except for one spot with a view of a small meadow beyond. Steam rose from the natural pool, curling up in the air, reminding Michi of the white flames on the old lady's jacket. At the edge of the water, closest to the slate path, there was ancient stonework, a crude bench, a stacked rock wall covered with moss, six foot by four, from which a thin waterfall splashed down into the rising heat of the onsen.

"Lovely," said Michi.

Riku nodded.

She left him and moved down along the side of the spring. He looked away as she stepped out of her sandals and removed her robe, which she hung on a nearby branch. He heard her sigh as she entered the water. When he removed his robe, her face was turned away, as if she were taking in the last light on the meadow. Meanwhile, Riku was taking Michi in, her slender neck, her long black hair and how it lay on the curve of her shoulder, her breasts.

"Are you getting in?" she asked.

He silently eased down into the warmth.

When Michi turned to look at him, she immediately noticed the tattoo on his right shoulder, a vicious swamp eel with rippling fins and needle fangs and a long body that wrapped around Riku's back. It was the color of the moss on the rocks of the waterfall.

Riku noticed her glancing at it. He also noticed the smoothness of her skin and that her nipples were erect.

"Who is your employer?" she asked.

"He's a good man," he said and lowered himself into a crouch, so that only his head was above water. "Now, pay attention," he said and looked out at the meadow, which was already in twilight.

"To what?" she asked, also sinking down into the water.

He didn't respond, and they remained immersed for a long time, just two heads floating on the surface, staring silently and listening, steam rising around them. At last light, when the air grew cold, the curlews lifted from their branches and headed for Australia. Riku stood, moved to a different spot in the spring, and crouched down again. Michi moved closer to him. A breeze blew through the pines, a cricket sang in the dark.

"Was there any inspiration?" he asked.

"I'm not sure," she said. "It's time for you to tell me your story of autumn." She drew closer to him, and he backed up a step.

"I don't tell stories," he said.

"As brief as you want, but something," she said and smiled.

He closed his eyes and said, "Okay. The autumn I was seventeen, I worked on one of the fishing boats out of Numazu. We were out for horse mackerel. On one journey we were struck by a rogue wave, a giant that popped up out of nowhere. I was on deck when it hit, and we were swamped. I managed to grab a rope, and it took all my strength not to be drawn overboard, the water was so cold and powerful. I was sure I would die. Two men did get swept away and were never found. That's my natural history of autumn."

She moved forward and put her arms around him. They kissed. He drew his head back and whispered in her ear, "When I returned to shore that autumn, I quit fishing." She laughed and rested her head on his shoulder.

They dined by candlelight, in their robes, in the alcove off the main room of the farmhouse. Grandmother Chinatsu served, and Ono followed a step behind, so that every time she leaned forward to put a platter on the table, there was the dog's leering face, tongue drooping. The main course was thin slices of raw mackerel with grated ginger and chopped scallions. They drank sake. Michi remarked on the appearance of the mackerel after Riku's story.

"Most definitely a sign," he said.

They discussed the things they each saw and heard at the spring as the sake bottle emptied. It was well past midnight when the candle burned out and they went down the hall to his room.

Three hours later, Michi woke in the dark, still a little woozy from the sake. Riku woke when she sat up on the edge of the bed.

"Are you alright?" he asked.

"I have to use the toilet." She got off the bed and lifted her robe from the mat. Slipping into it, she crossed the room. When she slid back the panel, a dim light entered. A lantern hanging in the center of the hallway ceiling bathed the corridor in a dull glow. Michi left the panel open and headed up the hallway. Riku lay back and immediately dozed off. It seemed only a minute to him before Michi was back, shaking him by the shoulder to wake up. She'd left the panel open and he could see her face. Her eyes were wide, the muscles of her jaw tense, a vein visibly throbbing behind the pale skin of her forehead.

She was breathing rapidly, and he could feel the vibration of her heartbeat.

"Get me out of here," she said in a harsh whisper.

"What's wrong?" he said and moved quickly to the edge of the bed. She kneeled on the mattress next to him and grabbed his arm tightly with both hands.

"We've got to leave," she said.

He shook his head and ran his fingers through his hair. It wasn't perfect anymore. He carefully removed his arm from her grip and checked his watch. "It's three a.m.," he said. "You want to leave?"

"I demand you take me out of this place, now."

"What happened?" he asked.

"Either you take me now or I'll leave on foot."

He gave a long sigh and stood up. "I'll be ready in a minute," he said. She went across the corridor to her room and gathered her things together.

When they met in the hallway, bags in hand, he asked her, "Do you think I should let Grandmother Chinatsu know we're leaving?"

"Definitely not," she said, on the verge of tears. She grabbed him with her free hand and dragged him by the shirtsleeve down the hallway. As they reached the main room of the house, she stopped and looked warily around. "Was it the dog?" he whispered. The coast was apparently clear, for she then dragged him outside, down the porch steps, to the silver car.

"Get in," he said. "I have to put the top up. It's too cold to drive with it down."

"Just hurry," she said, stowing her overnight bag. She slid into the passenger seat just as the car top was closing. He got in behind the wheel and reached over to latch the top on her side before doing his.

Michi's window was down and she heard the creaking of planks from the porch. She leaned her head toward her shoulder and looked into the car's side mirror. There, in the full moonlight, she could see Grandmother Chinatsu and Ono. The old lady was waving and laughing.

"Drive," she shrieked.

Riku hit the start button, put the car in gear, and they were off into the night, racing down a rutted dirt road at fifty. Once the farmhouse was out of sight, he let up on the gas. "You've got to tell me what happened," he said.

She was shivering. "Get us out of the woods first," she said. "To a highway."

"I can't see a thing, and I don't remember all the roads," he said. "We might end up lost." He drove for more than an hour before he found a road made of asphalt. His car had been brutalized by the crude paths and branches jutting into the roadway. There would be a hundred scratches on his doors. During that entire time, Michi stared ahead through the windshield, breathing rapidly.

"We're on a main road. Tell me what happened," he said.

"I got up to use the toilet," she said. "And I did. But when I stepped back out into the hallway to return, I heard a horrible grunting noise. I swear it sounded like someone was choking Grandmother Chinatsu to death in her room. I moved along the wall to the entrance. The panel was partially open, and there was a light inside. The noise had stopped so I peered in, and there was the shriveled old lady on her hands and knees on the floor, naked. Her forearms were trembling, her face was bright red, and she began croaking. At first I thought she was ill, but then I looked up and realized she was engaged in sexual relations."

"Grandmother Chinatsu?" he said and laughed. "Who was the unlucky gentleman?"

"That disgusting dog."

"She was doing it with Ono?"

"I almost vomited," said Michi. "But I could have dealt with it. The worst thing was Ono saw me peering in and he smiled at me and nodded."

"Dogs don't smile," he said.

"Exactly," she said. "That place is haunted."

"Well, I'll figure out where we are eventually, and we'll make it back to Numazu by morning. I'm sorry you were so frightened. The field trip seemed a great success until then."

She took a few deep breaths to calm herself. "Perhaps that was the true spirit of autumn," she said.

"'The Story of a Ghost,'" he said.

The silver car sped along in the moonlight. Michi was leaning against the window, her eyes closed. Riku thought he was heading for the coast. He took a tight turn on a narrow mountain road and something suddenly lunged out of the woods at the car. He felt an impact as he swerved, turning back just in time to avoid the drop beyond the lane he'd strayed into.

Michi woke at the impact and said, "What's happening?"

"I think I grazed a deer back there. I've got to pull over and check to see if the car is okay."

Michi leaned forward and adjusted the rearview mirror so she could look out the back window.

"Too late to see," he said. "It was a half-mile back." He eased down on the brake, slowing, and began to edge over toward the shoulder.

"There's something chasing us," she said. "I can see it in the moonlight. Keep going. Go faster."

He downshifted and took his foot off the brake. As he hit the gas, he reached up and moved the mirror out of her grasp so he could see what was following them.

"It's a dog," he said. "But it's the fastest dog I ever saw. I'm doing forty-five and it's gaining on us."

They passed through an area where overhanging trees blocked the moon.

"Watch the road," she said.

When the car moved again into the moonlight, he checked behind them and saw nothing. Then they heard a loud growling. Each searched frantically to see where the noise was coming from. Swerving out of his lane, Riku looked out his side window and down and saw the creature running alongside, the movement of its four legs a blur, its face perfectly human.

"Kuso! Open the glove compartment. There's a gun in there. Give it to me."

"A gun?"

"Hurry," he yelled. She did as he instructed, handing him the sleek nine millimeter. "You were right," he said. "The place was haunted." He lowered his side window, switched hands between gun and wheel. Then, steadying himself, he hit the brake. The dog looked up as it sped past the car—a middle-aged woman's face, bitter, with a terrible underbite and a beauty mark beneath the left eye, riding atop the neck of a mangy gray mutt with a naked tail. As soon as it moved a foot ahead of the car, Riku thrust the gun out the window and fired. The creature suddenly exploded, turning instantly to a shower of salt.

"It had a face," he said, maneuvering the car out of its skid. "A woman's face."

"Don't stop," she said. "Please."

"Don't worry."

"Now," she said, "who is your employer? Why would he send you to such a place?"

"Maybe if I tell you the truth it'll lift whatever curse we're under."

"What is the truth?"

"My employer is a very powerful businessman, and I have heard it said that he is also an onmyoji. You know him. In a moment of weakness he told you a story about an affair he had. Afterward, he worried that you might be inclined to blackmail him. If the story got out, it would be a grave embarrassment for him both at home and at the office. He told me, spend time with her. He wanted me to judge what type of person you are."

"And if I'm the wrong kind of person?"

"I'm to kill you and make it look like an accident," he said.

"Are you trying to scare me to death, you and the old woman?"

"No, I swear. I'm as frightened as you are. And I couldn't harm you. Believe me. I know you would never blackmail him." She rested back against the car seat and closed her eyes. She could feel his hand grasp hers. "Do you believe me?" he said. In the instant she opened her eyes, she saw ahead through the windshield two enormous dogs step onto the highway thirty yards in front of the car.

"Watch out," she screamed. He'd been looking over at her. He hit the brake before even glancing to the windshield. The car locked up and skidded, the headlights illuminating two faces—a man with a thin black mustache and wire-frame glasses, whose mouth was gaping open, and a little girl, chubby, with black bangs, tongue sticking out. On impact, the front of the car crumpled, the air bags deployed, and the horrid dogs burst into salt. The car left the road and came to a stop on the right-hand side, just before the tree line.

Riku remained conscious through the accident. He undid his seatbelt and slid out of the car, brushing glass off his shirt. His forehead had struck the rearview mirror, and there was a gash on his right temple. He heard growling, and, pushing himself away from the car, he headed around to Michi's side. A small pot-bellied dog with the face of an idiot, sunken eyes, and swollen lower lip was drooling and scratching at Michi's window. Riku aimed, pulled the trigger, and turned the monstrosity to salt.

He opened the passenger door. Michi was just coming around. He helped her out and leaned her against the car. Bending over, he reached into the glove compartment and found an extra clip for the gun. As he backed out of the car, he heard them coming up the road, a pack of them, speeding through the moonlight, howling and grunting. He grabbed her hand and they made for the tree line.

"Not the woods," she said and tried to free herself from his grasp.

"No, there's no place to hide on the road. Come on."

They fled into the darkness beneath the trees, Riku literally dragging her forward. Low branches whipped their faces and tangled Michi's hair. Although ruts tripped them, they miraculously never fell. The baying of the beasts sounded only steps behind them, but when he turned and lifted the gun, he saw nothing but night.

Eventually they broke from beneath the trees onto a dirt road. Both were heaving for breath, and neither could run another step. She'd twisted an ankle and was limping. He put one arm around her, to help her along. She was trembling; so was he.

"What are they?" she whispered.

"Jinmenken," he said.

"Impossible."

They walked slowly down the road, and, stepping out from beneath the canopy of leaves, the moonlight showed them, a hundred yards off, a dilapidated building with boarded windows.

"I can't run anymore," he said. "We'll go in there and find a place to hide."

She said nothing.

They stood for a moment on the steps of the place, a concrete structure, some abandoned factory or warehouse, and he tried his cell phone. "No reception," he said after dialing three times and listening. He flipped to a new screen with his thumb and pressed an app icon. The screen became a flashlight. He turned it forward, held it at arm's length, and motioned with his head for Michi to get close behind him. With the gun at the ready, they moved slowly through the doorless entrance.

The place was freezing cold and pitch black. As far as he could tell there were hallways laid out in a square, with small rooms off it to either side.

"An office building in the middle of the woods," she said.

Each room had the remains of a western-style door at its entrance, pieces of shattered wood hanging on by the hinges.

When he shone the phone's light into the rooms, he saw a window opening boarded from within by a sheet of plywood, and an otherwise empty concrete expanse. They went down one hall and turned left into another. Michi remembered she had the same app on her phone and lit it. Halfway down that corridor, they found a room whose door was mostly intact but for a corner at the bottom where it appeared to have been kicked in. Riku inspected the knob and whispered, "There's a lock on this one."

They went in, and he locked the door behind them and tested its strength. "Get in the corner under the window," he said. "If they find us, and the door won't hold, I can rip off the board above us and we might be able to escape outside." She joined him in the corner and they sat, shoulders touching, their backs against the cold concrete. "We're sure to be safe when the sun rises."

He put his arm around her, and she leaned into him. Then neither said a word or made a sound. They turned off their phones and listened to the dark. Time passed, yet when Riku checked his watch, it read only 3:30. "All that in a half-hour?" he wondered. Then there came a sound, a light tapping, as if rain was falling outside. The noise slowly grew louder, and seconds later it became clear that it was the sound of claws on the concrete floor. That light tapping eventually became a clatter, as if a hundred of the creatures were circling impatiently in the hallway.

A strange guttural voice came from the hole at the bottom corner of the door. "Tomodachi," it said. "Let us in."

Riku flipped to the flashlight app and held the gun up. Across the room, the hole in the bottom of the door was filled with a fat, pale, bearded face. One eye was swollen shut and something oozed from the corner of it. The forehead was too high to see a hairline. The thing snuffled and smiled.

"Shoot," said Michi.

Riku fired, but the face flinched away in an instant, and once the bullet went wide and drilled a neat hole in the door, the creature returned and said, "Tomodachi."

"What do you want?" said Riku, his voice cracking.

"We are hunting a spirit of the living," said the creature, the movement of its lips out of sync with the words it spoke.

"What have we done?" said Michi.

"Our hunger is great, but we only require one spirit. We only take what we need—the other person will be untouched. One spirit will feed us for a week."

Michi stood up and stepped away from Riku. He also got to his feet. "What are you doing?" she said. "Shoot them." She quickly lit her phone and shone it on him.

Instead of aiming the gun at the door, he aimed it at her. "I'm not having my spirit devoured," he said to her.

"You said you couldn't hurt me."

"It won't be me hurting you," he said. She saw there were tears in his eyes. The hand that held the gun was wobbling. "I'm giving you the girl," he called to the Jinmenken.

"A true benefactor," said the face at the hole.

"No," she said. "What have I done?"

"I'm going to shoot her in the leg so she can't run, then I'm going to let you all in. You will keep your distance from me or I'll shoot. I have an extra clip, and I'll turn as many of you to salt as I can before you get to me."

Turning to Michi, he said, "I'm so sorry. I did love you."

"But you're a coward. You don't have to shoot me in the leg," she said. "I'll go to them on my own. My spirit's tired of this world." She moved forward and gave him a kiss. Her actions disarmed him, and he appeared confused. At the door, she slowly undid the lock on the knob. Then, with a graceful, fluid motion, she pulled the door open and stepped behind it against the wall. "Take him," he heard her call. The Jinmenkin bounded in, dozens of them, small and large, stinking of rain, slobbering, snapping, clawing. He pulled the trigger till the gun clicked empty, and the room was filled with smoke and flying salt. His hands shook too much to change the clip. One of the creatures tore a bloody chunk from his left calf, and he screamed.

Another went for his groin. The face of Grandmother Chinatsu appeared before him and devoured his.

The following week, in a private room at the Limit, Michi sat at a blond-wood table, staring out the open panel across the room at the pines and the coast. Riku's employer sat across from her. "Ingenious, the natural history of autumn," he said. "And you knew this would draw him in?"

She turned to face the older man. "He was a unique person," she said. "He'd faced death."

"Too bad about Riku," he said. "I wanted to trust him."

"Really, the lengths to which you'll go to test the spirit of those you need to trust. He's gone because he was a coward?"

"A coward I can tolerate. But he said he loved you, and it proved he didn't understand love at all. A dangerous flaw." He took an envelope from within his suit jacket and laid it on the table. "A job well done," he said. She lifted the envelope and looked inside.

A cold breeze blew into the room. "You know," he said, "this season always reminds me of our time together."

As she spoke she never stopped counting the bills. "All I remember of that," she said, "is the snow."

Blood Drive

For Christmas our junior year of high school, all of our parents got us guns. That way you had a half a year to learn to shoot and get down all the safety garbage before you started senior year. Depending on how well off your parents were, that pretty much dictated the amount of firepower you had. Darcy Krantz's family lived in a trailer, and so she had a pea-shooter, .22 Double Eagle derringer, and Baron Hanes's father, who was in the security business and richer than God, got him a .44 Magnum that was so heavy it made his nutty kid lean to the side when he wore the gun belt. I packed a pearl-handled .38 revolver, Smith & Wesson, which had originally been my grandfather's. It was old as dirt, but all polished up, the way my father kept it, it was still a fine-looking gun. It was really my father's gun, and my mother told him not to give it to me, but he said, "Look, when she goes to high school, she's gotta carry, everybody does in their senior year."

"Insane," said my mom.

"Come on," I said. "Please . . ."

She drew close to me, right in my face, and said, "If your father gives you that gun, he's got no protection, making his deliveries." He drove a truck and delivered bakery goods to different diners and convenience stores in the area.

"Take it easy," said my dad, "all the crooks are asleep when I go out for my runs." He motioned for me to come over to where he sat. He put the gun in my hand. I gripped the handle and felt the weight of it. "Give me your best pose," he said.

I turned profile, hung my head back, my long chestnut hair reaching halfway to the floor, pulled up the sleeve of my T-shirt, made a muscle with my right arm, and pointed the gun at the ceiling with my left hand. He laughed till he couldn't catch his breath. And my mom said, "Disgraceful," but she also laughed.

I went to the firing range with my dad a lot the summer before senior year. He was a calm teacher, and never spoke much or got too mad. Afterward, he'd take me to this place and buy us ice cream. A lot of times it was Friday night, and I just wanted to get home so I could go hang out with my friends. One night I let him know we could skip the ice cream, and he seemed taken aback for a second, like I'd hurt his feelings. "I'm sorry," he said and tried to smile.

I felt kind of bad, and figured I could hug him or kiss him or ask him to tell me something. "Tell me about a time when you shot the gun not on the practice range," I said as we drove along.

He laughed. "Not too many times," he said. "The most interesting was from when I was a little older than you. It was night, we were in the basement of an abandoned factory over in the industrial quarter. I was with some buds and we were partying, smoking up and drinking straight, cheap vodka. Anyway, we were wasted. This guy I really didn't like who hung out with us, Raymo was his name, he challenged me to a round of Russian roulette. Don't tell your mother this," he said.

"You know I won't," I said.

"Anyway, I left one bullet in the chamber, removed the others, and spun the cylinder. He went first—nothing. I went, he went, etc, click, click, click. The gun came to me, and I was certain by then that the bullet was in my chamber. So, you know what I did?"

"You shot it into the ceiling?"

"No. I turned the gun on Raymo and shot him in the face. After that we all ran. We ran and we never got caught. At the time there was a gang going around at night shooting people and taking their wallets, and the cops put it off to them. None of my buds were going to snitch. Believe me, Raymo was no great loss to the world. The point of which is to say, it's a horrible thing to shoot someone. I see Raymo's expression right before the bullet drilled through it just about every night in my dreams. In other words, you better know what you're doing when you pull that trigger. Try to be responsible."

I was sorry I asked.

To tell you the truth, taking the gun to school at first was a big nuisance. The thing was heavy, and you always had to keep an eye on it. The first couple of days were all right, 'cause everyone was showing off their pieces at lunchtime. A lot of people complimented me on my gun. They liked the pearl handle and the shape of it. Of course the kids with the new, high-tech 9 millimeter jobs got the most attention, but if your piece was unique enough, it got you at least some cred. Jody Motes, pretty much an idiot with buck teeth and a fat ass, brought in a German Luger with a red swastika inlaid on the handle, and because of it started dating this really hot guy in our English class. Kids wore them on their hips, others, mostly guys, did the shoulder holster. A couple of the senior girls with big breasts went with this over-the-shoulder bandolier style, so their guns sat atop their left breast. Sweaty Mr. Gosh in second period math said that look was "very fashionable." I carried mine in my Sponge Bob lunch box. I hated wearing it; the holster always hiked my skirt up in the back somehow.

Everybody in the graduating class carried heat except for Scott Wisner, the King of Vermont, as everybody called him, I forget why 'cause Vermont was totally far away. His parents had given him a stun gun instead of the real thing. Cody St. John, the captain of the football team, said the stun gun was fag, and after that Wisner turned into a weird loner, who walked around carrying a big jar with a floating mist inside. He asked all the better looking girls if he could have their souls. I know he asked me. Creep. I heard he'd stun anyone who wanted it for ten dollars a pop. Whatever.

The teachers in the classes for seniors all had tactical 12-gauge short-barrel shotguns; no shoulder stock, just a club grip with an image of the school's mascot (a cartoon, rampaging Indian) stamped on it. Most of them were loaded with buckshot, but Mrs. Cloder, in human geography, who used her weapon as a pointer when at the board, was rumored to rock the breaching rounds, those big slugs cops use to blow doors off their hinges. Other teachers left the shotguns on their desks or lying across the eraser gutter at the bottom of the board. Mr. Warren, the vice principal, wore his in a holster across his back, and for an old fart was super quick in drawing it over his shoulder with one hand.

At lunch, across the soccer field and back by the woods, where only the seniors were allowed to go, we sat out every nice day in the fall, smoking cigarettes and having gun-spinning competitions. You weren't allowed to shoot back there, so we left the safeties on. Bryce, a boy I knew since kindergarten, was good at it. He could flip his gun in the air backwards and have it land in the holster at his hip. McKenzie Batkin wasn't paying attention and turned the safety off instead of on before she started spinning her antique Colt. The sound of the shot was so sudden, we all jumped, and then silence, followed by the smell of gun smoke. The bullet went through her boot and took off the tip of her middle toe. Almost a whole minute passed before she screamed. The King of Vermont and Cody St. John both rushed to help her at the same time. They worked together to staunch the bleeding. I remember noticing the football lying on the ground next to the jar of souls, and I thought it would make a cool photo for the yearbook. She never told her parents, hiding the boots at the back of her closet. To this day she's got half a middle toe on her right foot, but that's the least of her problems.

After school that day, I walked home with my new friend, Constance, who only came to Bascombe High in senior year. We crossed the soccer field, passed the fallen leaves stained red with McKenzie's blood, and entered the woods. The wind blew and shook the empty branches of the trees. Constance suddenly stopped walking, crouched, drew her Beretta Storm and fired. By the time I could turn my head, the squirrel was falling back, headless, off a tree about thirty yards away.

She had a cute haircut, short but with a lock that almost covered her right eye. Jeans and a green flannel shirt, a calm, pretty face. When we were doing current events in fifth period social studies, she'd argued with Mr. Hallibet about the cancellation of child labor laws. Me, I could never follow politics. It was too boring. But Constance seemed to really understand, and although on the TV news we all watched, they were convinced it was a good idea for kids twelve and older to now be eligible to be sent to work by their parents for extra income, she said it was wrong. Hallibet laughed at her and said, "This is Senator Meets we're talking about. He's a man of the people. The guy who gave you your guns." Constance had more to say, but the teacher lifted his shotgun and turned to the board. The thing I couldn't get over is that she actually knew this shit better than Hallibet. The thought of it, for some reason, made me blush.

By the time the first snow came in late November, the guns became mostly just part of our wardrobes, and kids turned their attention back to their cell phones and iPods. The one shot fired in the school before Christmas vacation was when Mrs. Cloder dropped her gun in the bathroom stall and blew off the side of the toilet bowl. Water flooded out into the hallway. Other than that, the only time you noticed that people were packing was when they'd use their sidearm for comedy purposes. Like Bryce, during English, when the teacher was reading *Pilgrim's Progress* to us, took out his gun and stuck the end in his mouth as if he was so bored he was going to blow his own brains out. At least once a week, outside the cafeteria, on the days it was too cold to leave the school, there were quick-draw contests. Two kids would face off, there'd be a panel of judges, and Vice Principal Warren would set his cell phone to beep once. When they heard the beep the pair drew and who-ever was faster won a coupon for a free thirty-two ounce soda at Babb's, the local convenience store.

One thing I did notice in that first half of the year. Usu-ally when a person drew their gun, even as a joke, they had a saying they always spoke. Each person had their own signature saying. When it came to these lines it seemed that the ban on cursing could be ignored without any problem. Even the teach-ers got into it. Mr. Gosh was partial to, "Eat hot lead, you little motherfuckers." The school nurse, Ms. James, used, "See you in Hell, asshole." Vice Principal Warren, who always kept his language in check, would draw, and while the gun was coming level with your head, say, "You're already dead." As for the kids, they all used lines they'd seen in recent movies. Cody St. John used, "Suck on this, bitches." McKenzie, who by Christmas was known as Half-toe Batkin, concocted the line, "Put up your feet." I tried to think of something to say, but it all seemed too corny, and it took me too long to get the gun out of my lunch box to really outdraw anyone else.

Senior year rolled fast, and by winter break I was wonder-ing what I'd do after I graduated. Constance told me she was going to college to learn philosophy. "Do they still teach that stuff?" I asked. She smiled. "Not so much anymore." We were sitting in my living room; my parents were away at my aunt's. The TV was on, the lights were out, and we were holding hands. We liked to just sit quietly with each other and talk. "So I guess you'll be moving away, after the summer," I said. She nodded. "I thought I'd try to get a job at Wal-Mart," I said. "I heard they have benefits now."

"That's all you're gonna do with your life?" asked Constance.

"For now," I said.

"Well, then when I go away, you should come with me."
She put her arm behind my head and drew me gently to her.
We just sat, holding each other for a long time while the snow
came down outside.

A few days after Christmas, I sat with my parents watching
the evening news after dinner. Senator Meets was on, talking
about what he hoped to accomplish in the coming year. He was
telling about how happy he was to work for minimum wage
when he was eleven.

"This guy's got it down," said my father.

I shouldn't have opened my mouth, but I said, "Constance
says he's a loser."

"Loser?" my father said. "Are you kidding? Who's this Constance, I don't want you hanging out with any socialists. Don't
tell me she's one of those kids who refuses to carry a gun. Meets
passed the gun laws, mandatory church on Sunday for all citi-
zens, killed abortion, and got us to stand up to the Mexicans . . .
He's definitely gonna be the next president."

"She's probably the best shot in the class," I said, realizing
I'd already said too much.

My father was suspicious, and he stirred in his easy chair,
leaning forward.

"I met her," said my mother. "She's a nice girl."

A gave things a few seconds to settle down and then
announced I was going to take the dog for a walk. As I passed
my mother, unnoticed by my dad, she grabbed my hand and
gave it a quick squeeze.

Back at school in January, there was a lot to do. I went to
the senior class meetings, but didn't say anything. They decided
for our "Act of Humanity" (required of every senior class), we
would have a blood drive. For the senior trip, we decided to
keep it cheap as pretty much everyone's parents were broke. A
day trip to Bash Lake. "Sounds stale," said Bryce, "but if we bring
enough alcohol and weed it'll be OK." Mrs. Cloder, our faculty
advisor, aimed at him, said, "Arrivederci, Baby," and gave him

two Saturday detentions. The other event that overshadowed all the others, though, was the upcoming prom. My mother helped me make my dress. She was awesome on the sewing machine. It was turquoise satin, short sleeve, mid-length. I told my parents I had no date, but was just going solo. Constance and I had made plans. We knew from all the weeks of mandatory Sunday mass, the pastor actually spitting he was so worked up over what he called "unnatural love," that we couldn't go as a couple. She cared more than I did. I just tried to forget about it.

When the good weather of spring hit, people got giddy and tense. There were accidents. In homeroom one bright morning, Darcy dropped her bag on her desk, and the derringer inside went off and took out Ralph Babb's right eye. He lived, but when he came back to school his head was kind of caved in and he had a bad fake eye that looked like a kid drew it. It only stared straight ahead. Another was when Mr. Hallibet got angry because everybody'd gotten into the habit of challenging his current events lectures after seeing Constance in action. He yelled for us all to shut up and accidently squeezed off a round. Luckily for us the gun was pointed at the ceiling. Mr. Gosh, though, who was sitting in the room a floor above, directly over Hallibet, had to have buckshot taken out of his ass. When he returned to school from a week off, he sweated more than ever.

Mixed in with the usual spring fever, there was all kinds of drama over who was going to the prom with who. Fist fights, girl fights, plenty of drawn guns but not for comedy. I noticed that the King of Vermont was getting wackier the more people refused to notice him. When I left my sixth-period class to use the bathroom, I saw him out on the soccer field from the upstairs hallway window. He turned the stun gun on himself and shot the two darts with wires into his own chest. It knocked him down fast, and he was twitching on the ground. I went and took a piss. When I passed the window again, he was gone. He'd started bringing alcohol to school, and at lunch, where again we were back by the woods hanging out, he'd drink a Red Bull and a half pint of vodka.

Right around that time, I met Constance at the town library one night. I had nothing to do, but she had to write a paper. When I arrived, she'd put the paper away and was reading. I asked her what the book was. She told me, "Plato."

"Good story?" I asked.

She explained it wasn't a novel, but a book about ideas. "You see," she said, "there's a cave and this guy gets chained up inside so that he can't turn around or move but only stare at the back wall. There's a fire in the cave behind him and it casts his shadow on the wall he faces. That play of light and shadow is the sum total of his reality."

I nodded and listened as long as I could. Constance was so wrapped up in explaining, she looked beautiful, but I didn't want to listen anymore. I checked over my shoulder to see if anyone was around. When I saw we were alone, I quickly leaned forward and kissed her on the lips. She smiled and said, "Let's get out of here."

On a warm day in mid-May, we had the blood drive. I got there early and gave blood. The nurses, who were really nice, told me to sit for a while, and they gave me orange juice and cookies. I thought about becoming a nurse for maybe like five whole minutes. Other kids showed up and gave blood, and I stuck around to help sign them up. Cody came and watched but wouldn't give. "Fuck the dying," I heard him say. "Nobody gets my blood but me." After that a few other boys decided not to give either. Whatever. Then at lunch, the King of Vermont was drinking his Red Bulls and vodka, and I think because he'd given blood, he was really blasted. He went around threatening to stun people in their private parts.

After lunch, in Mrs. Cloder's class, where we sat at long tables in a rectangle that formed in front of her desk, Wisner took the seat straight across from her. I was two seats down from him toward the windows. Class started, and the first thing

Mrs. Cloder said, before she even got out of her seat, was to the King. "Get that foolish jar off the table." We all looked over. Wisner stared, the mist swirled inside the glass. He pushed his seat back and stood up, cradling the jar in one arm and drawing his stun gun. "Sit down, Scotty," she said, and leveled her riot gun at him. I could see her finger tightening on the trigger. A few seconds passed, and then one by one all the kids drew their weapons, but nobody was sure whether to aim at Mrs. Cloder or the King, so about half did one and half the other. I never even opened my lunch box, afraid to make a sudden move.

"Put down your gun and back slowly away from the table," said Mrs. Cloder.

"When you meet the Devil, give him my regards," said Wisner, but as he pulled the trigger, Mrs. Cloder fired. The breeching slug blew a hole in the King of Vermont's chest, slamming him against the back wall in a cloud of blood. The jar shattered, and glass flew. McKenzie, who had been sitting next to Wisner, screamed as the shards dug into her face. I don't know if she shot or if the gun just went off, but her bullet hit Mrs. Cloder in the shoulder and spun her out of her chair onto the ground. She groaned and rolled back and forth. Meanwhile, Wisner's stun-gun darts had gone wild, struck Chucky Durr in the forehead, one in each eyebrow, and in his electrified shaking, his gun went off and put a round right into Melanie Storte's Adam's apple. Blood poured out as she dropped her own gun and brought her hands to her gurgling neck. Melanie was Cody St. John's "current ho," as he called her, and he didn't think twice but fanned the hammer of his pistol, putting three shots into Chucky, who went over onto the floor like a bag of potatoes. Chucky's cousin, Meleeba, shot Cody in the side of the head, and he fell, screaming, as smoke poured from the hole above his left ear. One of Cody's crew shot Meleeba, and then I couldn't keep track anymore. Bullets whizzed by my head, blood was spurting everywhere. Kids were dropping like pins at the bowling alley. Mrs. Cloder clawed her way back into her seat, lifted the gun and aimed it. Whoever was left fired on her and then she fired, another shotgun blast, like an explosion. When the ringing in my ears went away, the room was perfectly quiet but for the drip of blood and the ticking of the wall clock. Smoke hung in the air, and I thought of the King of Vermont's escaped souls. During the entire thing, I'd not moved a single finger.

The cops were there before I could get myself out of the chair. They wrapped a blanket around me and led me down to the principal's office. I was in a daze for a while, but could feel them moving around me and could hear them talking. Then my mother was there, and the cop was handing me a cup of orange juice. They asked if they could talk to me, and my mother left it up to me. I told them everything, exactly how it went down. I started with the blood drive. They tested me for gunpowder to see if there was any on my hands. I told them my gun was back in the classroom in the lunch box under the table, and it hadn't been fired since the summer, the last time I went to the range with my dad. It was all over the news. I was all over the news. A full one-third of Bascombe High's senior class was killed in the shootout.

Senator Meets showed up at the school three days later and got his picture taken handing me an award. I never really knew what it was for. Constance said of it, "They give you a fucking award if you live through it," and laughed. In Meets's speech that day to the assembled community, he blamed the blood drive for the incident. He proclaimed Mrs. Cloder a hero, and ended reminding everyone, "If these kids were working, they'd have no time for this."

The class trip was called off out of respect for the dead. Two weeks later, I went to the prom. It was to be held in the high school gymnasium. My dad drove me. When we pulled into the parking lot, it was empty.

"You must be early," he said, and handed me the corsage I'd asked him to get—a white orchid.

"Thanks," I said and gave him a kiss on the cheek. As I opened the door to get out, he put his hand on my elbow. I turned, and he was holding the gun.

"You'll need this," he said.

I shook my head, and told him, "It's OK." He was momentarily taken aback. Then he tried to smile. I shut the door and he drove away.

Constance was already there. In fact, she was the only one there. The gym was done up with glittery stars on the ceiling, a painted moon, and clouds. There were streamers. Our voices echoed as we exchanged corsages, which had been our plan. The white orchid looked good on her black plunging neckline. She'd gotten me a corsage made of red roses, and they really stood out against the turquoise. In her purse, instead of the Beretta, she had a half pint of Captain Morgan. We sat on one of the bleachers and passed the bottle, talking about the incidents of the past two weeks.

"I guess no one's coming," she said. No sooner were the words out of her mouth than the outside door creaked open and in walked Bryce carrying a case in one hand and dressed in a jacket and tie. We got up and went to see him. Constance passed him the Captain Morgan. He took a swig.

"I was afraid of this," he said.

"No one's coming?" I said.

"I guess some of the parents were scared there'd be another shootout. Probably the teachers too. Mrs. Cloder's family insisted on an open casket. A third of them are dead, let's not forget, and the rest, after hearing Meets talk, are working the late shift at Wal-Mart for minimum wage."

"Jeez," said Constance.

"Just us," said Bryce. He went up on the stage, set his case down, and got behind the podium at the back. "Watch this," he said, and a second later the lights went out. We all laughed. A dozen blue searchlights appeared, their beams moving randomly around the gym, washing over us and then rushing away to some dark corner. A small white spotlight came on above the mic that stood at the front of the stage. Bryce stepped up into the glow. He opened the case at his feet and took out a saxophone.

"I was looking forward to playing tonight," he said. We walked up to the edge of the stage, and I handed him the bottle. He took a swig, the sax now on a chain around his neck. Putting the bottle down at his feet," he said, "Would you ladies care to dance?"

"Play us something," we told him.

He thought for a second and said, "Strangers in the Night."

He played, we danced, and the blue lights in the dark were the sum total of our reality.

A Terror

Emily woke suddenly in the middle of the night, sitting straight and gasping as if finally breaching the surface of Puffer's Pond. The last thing she could remember was the shrill cry of the 6:00 a.m. whistle from the factory down Main Street in The Crossing. Then a sudden shuddering explosion behind her eyes; a shower of sparks.

She pulled back the counterpane and moved to the edge of the bed. There, she rested; her bare feet on the cold floor, letting the night's hush, like between the heaves of storm, settle her. Only when a fly buzzed against the windowpane did she remember everything.

Her health had been bad, her spirit low. She'd felt so weak for days on end that she could barely make it out into the garden to cull wilted blossoms. Her pen, which usually glided over a page, sowing words to correspondents or conjuring a poem, had become a weight nearly too burdensome to bear. At her father's insistence, the doctor had come the previous week and demanded to examine her. She'd reluctantly allowed it, in her way. He stood in the upstairs hallway, peering through the partially open door of her room as she shuffled past the entrance, back and forth, three times, fully clothed. He'd called out to her, "Emily, how can I diagnose anything other than a case of mumps in this manner?" but she was loathe to see him, to have him or any other stranger to the Homestead near her.

All that had somehow passed, though, and she no longer felt a slave to gravity. Gone was the perpetual headache like the beating of a drum, gone the labored rasping for breath. That frantic confusion of thought that had plagued her seemed only a fading nightmare, as if now, at the start of autumn, there'd been a spring cleaning in her mind. Before standing, she took stock to make sure she wasn't deluding herself, but no, she felt calm and rested. She stood and stretched, noticing a dim reflection of her loose white nightgown in the window glass, a floating specter that made her smile.

Moonlight sifted in through the two windows and showed her the way to her writing table. There, she lit the taper in the pewter candlestick and took it up to lead her through the darkened house. She wanted to let them know that she'd recovered from her spell. Turning right, down the hallway, she stopped first at Lavinia's room. A tapping at the door brought no response. She rapped louder, but still couldn't raise Vinnie from sleep. Quietly, she opened the door and crossed the dark expanse. Bringing the candlestick down in order to light her sister's form, she was surprised to find the bed still made, empty. She left that room and hurried farther down the hall to her parents'. Her mother had been in the poorest health, and Emily was reluctant to wake her, but concern for Vinnie overcame her caution and she knocked heavily three times. Silence followed.

The raised lantern revealed her parents' bed to also be empty, still made from the day. She hurried back up the hall to the top of the stairs and called out for her father. The glow of the candle only reached halfway down the steps. Beyond was a quiet darkness from which no answer came. She felt the nettle sting of fear in her blood and called again, this time for Carlo, her dog. At any other time the Newfoundland would have been right by her side. Slowly, she backed away and returned to her room. She set down the candlestick on her writing table and stepped toward the bed. After a quick look over each shoulder, and a moment of just listening, she pulled the nightgown off and tossed it on her pillow. She was paler than the garment she discarded, glowing within the glow of the candlelight. From the closet, she removed her white cotton day dress from its hanger and slipped it on with nothing beneath. She found her walking boots in the shadow at the end of the bed and guided her bare feet into them while standing. Not bothering to tie the laces, she picked up the candlestick and left the room.

The untied boots made a racket on the steps—better, she thought, than having to utter a warning to whatever revelation lurked in the dark. She discovered that the clock on the mantel in the downstairs parlor had stopped at 2:15. Stillness reigned in every room, from her father's library to the kitchen. She fled to the conservatory, to her gardens, for comfort. As soon as she crossed the threshold from the house into the growing room, the aroma of the soil soothed her. An Aeolian harp in the one open window made music, and she turned to the plants, desperate for a moment's distraction.

It seemed to her like it had been weeks since the last time she'd inspected the exotics. September had definitely come and was drawing the summer out of blossoms. The peonies, gardenias, jasmine drooped dejectedly, their closed petals half wilted. The summer gentian were long shriveled, and she knew she must pick them before they fell in order to make the purple tea she'd dreamed of. Resting the candle in a patch of thyme, she leaned over pots of oregano to reach the plants and pinch the desiccated flowers from their stems. Only when she had a handful did she recall that her family had vanished in the night. She shook her head, muttering recriminations at herself, put the petals in the pocket of her dress, and blew out the candle. Her eyes had adjusted to the moonlit night.

Before leaving through the door at the end of the conservatory, she grabbed from a peg the tippet of tulle she often wrapped around her shoulders when walking or working in the outdoor gardens. It was a flimsy wrap, and did little to warm her against the wind that shook the trees in the orchard. She thought of it more as a familiar arm around her shoulders. She kept to the path and called out in a whisper for her father and then Vinnie.

Upon reaching the heart of the gardens, she rested upon the log bench her brother, Austin, had built when just a boy. She resolved to go next door to The Evergreens, Austin's house, and get help. She had a choice to either reach it by traversing a lonely thicket or going round to the street. For the first time ever, she chose the street.

She hadn't been in front of the Homestead in over a year, and the thought of being seen drained her will. She found it ever preferable to be in her room, sitting at her writing table, watching, through the wavy window glass, the traffic of Main Street. For long stretches in the afternoon, before she'd put pen to paper again, she'd watch her neighbors come and go. Her imagination gave her their names and their secrets, but she felt in her bones that only at a distance could she know them.

It was different when the children came into the yard and stood beneath her window. They could smell that she'd been baking. When the cookies cooled, she'd slip them in a crude envelope she made from butcher wrap and then attach a parachute of green tissue paper her mother had been saving and forbade anyone to use. There'd be three or four children on the lawn, looking up at the white form behind the glass, a mere smudge of a phantom. Opening the window, she'd say nothing, but launch the cookies, the green paper cupping the air. The parcel would float gracefully down into their grasping hands. They'd hear her breathy laughter, the window would slam shut, and they'd scurry in fear.

She opened the wrought-iron gate of the fence that ran between the property and the sidewalk, cringing with the squeal of its hinges. Looking around, she waited for someone or something to come at her out of the dark. She left the gate open so as not to make it cry again and headed right, toward The Evergreens. The wind pushed against her, and dry leaves scraped the street. She shifted the tippet on her shoulders but it could do no better. It was only early September, yet she smelled a hint of snow and felt winter in her brain. A line from a poem she'd written surfaced, and she spoke it under her breath: "Great streets of silence led away . . . ."

She'd taken no more than fifty steps, head down, anticipating the comfort she'd find in the presence of Austin and the arms of his wife, Susan, when from the street behind her rose the sound of horses' hooves, the clickety-whir of carriage wheels. The noise slowed and then stopped her; zero at the bone. She dared not turn to look, and hoped the late-night travelers would pass her without notice. From the corner of her left eye she saw the contrivance pull just ahead of her and stop. It was an elegant black brougham with a driver's seat, a cab, and two white horses dappled with dark spots like a leopard's markings.

Emily turned and lifted her head but couldn't make out the driver beyond his silhouette. He was dressed in a heavy coat, collar up, a wide-brimmed hat, and gloves. He turned and lit the two lanterns that were attached to the front of the cab and then resumed his slumped posture. The door swung open and a male voice called out of the dark compartment, "Miss Emily Dickinson?" She blushed as she always did when confronted by a stranger. A man stepped out of the brougham. She took two steps back.

In that instant, she hoped and then thought for certain it was Sam Bowles, editor of *The Springfield Republican* and her clandestine correspondent. His stream of letters had dried up since his wife had discovered that he and Emily referred to her as "the hedgehog." Emily missed him so dearly since his departure for the sanitorium to treat his nervous condition. It would be like him to surprise her with his return in this way. But just as quickly she saw the features weren't Bowles', and her joy curdled.

It was a gentleman, finely dressed in a black tailcoat and trousers, a spotless white shirt. There was a lovely white rose in his lapel. He wore leather gloves and carried a walking stick. The last she dared to take in was his face, which was adorned by a thin mustache but otherwise smoothly shaven. His eyes were dark yet glimmered with the light of the lanterns. His smile was, considering her anxiety, enormously appealing. He took a gold watch from his vest pocket and held it on its chain up close to his eyes. "We're running late," he muttered, as if to himself, but loud enough for her to hear. This fact didn't seem to distress him in the least. In fact, he smiled more broadly.

Her manners obliterated, she called out louder than she'd intended, "Who are you?"

The gentleman stepped up out of the street and onto the sidewalk. "I'm nobody, who are you?" he said and laughed. "You know me," he added.

He wore some subtle cologne that reminded her exactly of the scent of the garden at the height of summer. The chill left her immediately and her breathing eased. "What do you want?" she asked, now more relaxed but still with a fading memory that she'd meant to be defensive.

"I'm here to bring you where you need to go," he said. "I know you're busy so I've taken it upon myself to come for you."

"I'm only going up the street to my brother's house."

"Oh, no, Miss Dickinson, you'll be going much farther than that."

"Please. I'm in a hurry. An emergency."

He took the glove off his left hand and held it in his right. She was incredulous at the effrontery when he reached down and lightly clasped her fingers. At his touch a blast of cold, like a January wind, ran through her body, lodging in her mind and causing a sudden confusion. He had no right to touch her. She meant to protest, to pull her hand away, but every time forgot what she'd intended and then remembered and forgot again.

"If I might call you Emily?" he said in a soothing voice.

"How civil," she thought while still searching within herself for the panic she expected. The cold that had invaded her slowly diffused into a sense of utter calm more comforting than an afternoon with Susan and the new baby. He gave a half-bow and led her toward the brougham as if her fears about him had never existed. She stepped off the curb convinced that a journey was precisely what was needed.

Emily woke to the movement of the carriage. The shades were up and the sunlight shone through the window to her left. She pushed against the hard bench to straighten her posture and yawned.

"You'll want to see this," said the gentleman, sitting opposite her.

He smiled cordially and her spine stiffened; a scream rendered numb fell to the bottom of her throat. He pointed out the sunlit window and his gaze insisted she look. The view was dizzying as the rig sped madly through town. She thought they were caught up in a twister, but then she was able to identify a section of street, and the whizzing scenery slowed to a crawl, as if it and not the carriage were moving. The sidewalks were empty in the late afternoon light, and the aroma of the oyster bar downstairs in the Gunn Hotel pervaded the cab. The very next thing she noticed was the spire of the First Congregational Church, and that was all wrong, for it should have been in the opposite direction.

They went a few more yards down the road and, impossibly, were passing the grounds of Amherst Academy. Whereas the church and hotel were steeped in the summer heat, the three-story school was surrounded by trees whose leaves had gone golden. There were children sitting on the steps of the building and some playing Ring A Rosie in the field out front. Emily remembered that the school had closed just that year, as a new public school had been built. She wondered what had brought the old place back to life. As the carriage rolled by, the children turned in the ring and she glimpsed the laughing face of her second cousin, Sophia.

She gasped and closed her eyes, averting her gaze from the window. "It can't be," she said.

"What's that?" asked her traveling companion.

"My cousin, Sophia. She died of typhus when we were children."

"You don't understand yet, do you?"

"You're taking me to my family, I thought."

"In a sense," he said.

"But then what is all this, this journey through the town all crossways and confusing?"

"You're taking the tour, Emily. Everybody gets the tour."

"The tour of what?" she begged, her voice raised.

"Why, your life, of course. A little summing up before nestling down into your alabaster chamber."

"How do you come to use my private words?"

"I can see you're beginning to see now," he said.

She turned quickly and caught a glimpse of Mount Holyoke Academy, miles away from Amherst, in the early evening, and right after it Amherst Town Hall, with its giant clock lit by morning light.

She looked back at him and asked, "What happened?"

"It comes to all, my dear. You were weak and had one of your seizures and . . . well . . . I have my job to do."

"But Vinnie and Mother and Father?"

"Oh, they're all as well as when you last saw them. It'll be a while more before they get the tour."

"I want to say good-bye to them." Tears formed in her eyes.

He shrugged and opened his gloved hands as if to indicate there was nothing that could be done.

"Where are we going?"

The gentleman banged on the ceiling of the cab with his cane, and the horses instantly set into a gallop. "Toward eternity," he said.

She fell back into the corner of the bench, her face turned toward the window. It was night, no stars visible. Only the bumping of the carriage and the sound of the horses' hooves gave any indication they were moving. They traveled on for what seemed hours and hours, and then she blinked and it was as if they'd arrived in a moment. In the carriage lantern's glow, she could see they'd halted in front of the Amherst Town Tomb, a stone structure built into the earth with a grassy hill of a roof and its cornice in the ground, like a sinking house.

"You are Death," said Emily.

Her fellow traveler sat in shadow. "Call me Quill." He leaned forward so that she could see his face and nodded. "Go ahead. I know you have questions."

Emily knew there was no point in trying to escape or cry out. Although she was terrified, her curiosity was intact. "Which direction am I heading once I'm interred?"

"That's the thing," said Quill, lighting a thin cigar. He swung open the carriage door to blow the smoke out. "I've got nothing to do with that. I don't know what happens after. That will always remain a mystery to me. My specialty is the moment *of*, so to speak, an entire life squeezed down into a flyspeck on the windowpane of the universe. I wish I could tell you more."

"I've done bold things in my life, as quiet as it might have seemed."

"You don't have to convince me, Emily," he said. "I know everything you've done and thought. You've nothing to be ashamed of. Even the falling sickness you tried to hide. It was nothing more than some twisted little knot in your brain work. You and Julius Caesar, my dear. Two emperors, one of men and one of words."

"My secret afternoons?" she whispered.

He shook his head. "I just deliver the spent to their rest."

"But why am I being put into the Town Tomb? It's only for the bodies of those who die in winter when the ground is too hard to dig a grave."

The gentleman clasped the cigar between his teeth and then removed his left glove with his right hand. He snapped his fingers. "There, look now," he said as he pulled the glove back on his hand.

She peered out the carriage window at a snowy scene, the wind howling, drifts having instantaneously formed around the entrance to the tomb.

Quill took a drag on his cigar and tossed it out the door of the cab. As he spoke his words traveled on curling smoke.

The brain is just the weight of God,
For, lift them, pound for pound,
And they will differ, if they do,
As syllable from sound.

"You see what I mean?" he asked. "It's metaphorical."

"What is?" she said.

"Everything. The world," he told her. "Come now, let's get to it." He reached his gloved hand out.

She appreciated his gentleness, his friendly manner, but still she pressed her back against the seat and didn't reach to meet his touch. "I'm only thirty-one. A dozen unfinished poems right now await me in my dresser drawer." Her breathing grew frantic.

"Unlike you, Emily, I never tell it slantwise."

"Is there nothing?"

He sat silently for a moment, and then reached out, grabbed the carriage door by the handle, and swung it shut. The sound of it latching brought a change to the scene outside the window. They were no longer in front of the tomb. It was early autumn again, twilight, and the carriage was moving along Russell Street, west, through Hadley, harvest fields to either side.

"Are you much for deals, Miss Dickinson?" asked Quill.

"Deals?" she asked.

"Yes, it so happens I'm in need of a poet. If you'll help me, I'll erase this evening and not bother you again until, uh . . ." He paused and reached into his jacket pocket for a small notebook.

Flipping the pages, he finally landed on one and stopped. Running his finger down a list of names, he said, "You'll have another quarter century. It's the best I can do."

"You're saying I can go home?"

"Yes, when we're finished with my errand. It's somewhat dangerous and there's a chance you still might wind up in the tomb if things go awry, but this is the only way."

Emily remembered from her reading of fairy tales the dangers of deals with Death, but she was flattered that he knew her as a poet. "What do I have to do?"

"I want you to help me kill a child," he said.

She shook her head vehemently.

"Hear me out, Miss Dickinson, hear me out," said Quill, and tapped his stick twice on the carriage floor.

"Speak," she said.

"First, keep in mind what I told you about the world being made of metaphor. I know you're an adherent of reality, a devotee of science. 'Microscopes are prudent in an emergency,' you write. Yes, sound advice, but there are those moments of—shall I call it magic? Sorcery? The supernatural, let us say . . . ."

"You mean something like a coach carrying Death, pulling up to take you hither and yon?"

"Well put," he said. "Now, this is where things stand—there's a child, a boy, who has for all intents and purposes died, succumbed to scarlet fever. But his mother has cast a spell upon him to keep him living."

"Can this be real?" she asked.

"It's real. I'm speaking of the power of words. Your father, a devout preacher, would be disappointed in you, not to mention what Reverend Wadsworth might think. In Genesis, God spoke the world and all that's in it. He said, 'Let there be light,' and there was."

"Sophistry," she said. "But go on."

"The fact that I'm prevented from taking the child has caused all manner of problems. In fact, I'd not have had to come for you so early if it wasn't for this one boy—you, and a dozen more whose times were not nigh. I've got to compensate for the aberration. It's not right."

"Why a poet?"

"The spell has to be undone. I'm not sure how, but word magic, I'm guessing, can best be subdued with words. You know, I almost decided to snatch Walt Whitman instead."

Emily winced. "The man's pen has dysentery."

"For me, there's a method to his madness," said Quill. "Like you, he writes about my work quite a bit. He writes that the grass is 'the beautiful uncut hair of graves.' Now that's the spirit. He writes, 'And to die is different from what any one supposed, and *luckier.*' You can see why I appreciate the gentleman."

"Please, allow Mr. Whitman the honor."

"For this task, though, I need a surgeon not a dervish."

She turned again to look out the window and noticed the road was lined with trees. "Where are we?"

"Just beyond Holyoke, heading toward the Horse Caves. The woman in question, the Widow Cremint, has a fine old home there in a clearing just a few hundred yards off the road. It's recently come to my attention that she's been advertising for domestic help in town. We will apply for the positions—a governess for the child and a laborer. No one else will dare to apply. They've all heard rumors and know what she is. I spread those rumors myself in the guise of a traveling preacher. She'll have to take us on."

"You're sure?"

"Nothing's a certainty, but I've been doing this for millions of years."

"Oh, my," said Emily, and brought her open palm to her mouth. "I just remembered one time when a very old woman came to the door of my father's house inquiring where she might find lodging in Amherst. This was when I still answered the door. I gave her directions that would eventually lead her to the cemetery, and told myself, this way she wouldn't have to move more than once in a year." She shook her head. "How I laughed at that mischief. I was laughing at myself."

She looked up for his reaction and noticed some commotion on his shadowed side of the compartment. There was a sound like the flapping of wings, and then something flew toward her. She closed her eyes and brought her arms up.

"Gather yourself," said Quill.

Emily lowered her arms and opened her eyes to morning sunlight. She blinked and then focused on a set of steps before her. When her gaze widened, she took in what she could see of a large, sprawling house that seemed to surpass the Homestead in size but not in upkeep. White paint was peeling, porch railing supports were missing, and one of the front windows had a meandering crack traversing its pane.

The suddenness of day forced her to adjust her balance, and she took a step back and then one forward. Quill, somehow she knew it was Quill, although he was no longer the gentleman of the brougham, stood next to her in front of the door. He was older, tired-looking, with a puffy, wrinkled face and white hair. His drab jacket and trousers were on the verge of tattered. She looked down and saw that she was now wearing a dark blue day dress, but thankfully her walking boots were her own.

"I wear white," she said.

"Not for this," he said, and stepped forward to rap on the door. "All that white you wear; I have a theory that it's symbolic of the blank page."

"Think again, Mr. Quill," she said.

"I hope you don't mind, I've supplied you with undergarments. White, by the way."

"I'll treat them like a blank page," she said, and noticed now that he was carrying a large sack over his shoulder.

The door opened and a tall young woman stood before them. Quill stepped forward and said, "Good day, Mrs. Cremint. I heard in town that you were looking for a laborer and a woman to watch your child. Allow me to introduce myself: I'm John Gullen, and this is my daughter, Dagmar."

Emily wondered if the witch would know there was treachery behind Quill's smile. She averted her gaze, but not before noticing the woman's voluminous hair and the inordinate length of her neck. When Emily looked down, she realized that she was wearing the very same blue day dress that Mrs. Cremint wore.

"You, there," said the woman. Emily looked up. "Do you have any experience with children? Have you cared for them before?" Her tone was demanding, and the poet was too nervous to answer. She merely nodded.

"We have a letter of recommendation from our last employer, Jessup Halstone, Albany, New York. A very wealthy and well-respected gentleman," said Quill. He handed Mrs. Cremint a piece of paper, folded in half. The woman took it and read through it quickly. She handed it back to Quill.

"You can see the place needs work," she said, her voice softening. "I'll take you on. But I want the young lady here—Dagmar, is it?—to know that my child is very frail. He has a serious condition that the doctors cannot diagnose. I should say, those from outside might think his demeanor something strange. If she thinks she can bring herself to treat him as she would any other child, she can have the position."

"I understand," said Emily.

Mrs. Cremint stepped beyond the doorway, approached Quill, leaned forward, and sniffed. She paused for a long spell as if contemplating his aroma while the breeze, laced with pine, played in the surrounding oaks and a chime sounded in the corner of the porch. Then it was Emily's turn, and the woman drew closer than the poet could tolerate. A lump formed in her throat but she dared not swallow. She feared that at any second, she'd tremble and give herself away. A few more moments of deep thought and the lady said, "Come in. I'll show you to your rooms."

She led them down a hallway, Quill directly behind Mrs. Cremint and Emily following. The hall they traversed was lined with the most magnificent paneling, a butterscotch wood with a thousand dark knots visible. There were daguerreotypes lining the walls; sienna portraits of an older gentleman with prodigious mutton chops and dressed in a military uniform. "The pictures are of my late husband, General Cremint," the woman called back. "You may call me Sabille."

"Sabille, very good," said Quill, and the party turned left into a large parlor. The furniture was plush, and the books and figurines were arranged neatly on the shelves, but all was cast with an indefinable dinginess, as if the very atmosphere and light had been corrupted. Emily wondered if nature itself might be in revolt against a child denied his death.

After Sabille had shown them to their separate rooms, and she'd briefly haggled with Quill over the terms of employment, she came to Emily and said, "Come and meet Arthur." Her tone was far more pleasant than before, almost conspiratorial. She led Emily back toward the front of the house and then mounted the steps leading to the second floor. "As you can see, there's a lot that needs to be done here. I just haven't had the strength to do everything since my husband died, and also watch the child. The accounts alone—my husband was a well-to-do gentleman—have been neglected, and I need to give them attention before I lose money. Your father will be a godsend in reviving the house."

At the end of the upstairs hallway, there was a door that Sabille waited at as Emily caught up to her. The woman reached out and gently touched the poet's shoulder to draw her near. She whispered, "The boy is very frail, very frail. He likes to hear stories and to play with his wooden soldiers. You'll see that his vitality diminishes with the day. By late afternoon, you'll not recognize him as the child of the morning." She opened the door.

The room was circular, no doubt a turret Emily had not caught a glimpse of in front of the house. There were five windows evenly spaced along the circumference. There was a small bed, a bookcase, a dresser, and a play table with a child's chair, all resting upon a large braided rug. In the miniature chair, there was a boy with his back to Emily. The first things that drew her eye were the intermittent clumps and strands of brown hair on the otherwise bald head. The sight of it depleted her.

He wore a red flannel shirt and a pair of overalls; moccasins on his feet. There must have been a hundred wooden soldiers, each the size of a thumb, arranged on the table as if on a parade ground, readied for inspection. The boy held one in each hand and mumbled to himself. Sabille cleared her throat and spoke. "Arthur, I want you to meet someone."

The boy turned at the sound of his mother's voice, and Emily desperately tried to stifle her astonishment, knowing her life depended on it. Still, an expression of awe escaped her lips, and she instantly recovered by turning the sound into the boy's name. "Arthur, I'm Emily, and I've come to keep you company."

His complexion was tinged green, and there were scabs and oozing scrapes across his cheeks and forehead. The whites of his eyes were yellowed and the pupils faded to white. Behind his crusted lips, his teeth were brown pegs. He looked to his mother and grunted. Cautiously, he left his chair and stepped across the room to hug Sabille's legs.

Emily lowered herself on her haunches to the child's height. The boy smelled like a muddy streambed, and there was something shiny dribbling from the side of his mouth. "I'm Emily," she said again. She reached out to take the child's scabbed hand, but at the last second he drew it quickly away. His sudden movement frightened her and she reared backward, nearly falling over. As she stood, he opened his horrid mouth at her. A second later, she realized he was laughing.

"A joke?"

Arthur nodded.

"Well," said Sabille, "I see you've got an understanding. I'll leave you two to get acquainted." The boy went back to his chair and soldiers. When the door closed, Emily took a seat on the bed and watched as if she were watching a neighbor through wavy glass on Main Street. The child seemed some kind of little beast sprung up from the forest floor. She worked to reconcile this with the fact that she could detect a child's spirit within the rotting husk. As horrid a figure as the boy cut, something about him reminded her of Austin and Susan's Ned, just born in June. *And I'm to kill him with words,* she thought.

Arthur mumbled continuously, the two soldiers in hand, facing his troops, for over an hour. She waited for something to happen, for war to break out or for the wooden men to suggest an adventure, but the game, in which he seemed entirely invested, was all talk. She listened to make out his words and heard nothing but low barks and burbling mumbles, occasionally a heave, like a fatalist's sigh.

"Arthur," she called to him. "What's happening to the soldiers?"

The boy stared at her over his shoulder. Emily waved to him. Then he turned, put the two soldiers in their empty places in the parade ground revue, and walked to the bookcase. He took a book down. She was horrified at his approach. She knew he would want her to take him in her lap and read him a story. No sooner had that realization dawned than she noticed his flesh had gone from a pale green to a light morbid blue. A clump of his hair fell out as he came across the room, a thin lock tumbled off his shoulder.

He held the book out and grunted. She took the volume from him, and then, holding her breath so as not to smell him, she reached out to take him into her lap. His flesh was the slick consistency of rotting mushrooms. When she began to read, she had to eventually breathe, and his aroma conjured in her mind an image of her holding a boy-sized toad. When Arthur made noise and pointed to the book's illustrations, she heard it as croaking.

Only a chapter into the story of Saint George and the Dragon, the boy fell asleep in her arms. His stillness won over her revulsion, and she grew accustomed to his weight and scent. She thought of a spring day a few years earlier when last she'd gone out walking. Carlo was at her side. Just beyond town, the meadow was full of black-eyed Susans. The day was warm and the sun bright. Across the meadow she and the dog moved in among the birch trees and continued on for a mile or more. As she approached a pond, leaves floating upon its surface, she felt a sharp pain in her breast, and woke to Arthur trying to bite her through her day dress.

She cried out and quickly set him on the floor. He showed her his big mouth full of brown shards and she smacked his face. The boy crumpled down onto the rug. She called out his name in a whisper, so as not to let his mother hear. He sprang up onto all fours, gave her another smile, and crawled in circles around the table and chair. To her horror, she noticed her handprint in pale green against the darker blue of his flesh. For the rest of the afternoon, he kept his distance from her and growled if she made any overture of contact.

Luckily, by dinner her handprint had vanished into the overall violet of his face. His flesh seemed to have come unstrung, sagging down in ripples around his neck and making cuffs at his wrists. His breathing had grown labored, and he cried out occasionally as if in pain. He sat, at the head of the dining room table, strapped into a high chair that was much too small for him. Sabille sat to his right and Emily to his left. For the sixth time his mother lifted a spoon of gruel into his mouth, forcing it far down his throat. The child gagged the portion into his stomach and a moment later Emily lifted the half-full bowl she held in order to catch his vomit. The process was repeated with each spoonful. "It's the only way," Sabille repeated as if saying a prayer. Emily was desperate to scream "The dead don't eat," but held her peace.

At the other end of the table was Quill in the guise of the old laborer, John Gullen. He watched the bizarre feeding, seemingly unable to touch his stew. At one point, Emily looked at him and caught his eye. In her mind she heard his young gentleman's voice say, "I've seen few things grimmer than this." "I'm nauseous," Emily told him in her thoughts. "At bedtime tonight, try to be near enough to them to hear the spell. If I have to spend another day here chopping wood, *I'll* expire."

The last spoonful had been loaded and returned, and Sabille said, "Dagmar, if you'll clean him and bring him upstairs in a minute, I'll prepare his bed."

"Yes, ma'am," said Emily.

Quill stood when the Widow Cremint left the table. Emily set to washing up Arthur, who was slick with gruel and vomit. She gagged more than once in the process. The entire time she worked on him, the boy mumbled at a furious pace, and every now and then released a weak howl of pain. When she was finished cleaning him, he pulled his thumbnail off. It came away from its bed easy as breathing. He dropped it into her open palm, and she put it in her pocket. She hugged him to her and thought she felt him kiss the spot he'd earlier bitten.

Sabille stripped the day's clothes from Arthur's sagging, violet body, and then she and Emily fitted him into the felt bag he slept in. His head stuck out of the end of the sack, and a drawstring was tied snugly around his neck. Carrying him to the bed, Sabille called him "my little caterpillar." When she set his head upon the pillow, strands of hair fell free. Emily waved and wished the boy a sweet night's sleep. She stepped back but didn't leave the room.

"You may go now," said Sabille.

"Yes, ma'am," said Emily, and exited but made sure to only close the door partway. She hid just outside in the darkened upstairs hallway and waited. Through the sliver of an opening, she watched as the mother knelt next to the bed, cooing and shushing the child who rocked frantically from side to side. After a time Arthur finally lay still. She watched Sabille lean over, her mouth near the child's ear.

Emily turned her own ear to the opening. Sabille's whisper was so very low, but each of the words of the spell registered in the poet's mind with utter clarity, like the tap of a pin against a crystal goblet. There were three stanzas, and she thought she knew them. She pulled away from the door and leaned back against the wall. "I've got it," she thought, hoping he would hear her.

His voice sounded behind her eyes. "Good. Now *run*," he yelled, and the words echoed through even her most distant memories. "Run to the road."

She slipped away from the open door and crept down the stairs, easing her boots down on each step so as not to be discovered. When she reached the door, her fear banished caution. She flung it open and trounced across the porch, knowing now she'd be heard. Emily hadn't run since she was a girl, but her walking in the woods with Carlo allowed her to keep a steady pace. She dashed along the winding, tree-lined path that led to the road. Only ten yards into her flight, she heard the ungodly baying of some creature. She ran faster, but before long heard the thing galloping behind her.

She pictured a muscular, sleek animal with six legs. When she turned to steal a look, she saw it in the moonlight. It was no beast, but the gentleman in the daguerreotypes, General Cremint. He was naked and wielding a saber. Both the sounds of galloping and baying issued from his open mouth. His eyes were missing, just two black holes. When he noticed Emily glance at him, Sabille's voice came forth, "*Spy*," she screamed. "*Spy*."

The old man gained on her, and she could feel the breeze of his flashing sword at the back of her neck. Up ahead she saw the end of the path and the silhouette of the brougham, waiting. Just then the carriage's lanterns blossomed with light. She was tiring, her legs cramping, and she heard Quill calling from the open door, "Lap the miles, Miss Dickinson. Lick the valleys up." She pushed harder but felt the sword tip slice through her hair. The brougham was only feet away.

As she reached for Quill's outstretched hands, Emily saw the driver stand in his box, his arm moving in a sudden arc. She heard the crack of his whip. General Cremint whimpered and fell behind. Quill grabbed her then beneath the arms and lifted her into the brougham. The horses sprang forth, the door of the carriage slammed closed, and they were off. Emily looked quickly to catch one more view of her assailant, the general, sitting in the road, crying, turning slowly to smoke. She moved to the bench across from Quill. Leaning back, catching her breath, she said, "I've forgotten the spell."

"Don't worry," said Quill, again a young gentleman, the rose still fresh in his lapel. "Once you heard it, *I* was able to hear it, and I've got it. Part of the spell was that every night when she used it on the boy I'd never be able to hear it. Once *you* heard it, though, I could hear it in your thoughts. Sabille is already weak. Evidence of that is the illusion of her dead husband she set on you. She must be going mad."

"An illusion?"

"A deadly illusion, but still conjured from nothing."

"It's inevitable she'll lose the child?" Emily asked.

"Exactly. And now you must get to work on the counterspell." The brougham came to a halt. She looked out the window to see that they'd returned to the Town Tomb. Again it was snowing and the drifts around the entrance to the sunken house were ever higher.

"Why are we here again? I've done what you asked."

"I certainly didn't recruit you for your running prowess," he said. "You're a poet, and now begins your work. Come see," he said. "I've brought your writing table from home." He'd removed his glove again. His fingers snapped.

She stood in freezing, damp darkness. She heard the wind howling as if at a distance, and then heard the scratch and spark of Quill lighting a match. The flame illuminated his face. He smiled at her, his breath a cloud of steam, and tossed the lit match over his shoulder. A moment later there was a hushed explosion, a sudden burst of flame, and the place came into view. At first she thought she was in a cave, but a moment later realized it was the Town Tomb.

Quill stood warming himself before a fireplace dug into the rock wall. She saw her writing table and chair. "See here," he said, and pointed to a swinging iron bar that could put a cauldron of water over the flame. "I've acquired your gold and white tea set. You can make tea. What type are you partial to? I'm guessing marble."

She glared at him. "Something strong, and I'll need a bottle of spirits."

"Spirits?"

"Whiskey," she said. "I'll need paper and a copy of the spell."

"There you are," he said, and pointed to her writing table, now complete with pen and inkwell and a stack of fresh paper. He turned and pointed again, and a few feet left of the fireplace there stood a wooden bar, a decanter of whiskey, and glasses. "If you need ice, you can go outside," he said. "It will always be winter while you're here."

"What exactly am I to do?"

"Create a counterspell to Sabille's spell."

"How is one to begin on something like this?"

"That's the challenge," said Quill.

"How long do I have?"

"Eternity, or until you succeed."

"Then I go back."

"For twenty-five years," he said.

"It's blackmail," she said.

"Laws don't apply here, Miss Dickinson. Death is no democracy." He walked toward the door of the tomb. "Might as well get started," he said.

"How will I know if I'm even close?"

"That'll be up to you." The huge door of the tomb slid open. As Quill went out, winter came in, snow flying and a wicked chill. With a distinct click, the door closed, and the wind and world were again distant. Emily took her seat at the writing table. She lit the taper in the candlestick for extra light and adjusted the tulle across her shoulders, a meager attempt at protection against the darkness of the tomb. She felt its blind depths like a breathing presence behind her. Lifting the page on which Quill had copied the spell, she noted his clear and elegant handwriting. The paper smelled of saffron. She read the words of the spell, but nothing registered. It didn't seem to be what she'd heard. Leaning over the scented page, as if to communicate with it as much as read it, she recited its stanzas in a whisper.

Stir, stir, stir
And stay
No leave to go away

Burn, burn, burn
And rise
The sun will be your open eyes

Stir, stir, stir
And stay
All of time to love and play.

After an hour of contemplation, Emily decided that the spell was useless to her. The magic of the words sprang from the traditions of a culture she knew nothing about. She surmised that her first solution, attempting to rearrange the words of the spell into a poem in order to counteract it, would have no effect. Dogmatic belief in anything was foreign to her. She crumpled the sheet of stanzas, got up, and threw it in the fire. The moment the flames licked the balled sheet black, she felt lighter, like a boat cutting loose its anchor and drifting. She made tea and put whiskey in it.

Sitting, sipping her brew, she noticed that she again wore her own white cotton day dress. She was clear that what she would do was simply write a poem, whatever came to her, and hope that somehow it would have some bearing on the spell. Presentiment, something she'd written about before—"The Notice to the startled Grass that darkness is about to pass"— was to be the order of the long night. She set a sheet of paper in front of her, moistened her pen in the inkwell and then sat there, staring, listening to the blizzard outside, searching for words in its distant shriek. An hour passed, maybe a day or year.

Later, she was brought to by the sound of a groan emanating from the dark back of the tomb where the winter's harvest lay frozen. When the enormous stillness had swallowed the noise, Emily was unsure if she'd really heard it or only heard it in her thoughts. She turned in her chair and looked into the shadows. "Hello?" she called. While she waited for a response, she realized that as long as she'd been in the tomb, she'd not been hungry, she'd not slept, and had no call for a chamber pot. No answer came back from the dark.

She put the tulle around her shoulders and opened the door of the tomb. She was surprised by how easily the enormous weight of it slid back. In a moment the blizzard was upon her. She took two steps out into a drift that reached to her thighs and looked up into the snow-filled night. It wasn't long before the fierce wind forced her to retreat. Once back inside, the tomb door closed, she swung the water cauldron out over the perpetual fire. Tea and whiskey were her only pleasures. She'd noticed that, when she wasn't looking, the decanter refilled itself.

Waiting for the water to come to a boil, she rubbed her hands together in front of the fire, and once they'd warmed she shoved them into her dress pockets. When first she felt the dried gentian petals, she thought them just some scrap of paper she'd jotted a line on at some point. But when she touched the child's nail, she remembered. The water boiled, and she made the tea she'd dreamed about, lacing the brew with a generous shot of whiskey to offset the taste of the boy's nail that twirled atop its plum-colored depths.

In the dream the gentian tea, tasting like the sweetest dirt, had made her mind race, and now too, beneath the ground, her mind raced. Phrases flew, their letters visible, from every grotto of her mind. She stood at the center of the storm, scythe in hand, cutting through the dross. Eventually she lifted the pen and drew ink. The first line came strong to the paper, and there was a pause—a moment, a day, a year—before she hesitantly began on the second line. Slowly, the poem grew. Midway she sat back and wondered which came first, the words or the visions. Her thoughts circled, and then she leaned forward and resumed her work. When she finished, she read the poem aloud.

> *The night woke in me—And I rose*
> *blindly wandering in a Snow*
> *To the Sunken house—*
> *its Cornice—in the ground.*
> *Parlor of shadows—in the ground*
> *The distant Wind—a lonely Sound*
> *Winter's orphans and Me*
> *Undoing knots with Gentian tea.*

The instant the last word was spoken, she rejected it; too obvious to undo a spell of life. She crumpled the sheet and tossed it into the fire. A belief in complexity and complication crept into her thoughts and with that the years fell like an avalanche. She drank tea, and stared at the blank sheet, went outside, and listened for groans in the dark back of the tomb. A million times, a place to begin arrived, and she would think of Arthur trapped in his high chair at dinner, and the line would vanish, too insubstantial to survive.

Later, she was brought to her senses by the sound of something shuffling in the dark behind her. She spun in her chair, her heart pounding. It sounded like weary footsteps. Realizing the sound was approaching, she stood and backed against the writing table. Out of the gloom and into the glow of the fireplace, a wasted figure staggered, an old woman, dressed in black, wearing a black muslin cap atop her white hair. Her face was wrinkled and powdered with dust, and there were patches of ice on her brow and sunken cheeks. She clutched a Bible in her crooked hands.

"Hello," said Emily, surprised as she did so. Even before the old woman stopped and looked up, the poet knew it was the same woman who'd come that time to the house for directions to a place she might stay.

"Excuse me, miss, could you tell me where I might seek lodging in town?" Her voice was low and rumbled in echoes through the tomb. Emily noticed part of the woman's nose had rotted away and that there was something alive in her glassy left eye by the way it bulged and jiggled.

"Go that way, into the dark," said the poet and pointed.

"Thank you for your kindness, dear." The woman turned and shuffled into the shadows.

Emily stood numb from the encounter. "Is the gentian tea still steering my mind?" she whispered.

"No," came the old woman's reply from the back of the tomb. "It's the rising tide of years."

Some piece of eternity later, she sat with pen poised above paper, her arm aching for how long it had been in that position. She barely recognized anymore the crackle of the fire, the distant wind. The pen's tip finally touched the blank sheet, and she heard a new sound that distracted her from her words. The nib made a fat black blotch, and she drew her hand back. "What was that noise?" she said. In her loneliness she now spoke all her thoughts. Finally it came again, something outside. "A person shouting?" No, it was the barking of a dog. She leaped up from the chair and rushed to the door of the tomb. Opening it, she stepped out into the blizzard.

Sitting a few feet off, up to his chest in snow, was Carlo, her Newfoundland, a bear of a dog. He barked again and bounded the drifts to reach her. She was overwhelmed and blinked her eyes to be certain he was there. But then she felt his furry head beneath her hand, and he licked her palm. It came to her as if in a dream that she was freezing, and she stepped back into the tomb. The dog followed. After closing out the winter, she sat in her writing chair, leaning forward, hugging Carlo to her. "You're good," she repeated, stroking his head. When she finally let go, the dog backed away and sat staring for a long while. His sudden bark frightened her.

"What?" she asked.

The dog barked three more times and then came to her and took the sleeve of her dress. Carlo tugged at her, long his sign for her to follow. It came to her, with his fourth tug and tenth bark, that he was there to take her back. "You know the way," she said to him. The dog barked. She turned to face the writing table and lifted her pen. She quickly scribbled on the blotched sheet, "Gone Home. Mercy." Dropping the pen, she stood and wrapped the tippet around her shoulders. The dog came to her side and she took hold of him by the collar. "Home," she said, and Carlo led her into the dark back of the tomb.

They walked forever and before long he led her by way of a narrow tunnel back into the world. When the moonlight bathed her, she felt the undergarments Quill had given her vanish like a breeze. The dog led her down a tall hill to the end of Main Street. Walking the rest of the way to the Homestead they encountered no one. Quietly, in the kitchen, she gave Carlo a cookie and kissed him between his eyes. After taking off her boots, she tiptoed up the stairs to her room. She removed the white dress and hung it in the closet. She swam into her nightgown and got back into bed.

As her eyes began to close, she felt a hand upon her shoulder. In her panic, she tried to scream but another hand covered her mouth. "Shhh, shhh," she heard in her ear, and feeling cold breath on the back of her neck knew it was Quill. "Lie still," he said. "Let's not wake your parents."

"Leave me alone," she said. She lay back on the pillow without getting a look at his face.

"I intend to," he said. "I merely wanted to tell you that the piece you left in the tomb worked the trick. Three simple words were the key to the spell's lock; a mad but marvelous thing. Arthur is resting peacefully, so to speak."

"So I owe you nothing."

"I'd like to ask you a question, if I may."

"What?"

"All these poems you've written and hidden—so many poems. Why?"

While she thought, morning broke and the birds sang in the garden. "Because I could not stop," she said, and he was gone.

---

*Story Note: In April of 1862, Emily Dickinson struck up a correspondence with the poet and war hero Thomas Wentworth Higginson in response to an article Higginson published in the *Atlantic Monthly*, offering advice to new poets. In her second letter to him she made this odd statement: "I had a *terror*—since September—I could tell to none." She is obviously referring to September of 1861, which is the setting of my story. The poem I'm riffing off of is one of her most famous, "Because I Could Not Stop For Death . . ." The earliest known version of this poem, of which there are many, was written, as far as I can tell, in 1863. I imagine the "terror" Emily refers to is her experience that plays out in my story. After mulling it for a year, I've imagined she decided to capture it in that famous poem.

Rocket Ship to Hell

Twelve years ago, I was at the Millennium Worldcon in Philly, and with the exception of the incident I'm about to relate, I only remember three other things about that long weekend.

1. I recall going to a cocktail party at night in a dinosaur museum.

2. Somewhere along the line, Michael Swanwick told me I should check out Fritz Leiber's *Our Lady of Darkness*.

3. I remember the walking. The convention center is enormous. I must have walked a hundred miles a day in that place—spacious, empty hallways with columns, rotundas, vestibules. With all the people attending, I couldn't believe I could trudge for twenty minutes along some dimly lit, marble concourse and never see a soul. I suppose I attended panels and maybe even did a reading, but I can't conjure one shred of an image of any of that—just the slogging from one distant point to another. Think Kafka's "An Imperial Message."

Somewhere in the middle of the third day, exhausted and confused, not having seen the sun since arriving at my hotel attached to the convention center, I found myself near an exit and seized the opportunity. I plunged into a hot, blue day and the light momentarily blinded me. A few moments later, when I could see again, I noticed there was a bar right across the street from where I'd exited. Unfortunately, the place was packed with fellow con-goers having lunch. I had a hangover from the dinosaur cocktail party the night before, and I needed a drink. Before I moved to Jersey, I'd lived in Philly for a while. I was almost certain that there was a little place called Honey's a few blocks east and then one south.

I found it wedged into the middle of a block of grimy storefronts. It was dark inside and air-conditioned, cool relief from the August day. The walls were covered in cheap wood paneling and the floor was a black-and-white checkerboard that must have been laid back in the thirties. There were a few tables and chairs, and the bar was covered in the same splintered wood paneling. There was no mirror behind it or decoration, just rows of bottles of cheap liquor. I took a seat and the young woman behind the bar told me she had forty-ounce Colt 45s as well as the hard stuff. I ordered one. She gave me a forty and a glass.

Other than the two of us, the place was empty. She looked to be in her early twenties, tall and thin, her hair shaved into a crew cut. The blue-gray T-shirt she wore bore the words *Cannibal Ox* and *The Cold Vein* and carried an image of what could have been astronauts with guns. She was busy, wiping things down with a wet rag, adjusting the placement of the bottles, drying glasses.

"Are you from the neighborhood?" she asked, her back to me.

"No, I'm in town for a thing at the convention center."

"The science fiction show?"

"That's it," I said. "Have you been over there?"

"I'd like to, but I'm working this whole weekend. My daddy's in the hospital, so I'm filling in for him."

"Oh, hope he's OK."

"He's got the prostate. You know what I mean?" She turned and looked at me.

"Not yet, but I'm sure someday I will."

She laughed, put her rag down, and walked through a door to the left.

While she was in the back, the front door of the place opened and I heard someone come in. I knew they were headed for the bar because their labored breathing grew closer. A moment later, an old, heavyset guy in a floppy brown suit and white shirt, yellow tie loosened to the point of uselessness, took a seat a few down from me. I looked over and he nodded his big potato head in my direction. He was mostly bald, but little squalls of hair erupted here and there across his scalp. His thick glasses were steamed, and sweat drenched his jowls.

"It's a fuckin' oven out there," he said.

Trying to avoid a conversation, I just nodded.

The bartender came back into the bar and, seeing him, asked, "What you want?"

He stopped gasping for a moment and said, "Gin, straight up, miss. Not a shot, a full glass."

She set a glass in front of him and poured right to the rim. Due to past martini experiences, the sight of it made me gag.

"Seven dollars," she said. He put two twenties on the bar and thanked her.

I knew that eventually the guy was going to start a conversation, and although I wasn't keen on talking to him, at the same time I had no intention of leaving Honey's until I'd finished a second Colt.

"You're at the convention? Right?" he finally said.

I wasn't wearing my badge and had a moment of panic over the fact that I could be so easily identified with that to which I belonged. There was no denying it, though. The bartender noticed my hesitation. "How'd you know?" I finally said.

"I saw you over there, walking the hallways." His voice was breathy and slightly high-pitched. There was a kind of weird resonance to it.

"Some hallways. Place is like a labyrinth."

"I had to rent one of those scooters," he said, and his laugh turned into a hacking cough.

"You a fan?"

"I'm a writer," I said.

"Me too," he confided and took a long drink.

"Two writers at once," said the bartender. "That might be a first for Honey's."

"It's not as auspicious as all that, my dear," he said. Then he looked at me and asked what I'd published.

"Last book of a trilogy came out this year," I said. "I've only been at it since ninety-seven."

"Live long and prosper," he said and flashed us the Spock split-finger deal. "My first publications were back in the late sixties."

"Novels or stories?" I asked.

"Always stories," he said. "I only wrote one novel, and you can't find that anywhere."

"I want to write stories," said the bartender. "I'm in my last semester at community college, and I'm going to Temple to take fiction writing."

"Three writers," said the old guy. He took a drink and smoothed his wispy islands of hair.

"You like SF?" I asked her.

"And fantasy," she said. "I'm taking a lit course this summer. We're reading Ellison, Butler, Moorcock, Tiptree, Dick."

"As long as you lay off that slipstream drivel—the lime Jell-O of subgenres," he said.

"That's next semester," she said. "Do you guys make a lot of money?"

We laughed.

"Money can be made," said the old guy. "But you can't make a living now writing stories."

I asked his name and he told me, "Cole Werber." It didn't ring a bell, but my knowledge of the genre was minimal. I told them my name, and the bartender told us hers was Breelyn.

"Where'd you publish your early stories?" I asked Werber.

"Back in the day, all over. *Galaxy*, *Amazing*, *F&SF*, *If*, and one you don't hear about now, *Venture*. I wrote a series of stories about this alien named Pirsute. He lived on the planet Borlox, and he was a kind of vegetable creature—but arms and legs and a head like a human. Skin the consistency of an eggplant, a mop of greenery for hair, a thistle beard, and eyes like cherries. He was a detective. I based him on Poe's Auguste Dupin. You know, ratiocination, etc. He had a sidekick, who was an orphaned Earth girl with a photographic memory."

"I love that kind of shit," said the bartender.

"That sounds cool," I said.

"Shit may be the operative word," said Werber. "But my plan was to link all the stories in what we used to call a fix-up and then publish my first novel."

"Oh, sorry. I didn't mean it like that," said Breelyn.

Werber waved his hand and smiled. "I'm just joking."

"How many stories did you have in the series?" I asked.

"Well, I published the first one in sixty-five, and by sixty-nine I had a dozen and a half published."

"Eighteen stories in four years? That's pretty impressive," I said.

"Not really, not for the time. Some of those writers back then cranked 'em out a couple a month. I think Silverberg published a hundred by the time he was this young lady's age. I was twenty when I published the first one."

"Did you have a lot of readers?" asked Breelyn.

"Actually, people liked them. They followed them from magazine to magazine. I'd get a lot of response when I'd go to the conventions."

"So then why'd nobody read the novel?" I asked.

"It wasn't that novel. The Pirsute novel was never put together. The one nobody read was called *Rocket Ship to Hell*."

"Great title," I said.

"Religion meets science," said Breelyn and made herself a whiskey on the rocks.

"Maybe not religion," said Werber, "but the whole thing reeked of mythology. I could tell you folks about it, but it'd take me a little while. It's a remarkable story, though, no lie. I never really told it to anyone before, but with my health the way it is now there's not much they could do to me."

"I'm not going anywhere," said Breelyn and took a long drink.

I could tell by this guy's shtick that if I went for his story, I could be there for an eternity. At the same time, the way he stared at me waiting for an answer, eyes big behind those thick lenses, it was almost as if he was offering a challenge, writer to writer—Are you going to go back and walk the empty corridors or are you going to stay right here where the story is?

Although I'd not yet finished my first, I ordered another forty. When Breelyn put it on the bar, I said, "OK, let's have it."

The old guy nodded with a look of satisfaction and polished off about three fingers of gin in a gulp. "It was 1969, and I'd run out of Pirsute stories. I tried to go in a different direction, and my imagination always wound up back on Borlox, following the vegetable detective and the girl with the photographic memory, but nothing ever happened. My imagination was shot. The bad part was that I was broke. I'd been trying to live off the money from the stories—late on rent, phone bill, car payments. I was a mess.

"The day after they repossessed my car, I got a phone call from this guy who said he wanted me to come and do a reading and talk for his club. I told him, OK, but that I had no car. He said, 'We'll send a car for you. And the event pays three hundred dollars.' I almost dropped the phone. For that kind of money, I'd have walked.

"Two days later, a limousine showed up in front of my apartment complex to the minute the guy on the phone, Mr. Masterson, had promised. The driver got out and opened the door for me. About twenty minutes later, we pulled up in front of this mansion. I don't know where it was. The place was gigantic, from some time in the nineteenth century. We got out, and the driver led me inside and through a series of hallways and rooms until we came to a closed door somewhere at the back of the house. The driver knocked; a voice inside said, 'Enter.' He opened the door, stood back, and I stepped in.

"There were books lining the walls, and in the center of the room was a well-polished table at which sat four old gentlemen, dressed to the nines, each holding what looked like toy rockets. They put their rockets down and stood when I entered. I made the rounds, shook hands, got their names, and took a seat at the head of the table. Across from me was Masterson, who seemed to be the head of the group. 'Welcome to the Rocket Club,' he said." Werber took a sip and said, "Are you with me?"

Breelyn lit a cigarette, and I pulled the second forty closer. She said, "Yeah," and he went back to it.

"I'll try to speed it up a little," he said. "The Rocket Club was these four old, white-haired farts. They were mad about science fiction. Knew just about everything going back to the thirties and could talk about any writer I mentioned. It was more an education for me than them. To top that, they asked me all kinds of intricate questions about the Pirsute stories. They remembered more about my own stuff than I did. I read them my most recent publication, 'Slaves of Dust.' Some solid vegetable love and death. When I was finished, they applauded so much I was afraid one of them would drop over. Instead, Masterson asked me if when I was a boy, I ever wanted to be an astronaut.

"I said, 'Probably,' and shrugged, but it was true, I'd dreamed of it when I was a kid. When I'd told my father, he'd said, 'You're a blockhead at math and you're afraid of heights. Forget it.' But I never did forget it.

"'How'd you like to make fifty thousand dollars instead of three hundred?' asked Masterson.

"I was stunned. I just sat there with my mouth open.

"'We're each exceedingly wealthy,' said the grandpa next to me with the white goatee and sideburns.

"'We can send you into outer space,' said the heavy one with the ruffled shirt collar.

"I was floored and a little worried they were dangerously insane. When all was said and done, though, this was the deal as proposed by Masterson: They were funding a secret joint project with NASA. Because they were putting up the bread, they called the shots on the mission and rocket design. What they wanted to do was put artists in outer space to witness the experience and then transcribe it to the populace through some work conceived on the journey. In addition to me, who they wanted to be the mission's official writer, they were looking for a painter and a musician. Four days in space, and I collected for writing a story about it.

"At first, all I could think about was the fifty thousand, but then it began to dawn on me that I wasn't in the best shape. I was seventy pounds overweight and smoked a couple packs a day. Besides that I didn't know how to do much else but make up stories about the vegetable detective. I actually said, 'Do you think I'm the best candidate?'

"Masterson looked at his cronies, and they nodded. 'Well,' he said, 'we tried to get Thomas Pynchon, but he turned us down.'"

"Come on," I said to Werber. "Is that for real?"

"I wouldn't mind doing that," said Breelyn.

"You'd be a lot more fit for it than I was," said Werber. "Is it real?" He took off his glasses and cleaned them on his shirt. "As God is my judge." He put the glasses back on.

"You say NASA was in on this?" I asked.

"Yes. They were supposed to build the rocket. They used it as an opportunity to test out some new things and to simplify the control mechanisms of the ship, all on the Rocket Club's dime."

"You did it, right?" asked Breelyn.

"Yeah," he said, pushed his glass forward, and took out a handkerchief to wipe his face. She filled him up with gin, and, after a prolonged coughing spree, he was off.

"I took it. I needed the fucking money. Oops, sorry, miss. I needed the money. We shook on it. Two weeks later, with a five-thousand-dollar advance in my bank account, I was in an apartment in downtown Vegas. I was there to train for the mission. My handler and apartment mate was an ex-astronaut named Maxwell Penfield. He was a sturdily built old man with a tan and a crew cut. At night, he'd sit by the air conditioner in his boxer shorts and drink a pint of bourbon while reading Herodotus. The night I arrived I told him I'd never seen his name mentioned in any of the NASA missions. He nodded and said, 'I only flew secret missions.' I questioned him about it, and he said, 'Do you think that every time the US puts men in space that it's going to be on TV? Seriously, now.'

"My training started the next day. We had a breakfast that Max prepared—every meal was fruit and meat. I was on the can twice a day. You could set the atomic clock by it. After breakfast, we walked for two hours before the real heat came on. Then it was lunch, downtown at a place called Hoppy's where we always had a burger, no bun, and the melon bowl. No time to digest, though, 'cause we were off to the Castaways Casino, where we climbed the stairs to the top floor. That took me an hour and was agonizing. Max was patient, though. I'd complain and he'd laugh. 'Come on, move that gravy,' he'd say as I gasped on every landing.

"The afternoons were given over to gambling. Max said it would test my stress levels. He made me gamble every day, with my own money. It was exhilarating and depressing, sometimes at the same time. I lost three thousand dollars in the first week and in the second won four thousand. At the end of the two weeks I'd lost some weight. Actually, considering the time, a good amount, but I was still fifty pounds overweight. My nightly push-up tally had gone from three to fifteen. On our last day in the apartment, Max told me he was going to give me a final exam.

"We were in the living room, our bags packed. He reached into his pocket and took out a crisp bill. He held it out so that I could see it was a fifty. He folded it in half, creasing the fold, and then flipped his two fingers and scaled it toward me so that it landed at my feet. 'If you can pick that up without bending your knees, you pass,' he said. 'And if you do, you can keep it.'

"I sucked my gut in, took a deep breath, stiffened my knees, and swept down on that note like a bald eagle grabbing a salmon out of a stream. Max said, 'You pass, Werber.' Then we were in the car, heading out to Groom Lake, what they now call Area Fifty-One." The old writer took a drink and wiped his face again.

"Did you really go into outer space?" asked Breelyn as she ran around the bar to grab a stool. She brought it back to her spot next to the liquor shelf and sat down.

"One of my personal rules for stories is no foreshadowing," he said.

In as amiable a tone as possible, I said, "This is getting pretty far-fetched."

"Patience, my esteemed colleague," he said. "The best or worst, depending on your point of view, is yet to come. For on that first day at the testing range, out in the middle of absolutely nowhere, I saw the rocket. Now, I knew what a NASA rocket looked like. They were using the Saturn Five at the time. This didn't look like any rocket I'd ever seen that made it into outer space. It looked way better than that, as if it had been designed by Frank R. Paul, Freas, or Finlay. It was a giant, pointy, silver bullet with four arcing fins at the back. There were three circular portholes lining two sides of the ship, and there was a window near the top in what I assumed was the control cabin. I didn't detect any stages to it, which meant the whole ship had to lift off into space and return in one piece. This is when I started to get nervous."

"Who's Finlay?" asked Breelyn.

"Those guys were magazine cover artists back before you were born. They did great rocket ships and aliens. Beautiful stuff," I told her.

"The future they drew was always more futuristic than what the future ever became," said Werber. "It was dreams and nightmares of the future."

"Still no flying car," I said.

"Yeah, but the Rocket Club had the money and influence to make it real. Masterson met us at the launch site. As I stood there gaping at what they'd wrought, he said, 'The name of the ship is the *Icarus*, do you know what that's from?'

"You mean the Greek myth? I asked.

"'No, last year's *Planet of the Apes* movie. That was the name of the ship in it. The club, to a man, thought that film spectacular.'

"The *Icarus* didn't sit well with me under either interpretation.

"'Both a hundred percent operational and a hundred percent sense of wonder,' said Masterson.

"A long day followed—from the launchpad into the complex, where I met my teachers who would deal with the technical aspects of the mission, and then on to my room. Max helped me bring my bags in from the car. He turned the air conditioner way up and called me into a corner behind the door.

"'What do you think of that rocket?' he asked in a whisper.

"'I can't believe it's for real.'

"'You ever hear of Operation Paperclip?'

"I knew about it, a move by the US to snatch up all the excellent German scientists after the Second World War ended. A lot of the people they brought in were Nazis. I nodded, wondering why he was whispering.

"'One of those guys designed that thing.'

"'Will it fly?'

"'Probably,' he said.

"'I'm just thinking of the fifty thousand,' I told him.

"'You need to put that in perspective,' he said. 'A good space chimp costs at least a hundred and fifty thousand and gets about a hundred hours more training.' He shook my hand, and as he went out the door he said over his shoulder, 'Keep doing those push-ups.'

"The next day I met the other two members of the crew. The musician was a guy who went by the name Owl Parson.

He composed for and played the theremin. Small stature and thin limbs, he had a haircut like Moe from The Three Stooges. During our initial conversation he used the word *naturally* a lot, like he was an expert on everything. Eventually he asked me what I wrote and I told him about Pirsute. He shook his head and said he only read pure science fiction like Tom Godwin's 'The Cold Equations.' What could I say? He could read whatever he wanted and strum the air till the cows came home; I just wanted to get paid.

"Anyway, the painter of our trio, Tracy (she had only one name), was a nice woman—a young divorcée from Kansas. 'I always had an artistic bent,' she told me. She showed me some of her paintings. She was a big bony woman with a strict jaw and a sweet face. Her voice had a raspy quality to it—too much dust on the Great Plains. She stood, statuesque, in the middle of her room, holding one after another of her works for me to see. With only a couple of minor adjustments, they were all basically the same thing—a flat background of a solid color, with a bare tree forking and branching upward in straight black. That was it. The kind of thing kids do in fourth grade. Really lousy.

"The next day we got into the onsite training. They spun me in a chair at a thousand miles an hour or something and I puked. They took us up in a big plane and made us weightless and I puked. They dropped us into a thirty-foot-deep pool in space suits and my claustrophobia kicked in. I was terrified and stood on the bottom like a statue while Parson and Tracy completed the mission of three laps back and forth across the bottom. As far as the technical stuff went, yawl and pitch, zero gravity, what all the lights and levers on the boards meant, I tried to pay attention but most of it went through me. It was clear that the ultimate mission was for us to experience space flight, four days in orbit around the Earth, and I did make an effort to listen when they told us how to use the toilet and also how to eat the brown toothpaste that passed for astronaut food."

"How was that stuff?" asked Breelyn.

"It'd say on the packet something along the lines of *Sunday Pot Roast Dinner at Mom's*, but it tasted like you scraped it off your shoe."

"Didn't they care that you did so poorly at all their tasks?" I asked.

"Nah," said Werber and laughed to himself. "Everything was smooth as snot on a doorknob. They just told me, 'We'll get somebody to clean up the mess. You could have done a lot worse.'"

"That doesn't sound like NASA," I said.

"It wasn't NASA. They just built the ship. The guys running the tests and teaching the technical stuff were on the Rocket Club's bankroll."

"How did the others do?" asked Breelyn.

"Parson was a little less hapless than me. Tracy excelled at everything and seemed to understand everything. She should have been an astronaut instead of a painter."

"That's what I'm talking about," said Breelyn and pointed at him with her cigarette between two fingers.

"Let me cut to the chase," said Werber. "The days passed. I avoided the insufferable Owl Parson and spoke to Tracy when she was free. She was usually busy, though, studying her notes and painting more of her pointless trees. In that time I conceived of an idea for a new book, describing in full the mission we were about to undergo. It was, as far as I knew, the first privately funded project to put astronauts into orbit. What a scoop. I didn't even have to make it science fiction. I could just tell exactly what happened and make a mint. I daydreamed about that book while the technicians lectured. And then the launch day was there, and they were strapping me into my suit. I woke up, so to speak, in a cold sweat to find the nightmare was real. I was actually going into outer space. It was a shame my old man had passed, 'cause I'd have liked to rub it in.

"The day of the launch we saw the inside of the *Icarus* for the first time. They waited till we were all suited up and ready to go. Somewhere there's a photo of the three of us with those ridiculous fishbowl helmets on. After that they gave us a walk-through. Suffice it to say things were tight, and I presented a major obstruction when in the one long passageway that made up the ship's center. The cabins were in two parts, half on one side of that main passage and half on the other. Bed and small closet on one side, and across the open expanse a work station. Both the bedroom and work station had round porthole windows. My writing desk had been set up so that when I sat at it I'd be staring into space.

"Remember now, we were on a ladder. This was prelaunch. The ladder retracted once weightlessness set in. I was seeing everything for the first time at a weird angle. The desk, like everything else welded in place, seemed to be hanging on the wall. They told us that when we were weightless it would all make sense. Parson's cabin was closest to the back. The only thing beyond it was the crapper. Next came my cabin and after it, Tracy's. Farther forward there was a storage spot and then the cockpit. They told us to strap into the three seats facing the large, rectangular window. They put Tracy in the middle, so she could handle the controls. All there was to it was a lever—you pushed it forward to go and back to slow down or stop—and a steering wheel that went up and down as well as around. I'd seen more complicated technology on the rides at Coney Island.

"While we were getting strapped into the chairs, I heard Masterson over my headset. He said, 'Something a little special for our travelers. I will reveal it now. The red button on the console in front of Tracy fires a laser beam. What space mission would be complete without one?' His wacky laughter crackled, echoing through my helmet, and I thought, behind him, I heard the rest of the Rocket Club applauding.

"The last thing the technicians said to us before they left the ship was that for liftoff we didn't have to do anything. 'We'll light the fuse for you,' one of them said and the others laughed.

"Parson yelled, 'What's that supposed to mean?'

"'It's a joke,' said Tracy, and then we heard the door to the outside clang shut. Instant nausea and trembling. At that moment, I knew the whole thing was a bad idea. Four old codgers with their musty heads full of pulps send a rocket into outer space. I mean, what would they call this in your class? Reality meets fantasy? Something like that? It looked to me like the former was gonna blow the latter to smithereens."

"We'd call that the unwilling suspension of disbelief," said Breelyn.

"This really happened?" I asked.

"I'm telling you," said Werber. "How could I make this shit up? When you get home, look up Project Icarus on the Internet. There's only two sites that have hearsay info about it. They're only passing off rumors, but rumors of something that really happened." Werber pushed his empty glass forward.

Lifting it, Breelyn said, "This'll be your third and your last. If I send you stumbling out of here and something happens to you, they'll shut us down."

"Here's a deal," he said. "Pour me that third, and I'll nurse it through the end of the story. If by then I'm not slurring my words too badly and you've enjoyed the story, you will pour me one more. What do you say?"

Breelyn poured his drink and then slid it toward him. "We'll see," she said.

"Prepare for liftoff," he said, and we all took a drink. "When they hit the switch, it felt like the whole damn thing was blowing up. I saw a flash of orange outside the window and then smoke. There was a thunderous rumbling, an infernal shaking, and I passed out. When I opened my eyes, all was silent. I looked over, and Tracy and Parson were gone from their chairs. Outside the window I saw stars. I unhooked my safety straps and was weightless. I drifted out of the command cabin and back down the center passage of the ship, floating like a ghost. Every now and then, I'd bump into the wall, and I learned early on to be careful how hard I pushed off.

"I found my crewmates both back at the crapper, minus their fishbowl helmets unscrewed, taking turns puking into the urination contraption. Upon seeing them, the nausea hit me. In between her bouts, Tracy told us it was SAS, Space Adjustment Syndrome, and it would take a while to get over. I screwed off my helmet and took my turn. We stayed there for an hour straight, and then made our way to our rooms. I was just about able to get out of the space suit and put on my jumpsuit before I had to go back for another round. It was a horrible feeling, like the vertigo I once had from an ear infection, like I'd been on a gin bender for two weeks.

"It's hard to breathe in space. Your nose gets totally plugged. So not being able to draw a decent breath and feeling sick as a dog with the claustrophobia ever on the verge of pouncing, I was miserable. I floated into my room and sat at the writing desk. There was a pad of paper affixed to the top, and the yellow pages flapped upward. My writing implement was a pencil. It sat in a special holder that kept it continuously, automatically, sharpened. I looked up and there was Earth, like a peeping Tom in my porthole window. I nearly gasped at the sight of it, and the first notes of the theremin drifted through the rocket—creepy, liquid sound. I wrote nothing.

"Sometime later, I'm not sure how long, Tracy floated by and said she was going to get dinner. I left my chair and followed her. Parson was right behind me. At the storage area, we divvied up the packets. I had Aunt Jo's Chicken and Dumplings—baby shit with streaks of carrot. Parson had Paradise Split-Pea Soup with Bacon and Potato—a pale green mess he pronounced to be 'Pond Scum.' Tracy chose the Coconut Shrimp, and I begged her not to eat it. 'My, it's tasty,' she said. Parson shook his head.

"More trips to the crapper followed, to be sure. We got a radio message from mission control, and all gathered in the command cabin to listen in. It was, as far as I could tell, a bunch of static and mumbling. 'All is well,' said Tracy. That was it, then they signed off and it was the silence of outer space. Every second, I was thinking, was a second too much. I felt buried alive out there, cramped and wheezing for every breath. The *Icarus* was a tomb as far as I was concerned. I went to my cabin and lay down with the book I'd brought—*The Butterfly Kid*. It had been up for a Hugo Award.

"When I strapped myself in and opened the book, something floated out of it. I grabbed it as it drifted overhead: a green square of paper. Then I remembered it was the fifty I'd gotten from Max. I'd put it in the book as a good-luck token for the trip. I unfolded it and looked at the face. For the first time I noticed that there was writing on it. In a very light ballpoint pen, someone had drawn a word balloon coming out of Grant's mouth. It contained two words in Max's handwriting: *Suicide Mission*.

"Tracy found me floating in my cabin, hyperventilating. She pulled me down to her cabin and strapped me to the wall. Across from me she secured one of her paintings, a bare black tree on a jade green background, on an easel that was bolted to the cabin. She told me to stare at the painting and breathe steadily. 'Concentrate on the life of the tree,' she said. I did. I was in shock and barely moved, but my mind was frantic with thoughts of suffocation and a sense that the walls were about to close in.

"The inanity of the painting actually brought me back around. Its simplicity was infectious. I eventually calmed down, and when my breathing had returned to normal, Tracy said, 'If you get scared, just think of the painting.' I swore to her that I wasn't scared, and she just gave me a flat midwestern chuckle. All this time, the theremin was playing, and now that I was free of my own fear, I began to notice how annoying the instrument was, like a relentless robot cat in heat with digestion problems.

"I wondered what Max was up to writing on that fifty. Besides my machinations about that and the yips it gave me, the second biggest problem over the next day and a half was that we were all space slobs. Man, by the second day there was all kinds of crap floating around the rocket ship. Tracy had this glass box they'd designed for her with gloves you put your hands in to work inside the enclosure. Inside, she had paint and a canvas. The thing was a disaster. The paint globbed up and went weightless, and the box was so full of bubbles of color you couldn't see the painting. The contraption started to leak. Every now and then, a small globe of cadmium yellow or scarlet drifted past my head like a miniature errant world.

"Other things in the slurry of atmosphere were a pair of Parson's jockey shorts, my copy of *The Butterfly Kid*, empty food packets, droplets of water, scraps of paper. At lunch on the second day, while I tongued a packet of Ham and Swiss on Rye, Tracy announced that we needed to police the area. 'You don't want to breathe this stuff in while you're sleeping,' she said. Parson said, 'You folks do it, I'm on the verge of a breakthrough.' We decided to let the cleanup wait till after dinner.

"Parson's breakthrough came a little later in the day. I didn't even notice it at first, as I'd finally gotten into writing something despite how awkward and annoying the process was in outer space. My imagination was hot on the trail of a tale about Pirsute's young female sidekick, Molly Molly. She was down an alley, her back to the wall, and the Surrogate of Fruition had her cornered with his claws and atom-strangling ray gun, when all of a sudden this noise drew me away. It was Parson and that infernal device. He was playing one single note over and over again. I mean nonstop.

"My head was being drilled out by that note. Eventually I unstrapped myself from my desk chair and went back to have a word with him. On the work side of his cabin, his feet in the metal shoes bolted down that grounded him to the ship, he was leaning over his electronic box and pinching the air with two fingers at the exact same place in the tone field. He had on an expression like he was passing ground glass, and droplets of sweat were being born and rolling upward off his brow. I called to him but he ignored me. I gave him a minute and then got right into his face and yelled his name. He suddenly looked up, angry, and said, 'What do you want, Werber?'

"'How about a different note?' I said.

"'Get out,' he told me. 'I've hit on the universal note of the universe. It's all there.'

"'Too bad you're not,' I said.

"He pinched the air again twice, achieving the exact same tone. I shoved him back out of his metal shoes, and he flew into the cabin wall, ricocheting upward. While he floated above me, I pulled the plug on the theremin. 'From now on hum it to yourself,' I said. He reached the opposite wall and then pushed off fast at me. We space-wrestled around his cabin, across the ceiling and walls, and wound up out in the core of the ship. On Earth I was a load and a half, but in space I was Bruce Lee. I did a flip, bounced off the wall, and kicked him right in his cold equations. He grimaced, looking back at me, as he flew down the central passage all the way to the control cabin.

"I pushed off to go after him, and he pushed off to come back at me. We met and tussled outside Tracy's painting area. She came out red in the face, with her arms folded, and sent us to our cabins, telling Parson to either move on with the music or turn it off, and asking me, 'How old are you?' Later, after dinner, I got a chance to apologize to her. We sat together in the control cabin staring out at the universe.

"'My ex-husband was always fighting,' she said. 'And drinking.'

"'What'd he think of your painting?' I asked.

"'He hated me going to the night classes.'

"'Why do you always paint black trees?'

"'It represents the darkness in my soul growing toward the sunlight,' she said and stared at me.

"'They're nice trees,' I told her.

"She smiled, and then things happened fast, in this order—Parson stuck his head into the control cabin and said, 'The toilet is broken.' When the last word was out of his mouth, there was a great shuddering throughout the ship, and a siren, like noon at a firehouse, sounded in the cabin. Parson and I looked to Tracy. 'We've been hit by something,' she said. 'Get into your space suits.' I grappled my way back to my cabin and suited up. 'Put your helmets on,' called Tracy as I was screwing mine into place. In less than four minutes we were back in the control cabin, and it immediately became clear what the danger was. Fist-size rocks, like a school of fish, were all around us. Very faintly, I could hear them banging off the outside of the *Icarus*.

"Parson pushed his way forward and brought his gloved hand down on the laser-beam button. We saw the red beacon flash outward. It took a few seconds to realize that the space rocks weren't even so much as sizzling. Mr. Universal Note kept banging on the button, though. 'Don't you get it?' I said to him. 'It's just a fucking toy.' Tracy tapped my shoulder, and I heard her voice in my helmet say, 'Push that blue one over your head.' I looked up and saw a button above me I'd never noticed before. I hit it. 'What is it?' I asked.

"'Abort mission,' she said.

"Instantly, I felt the thrust of the boosters and had to hold on. I remembered them telling us that once that button was pushed, the rocket ship would immediately return to Earth. Our sudden speed caused the rocks to hit us with more force, and the ship jerked from side to side and up and down. From what I could see ahead, we seemed to be veering out of the rubble field, and as we did the pummeling eased. From out of that growing calm, a loud screeching noise was heard, and the ride got instantly rougher. 'We've lost a fin,' said Tracy. She hailed mission control and said, 'Mayday, *Icarus* is falling. I repeat, *Icarus* is falling. We are aborting mission, leaving orbit.'

"I heard the transmissions in my helmet. A crackling response from the ground crew was half-garbled. All I could make out were the words *escape pods*.

"'There are escape pods on board?' I asked.

"Tracy never got a chance to respond, because a small, clear stone, a space diamond, shot through the window glass like a bullet, shattered her fishbowl, and hit her right between the eyes.

"'Oh, fuck,' I heard Parson say.

I immediately felt the current of the atmosphere whistling out of the ship. Tracy's lifeless body was sucked against the windshield, which was slowly cracking, a pattern of fractures in the glass growing out from her like those trees branching in her paintings.

"'Where are the escape pods?' I asked Parson as we clawed our way back along the passage. I couldn't even recall them mentioning escape pods in our training. Ahead of us, his last movement bobbed like a flying mud slide in midair. 'What the hell?' I said as it hit us.

"'I told you the toilet was broken,' he said. His helmet needed a windshield wiper.

"'The escape pod—where and how?' I managed to get out. Fighting a vacuum is hard work. My trips to the top floor of the casino kept me moving. I was sweating, and the water was pooling in my suit. There was something bad about that, but I couldn't recall what it was.

"Parson was losing ground; his spindly theremin-playing arms weren't enough for the job. 'It's the bed,' he yelled.

"'How do I activate it?'

"'Save me,' he yelled and grabbed my foot with both his hands.

"'Activation?'

"'You gotta take your helmet off and say, "Take me home."' There was a pause. 'It's voice activated.'

"I tugged him a couple of feet, and just when I made it to the cabin, I looked back and the control cabin window gave out completely. Amid a cluster of glass shards, Tracy flew off into outer space. I got a burst of adrenalin from fear of death and kicked hard with my leg to shake off Parson.

"'You bitch,' he yelled back at me as he flew away.

"I put everything into it and was able to get into the bed, strap myself down, and take my helmet off. The atmosphere was leaving the ship at hurricane force. I screamed, 'Take me home.' Nothing happened. 'Take me home,' I repeated, and this time my desperation increased my volume and it managed to overcome the rush of air. From the wall side of the bed, a covering arced over my body and encapsulated me. My helmet was gone and I couldn't breathe, but soon enough an emergency source of air came on. It was pitch black inside, and the fit was tight. The ship was shaking and seemed to be tumbling end over end. The pod vibrated like a washer on the spin cycle. And of course my claustrophobia was stuffed in there with me.

"The last thing I heard before passing out was Parson's voice from some speaker in the pod. He said, 'I *am* the universal note,' and his crazy cosmic bellowing followed me into unconsciousness. The next thing I knew, there was a terrible jarring, a shuddering thump, and the cover of the pod drew back. I saw before me a field of pure white. I was dizzy, fading in and out. I thought for sure I'd made it to heaven. I went out cold, and when I came back again the white field drew back and there were two huge men in dark suits and dark glasses. Behind them stood Masterson wearing a sour expression and shaking his head.

"They helped me out of the pod. We weren't in heaven, but rather the white field I beheld was a parachute. We were in the Nevada desert. We walked over a small rise to a black limousine parked there in the middle of nowhere. The two big guys got in front, and Masterson and I got in the back. Thank God the car was air-conditioned. 'What happened?' I said, resting my head back. The driver started the car, and we were off. There was silence until we reached a paved road.

"'What happened, sir, was that you have severely deflated my sense of wonder.'

"I laughed, thinking he was joking, but when I looked at him, his face was red with anger. 'Sorry' was all I said, because already I was thinking about the fifty thousand. When we came to a midsize desert town, a place called Numa, the car pulled over at a street corner and parked. Masterson handed me a bank roll. He said, 'Here's two thousand dollars. Buy some clothes, get a place to stay, and lay low for a while.'

"'Out here?' I said. 'You're dropping me off?'

"'That's right, and remember, do not mention the *Icarus* to anyone. If you do there will be regrettable consequences.'

"'But my fifty grand,' I said.

"'We have to wait till things cool down. Check your bank account in three months. It will be there. Now get out.'

"'I just came back from space,' I said. The guy in the driver's seat opened his door, and I knew he was coming to drag me out. 'OK, OK,' I said. I got out of the car. It was hot as hell on the street, and I wasn't used to standing under the influence of gravity. I fell to my knees on the curb. 'Your rocket ship was crummy,' I yelled as the door closed. The black car drove off."

"They just left you there?" I asked.

Werber nodded and stared off at the liquor shelf as if he couldn't believe it either. He finished his third gin and pushed the glass forward. "Well?" he said.

"Is that all of it?" asked Breelyn.

"Well, there's the fact that I never got paid."

"Get out," she said.

"Never got another dime out of the Rocket Club. I went back east and lived for a while on the remainder of the initial five thousand in my account and what was left of the roll Masterson had handed me. A few months after the bank deadline came and went with no payment, I decided to write a fictional account of the mission. I figured if it was fiction, who would care? I really got into it. My best work ever. I sold it to ACE for one half of a double. Remember when ACE did the doubles?"

"I used to get them off a spinning rack at the local newspaper shop when I was a kid," I said.

"This was two books in one?" asked Breelyn.

"Yeah," I said. "A cover and story on one side, and then you flipped it over and there was another cover on the back and another story that read to the middle of the book. You can definitely still find them."

"I made, for me, good-enough money on that book. The production went along. They sent me a finished copy of it a few weeks before it was to hit the bookstores, and then, all of a sudden, I get a call from the editor, and he tells me, 'We're pulling the book.' I was heartbroken. When I asked why, I was told, 'We had a visit here from some of your friends in the federal government. They told us the book never existed. They confiscated all copies before they shipped to the stores.' A few days later, I was rolled on the street not far from my apartment. Four guys with dark suits and glasses roughed me up, bloodied my nose, and warned me that if I didn't keep the *Icarus* thing quiet, I would permanently disappear."

"I don't know," said Breelyn. "I've got a hard time believing."

"I'll say," I added.

Werber reached into his jacket pocket, pulled out a paperback book, and tossed it on the bar. "All aboard," he said. And there it was, staring up at us. A picture of a rocket ship streaking through space, and in the background, a visage of Satan, laughing. The title was in red saber-style across the top and in the corner was the ACE logo. The ship was the same as the one Werber described in his story.

Breelyn poured the old man a fourth straight gin.

"Who's on the other side?" I asked and turned the book over. On that side there was an illustration of a guy, at night, crouched down under a tree, holding a futuristic-looking rifle while overhead in the starry sky a spacecraft in a shape sort of like a telephone searched the ground in the distance with a beacon of green light. The title on this side was in block letters in the same sea green as that of the searchlight. It read *Six Against the Mind Barons by Tom Purdom*. Breelyn picked the book up and turned it over to see Werber's side again.

"Purdom lives in Philly," I said. "He's probably here at the convention."

"That guy's got a story in *Asimov's* this month," said Breelyn. She looked at the ceiling. "I think it's called 'Civilians.'"

"You can't mention this book to him. He'll say nothing about it. In 1983, I ran into him at the Worldcon in Baltimore. He told me how important that confiscated work was to him. He rewrote it, taking all the space opera elements out and setting it on Earth in the twenty-first century. I think ACE was gonna publish it as a stand-alone, but Purdom was so set back by them initially pulling the title that he missed the deadline by three months and that was it. Having *Mind Barons* confiscated was a kick in the nuts. I didn't have it in me to tell him the truth, about the *Icarus* and everything."

Breelyn put the book back on the bar and slid it toward me. I picked it up, took one more look at each side, and handed it toward Werber. I was amazed to see that the fourth gin was already gone. He waved his hands in front of him and said, "You keep it. I don't want it anymore."

"Sure you do," I said.

He slurred his words. "Seriously, I'm through with it," he said and belched. He smiled and put his head down on the bar. An instant later, he was out cold. Breelyn called the cab company. While we waited, she swept up and wiped down the bar. I sat there and finished my second forty. The taxi finally arrived and I helped her cart Werber to it. He'd roused a little by then and almost walked on his own. He shook our hands, and we poured him into the backseat of the cab. Breelyn told me that her father didn't want her working in the bar by herself at night. The sun was starting to go down, and it's not like there was a mob of customers, so she decided to close up. She went inside and turned the lights out. After closing the door behind her, she pulled the metal curtain across the front of the bar and padlocked it.

She walked along with me back toward the convention.

Jeffrey Ford

"That's one buggin' white man," she said. "Like what's a *space diamond?*"

"Yeah, he's a hundred percent sense of wonder, but what about the book?" I said.

"That is weird."

We walked a block in silence, and at the next corner she had to turn left. I held *Rocket Ship to Hell* out to her and said, "Do you want it?"

She shook her head. "I've got other destinations in mind."

"Fair enough," I said. Then I told her, "I'll look for your name in the magazines."

"I'll look for yours," she said. She flashed me a Spock and was off down the street.

Before heading back to Jersey the next day, I went to the dealer's room at the convention. The bookseller Joe Berlant had a long table stocked three rows deep with old paperbacks. When no one was looking, I took the book out of my back pocket, shoved it in between two others, and walked away. Now, a dozen years later, and well into the new century, I sit by the window and dream of that book when evening comes on.

*Story Note: A tip of the hat to my friend Tom Purdom, who let me use his good name in this story. Tom's been writing and publishing science fiction since 1957. Back in the '60s, he actually did have three short novels appear as ACE doubles. His recent work has appeared in *Asimov's Magazine* and Gardner Dozois' *Year's Best Science Fiction,* and an excellent career retrospective story collection, *Lovers & Fighters, Starships & Dragons,* has recently been published.

The Fairy Enterprise

Once upon a time, prior to the mastication of mill gears, the clang and hellfire of factories, before smog and black snow, fairies grew up naturally from out of the earth, out of the bodies of the dead, and found life again in one of the four elements. They gamboled invisibly but oft enough appeared as lovely women or tiny men or a demon come to lead you astray.

Their boons and curses were a thread of magic in our lives. It was just the old world's way of showing us its dreams. But fairies can't survive on soot and fetid water. Cold iron is murder to them. Manufacture drove them away, to the desolate places, where, eventually, the miasma of commerce found them and cast its deadly spell.

From the street to the palace, the fall of the fairy realm was roundly lamented, all the while industry spread like the cholera. Where others saw an unavoidable tragedy, though, and looked away, Mr. Hollis Lackland Benett, a man of a peculiar nature and vast capital, saw opportunity. It came to him on a carriage ride one mid-December night. The wind was frigid and the driving black snow gave the streets a grimly festive appearance.

When leaving the industrialists' soiree at Thrashner's mansion, Benett gave orders to his shivering driver, Jib, who held the carriage door. "Take the long way home, old man, I need a rest." It was said of Benett that his mind was steady as the movement of a watch but one whose gears were greased to speed ahead of the thoughts of others. He found it difficult to sleep at night. Only while the wheels of the carriage turned, pulling him ever forward, was he content to lay aside his ambition for a few hours. Sleep for Benett was utter darkness; he never dreamed.

Wrapped in a bearskin throw, he leaned into the corner of the carriage and closed his eyes. For a few moments he was aware of the sounds of the wheels on cobblestones, Jib's chattering teeth, the murmur of the wind, the hard snow pelting the window he leaned upon . . . and then he wasn't. Sometime later, he woke suddenly and sat forward. Rubbing his eyes, he ducked his head to look out the window and immediately realized they were passing Milner's Bakery. Then he noticed, only for a flashing instant, a tiny white figure of a man, no bigger than a finger, ice-skating horizontally across the place's window pane, leaving a gleaming streak in his wake.

Before Benett could register his amazement, the scene was out of sight, the carriage moving on. He banged three times on the ceiling with his walking stick, a signal to Jib to now head directly home. His mind was sprinting forward toward the assumption that the strange sight was merely an optical illusion caused by the snow blowing through the light of the street lamp until somewhere in its course it tripped and fell into a memory.

He was in his childhood bed, the counterpane pulled up to his chin. The elm outside the open window rustled and a soft breeze blew in to gutter the candle flame. His mother rested back in the rocker, and like every night, when she returned late from the mill, she told him stories. If he woke early enough before dawn, he might find her gaunt figure, like a ghost in the moonlight, asleep in the chair. The gleaming creature he'd seen on the baker's window was like something from one of her tales.

The memory of his mother faded into a memory from the gathering earlier that evening, at Thrashner's. Binsel, the butler, freshened every one's brandy, and the conversation turned to predictions of the next development in the bounding evolution of industry. Cottard spoke of electricity and the experiments of Edison. Dodin resurrected the specter of Malthus before suggesting that a factory-like approach to thinning the herds of the poor might catch on with the moneyed set. The economic theories of Mills and Carey made the rounds until Thrashner laughed aloud. "Bollocks to all that rubbish," he said. "It's simple. Ask yourselves, 'What is it people want?' People with money, that is."

The vision of the fairy, the two odd memories, seeped and mingled together behind Benett's eyes. Perspiration on his mustache, a prickling of his scalp, were definite signs forecasting a brainstorm. His mind sped to meet it. When the carriage finally came to a halt outside Whitethorn Hall, he looked up to see the sun shining. Jib had driven in circles all night through the storm. Upon disembarking the carriage, Benett discovered his man frozen solid, icicles hanging from the eyes and nostrils, the ends of the hair. It was the horses who had eventually brought them home. He petted their snouts, and, taking a last look at Jib, whispered, "A pity, old boy," and then went in to warm up.

After a nap, a bit of lamb stew and a bath, Benett, wearing his yellow silk lounging attire, settled down at the desk in his study with a pot of tea by his side. He lifted his pen and began to jot down the plans for his new factory. He worked all afternoon and was only disturbed once, by his butler, Jennings, who approached to inform him that Jib could not be buried; the ground was frozen.

"Put him in one of those old whisky barrels, sprinkle some kerosene on him, and torch the blighter," said Benett impatiently. In a second, he was back to work. Jennings cleared his throat and timidly asked, "And what, sir, should we tell his family?" "Good question," said the master of the house, and looked out the window. "Send them three farthings and my condolences." The pen went back to the paper.

He was finished work for the day, sitting by the window, with a glass of port and his pipe. Through the twilight, he could make out Jennings and son, rolling a barrel into the courtyard. This was set upright on the snow-covered walk. Next they passed his view carrying the pale Jib, stiffened in the posture of the driver's box. Benett heard a terrible crack as they shoved the corpse into the barrel. Then Jennings' boy had the kerosene and Jennings had the matches.

A moment later, Benett was outside, in only his slippers and billowing yellow silk, waving his walking stick and directing the immolation of Jib. "Don't be cheap with the kerosene, boy," said the master. For the lad's trouble, he slapped him across the backs of his thighs with the stick. "Three matches at once, you dolt," he yelled at Jennings. The butler threw the lit matches, and there was a sudden puff of flame. A few minutes later, Jib began smoldering. "Good Lord, he smells like the queen's own turd," cried Benett. "Quite," said Jennings, whose son nodded.

More cans of kerosene were called for, and when Jennings threw the matches this time, there was a great whoosh of flame reaching eight feet into the night. It quickly settled down to merely a steady fire, and the three of them moved closer to it for warmth. They each stared into the burning barrel at where Jib's left leg jutted up. The ankle turned black; the old shoe melted. Suddenly there was a great pop, and Benett jumped back a step.

"That'd be the head popping. Right, Pa?" said the boy.

"For certain," said Jennings. "Now watch for the libban." He and his son stood leaning forward in anticipation.

"What are we looking for?" asked Benett.

"A certain spark that always flies up when the skull cracks in the heat. The libban. The other sparks die out just above you, but this one stays lit, no matter how high or far it goes. As long as you can see it, it burns. From the soft core of the nut," said Jennings and knocked twice on his forehead with his knuckle.

"There now!" said the boy and pointed up.

Benett cocked back his head and caught sight of the so-called libban. He watched for a long while as the winter wind carried it high away over the dark silhouette of treetops.

"Like a soul?" he asked, still staring into the distance.

"Like a seed," said Jennings.

"From a will-o'-the-wisp," said Jennings' son as if reciting.

The master wondered just how many bodies the boy had seen burned.

For the remainder of the winter and well into spring, Benett applied himself as a student of the vanished fairy realm. He spent a small fortune on books, most of them ancient, their yellowed pages crumbling to dust once read and turned. The gears of his mind became tarred with fairy lore, and the mechanism slowed to a crawl. He was struck by long bouts of lassitude and imagination. These creatures that were the object of his scrutiny were elusive, and understanding came to him only in glimpses. He persevered, though, through long hours, pots of tea and pipes, and eventually reached a point where his natural disdain for the fanciful turned to admiration and respect.

The natural settings of the tales and histories he consumed made him long for a journey to the forest. So, in the first fair days of May, he set out in the carriage, his new driver the Jennings boy, and headed south, away from the city, toward a small village, Ilferin, on the edge of the wild. Enormous stones stood in a meadow nearby. A steady stream of fairy sightings had poured forth from the place, down through the ages.

They found lodging at the Inn of the Green Dog, Benett renting out the entire second floor of rooms, young Jennings getting a tattered blanket and a half bushel of hay in a corner of the stable. Mr. Yallerin, the owner of the establishment, was delighted to have Mr. Benett and Mr. Benett's money staying beneath his roof. Over a welcoming glass of spirits on the front porch, the industrialist asked his host where he might find someone who could speak to the local fairy lore. Yallerin rubbed his bald pate, drew on his pipe, and said, "We call her the crone, just for a laugh, of course. They say she's over a hundred. Lives out past the meadow in an ancient stone cottage next to the stream."

"And you," said Benett, "have you seen the good folk in your years here?"

"As a scamp, I saw them once," said the innkeeper. "My grandpa was laid out for burial in the sitting room of our house. His box, lid off, rested atop two sawhorses next to the hearth. I woke in the middle of the night from a frightener in which the old man called to me. I crawled out of bed, lit a candle, and crept out to where he lay. I didn't want to, but I did hold the candle high to see one last time his death expression. Shock, sir, shock and zero to the bone when I discovered a half-dozen tiny violet men with pointed heads perched upon his forehead, cheekbones, and chin, using long-handled spades to dig out his eyeballs. Only for a moment before the candle blew out, and then I fell through the dark."

"His eyes?" asked Benett and took a small notebook and pencil from his jacket.

"The next morning, I found myself in bed. When I went out into the sitting room, the lid was on the box and my ma and pa were crying."

"Did they explain?"

"I knew not to speak of it."

"What did it mean, their taking his eyes?"

"Mr. Benett, even a brilliant gentleman such as yourself can never know the ways of the fairies. They seem to us crazy as a mad woman's poo."

The industrialist jotted down *mad woman's poo*.

The next morning, after a hardy breakfast of bacon and potatoes for the master and a dry biscuit and a hunk of cold fat for his driver, the two set out on foot. The sun was warm, the sky was blue, and there was a breeze coming out of the forest, carrying the scent of blooming life. Benett had had a suit of clothes made for this very occasion—a jacket and trousers, a shirt and vest—all the same color of grass. He swung his walking stick and whistled. The boy ran to keep up with him.

They set out across the meadow. At the very center of the rings of silent sentinels, there stood a thin, ten-foot-high pointed stone, like a crooked finger, accusing the sky. Here Benett stopped and put his arms around the crude obelisk. Young Jennings watched as his employer touched his lips against the hard rock. When he was finished, he wiped his mouth and told the boy to do as he had done. The lad stood wide-eyed, unable to move. Benett employed the stick. "Kiss it good," he commanded. "Hug it tight."

When the boy completed his duty, his master inquired, "So, did you feel the enchantment?"

"I don't know, sir," said Jennings.

"You're a chip off your father's block head," said Benett.

"I should hope so, sir."

Across the meadow, at the tree line, they found a path that led in amid the Wych Elms and Ashes. Sunlight dappled the forest floor as the leaves rustled. Benett breathed deeply, taking in the heady green fizz of nature. Before long, they came upon a brook, and the sound of the water moving swiftly over the rocks reminded him of his mother's voice, when, with eyes closed, she'd continue to murmur her tales from the other side of sleep.

At the brook they turned west as instructed by Mr. Yallerin of the Green Dog, and before long they came upon a small clearing inhabited by a trio of deer. "Be gone, demons," said Benett and swung his stick over his head. The gentle creatures fled, clearing a pathway to the stone cottage. Smoke issued from the chimney, a grumbled song from the open window. Just before reaching the steps to the door of the place, the industrialist put his hand on the boy's shoulder and stayed him. "Take this," he said, a silver derringer in his hand. "It's loaded. Remain outside here and keep an eye. If I call for help, you must rush to my assistance. Should the necessity arise, you'll be ready to shoot?"

The boy took the gun and put it in his coat pocket. "Yes," he said.

"There's hope for you, Jennings," said Benett and took the steps. He knocked. There was movement inside, and then the door slowly opened. A squat old woman with white hair and large forearms appeared. Her simple gray dress was much mended, her kindly smile was a grimace. "You're the gentleman about the fairies," she said in a gruff voice. "I had word you were coming."

The hair on her pointed chin was disconcertingly long, and it took Benett a moment to focus. "From whom?" he asked.

She turned slowly and retreated back into the place. He followed her inside and shut the door behind him. There was a large room at the front of the cottage, and they settled down at a table by its window. A steaming pot of tea, cups and saucers, awaited them. She lit her clay pipe and moved it to the side of her mouth. "Name, sir," she said, squinting at him.

"Hollis Lackland Benett," he said.

"Tima Loorie." She nodded.

"I heard it said in the village that you're over a hundred."

"Are you a gullible man, Mr. Benett?"

"Not usually."

"Then there's no reason to begin now. Give me your hand," she demanded.

He reluctantly offered it to her.

She squeezed his wrist with a powerful grip and turned it so his palm was facing her. "I see you're a self-made man," she said, "Come from the salt and now a king of factories. Wealthy. When you sleep, unbeknown to yourself, you call out in the dark. Always the same word."

"Progress?" he asked and smiled.

She shook her head. "You're not to know."

"All right then," said Benett. "Tell me something else. I want you to tell me where fairies come from."

"They come from whereever they are," she said.

"No, what is the process by which they're created? Do you understand?"

"I might."

"I intend to manufacture fairies. I want to make the household fairies, the ones that help with chores and play mischievous fun on their adopted families. There's a need for them in the city. Playthings for the wealthy, helpmates for the poor."

"A fairy's a living thing," she said. "These aren't brass hinges we're discussing."

"I've done my research. I know they won't thrive in an environment of iron and smoke. My plan is for an organic process, beginning with the libban."

Tima Loorie laughed loud, flashing her one tooth. "You're barmy, Mr. Benett," she said. "A fairy factory?"

"I'm also wealthy enough to make you wealthy as well. I've brought a substantial amount of capital with me, and it is now locked away in the safe at the Green Dog.

"How much of the filthy soft have you brought?" She poured him a cup of tea.

"Two hundred pounds, if you have the answer I'm looking for," he said and took a sip.

"Drink up and I'll take you to a fairy circle. It'll be easier to explain."

He finished his tea and they left the cottage. As they moved into the trees, the boy followed them. Tima turned to Benett and said, "The boy can't go."

"Jennings, there, is my protection."

"From a hundred-year-old woman?"

"Go back and guard the cottage," he said to the boy.

Tima was none too fast on her feet, but she inched ever deeper into the forest. It seemed that the dial of the day moved with the speed of Benett's mind, passing them. It seemed they went far but walked little. As they strode through morning and afternoon, she spoke intermittently, dispensing fairy knowledge. He jotted it all down in his notebook.

"The fairies you spoke of, household fairies, hobs, goblins, they're of the earth, a mix of dirt and the freed crux of a corpse's being. This seed sprouts into the fruiting body. Like here," she said and pointed at the ground.

Benett looked away from his notes. It was late afternoon and the forest was filling with shadow. They stood on a particularly shaded byway, beneath a giant oak. He followed Tima's direction and looked down to see a circle of strange mushrooms growing out of the forest floor. They were pale like a toad's belly, with brown spots, and their heads were large fleshy globes. He watched as Tima bent over and picked one of them. She handed it to him. "*Glasfearballas*, they're called." He took it from her.

"A fairy factory," she said.

In the dim light of the path, it appeared to him that there was something moving inside the globe of the mushroom. He brought it closer for a better look, and with a whisper, it suddenly burst open, spewing a black powder at his face. In an instant, he lost his balance and dropped to his knees, coughing. When he blinked to clear his eyes, he went blind. "Help me," he managed to choke out.

"There is no money in the safe at the Green Dog, is there?" he heard her say. "Be honest or I'll let you die."

He shook his head and began to drool uncontrollably.

"For that, you shall have your wish."

Benett managed one more strangled "Help," and a moment after there was a loud bang. His sight returned at once and he found himself sitting at the table in Tima Loorie's cottage. It was late morning. The door was open and the boy stood in the entrance holding the derringer aimed forward. A trail of smoke issued from the short barrel of the gun.

"How did I get back here?" he said to Jennings.

"You never left, sir. A few minutes went by and you called for help. I come through the door, sir, and this rabbit I shot come running at me."

"A rabbit?" said Benett. He stood and moved around from behind the table to see the boy's kill. A large gray rabbit lay on the floor with a trickle of blood coming from its blasted face. "Where's the crone?"

"She must have gone out the back," said Jennings.

"She put something in the tea, no doubt, the hag." Benett reached for his jacket pocket and retrieved his notebook. Opening it, he frantically flipped through the pages and found he'd recorded every word Tima Loorie had spoken on their journey through the dream day. He snapped shut the book. "I've got it," he said. "Well done," said the boy. By that afternoon, they were in the carriage, heading back toward the city.

After his journey to the wild, the master of Whitethorn secreted himself away for months only to emerge in late August for a business meeting with Thrashner. Benett had the collateral for the factory, but he needed Thrashner's powerful connections both political and local to make its construction move at the rapid pace he desired. The meeting took place on the gruff old industrialist's veranda, beneath the summer stars. Benett arrived promptly at seven. The night was stifling save for an occasional breeze rolling through the back gardens. "All right, Benett," said Thrashner when both men were seated, "you know I don't like a lot of dither. Cut through and let's get to the meat of it."

"I aim to construct a new type of factory, and I need you to help me grease the palm of government so I don't get tripped up by deeds and inspections. My plan would also benefit from the availability of some of your private work crews."

"Not impossible, by any means," said Thrashner. "But what are you making, and what's in it for me?"

"What I'll be making is fairies."

"Did you say fairies?"

"You asked the question at the industrialist's soiree months ago, 'What do people want?' I've determined they want fairies."

"I'm not a good man for a joke, Benett. I'd have thought you'd known that by now."

"No joke. I've studied the process. It starts with fresh corpses."

"Benett, are you having some sort of episode of hysterics? You look pale."

"Fresh corpses, not left to lie past the dawn following their moment of demise. We need the heads."

Thrashner's eyes widened. He smoothed his mustache. "Corpses! Where does one acquire corpses for manufacture?"

"Believe me sir, deals can be made with the morgues, etc. Out of a sense of morality, so that all's on the up and up, we'd only use those without close kin. The lonely dead."

"So your factory will run on the remains of the lonely dead?"

"No, we will burn their heads to release the libban, which we will gather through a vacuum sitting at the vaulted ceiling of the libban silo."

"Libban?" asked Thrashner.

"The soul or seed of the dead. A kernel of life that flies off once the head pops open in a fire."

"I believe I may have heard the term."

"Of course you have," said Benett. "The libban are gathered up at the top of the silo and then pushed through a tube into a chamber where they are blasted with the powdered dirt of the earth. This mix of spirit and dust is then spewed out across the fruiting vats of the factory, wherein will grow large, globe-headed mushrooms. When they succeed to a certain plumpness, these fungi will burst and fairies will be born."

"You've gone 'round the bend, Bennet. You're completely off your chump."

"We use the dirt because we're making hobs and goblins, brownies, household fairies that help with chores. It's not that people need fairies, Thrashner, it's that they want them."

"Even if you could make them, how do you intend to sell them?" The old man laughed at himself for not having thrown Benett out.

"When they burst forth from the mushrooms, they're invisible—the natural fairy state. Then comes my secret technique of gathering them up and capturing them individually in colored glass balls. These are sold to the public, and they are instructed to take them home and smash them on the kitchen floor, which will release the hobs into their homes."

Thrashner leaned across the table that separated them. He facetiously whispered, "What is the secret?"

Benett also leaned in. "The secret is, there are no fairies."

"You mean you're selling humbug?" Thrashner smiled from ear to ear.

Benett nodded. "That's why the process must be both gruesome and a tad mysterious. The better the show on that end, the more empty glass balls we can sell to the hopeful."

"A moment ago, I was certain you were mad, but now I'm certain you're a genius."

"We'll need a good artist. The advertisements will be important. Once we fill every house with a hob, we'll start turning out sylphs. I've envisioned a demon that I'm sure will catch on with those who consider themselves naughty. The skeptics, of course, will scowl, but I predict it will be all the rage.

"The factory will cost money, as will the fruiting vats and the mushrooms. I thought we'd make the latter out of rubber and paint them. Have two or three automated ones that burst and spew black powder on cue. We'll give tours of the factory once a week and charge a few coins. A hoax the customer will long to have perpetrated upon him."

"The appearance of industry and yet the manufacture of nothing," said Thrashner, closing his eyes in delight.

By the time Benett left Thrashner's veranda, he had the old man's agreement of political and labor support but also a promise of cash for a share in the enterprise. After a year of work, Benett's scheme was beginning to take shape. He felt so good, he gave an order to the Jennings lad to troll the city streets for a pretty, young dolly mop for hire. "Be courteous, boy," he reminded the driver. "We must respect how these women have turned themselves into factories."

Down by the waterfront, the carriage slowed to a crawl. Benett slid back the glass of the window and leaned out. Up ahead a few feet, standing to the side of the cobblestone lane beneath a dim gas lamp, was a young woman with her blond hair in barley curls. He quickly checked the condition of her clothing, which let him know how long she'd been on the street plying her trade. When he decided he could live with their degree of shabbiness, he said, "Young miss, would you like a ride?"

"Where will you take me?" she asked.

He noticed she was wearing boots without socks and this put him off, but her face was lovely. "I'm inviting you to my mansion to drink champagne and to celebrate."

"A party?" she said.

"Of course," said Benett and did his best to smile. "Come now."

She nodded and stepped toward the carriage. Jennings held the horses still for her to get in. As the girl was getting situated on the bench next to Benett, he banged on the ceiling of the cab five times to indicate to the driver to go as fast as possible. "What's your name, miss?" he said. The horses lurched forward and threw the passengers together. Gas lamps seemed to fly past the windows, and the racket of the wheels on the stones was hellish.

"My name is Tima Loorie," she said.

"What?" said Benett, and put his hand behind his ear to hear her better.

She pulled him to her and brought her face close to his as if expecting a kiss. Benett acquiesced and opened his mouth in preparation. He waited for her lips to touch his, and then she spit directly into his mouth. He was paralyzed with astonishment, and before he could utter a groan, he felt the thing slide down his throat with the heft of an oyster, tasting of bile and rot.

"Tima Loorie," she shouted.

This time he heard her and lunged, brandishing the stick, but with one graceful move she opened the carriage door and leaped out. Benett managed to close the door and bang on the ceiling once for Jennings to stop. When the horses came to a halt, he called up to the boy, "Head slowly back the way we've come. The fool girl jumped out. We need to find her."

"Yes, sir," said the boy.

"And Jennings, have you got the derringer?"

"In my pocket and loaded."

They drove slowly back along the streets they'd galloped through, but saw no one. Eventually, Benett had to satisfy himself with the idea that the carriage was moving so fast that she'd no doubt broken her neck in the fall. He finally signaled for Jennings to head back to Whitethorn. The moment he got into his study, he downed three quick glasses of whisky in hopes it might kill the witch's scurvy spit he could feel swimming in his stomach. That night he needed no further driving in the carriage to sleep. He fell into utter darkness, fully clothed, in the chair by the window.

He woke late the next morning, unusual for him, yet still felt exhausted. Using a hand mirror, he gazed upon the dark circles surrounding his eyes, his pale complexion. His gut was in a turmoil, and every time he thought back to the spit, he grew nauseous. He went to his bedchamber and got beneath the counterpane, pulling it up to his chin. Farting and shivering, he closed his eyes and tried to sleep, but the phrase "fruiting body" repeated in his thoughts in the voice of Tima Loorie. At noon, the elder Jennings came in to deliver a message that had just been brought by Thrashner's man, Binsel.

My Good Benett,

I've been up and at work early today on the fairy enterprise. Drinks at my place this afternoon at 3:00 with Lord Smith. He'll take our money in the long run, but he'll want us to grovel a bit in his presence. We can't do anything without him on board. I've invited a few others so as not to make the scene too awkward.

Your Partner In Manufacture,

Thrashner

He needed both Jennings and Jennings to pull him out of bed and get him into his formal attire. He said little but belched profusely, and the father and son, one on each arm, led him to the carriage. In the fresh air, he felt a bit better and managed to get into his seat by himself.

"Shall I accompany you?" asked the elder Jennings.

"Don't be a fool. The boy will take me."

Only moments after pulling away from Whitethorn, Benett grew worse. Waves of nausea and difficulty breathing through his nose. He pulled out a handkerchief and blew. For a moment, it felt as if he was bleeding, and he looked into the folded handkerchief to check. What he found there wasn't the red stain he feared, but a tiny green man, struggling to be free. The creature scurried across the expanse of material and then leaped to Benett's knee. He felt the thing land and brought his fist down, but too late. It had already hopped into the shadows below. For over a quarter mile, Benett stamped his feet around the floor, hoping to crush the thing he'd convinced himself was an insect.

The affair at Thrashner's was crowded with important people who no doubt sensed palm-greasing in the offing. Benett struggled from room to room, meeting the highwaymen of the aristocracy. The most difficult thing for him was smiling. His guts were twisting like a pin wheel, and the sweat was pouring off him. Before he'd yet run into Thrashner, Bensil handed him a brandy and introduced him to Lord and Lady Smith.

Benett knew he needed to rise to the occasion, so he stretched his smile another agonizing jot and took a sip of his drink to seem debonair. "A pleasure to meet you both," he said. The brandy set fire to his insides.

"Likewise," said Lord Smith, a stately man whose eyes barely opened. "Lady Smith and I would like you to do us a courtesy, if you would. To the gathering today my dear lady has brought a new dish she has invented. She's a culinary expert, of course, you know. In the French tradition. She'd like you to have a taste and give her your unmitigated opinion."

Benett looked to Lady Smith and bowed slightly, for the first time noticing the platter she held in her arms. The aroma struck him, and he felt the saliva coursing to the corners of his mouth. He knew he dared not look, but he did. Slices of gray meat in what appeared a dishwater sauce. Breathing deeply, he managed to regain a modicum of composure.

"Orange goose," she said. Her outfit, to Benett, made her look like some kind of circus performer. The sparkle of her diamonds prevented him from seeing any more of her. She stabbed a slice of goose with a long thin silver fork and held it up to his mouth.

Lord Smith looked on, smiling. Thrashner suddenly appeared behind the lord and gave a quick hand motion and a wink to convey the message, "Eat it and like it." Benett closed his eyes and opened his mouth. He couldn't help a slight gag when it touched his tongue. Slowly he chewed it as it seemed every guest looked on. The goose was tough as gristle. It became evident during that eternity of chewing that he'd need a visit to the crapper post haste. Through clenched teeth, he announced, "Delicious," and then excused himself for a moment.

He could have thrashed Thrashner with his stick, he was so angry with him. "No wonder Lord Smith's smile had no sign of pleasure," he grumbled, scuttling down a long hallway. One thing he could say for his business partner, though, he had the state of the art in toilets. Benett locked the door, hung up his jacket, undid his trousers and settled onto the bowl. He was breathing heavily and his heart was racing. There were periods where the dizziness swirled toward a blackout and then pulled back. He leaned forward and strained to free the beast. Trickles of sweat fell from his forehead. As they tumbled through the air, they became tiny blue women, who landed in a crouch on his bare knees and then sprang away onto the floor.

He cried, and his tears became fairies that he brushed away into flight. A belch became a will-o'-the-wisp, glowing as it issued from the cave of his open mouth. He felt them crawling from his ears, down his cheeks to his shoulders. Then turmoil below, and a riotous gang of goblins clawed their way out of his quivering hindquarters with a cumulative birth shriek. He heard them laughing and swimming in the water beneath him.

Jennings was sitting on the driver's box when Benett appeared from behind a hedge. One quick glance and the boy leaped down and caught his tipping employer by the sleeve of his jacket.

"What's wrong, sir? You look horrible."

"I shat a populace."

"Yes, sir."

"Get me home, lad."

As soon as Jennings managed to get him in the carriage and start on the way, Benett felt their pointy heads poking up through the pores of his skin like a living, writhing beard. He whimpered as they bored and poured out of him from every conceivable egress. It was like his body was turning inside out, and the agony of it was mythic. He beat himself all over and clawed at his own face. Then he felt the spades dig in at the corners of his eyes, and the light failed.

Back at Whitethorn, when young Jennings opened the door of the carriage, he saw no fairies, though in the course of the ride Benett had manufactured thousands. A strong, sulfurous breeze blew out of the box, and behind it sat the master's corpse, desiccated, full of holes, the sockets empty. The boy ran to the house to get his father.

It's said that Benett's fairies spread out around the city and multiplied. They weren't the good ones that he'd intended to produce but were ones who thrived in soot and took energy from iron. They found homes in all of the myriad factories and worked their enchantment to cause accidents, sabotage machinery, create explosions, set fires, and generally gum up the works. They were responsible for more than one industrialist, of his own volition, leaping into a smokestack.

As for Benett, Jennings and his son found an old whisky barrel and rolled it into the courtyard. They didn't spare the kerosene. When the elder threw the three matches, a pillar of fire shot up into the night. Eventually the flames settled down and the skull popped in due course. Jennings retired just past midnight, but the boy sat alone by the barrel and waited for the libban until the dawn revealed a smoking heap of ashes and bones.

The Last Triangle

I was on the street with nowhere to go, broke, with a habit. It was around Halloween, cold as a motherfucker, in Fishmere, part suburb/part crumbling city that never happened. I was getting by, roaming the neighborhoods after dark, looking for unlocked cars to see what I could snatch. Sometimes I stole shit out of people's yards and pawned it or sold it on the street. One night I didn't have enough to cop, and I was in a bad way. There was nobody on the street to even beg from. It was freezing. Eventually I found this house on a corner and noticed an open garage out back. I got in there where it was warmer, laid down on the concrete, and went into withdrawal.

You can't understand what that's like unless you've done it. Remember that *Twilight Zone* where you make your own Hell? Like that. I eventually passed out or fell asleep and woke, shivering, to daylight, unable to get off the floor. Standing in the entrance to the garage was this little old woman with her arms folded, staring down through her bifocals at me. The second she saw I was awake, she turned and walked away. I felt like I'd frozen straight through to my spine during the night and couldn't get up. A splitting headache, and the nausea was pretty intense too. My first thought was to take off, but too much of me just didn't give a shit. The old woman reappeared, but now she was carrying a pistol in her left hand.

"What's wrong with you?" she said.

I told her I was sick.

"I've seen you around town," she said, "you're an addict." She didn't seem freaked out by the situation, even though I was. I managed to get up on one elbow. I shrugged and said, "True."

And then she left again, and a few minutes later came back, toting an electric space heater. She set it down next to me, stepped away, and said, "You missed it last night, but there's a cot in the back of the garage. Look," she said, "I'm going to give you some money. Go buy clothes. You can stay here, and I'll feed you. If I know you're using, though, I'll call the police. I hope you realize that if you do anything I don't like, I'll shoot you." She said it like it was a foregone conclusion, and, yeah, I could actually picture her pulling the trigger.

What could I say. I took the money and she went back into her house. My first reaction to the whole thing was I laughed. I could score. I struggled up all dizzy and bleary, smelling like the devil's own shit, and stumbled away.

I didn't cop that day, only a small bag of weed. Why? I'm not sure, but there was something about the way the old woman talked to me, her unafraid, straight-up approach. That, maybe, and I was so tired of the cycle of falling hard out of a drug dream onto the street and scrabbling like a three-legged dog for the next fix. By noon, I was pot high but still feeling shitty, downtown, and I passed this old clothing store. It was one of those places like you can't fucking believe is still in operation. The manikin in the window had on a tan leisure suit. Something about the way the sunlight hit that window display, though, made me remember the old woman's voice, and I had this feeling like I was on an errand for my mother.

I got the clothes. I went back and lived in her garage. The jitters, the chills, the scratching my scalp and forearms were bad, but, when I could finally get to sleep, that cot was as comfortable as a bed in a fairy tale. She brought food a couple times a day. She never said much to me, and the gun was always around.

The big problem was going to the bathroom. When you get off the junk, your insides really open up. I knew if I went near the house, she'd shoot me. Let's just say I marked the surrounding territory. About two weeks in, she wondered herself and asked me, "Where are you evacuating?"

At first I wasn't sure what she was saying. "Evacuating?" Eventually, I caught on and told her, "Around." She said that I could come in the house to use the downstairs bathroom. It was tough, 'cause every other second I wanted to just bop her on the head, take everything she had, and score like there was no tomorrow. I kept a tight lid on it till one day, when I was sure I was going to blow, a delivery truck pulled up to the side of the house and delivered, to the garage, a set of barbells and a bench. Later, when she brought me out some food, she nodded to the weights and said, "Use them before you jump out of your skin. I insist."

Ms. Berkley was her name. She never told me her first name, but I saw it on her mail, "Ifanel." What kind of name is that? She had iron-gray hair, pulled back tight into a bun, and strong green eyes behind the big glasses. Baggy corduroy pants and a zip-up sweater was her wardrobe. I definitely remember a yellow one with flowers around the collar. She was a busy old woman. Quick and low to the ground. Her house was beautiful inside. The floors were polished and covered with those Persian rugs. Wallpaper and stained-glass windows. But there was none of that goofy shit I remembered my grandmother going in for, suffering Christs, knitted hats on the toilet paper. Every room was in perfect order and there were books everywhere. Once she let me move in from the garage to the basement, I'd see her reading at night, sitting at her desk in what she called her "office." All the lights were out except for this one brass lamp that was right over the book that lay on her desk. She moved her lips when she read. "Good night, Ms. Berkley," I'd say to her and head for the basement door. From down the hall I'd hear her voice come like out of a dream, "Good night." She told me she'd been a history teacher at a college. You could tell she was really smart. It didn't exactly take a genius, but she saw straight through my bullshit.

One morning we were sitting at her kitchen table having coffee, and I asked her why she'd helped me out. I was feeling pretty good then. She said, "That's what you're supposed to do. Didn't anyone ever teach you that?"

"Weren't you afraid?"

"Of you?" she said. She took the pistol out of her bathrobe pocket and put it on the table between us. "There's no bullets in it," she told me. "I went with a fellow who died, and he left that behind. I wouldn't know how to load it."

Normally I would have laughed, but her expression made me think she was trying to tell me something. "I'll pay you back," I said. "I'm gonna get a job this week and start paying you back."

"No, I've got a way for you to pay me back," she said and smiled for the first time. I was 99 percent sure she wasn't going to tell me to fuck her, but, you know, it crossed my mind.

Instead, she asked me to take a walk with her downtown. By then it was winter, cold as a witch's tit. Snow was coming. We must have been a sight on the street. Ms. Berkley, marching along in her puffy ski parka and wool hat, blue with gold stars and a tassel. I don't think she was even five foot. I walked a couple of steps behind her. I'm 6-4, I hadn't shaved or had a haircut in a long while, and I was wearing this brown suit jacket that she'd found in her closet. I couldn't button it if you had a gun to my head, and my arms stuck out the sleeves almost to the elbow. She told me, "It belonged to the dead man."

Just past the library, we cut down an alley, crossed a vacant lot, snow still on the ground, and then hit a dirt road that led back to this abandoned factory. One story, white stucco, all the windows empty, glass on the ground, part of the roof caved in. She led me through a stand of trees around to the left side of the old building. From where we stood, I could see a lake through the woods. She pointed at the wall and said, "Do you see that symbol in red there?" I looked but all I saw was a couple of *fucks*.

"I don't see it," I told her.

"Pay attention," she said and took a step closer to the wall. Then I saw it. About the size of two fists. It was like a capital *E* tipped over on its three points, and sitting on its back, right in the middle, was an *o*. "Take a good look at it," she told me. "I want you to remember it."

I stared for a few seconds and told her, "OK, I got it."

"I walk to the lake almost every day," she said. "This wasn't here a couple of days ago." She looked at me like that was supposed to mean something to me. I shrugged; she scowled. As we walked home, it started to snow.

Before I could even take off the dead man's jacket, she called me into her office. She was sitting at her desk, still in her coat and hat, with a book open in front of her. I came over to the desk, and she pointed at the book. "What do you see there?" she asked. And there it was, the red, knocked over *E* with the *o* on top.

I said, "Yeah, the thing from before. What is it?"

"The Last Triangle," she said.

"Where's the triangle come in?" I asked.

"The three points of the capital *E*, stand for the three points of a triangle."

"So what?"

"Don't worry about it," she said. "Here's what I want you to do. Tomorrow, after breakfast, I want you to take a pad and a pen, and I want you to walk all around the town, everywhere you can think of, and look to see if that symbol appears on any other walls. If you find one, write down the address for it—street and number. Look for places that are abandoned, run down, burned out."

I didn't want to believe she was crazy, but . . . I said to her, "Don't you have any real work for me to do—heavy lifting, digging, painting, you know?"

She shook her head. "Just do what I ask you to do."

Ms. Berkley gave me a few bucks and sent me on my way. First things first, I went downtown, scored a couple of joints, bought a 40 of Colt. Then I did the grand tour. It was fucking freezing, of course. The sky was brown, and the dead man's jacket wasn't cutting it. I found the first of the symbols on the wall of a closed-down bar. The place had a pink plastic sign that said *Here It Is* with a silhouette of a woman with an afro sitting in a martini glass. The *E* was there in red on the plywood of a boarded front window. I had to walk a block each way to figure out the address, but I got it. After that I kept looking. I walked myself sober and then some and didn't get back to the house till nightfall.

When I told Ms. Berkeley that I'd found one, she smiled and clapped her hands together. She asked for the address, and I delivered. She set me up with spaghetti and meatballs at the kitchen table. I was tired, but seriously, I felt like a prince. She went down the hall to her office. A few minutes later, she came back with a piece of paper in her hand. As I pushed the plate away, she set the paper down in front of me and then took a seat.

"That's a map of town," she said. I looked it over. There were two dots in red pen and a straight line connecting them. "You see the dots?" she asked.

"Yeah."

"Those are two points of the Last Triangle."

"OK," I said and thought, "Here we go. . . ."

"The Last Triangle is an equilateral triangle. All the sides are equal," she said.

I failed math every year in high school, so I just nodded.

"Since we know these two points, we know that the last point is in one of two places on the map, either east or west." She reached across the table and slid the map toward her. With the red pen, she made two dots and then made two triangles sharing a line down the center. She pushed the map toward me again. "Tomorrow you have to look either here or here," she said, pointing with the tip of the pen.

The next day I found the third one, to the east, just before it got dark. A tall old house, on the edge of an abandoned industrial park. It looked like there'd been a fire. There was an old rusted Chevy up on blocks in the driveway. The *E* and *o* thing was spray painted on the trunk.

When I brought her that info, she gave me the lowdown on the triangle. "I read a lot of books about history," she said, "and I have this ability to remember things I've seen or read. If I saw a phone number once, I'd remember it correctly. It's not a photographic memory; it doesn't work automatically or with everything. Maybe five years ago I read this book on ancient magic, *The Spells of Abriel the Magus*, and I remembered the symbol from that book when I saw it on the wall of the old factory last week. I came home, found the book, and reread the part about the last triangle. It's also known as Abriel's Escape or Abriel's Prison.

"Abriel was a thirteenth century magus . . . magician. He wandered around Europe and created six powerful spells. The triangle, once marked out, denotes a protective zone in which its creator cannot be harmed. There are limitations to the size it can be, each leg no more than a mile. At the same time that zone is a sanctuary, it's a trap. The magus can't leave its boundary, ever. To cross it is certain death. For this reason, the spell was used only once, by Abriel, in Dresden, to escape a number of people he'd harmed with his dark arts who had sent their own wizards to kill him. He lived out the rest of his life there, within the last triangle, and died at one hundred years of age."

"That's a doozy."

"Pay attention," she said. "For the last triangle to be activated, the creator of the triangle must take a life at its geographical center between the time of the three symbols being marked in the world and the next full moon. Legend has it, Abriel killed the baker Ellot Haber to induce the spell."

It took me almost a minute and a half to grasp what she was saying. "You mean, someone's gonna get iced?" I said.

"Maybe."

"Come on, a kid just happened to make that symbol. Coincidence."

She shook her head. "No. Remember, a perfect equilateral triangle, each one of the symbols exactly where it should be." She laughed, and, for a second, looked a lot younger.

"I don't believe in magic," I told her. "There's no magic out there."

"You don't have to believe it," she said. "But maybe someone out there does. Someone desperate for protection, willing to believe even in magic."

"That's pretty farfetched," I said, "but if you think there's a chance, call the cops. Just leave me out of it."

"The cops," she said and shook her head. "They'd lock me up with that story."

"Glad we agree on that."

"The center of the triangle on my map," she said, "is the train station parking lot. And in five nights there'll be a full moon. No one's gotten killed at the station yet, not that I've heard of."

After breakfast she called a cab and went out, leaving me to fix the garbage disposal and wonder about the craziness. I tried to see it her way. She'd told me it was our civic duty to do something, but I wasn't buying any of it. Later that afternoon, I saw her sitting at the computer in her office. Her glasses near the end of her nose, she was reading off the internet and loading bullets into the magazine clip of the pistol. Eventually she looked up and saw me. "You can find just about anything on the internet," she said.

"What are you doing with that gun?"

"We're going out tonight."

"Not with that."

She stopped loading. "Don't tell me what to do," she said.

After dinner, around dusk, we set out for the train station. Before we left, she handed me the gun. I made sure the safety was on and stuck it in the side pocket of the brown jacket. While she was out getting the bullets, she'd bought two chairs that folded down and fit in small plastic tubes. I carried them. Ms. Berkley held a flashlight and in her ski parka had stashed a pint of blackberry brandy. The night was clear and cold, and a big waxing moon hung over town.

We turned off the main street into an alley next to the hardware store and followed it a long way before it came out on the south side of the train station. There was a rundown one-story building there in the corner of the parking lot. I ripped off the plywood planks that covered the door, and we went in. The place was empty but for some busted-up office furniture, and all the windows were shattered, letting the breeze in. We moved through the darkness, Ms. Berkley leading the way with the flashlight, to a back room with a view of the parking lot and station just beyond it. We set up the chairs and took our seats at the empty window. She killed the light.

"Tell me this is the strangest thing you've ever done," I whispered to her.

She brought out the pint of brandy, unscrewed the top, and took a tug on it. "Life's about doing what needs to get done," she said. "The sooner you figure that out, the better for everyone." She passed me the bottle.

After an hour and a half, my eyes had adjusted to the moonlight and I'd scanned every inch of that cracked, pot-holed parking lot. Two trains a half hour apart rolled into the station's elevated platform, and from what I could see, no one got on or off. Ms. Berkley was doing what needed to be done, namely, snoring. I took out a joint and lit up. I'd already polished off the brandy. I kept an eye on the old lady, ready to flick the joint out the window if I saw her eyelids flutter. The shivering breeze did a good job of clearing out the smoke.

At around three a.m., I'd just about nodded off when the sound of a train pulling into the station brought me back. I sat up and leaned toward the window. It took me a second to clear my eyes and focus. When I did, I saw the silhouette of a person descending the stairs of the raised platform. The figure passed beneath the light at the front of the station, and I could see it was a young woman, carrying a briefcase. I wasn't quite sure what the fuck I was supposed to be doing, so I tapped Ms. Berkley. She came awake with a splutter and looked a little sheepish for having corked off. I said, "There's a woman heading to her car. Should I shoot her?"

"Very funny," she said and got up to stand closer to the window.

I'd figured out which of the few cars in the parking lot belonged to the young woman. She looked like the white Honda type. Sure enough, she made a beeline for it.

"There's someone else," said Ms. Berkley. "Coming out from under the trestle."

"Where?"

"Left," she said and I saw him, a guy with a long coat and hat. He was moving fast, heading for the young woman. Ms. Berkley grabbed my arm and squeezed it. "Go," she said. I lunged up out of the chair, took two steps, and got dizzy from having sat for so long. I fumbled in my pocket for the pistol, grabbed it, and groped my way out of the building. Once I hit the air, I was fine, and I took off running for the parking lot. Even as jumped up as I was, I thought, "I'm not gonna shoot anyone," and left the gun's safety on.

The young woman saw me coming before she noticed the guy behind her. I scared her, and she ran the last few yards to her car. I watched her messing around with her keys and didn't notice the other guy was also on a flat-out run. As I passed the white Honda, the stranger met me and cracked me in the jaw like a pro. I went down hard but held on to the gun. As soon as I came to, I sat up. The guy, I couldn't get a good look at his face, drew a blade from his left sleeve. By then the woman was in the car, though, and it screeched off across the parking lot.

He turned, brandishing the long knife, and started for me. You better believe the safety came off then. That instant, I heard Ms. Berkley's voice behind me. "What's the meaning of this?" she said in a stern voice. The stranger looked up, and then turned and ran off, back into the shadows beneath the trestle.

"We've got to get out of here," she said and helped me to my feet. "If that girl's got any brains she'll call the cops." Ms. Berkley could run pretty fast. We made it back to the building, got the chairs, the empty bottle, and as many cigarette butts as I could find, and split for home. We stayed off the main street and wound our way back through the residential blocks. We didn't see a soul.

I couldn't feel how cold I was till I got back in the house. Ms. Berkley made tea. Her hands shook a little. We sat at the kitchen table in silence for a long time.

Finally, I said, "Well, you were right."

"The gun was a mistake, but if you didn't have it, you'd be dead now," she said.

"Not to muddy the waters here, but that's closer to dead than I want to get. We're gonna have to go to the police, but if we do, that'll be it for me."

"You tried to save her," said Ms. Berkley. "Very valiant, by the way."

I laughed. "Tell that to the judge when he's looking over my record."

She didn't say anything else, but left and went to her office. I fell asleep on the cot in the basement with my clothes on. It was warm down there by the furnace. I had terrible dreams of the young woman getting her throat cut but was too tired to wake from them. Eventually, I came to with a hand on my shoulder and Ms. Berkley saying, "Thomas." I sat up quickly, so sure I'd forgotten to do something. She said, "Relax," and rested her hand for a second on my chest. She sat on the edge of the cot with her hat and coat on.

"Did you sleep?" I asked.

She shook her head. "I went back to the parking lot after the sun had come up. There were no police around. Under the trestle, where the man with the knife had come from, I found these. She took a handful of cigarette butts out of her coat pocket and held them up.

"Anybody could have left them there at any time," I said. "You read too many books."

"One of them was still warm," she said.

"You mean he went back under the trestle and waited for someone after we'd chased him away?"

She nodded. "This is a serious man," she said. "Say he's not just a lunatic but an actual magician?"

"Magician," I said and snorted. "More like a creep who believes his own bullshit."

"Watch the language," she said.

"Do we go back to the parking lot tonight?" I asked.

"No, there'll be police there tonight. I'm sure that girl reported the incident. I have something for you to do. These cigarettes are a Spanish brand, Ducados. I used to know someone who smoked them. The only store that sells them in town is over by the park. Do you know Maya's News Stand?"

I nodded.

"I think he buys his cigarettes there."

"You want me to scope it? How am I supposed to know whether it's him or not? I never got a good look at him."

"Maybe by the imprint of your face on his knuckles?" she said.

I couldn't believe she was breaking my balls, but when she laughed, I had to.

"Take my little camera with you," she said.

"Why?

"I want to see what you see," she said. She got up then and left the basement. I got dressed. While I ate, she showed me how to use the camera. It was a little electronic job, but amazing, with telephoto capability and a little window you

186

could see your pictures in. I don't think I'd held a camera in ten years.

I sat on a bench in the park, next to a giant pine tree, and watched the newsstand across the street. I had my 40 in a brown paper bag and a five-dollar joint in my jacket. The day was clear and cold, and people came and went on the street, some of them stopping to buy a paper or cigs from Maya. One thing I noticed was that nobody came to the park, the one nice place in crumbling Fishmere.

All afternoon and nothing criminal, except for one girl's miniskirt. She was my first photo—exhibit A. After that I took a break and went back into the park where there was a gazebo looking out across a small lake. I fired up the joint and took another pic of some geese. Mostly I watched the sun on the water and wondered what I'd do once the last triangle hoo-doo played itself out. Part of me wanted to stay with Ms. Berkley and the other part knew it wouldn't be right. I'd been on the scag for fifteen years and was now somebody making break-fast and dinner every day. Things like the camera, a revelation to me. She even had me reading a book, *The Professor's House*, by Willa Cather—slow as shit, but somehow I needed to know what happened next to old Godfrey St. Peter. Staying off the hard stuff, the food and the weights, made me strong.

Late in the afternoon, he came to the newsstand. I'd been in such a daze, the sight of him there, like he just materialized, made me jump. My hands shook a little as I telephoto'd in on him. He paid for two packs of cigs, and I snapped the picture. I wasn't sure if I'd caught his mug. He was pretty well hidden by the long coat's collar and the hat. There was no time to check the shot. As he moved away down the sidewalk, I stowed the camera in my pocket and followed him, hanging back fifty yards or so.

He didn't seem suspicious. Never looked around or stopped, but just kept moving at the same brisk pace. Only when it came to me that he was walking us in a circle did I get that he was on to me. At that point, he made a quick left into an alley. I followed. The alley was a short one with a brick wall at the end. He'd vanished. I walked cautiously into the shadows and looked around behind the dumpsters. There was nothing there. A gust of wind lifted the old newspapers and litter into the air, and, I'll admit, I was scared. On the way back to the house, I looked over my shoulder about a hundred times.

I handed Ms. Berkley the camera in her office. She took a wire out of her desk drawer and plugged one end into the camera and one into the computer. She typed some shit, and then the first picture appeared. It was the legs.

"Finding the focus with that shot?" she asked.

"Every one's a suspect," I said.

"Foolishness," she murmured. She liked the geese, said it was a nice composition. Then the one of the guy at the newsstand came up, and, yeah, I nailed it. A really clear profile of his face. Eyes like a hawk and a sharp nose. He had white hair and a thick white mustache.

"Not bad," I said, but Ms. Berkley didn't respond. She was staring hard at the picture, and her mouth was slightly open. She shook her head and then reached out and touched the screen.

"You know him?" I asked.

"You're wearing his jacket," she said. Then she turned away, put her face in her hands.

I left her alone and went into the kitchen. I made spaghetti the way she'd showed me. While stirring the sauce, I said to my reflection in the stove hood, "Now the dead man's back and he's the evil magician?" Man, I really wanted to laugh the whole thing off, but I couldn't forget the guy's disappearing act.

I put two plates of spaghetti down on the kitchen table and then went to fetch Ms. Berkley. She told me to go away. Instead I put my hands on her shoulders and said, "Come on, you should eat something." Then, applying as little pressure as possible, I sort of lifted her as she stood. In the kitchen, I held her chair for her and gave her a cup of tea. My spaghetti was undercooked and the sauce was cold, but, still, not bad. She used her napkin to dry her eyes.

"The dead man looks pretty good for a dead man," I said.

"It was easier to explain by telling you he was dead. Who wants the embarrassment of saying someone left them?"

"I get it," I said.

"I think most people would, but still . . ."

"This clears something up for me," I told her. "I always thought it was pretty strange that two people in the same town would know about Abriel and the last triangle. I mean, what's the chances?"

"The book is his," she said. "Years after he left, it just became part of my library, and eventually I read it. Now that I think of it, he read a lot of books about the occult."

"Who is he?"

"His name is Lionel Brund. I met him years ago, when I was in my thirties. I was already teaching at the college, and I owned this house. We both were at a party hosted by a colleague. He was just passing through and knew someone who knew someone at the party. We hit it off. He had great stories about his travels. He liked to laugh. It was fun just going to the grocery store with him. My first real romance. A very gentle man."

The look on her face made me say, "But?"

She nodded. "But he owned a gun, and I had no idea what kind of work he did, although he always had plenty of money. Parts of his life were a secret. He'd go away for a week or two at a time on some 'business' trip. I didn't mind that, because there were parts of my life I wanted to keep to myself as well. We were together, living in this house for over two years, and then, one day, he was gone. I waited for him to come back for a long time and then moved on, made my own life."

"Now you do what needs to get done," I said.

She laughed. "Exactly."

"Lionel knows we're onto him. He played me this afternoon, took me in a circle and then was gone with the wind. It creeped me."

"I want to see him," she said. "I want to talk to him."

"He's out to kill somebody to protect himself," I said.

"I don't care," she said.

"Forget it," I told her and then asked for the gun. She pushed it across the table to me.

"He could come after us," I said. "You've got to be careful." She got up to go into her office, and I drew the butcher knife out of its wooden holder on the counter and handed it to her. I wanted her to get how serious things were. She took it, but said nothing. I could tell she was lost in the past.

I put the gun, safety off, on the stand next to my cot and lay back with a head full of questions. I stayed awake for a long while before I eventually gave in. A little bit after I dozed off, I was half wakened by the sound of the phone ringing upstairs. I heard Ms. Berkley walk down the hall and pick up. Her voice was a distant mumble. Then I fell asleep for a few minutes, and the first thing I heard when I came to again was the sound of the back door closing. It took me a minute to put together that he'd called and she'd gone to meet him.

I got dressed in a flash, but put on three T-shirts instead of wearing Lionel's jacket. I thought he might have the power to spook it since it belonged to him. It took me a couple of seconds to decide whether to leave the gun behind as well. But I was shit scared so I shoved it in the waist of my jeans and took off. I ran dead-out to the train station parking lot. Luckily there were no cops there, but there wasn't anybody else either. I went in the station, searched beneath the trestles, and went back to the rundown building we'd sat in. Nothing.

As I walked back to the house, I tried to think of where he would have asked to meet her. I pictured all the places I'd been to in the past few weeks. An image of Ms. Berkley's map came to mind, the one of town with the red dots and the triangles, east and west. I'd not found a triangle point to the west, and as I considered that I recalled the point I had found in the east, the symbol spray painted on the trunk of an old car up on blocks. It came to me—say that one didn't count because it wasn't on a building, connected to the ground. That was a fake. Maybe he knew somehow Ms. Berkley would notice the symbols and he wanted to throw her off.

Then it struck me, what if there was a third symbol in the west I just didn't see? I tried to picture the map as the actual streets it represented and figure where the center of a western triangle would be. At first it seemed way too complicated, just a jumble of frustration, but suddenly, into my head popped a memory of the geese in the park across the street from Maya's News Stand. The park was a hike, and I knew I had to pace myself, but the fact that I'd figured out Lionel's twists and turns gave me a burst of energy. What I really wanted was to tell Ms. Berkley how I'd thought it through. Then I realized she might already be dead.

Something instinctively drew me toward the gazebo. It was a perfect center for a magician's prison. The moonlight was on the lake. I thought I heard them talking, saw their shadows sitting on the bench, smelled the smoke of Ducados, but when I took the steps and leaned over to catch my breath, I realized it was all in my mind. The place was empty and still. The geese called from out on the lake. I sat down on the bench and lit a cigarette. Only when I resigned myself to just returning to the house, it came to me I had one more option, to find the last point of the western triangle.

I knew it was a long shot at night, looking, without a flashlight, for something I couldn't find during the day. My only consolation was that since Lionel hadn't taken Ms. Berkley to the center of his triangle, he might not intend to use her as his victim.

I was exhausted, and although I set out from the gazebo, jogging toward my best guess as to where the last point was, I was soon walking. The street map of town with the red triangles would flash momentarily in my memory and then disappear. I went up a street that was utterly dark, and the wind followed me. From there, I turned and passed a row of closed factory buildings. The symbol could have been anywhere, hiding in the dark. Finally, there was a cross street and I walked down a block of row homes, some boarded, some with bars on the windows. That path led to an industrial park. Beneath a dim streetlight, I stopped and tried to picture the map, but it was no use. I was totally lost. I gave up and turned back in the direction I thought Ms. Berkley's house would be.

One block outside that industrial park, I hit a street of old four-story apartment buildings. The doors were off the hinges, and the moonlight showed no reflection in the shattered windows. A neighborhood of vacant lots and dead brick giants. Halfway down the block, hoping to find a left turn, I just happened to look up and see an unbroken window, yellow lamp light streaming out. From where I stood I could only see the ceiling of the room, but faint silhouettes moved across it. I took out the gun. There was no decent reason why I thought it was them, but I felt drawn to the place as if under a spell.

I took the stone steps of the building, and when I tried the door, it pushed open. I thought this was strange, but I figured he might have left it ajar for Ms. Berkley. Inside, the foyer was so dark, and there was no light on the first landing. I found the first step by inching forward and feeling around with my foot. The last thing I needed was three flights of stairs. I tried to climb without a sound, but the planks creaked unmercifully. "If they don't hear me coming," I thought, "they're both dead."

As I reached the fourth floor, I could hear noises coming from the room. It sounded like two people were arguing and wrestling around. Then I distinctly heard Ms. Berkley cry out. I lunged at the door, cracked it on the first bounce, and busted it in with the second. Splinters flew and the chain lock ripped out with a pop. I stumbled into the room, the gun pointing forward, completely out of breath. It took me a second to see what was going on.

There they were, in a bed beneath the window in the opposite corner of the room, naked, frozen by my intrusion, her legs around his back. Ms. Berkley scooted up and quickly wrapped the blanket around herself, leaving old Lionel out in the cold. He jumped up quick, dick flopping, and got into his boxers.

"What the hell," I whispered.

"Go home, Thomas," she said.

"You're coming with me," I said.

"I can handle this," she said.

"Who's after you?" I said to Lionel. "For what?"

He took a deep breath. "Phantoms more cruel than you can imagine, my boy. I lived my young life recklessly, like you, and its mistakes have multiplied and hounded me ever since."

"You're a loser," I said, and it sounded so stupid. Especially when it struck me that Lionel might have been old but he looked pretty strong.

"Sorry, son," he said and drew that long knife from a scabbard on the nightstand next to the bed. "It's time to sever ties."

"Run," said Ms. Berkley.

I thought, "Fuck this guy," and pulled out the gun.

Ms. Berkley jumped on Lionel, but he shrugged her off with a sharp push that landed her back on the bed. "This one's not running," he said. "I can tell."

I was stunned for a moment by Ms. Berkley's nakedness. But as he advanced a step, I raised the gun and told him, "Drop the knife."

He said, "Be careful, you're hurting it."

At first his words didn't register, but then, in my hand, instead of a gun I felt a frail wriggling thing with a heartbeat. I released my grasp and a bat flew up to circle around the ceiling. In the same moment, I heard the gun hit the wooden floor and knew he'd tricked me with magic.

He came toward me slowly, and I whipped off two of my T-shirts and wrapped them around my right forearm. He sliced the air with the blade a few times as I crouched down and circled away from him. He lunged fast as a snake, and I got caught against a dresser. He cut me on the stomach and the right shoulder. The next time he came at me, I kicked a hassock in front of him and managed a punch to the side of his head. Lionel came back with a half-dozen more slices, each marking me. The T-shirts on my arm were in shreds, as was the one I wore.

I kept watching that knife, and that's how he got me, another punch to the jaw worse than the one in the station parking lot. I stumbled backward and he followed with the blade aimed at my throat. What saved me was that Ms. Berkley grabbed him from behind. He stopped to push her off again, and I caught my balance and took my best shot to the right side of his face. The punch scored, he fell backward into the wall, and the knife flew in the air. I tried to catch it as it fell but only managed to slice my fingers. I picked it up by the handle, and when I looked, Lionel was steamrolling toward me again.

"Thomas," yelled Ms. Berkley from where she'd landed. I was stunned, and automatically pushed the weapon forward into the bulk of the charging magician. He stopped in his tracks, teetered for a second, and fell back onto his ass. He sat there on the rug, legs splayed, with that big knife sticking out of his stomach. Blood seeped around the blade and puddled in front of him.

Ms. Berkley was next to me, leaning on my shoulder. "Pay attention," she said.

I snapped out of it and looked down at Lionel. He was sighing more than breathing and staring at the floor.

"If he dies," said Ms. Berkley, "you inherit the spell of the last triangle."

"That's right," Lionel said. Blood came from his mouth with the words. "Where ever you are at dawn, that will be the center of your world." He laughed. "For the rest of your life you will live in a triangle within the rancid town of Fishmere."

Ms. Berkley found the gun and picked it up. She went to the bed and grabbed one of the pillows.

"Is that true?" I said and started to panic.

Lionel nodded, laughing. Ms. Berkley, took up the gun again and then wrapped the pillow around it. She walked over next to Lionel, crouched down, and touched the pillow to the side of his head.

"What are you doing?" I asked.

Ms. Berkley squinted one eye and steadied her left arm with her right hand while keeping the pillow in place.

"What else?" said Lionel, spluttering blood bubbles. "What needs to be done."

The pillow muffled somewhat the sound of the shot as feathers flew everywhere. Lionel dropped onto his side without magic, the hole in his head smoking. I wasn't afraid anyone would hear. There wasn't another soul for three blocks. Ms. Berkley checked his pulse. "The last triangle is mine now," she said. "I have to get home by dawn." She got dressed while I stood in the hallway.

I don't remember leaving Lionel's building, or passing the park or Maya's News Stand. We were running through the night, across town, as the sky lightened in the distance. Four blocks from home, Ms. Berkley gave out and started limping. I picked her up and, still running, carried her the rest of the way. We were in the kitchen, the tea whistle blowing, when the birds started to sing and the sun came up.

She poured the tea for us and said, "I thought I could talk Lionel out of his plan, but he wasn't the same person anymore. I could see the magic's like a drug. The more you use it, the more it pushes you out of yourself and takes over."

"Was he out to kill me or you?" I asked.

"He was out to get himself killed. I'd promised to do the job for him before you showed up. He knew we were on to him and he tried to fool us with train-station scam, but once he heard my voice that night, he said he knew he couldn't go through with it. He just wanted to see me once more, and then I was supposed to cut his throat."

"You would have killed him?" I said.

"I did."

"You know, before I knifed him?"

"He told me the phantoms and fetches that were after him knew where he was and it was only a matter of days before they caught up with him."

"What was it exactly he did?"

"He wouldn't say, but he implied that it had to do with loving me. And I really think he thought he did."

"What do you think?" I asked.

Ms. Berkley interrupted me. "You've got to get out of town," she said. "When they find Lionel's body, you'll be one of the usual suspects what with your wandering around drinking beer and smoking pot in public."

"Who told you that?" I said.

"Did I just fall off the turnip truck yesterday?"

Ms. Berkley went to her office and returned with a roll of cash for me. I didn't even have time to think about leaving, to miss my cot and the weights, and the meals. The cab showed up and we left. She had her map of town with the triangles on it and had already drawn a new one, it's center, her kitchen. We drove for a little ways, and then she told the cab driver to pull over and wait. We were in front of a closed-down gas station on the edge of town. She got out and I followed her.

"I paid the driver to take you two towns over to Willmuth. There's a bus station there. Get a ticket and disappear," she said.

"What about you? You're stuck in the triangle."

"I'm bounded in a nutshell," she said.

"Why'd you take the spell?"

"You don't need it. You just woke up. I have every confidence that I'll be able to figure a way out of it. It's amazing what you can find on the internet."

"A magic spell?" I said.

"Understand this," she said, "spells are made to be broken." She stepped closer and reached her hands to my shoulders. I leaned down. She kissed me on the forehead. "Not promises, though," she said and turned away, heading home.

"Ms. Berkley," I called after her.

"Stay clean," she yelled without looking.

Back in the cab, I said, "Willmuth," and leaned against the window. The driver started the car and we sailed through an invisible boundary into the world.

Spirits of Salt: A Tale of the Coral Heart

The saga of Ismet Toler can only be told in pieces. Like a victim of his battle craft transformed to red coral by a nick from his infamous blade only to be shattered with a well-placed kick and strewn in a thousand shards, the swordsman's own life story is scattered across the valley of the known world and so buried in half-truth and legend that a scholar of the Coral Heart, such as myself, must possess the patience and devotion of a saint. It's a wonder I've not yet succumbed to the hot air of the yarn-spinners of inns and royal courts. Oh, they have wonderful tales to tell—fanciful, heroic, daunting adventures—but their meager imaginations could never match the truth of what actually transpired.

Many of them will recount for you, as if they were there, the Coral Heart's battle on the island of Saevisha, against the cyclopean ogre Rotnak, tall as a watchtower and ever ravenous for human flesh. They'll supply the details, no doubt—the whistling wind from the swing of the giant's club, the tremble of the earth in the wake of his monstrous stride, Toler's thrust to that single eye, and the whole massive body crackling into a weight of red coral the size of a merchant ship. I hate to disabuse you, but the incident never happened. Please, an ogre? Remember we live in the world, dear reader, not a children's bedtime story.

One of the aspects of Toler's life most abused by these fabrications is the story of his upbringing in the Sussuro Mountains. Yes, they manage to capture well enough the location and the fact that he lived out his childhood in a cave in the side of a cliff—common knowledge—but that's about the extent of any accuracy. All of these tale-tellers have him raised by a hermit, who taught him the art of swordsmanship. The old man was a master of the blade, a fallen knight who had fled the world for a life of contemplation. And even some of this is truth, because Toler was raised by a hermit. The difference between legend and truth, though, is that the hermit was a woman—an assassin who had spent half her life killing for the Alliance of the Back of the Hand, a clandestine society of the very wealthiest of aristocrats who pulled the strings of commerce and manipulated the fate of the powerless.

She was known, or more her work was known, under the alias, -I-. Even those in the secret council of the Alliance, those who sent her on her missions, had never seen her face. What they knew was her black cloak, her silk boots, the speed and grace of her sword. And they knew her mask, a blank white shell with two small circular eye holes and a small circle for a mouth. She killed swiftly, simply, and accurately and moved like an eel through a sunken pasture in the escape. Most of her victims practiced sorcery. The Alliance had secretly declared war on all magic, fearing its promise of hope to the powerless. In -I-'s years of killing, her prey had thrown spells at her, frightening illusions, distracting dreams, creatures of the imagination. She trusted in her sword, her darts, her leather club, and dagger. Once she parried with an enchanted hog, wielding a sword. Once she wrestled with an angel in the heat of the afternoon. She kept her focus as sharp as the blade, able to cut through illusion, sharper than magic.

In the summer of her fortieth year, she was sent on a mission to kill a witch, the crone of Aer, who lived on the outskirts of the city of Camiar. There, in a small cottage, she kept a vast flower garden from which she drew her sorcery. The warm sun and cloudless blue skies did their best to distract the assassin as she rode out of the city to the edge of the Forest of Sans. Along the way, she repeatedly caught herself daydreaming. When she neared the spot where the council had told she'd find the witch's cottage, she slipped off her horse and sent it silently away to graze in the pasture of tall grass. Moving against the breeze, she crept amid six-foot stalks swarming with yellow butterflies. Some small pest stung her on the back of the neck but she ignored the distraction. At the edge of the pasture, with the place finally in sight, she drew her sword.

She found the door of the cottage wide open and a black cat sitting on the top of three short steps. It never so much as cast a glance her way. Stepping through into the cool shadows of the cottage, she felt the adrenalin pulse and crouched into the fighting stance known as the fly trap. Her eyes immediately adjusted and she noted the basket of fruit on the table, the collections of animal skulls and cleaved rocks displaying green and purple crystals at their centers. Melted candles and crudely fashioned furniture made from tree branches. Crystals hung by twine in the place's one window; blown glass bottles on the sill held nasturtiums. -I- moved cautiously from one room to the next till she'd searched all three. Then from the kitchen, through a back door, she let herself into the garden.

The aroma of the blossoms was relaxing. She felt the muscles in her sword arm slacken and released a sigh she'd not intended, which she knew was enough of a slip to get her killed. The garden had a fountain and diverging paths lined with egg-like stones shining in the summer sun and radiating warmth through the soles of her boots. More butterflies and grasshoppers and thickets of flowers of all types and colors spilling onto the edges of the walk. Passing a shock of blue daffodils twice her height, she was startled by a figure standing amid a bed of foxglove. Her blade instantly swept through the air and stuck with a knock three inches in the neck of a wooden statue. Its eyes were seashells, its heart a puffball. She pulled the sword free and spun around to see if anyone had heard. There was only a breeze and the sun in the sky.

-I- found her target farther down the path, sitting in a wicker chair beneath an awning of huge, broad leaves. Beside the old woman there was a table on which sat a teapot, two cups, a lit taper, and a pipe. Upon noticing -I-, the witch smiled and motioned for the assassin to join her. She pointed to the empty wicker chair across from hers. -I- was startled by the realization that she'd let herself be detected.

The witch pushed her gray hair behind her ears and said, "Come sit down. There'll be plenty of time for killing later. And take that ridiculous mask off."

Disarmed as she was, realizing that any chance of surprise was gone, she walked forward, sheathed her sword, and sat down. "Did you hear me coming?" she asked.

"I smelled you two days off," said the witch. "Sweet enough but somewhat musty. Please, dear, the mask."

"Brave for a woman who's about to die," said -I-, unable to believe she was speaking to her prey. Until that moment, she'd never have conceived of the possibility. By every measure, it was bad form. Still, she removed her mask and set it on the table. The witches' glance made her blush. "Do you mean me or you?" asked the crone of Aer.

"You intend to kill me?" -I- went for her sword.

"Easy, dearest," said the witch. "For someone who's killed so often, you know little of death."

-I- returned her sword and sat back. From her years of assessing her prey, her glance instantly registered the woman's lined face and hunched form, noted her strange beauty—ugliness made a virtue—and the grace with which she poured a cup of tea.

"If I'd wanted you dead, I'd have sent a thought-form servant with a silver rope to strangle you in your sleep two days ago," said the witch. She pushed the steaming tea cup across the table.

-I- shook her head at the offering.

"Drink it."

She reached for the teacup at the same time she wondered which poison the old lady had used. Bringing it to her lips, -I-'s senses were enveloped with the aroma of the pasture, its steam misting her vision. She meant to ask herself what she was doing but felt it would have to wait until after she'd tasted the tea. It was soothing and made her body feel cool in the breeze of the hot day. Drinking in small sips, she quickly downed the cup while the witch packed a pipe with dried leaves from a possum-hair pouch.

As -I- placed the empty cup back on the table, the witch handed her the smoldering pipe—a thin, hollowed-out tibia with a bowl carved to resemble the form of an owl.

"What was the tea? And what is this?" asked the assassin.

"The tea was clippings from the garden, stored underground through a frost, drying in sugar. The smoke is Simple Weed."

"It makes you simple?"

"Does everything need to be complicated?"

-I- laughed and accepted the pipe and candle with which to spark it. She forsook caution, drew deeply, and woke in the middle of the night, the stars shining overhead. She sat up suddenly, confused, her joints aching from the cold ground she'd slept upon. She staggered to her feet and drew her sword only to find she was completely alone. The starlight was enough to show her she'd lain among the ruins of an old stone building, roof gone and walls three-quarters shattered. Grass grew up around the fallen masonry and crickets sang.

She reached her free hand to the back of her neck and found the tiny dart she'd put off to an insect still lodged there. It was instantly clear that she'd been out cold since the moment she'd felt the sting amid the tall grass, and all else had been a dream. She called for her horse, and it approached from the pasture. Mounting it, she rode fiercely toward Camiar, and within the first mile realized the witch in the dream was her future-self. It was then she decided to assassinate all in the secret council of the Alliance of the Back of the Hand.

And she did just that. Five fat, miserable old men. She stalked them and dispatched them without remorse. Each of the three remaining after the first councilor was found, his head stuffed in his hindquarters, hired his own small army of bodyguards and assassins, but -I- cut through all of them. It was a time known to those in the know as the "Hemorrhage," for there was a great bleeding although none of the blood seeped into public view. She killed the councilors and their minions, quietly, secretly, each assassination merely a whisper. She killed the head of the Alliance, the so-called "middle finger of the Back of the Hand," so exquisitely that it took him an hour to realize he was dead before dropping over. And when the last was opened like a mackerel to let the insides become the outside, she rode out of Camiar and lost herself in the Sussuro Mountains.

She ate what hermits eat, locusts and honey, weeds and flowers, fruit and fish. She hunted with her sword, facing off against mountain goats, bears, wildcats, badgers. Those she assassinated for the Alliance rarely had a chance to fight back, but these creatures were cunning and fast and fought to the death every time. Her style of engagement became more calculated than ever, seeing that the fierceness in creatures was a mask of fear. While they pounced, she analyzed and then in the last instant struck with accuracy—one thrust of the blade to let the fear out.

Her dagger trimmed the hide from the meat, which she wrapped in an animal skin and dragged back to her cave. There she had fire and fresh clothes she stole on raids of Camiar's clotheslines. At night she read her only book, *The Consolation of the Constellations,* by the light of a lantern that cast a silhouette of an ibis on the wall of the cave. When reading wouldn't do, she worked through her imagination to create a thought-form servant like the one mentioned by her dream witch.

When she finally climbed into her sleeping bag nestled upon willow branches, let the fire burn low, and closed her eyes, she always wondered who it was who'd cast the dart that day she'd gone to kill "the witch." She wondered if there'd ever been such a sorceress as the crone of Aer or if the whole thing had been an ambush. Since she wasn't killed, she believed that perhaps a larger spell had been cast that might strike a blow against the Alliance and remove her deadly art from the covert war between the powerful and the people. The longer she stayed away from Camiar, the more she considered that dart an act of kindness.

In spring of her second year in the mountains, while chasing down a stag, she followed the creature into a place she'd never been before. It led her down a canyon as wide as an alley to the floor of a gorge. There, things opened up to a vast mudflat shadowed by three-hundred-foot vertical walls of granite. She looked up and saw the blue sky over the rim of the cliffs, and the sight of it made her cold. In an instant, she felt that the place was haunted and she turned to flee. It was then that she noticed the bodies, lying here and there, dressed in finery, decomposing in the mud. They were badly broken, limbs in odd twisted positions, obviously having fallen from the cliffs.

Seeing the manner in which the corpses were dressed, she remembered from her days with the Alliance having heard of a place in the mountains where people were coaxed to commit suicide by leaping to their deaths. The natural setting of the gorge was staggeringly beautiful, and so the secret council gave some of their victim's the choice—either -I- could come for them or they could willingly take the plunge at Churnington's Gorge surrounded by nature and with a modicum of dignity. When she realized who the dead were, she rifled their pockets and took the mink coat of a recent arrival. Her fear of spirits was strong every second she delayed to pillage them, and eventually she left behind a string of pearls she easily could have had and ran, heart pounding, back through the narrow canyon.

That night, lying in the cave, the fire burning low, -I- remembered looking up to the cliffs and seeing that sliver of blue sky. With that image in mind, she had an idea that wealthy people about to jump might leave something behind for the world to remember them by. She daydreamed a large man in a violet suit, brandishing a cane, leaving behind a short stack of books before stepping over the side, and realized she would go there, to the top of the gorge and see what treasures could be found.

The journey was arduous, the trail leading over a mountain and then a descent to the plateau that ended at Churnington's. What she found at the edge of the cliff was a small boy, sitting, staring out at the afternoon sun. In his pocket, she found a note that read, "I am Ismet Toler." She judged him to be three years old. When she leaned down to him and reached out her hand, he took it. "Come," she said, and led him back to the cave where she raised him.

Little is known about Toler's younger years. Although there are many opinions about what kind of mother -I- made for the boy, or what kinds of qualities he'd carried over from the poor soul who'd chosen to leap to his doom, there exists no proof for any of it. The only verifiable record from this time was a letter written by a sixteen-year-old Toler to himself about his training in swordsmanship. There were cadavers dragged from the gorge and strapped to the trunks of trees or hung by a rope from a branch—lifelike dummies on which one could practice the precise arc and velocity necessary to slice the heel tendon of a large man. There was dance. There was acrobatics and con-templation. About sparring with -I-, he confessed to himself, he couldn't conceive of victory.

The only other verifiable incident from Toler's youth was related to me by Lady Etmisler, who had heard it from The Coral Heart himself at a banquet they'd both attended in the palace at Camiar. He told her that when he became masterful with the sword, -I- told him that he'd reached the second of three levels of development. She told him to leave the cave and go out in the world and ply his trade. He wanted to know when the third level began, and she told him, "In five years, you can return to me if by then you've renounced the sword. We can only continue if you forsake it."

That night she told him the story of how she came to the mountains and discovered him on the ledge at Churnington's Gorge. In the morning, he kissed her good-bye, and she told him that at the end of five years she would send a thought-form servant to him to ask if he'd renounced the sword and was returning. He nodded as he walked away, his sword upon his back. In the valley of the known world, he soon found employment as a bodyguard to a corrupt bishop who was often the target of assassination attempts. From there his reputation as a swordsman grew. He moved on to work as a mercenary and fought for the side that paid the most in any conflict, often changing sides in mid-battle for the promise of better. By his fourth year away from the mountains, Ismet Toler was a name to be reckoned with.

But as that fourth year drew to a close, after proving the effectiveness of his blade, he felt he'd had enough of slaughter. The disfigurement of his victim's bodies, the blood and severed flesh, had become nauseating to him. It was all too much of the same gore, and he felt a need to move on to the next level. His diary from this time proves he was on the verge of renouncing the sword and returning to -I-. For the remaining months of the year, he decided to leave his position, training assassins for the Igridot royalty, and head for Camiar, where he would rent rooms, live off the spoils of his killing, and wait for -I-'s servant to appear.

In that brief space of days that he travelled north on the road to Camiar, Fate in all its bad timing and low humor stepped in, and he somewhere, somehow, acquired the Coral Heart, the blade, whose magical properties would eventually make him a legend. Toler swore to never reveal how he came by it, and so this crucial juncture in the story is blank. I constantly comb the valley of the known world for clues to those few days he spent retreating along that road, and have found nothing. I could spin a fanciful tale, but instead, I merely direct you to where the trail of known fact resumes.

By the time Toler entered the city, he'd already turned to red coral a band of highwaymen who'd foolishly tried to rob him and take his horse. It was the trio of palace guard, though, who confronted him in the marketplace at Camiar and wound up red statues of their former selves, that caused the trouble. He knew he would have to flee. Learning the feel of the sword, he was eager to use it, but he'd not yet mastered its extra weight or reckoned the sharpness or balance to the point where he could yet defeat the entirety of the royal guard of the palace of Camiar. He left the city by night as door-to-door torch-light searches for him were being conducted. There had been witnesses.

Two days later, he arrived in a village, a hundred miles away, separated from Camiar by the Forest of Sans. He chose Twyse as his hideout as it was off the main trails that linked the palaces of the realm. If the snowy, sleepy place had any reputation it was as a home for hunters who stalked the forests that lay just beyond. The furs and skins of Twyse were renowned among the royalty, but its inhabitants cared little for news from outside its borders and would have cheered a tale of the demise of three of the royal guard of Camiar. Toler had stayed there once before and came to know the people as that rare stock who could mind their own business.

He paid handsomely for the use of a barn at the edge of the village with a fireplace and a loft to sleep in, and paid extra for the owner to keep his mouth shut. Then once the great wooden doors were secured, he unwrapped the Coral Heart, which he'd hidden beneath an extra cloak, and began a regimen of daily practice. His diary attests that every hour he felt his ability with the sword growing. As he wrote, "The weapon has a personality, and if I'm not mistaken a will, which I am learning to merge with mine."

At night, after a full day of training, Toler would go to the Sackful, the town's one inn, sit in a dark corner, drinking honeycomb rye, and contemplate what he would tell -I-'s mysterious servant when it materialized. Only days earlier, he'd planned to renounce the sword, but now he meant to tell her through her messenger of the nature of the enchanted weapon and how it was changing him. He wanted to tell her that it took the art of the blade to a new level, one he wished to explore. He'd beg her for a reply in which she would tell him her thoughts about his decision.

The days passed in Twyse, overcast but with no visits from the royal guard or news of local manhunts. Toler continued his exercises and imaginary battles and now had begun to move around the entire expanse of the barn in a lunatic dance that made even him doubt his sanity at times. Still, it was exciting and he'd burst out laughing when the sword would show him something new. Now when he held the coral heart of the grip, he felt a pulsing in his palm that matched the beating of his heart. As Toler reminds us in a diary entry, all he wrote for that particular day—"This sword has slain monsters."

As his confidence grew through his daily practice, he became bolder at night as well, conversing and drinking with the people of the village at the Sackful. They told him of their hunting and he recounted some of his exploits as a mercenary, failing, of course, to mention his name. The moment that marked a monumental transition in the life of Ismet Toler was the night, before leaving for the inn, that he removed his old sword from its sheath and replaced it with the Coral Heart. From the moment it hung at his side, he felt a great sense of calm and a new shrewd reserve, an intuitive calculation.

That night he drank more than his fill and revealed too much about himself. Halfway into the evening, while the inn crowd was listening to a young girl sing a hunter's hymn, he realized that all his newfound energy and personality, his reserve, was as a result of his yearning to use the sword again in a battle. The charm of practice had just about reached its limits and he was eager for the fray. To build the energy, he decided to hold off using the Coral Heart for another two weeks, and then, if the occasion arose, or he were to coax one into happening, he would draw the weapon and turn the world red.

That night, soon after he'd made his decision to continue to lay low, the chatter of the Sackful died down for an instant and the patrons were able to hear a horse approaching on the frozen road. All eyes glanced at the door, including Toler's. A moment passed and then a hooded figure strode in dressed warmly against the winter night—gloves and leggings, a thick cloak. The swordsman noticed first, of course, the stranger's sword hilt, which appeared to be made of clear crystal. The man strode to the bar, and the inn crowd, out of a sense of rural politeness, tried to avert their glances. They were soon drawn back to the figure, though, when the innkeeper, after inquiring if the stranger would have a cup of holly beer, gasped aloud.

What he alone was seeing, all beheld a moment later, when the man who'd just arrived, drew back his hood—a face and neck and even hair of a deep red hue. Toler went weak where he sat, realizing from the smooth, shiny consistency of that face, that the fellow was made of red coral. He wondered if this was one of his recent victims having chased him down for revenge. But there was nothing in the legend of the Coral Heart to suggest that its prey returned to life as breathing statues.

"I want whiskey," said the stranger, and although he looked to be made of polished coral his mouth moved pliantly and his lips slipped into a smile without cracking his face. He pulled off his gloves, and yes, his fingers and palms too were red coral and flexed easily, although when he set one down upon the bar there was a sound as if he'd dropped a rock. He lifted off his cloak and set it on a chair. None were prepared for a statue come to life.

Toler, like the rest of his Sackful compatriots, couldn't move, so stunned was he at the sight. "What manner of creature are you?" asked the innkeeper, backing away.

"My name is Thybault, and I, like you, am a man, of course."

"How'd you come by that color?" asked one of the more brazen patrons, lifting the hatchet from a loop in his belt. "That's the color of the devil."

"The devil? You're an idiot," said Thybault.

The hunter with the axe stood, his weapon now firmly in his grip. "An idiot I may be," he said, "but at least I know God never made a man out of red stone." This said, two of his fellow hunters rose behind him.

"Coral," said the red man.

Toler would later recount in his diary that it was at this moment that he realized the stranger had come for him. He cautiously moved his cloak up to cover the hilt of the Coral Heart. A tightness in his chest told him not to get involved in what was about to happen. The anticipation of battle in the room was palpable. The hunters slowly advanced toward Thybault, who turned to the innkeeper and said, "Where's my drink?"

While he was looking away, they lunged. When they saw the speed with which he drew his sword, it was visible in their faces that they knew they'd made a mistake. The lead hunter raised the hatchet high, but the crystal sword had already punctured his throat, and in an eyeblink later he disintegrated into salt that showered down into a pile on the wooden floor. There were screams of fear and wonder from the patrons. The two other hunters' eyes were wide. The shock made them living statues as Thybault became a statue alive, spinning into a crouch and running one through, exploding him into salt. Then an upward motion and the crystal blade buried itself in the underside of the third man's chin. Again, it rained salt onto which fell the empty garments.

The innkeeper put Thybault's drink on the bar. There was silence as the coral man returned his glistening sword to its sheath and lifted his whiskey. The only one to move was a young woman who, getting to her knees, gathered in her apron the salt that had been the hunters. Toler was frightened, and he hated the feeling. He'd trained for weeks to reach the condition he was in, and the first instance where he might have tried out the Coral Heart, fate threw at him an enemy who was a superior swordsman and made of red coral. He knew it could only be magic.

Thybault finished his drink and smashed the clay cup on the floor. He turned and stared out at the patrons cowered into the corners of the inn. The candles' glow against his polished complexion set him in a bright red haze. He put on his left glove. "If anyone knows of a man, Ismet Toler, tell him I challenge him to a duel out in this latrine of a street tomorrow morning when the church bell chimes. Every day he doesn't meet me, I'll turn another three of you to salt. We'll start with the children." He put on his other gloves, wrapped his cloak around him, lifted his hood, and was gone. In the silence that followed, they heard his horse, which must have been massive from the percussion of its hoofbeats, moving away into the sound of the winter wind.

Someone cursed, and then the inn erupted into a den of chatter. Toler was so scared he could barely move. Still, he managed to stand and slowly make his way to the door. He didn't want to run, which would, although they didn't know his name, identify him as Ismet Toler. When he neared the entrance, he turned around and shuffled backward, a little at a time, until he was free of the place. The cold air helped him to think, and he realized that it wouldn't be long before the people of Thyse gave him up to the crystal sword. As he ran toward the barn, he made the decision to ride out that night, take to the forest, and escape.

In his diary entry that was made apparently just before setting out on horseback, he wrote, "Something powerful is after me. I'm running away." Then he fled into the night forest, stopping and listening every now and then to make sure Thybault and his giant horse weren't following. There was no moon, and the sky was overcast. Toler stayed off the trails, and that made the journey slow and difficult. The temperature dropped well below freezing and before he was even an hour into his escape, it began to snow. Still, he kept moving forward, but for every few yards he'd cover the white wind pushed harder against him. By the end of another hour, he was sure he'd freeze—a statue in a saddle. An hour farther on and the snow was so blinding, he was sure they'd been traveling in circles for the last five miles. His hands were so cold, he was losing his grip on the reins; his face was all but numb. The incessant pummeling of his eyes by the small hard flakes made him ride with them closed, and what he saw behind the lids was more snow driving down within his mind. In his confusion he mistook the sound of the wind for that of a children's choir, and it made him recall Thybault threatening, "We'll start with the children." The only thought that stayed fixed in his mind was that he was a coward.

It came to him at one point in the storm that the horse was no longer moving. He looked up into the squall to see what had happened and felt a pair of hands grasp his arm. Their touch was so wonderfully warm. He squinted against the snow and saw a small form in a black cloak standing beside his horse, reaching up to him. "Come with me," said a female voice. Ice cracked off him as he climbed down. He turned back to the animal to see if it was still alive. "Don't worry, your mount will be fine." Somehow he heard her voice clearly beneath the howl of the wind. She pulled him gently by the arm, and he followed.

A few minutes later they entered a cottage built beneath giant pines whose boughs blocked some of the blizzard. He groaned slightly when he heard the door close behind him and felt the warmth of a fire. "You saved me," he said finally, turning to his host. The young woman had already removed her cloak and was hanging it on a peg near the door. When she looked up and smiled, he knew he'd seen her before. "Where do I know you from?" he asked, his hand dropping to the coral hilt.

"I was at the inn tonight when the red man came," she said.

"Ahh," said Toler. "I saw you gather up the remains of the hunters he, what would you call it, killed?"

"Yes."

"How did you find me in the storm? How did you know I was out there?"

"Do you know who I am?" she said.

Toler began to sweat. He shook his head and gripped his sword. "Are you my mother's servant?"

The young woman laughed. "Perish the thought. I'm the crone of Aer."

"The crone of Aer?" said Toler, knowing he'd heard the title before. "Where's Aer?"

"At the end of the valley of the known world," she said.

"You don't look like a crone," he told her.

"To each her crone," she said.

"And so I'm to assume you sent this hellish swordsman after me? Made him of coral so as to cancel the magic of my weapon?"

"That monstrosity isn't mine," she said. "I want to help you defeat it."

"There's not going to be a battle," said Toler. "I'm fleeing for my life. I'm not prepared to meet such an opponent."

"Because he has an advantage like the one your sword, in any other duel, would give to you?"

"Precisely," he said.

"You will fight him," she said.

"I can't."

"I've made you something that will help." She walked past him and the glow of the fireplace into the shadows of the cottage.

Toler sweated profusely; the so recently welcomed warmth was now oppressive. He didn't trust anything. A sword that turns opponents to coral, a red coral man with a crystal sword that turns opponents to salt, and a witch in a cottage in the middle of a blizzard. "Wake up," he whispered to himself, and then the crone of Aer returned, holding a large goose egg out toward him. He took a step back from this new strangeness.

"This egg holds your salvation in a duel with Thybault. Do you remember the salt I gathered at the inn?"

"Yes."

"I mixed it with green vitriol and derived the spirits of salt. They're here in the egg. Merely crack this in the face of Thybault and you will have gained back the advantage."

"What will happen?"

"The spirits will be released."

"I'm going back into the storm," he told her. "I don't trust you. I remember the story my mother told me about you."

"Your mother, who was sent to assassinate me? That demon we saw at the inn tonight, that wasn't my doing."

Toler moved toward the door. His hand touched the knob and he felt a sudden sting at the back of his neck. He tottered for a spell and then fell into the heat of the cottage. The crone spoke directly into his ear. "It's your mother's servant." He woke in the street, the Coral Heart drawn and in his hand, a crowd surrounding him. He heard the church bells and in a second realized he was back in Thyse. He pulled himself up off the frozen mud, and the crowd retreated a few steps. Freezing to the point of shivering and totally confused, he turned to look for an escape from the people, and saw Thybault charging, the crystal blade above his head. He wore no shirt or shoes; the cold meant nothing to him.

Toler crouched and brought his weapon up to block the downward chop of the crystal blade. The crystal clanged off the metal of his weapon, hard as blade steel. He absorbed the blow and rolled away, two somersaults backward and then into a standing position. As he lifted the Coral Heart in defense, he felt the beat of the pulse in his palm. His heart regulated it and regulated the sword. The training he'd done was paying off. Thybault came after him, swinging wildly, massively, as if to cut Toler in half. The red man's blade caught a bystander on the earlobe and made her a cloud of salt. The sight of it distracted the Coral Heart and it was everything he could do to gather in his wonder and counter a thrust of the crystal death.

The duel became fierce, a crazy clash of swords amid the thronging crowd. The pair moved around the street, attacking and defending. At one point, Toler could have sworn that he'd been cut by Thybault. In fact he stopped to look along his side where his shirt was ripped. "Don't you get it," said the red man. "You'll know when I cut you because you'll be a pile of salt." With this, Toler's opponent punched him in the mouth, those polished coral knuckles like a hammer, and sent him stumbling backward into the crowd. Afraid to be caught by an errant blade from the red man, the crowd retreated and let their defender fall on his back in the street.

Again, Thybault advanced, this time more deliberately, as if confident he could finish the duel at will. Someone behind Toler helped him to his feet. As he regained his stance, he felt something smooth slip into his free hand. It could have been a stone by its size, but it lacked the weight. He cantered to the left and began circling Thybault. The red man swung, every time just a second behind the moving target. When Toler stopped abruptly, Thybault kept turning and swinging, and this gave the Coral Heart a chance to look down at the object he held; the crone's goose egg.

He got in two good slashes to the red man's neck, but his blade had little effect upon the coral. Tiny slivers chipped away, leaving barely visible creases. One thing he was sure of was that the longer he could stay alive the better his chances were.

The red man, carrying and swinging the crushing weight of red coral arms, was growing winded. He redoubled his efforts to finish off Toler and came with a barrage of lunges and half fades that pressed the youth back nearly to the wall of the inn.

Thybault then executed an empty fade and instead of retreating lunged with his foot drawn up. He caught Toler in the chest with a kick and slammed him against the wall, knocking the air out of him. He slid down to a sitting position. The Coral Heart had sprung free from Toler's grasp, and the crystal sword advanced, slashing the air.

Thybault stood now above his prey, leering down. The crowd cheered, shifting allegiance upon seeing that Toler was doomed and fearing reprisals from the apparent victor for having initially cheered against him. The red man lifted the gleaming blade into the air for the final blow, and it was here that Toler threw the egg that was still in his hand. It hit his opponent in the face and cracked. Something wet inside spilled across the coral man's visage. He laughed at Toler's desperate attempt at defense, and the crowd joined him.

Then Thybault's face began to smoke and fizz, and a chunk of his chin slid off. The coral man's laughter turned to screams, and the crowd, not knowing how to react, screamed as well. Toler gathered his wits and rolled to where the Coral Heart lay. As he sprang up with his weapon in his grip, Thybault dropped the crystal sword and clawed at his face, more slivers and chunks bubbling pink and fizzing away, coming loose. The Coral Heart didn't rely on the magical properties of his sword but just its strong steel blade, and with a mighty arcing swing, the air singing against the blood groove, he took off his opponents already rotted head. It fell on the ground smoking. A moment later the massive weight of the coral body tipped over and smashed to pieces in the frozen street. The crowd cheered for Toler.

Toler stared at the smoldering face and, in awe, noticed the lips moving. He got down on his knees and put his ear to them. To his astonishment, the sound that came forth was his mother's, -I-'s, voice. "You have now ascended to the third level," she said. "I thought I was to renounce the sword," whispered Toler. "Don't be a fool," were her last words. Then the crowd swarmed him and took him on their shoulders into the inn to celebrate his victory.

Late that night, when he returned to the barn to prepare his things for a journey back to Camiar in the morning, the crone of Aer was waiting for him. She stepped out of the shadows, and her sudden presence made him draw the Coral Heart.

"I noticed Thybault's crystal sword disappeared soon after the duel," he said to her.

"I took it and hid it away. No one will find it. You now have no equal."

"I don't understand my mother's creation."

"She was testing you. She may live in a cave in the mountains, but in her heart she'll always be an assassin."

"But didn't you put a spell on her and change her?"

"That was all just a dream she had, twice deluding herself. You can create incredible, deadly thought-form servants and raise a child while surviving in the mountains, but you can't change what's in your heart."

"So you helped me because she once intended to kill you?"

"From what I saw today," said the crone, "it looks like she intended to kill you as well."

"You said no one else knows where the crystal sword is?" asked Toler.

It was only hours after he'd left the village, riding on a main trail through the Forest of Sans, that the owner of the barn Toler had stayed in found the red coral statue of a young woman with long hair. The man was surprised and perplexed by it for a few years until news of the hard red slaughter reached even Thyse. Upon learning of the Coral Heart, he told his daughter how the ancients once believed that the planet Mars was made of red coral.

The Thyme Fiend

In July of 1915, in Hardin County, Ohio, the normally reliable breeze of the plains that through eons could be counted on for at least a modicum of relief during the most dire of summer days—a wave in the wheat, a whisper in the cornfield—without warning up and died. The relentless blue skies and humidity were merciless; the dream-white clouds, palatial and unmoving. Over ninety degrees every day, often over a hundred, no hint of rain. Fear of crop failure turned like a worm in the heart. Farm folk sweated and burned at their labor, and at night took to either the Bible or the bottle or both. Some children were sent to the evaporating creek to try to catch memories of coolness; some to the distant windbreaks, those thickets of trees, like oases in the vastness of cornfields, to play Desert Island and loll in the shade until the sun went down. More than one mother fainted from the heat of a stove. Nights were better for being dark but offered no relief from the sodden stillness that made sleep so hard to achieve.

On the hottest of the days in that long spell, sometime just before noon, when the sun was at its cruelest, fourteen-year-old Emmett Wallace mounted his bike and, leaving the barnyard, headed out on the dirt road that ran all the way to Threadwell or Mount Victory, depending on which direction you chose. He pedaled slowly west, toward the former, passing between fields of drooping wheat. Turkey vultures circled, casting their shadows on him, and the long straight path he traveled dissolved at a distance into a rippling mirage.

The bike wasn't new, but it was new to him, his first, and the joy of powering himself along, the speed of it, hadn't yet become old hat. It had been a birthday gift from his father not but five days earlier. Bought used, it was a Hercules; a rash of rust across its fading red paint, splintered wooden rims, an unpadded shoehorn of a seat with a saddlebag behind it. There was a small oil lantern with a glass door attached to the handlebars, but the burner was missing.

Nothing was said, but the boy knew the bike had come to him as reparation for an incident that happened in spring. It was after a day of ploughing, dusk coming on, and father and son stood in the barnyard, unhitching the horses. They'd worked for days, from one end of their land to the other. Emmett sensed that he was, for the first time, more an asset in the fields than a distraction and felt a closeness to his father that had been missing in recent months. In that instant it came to him to try to explain just why he needed his cup of tea before bed. The old man had deemed the practice a vain pretension and ordered his wife not to continue it.

Emmett's mother disagreed. "You're not the one who has to get up in the middle of the night and calm the boy down," she said. His father grumbled but knew his place, and she kept on brewing the herbal drink, filling the steel tea ball with thyme from the kitchen garden. It was a remedy for nightmares brought over from the old country.

"I get the terrors otherwise," Emmett explained.

His father stopped and turned to stare at him.

"My skull gets jammed to cracking with demons. Fire. Blood. People crying." He shook his head as he spoke, hoping to better convey his dread.

With a sudden lunge, his father clipped him across the side of the face with the back of his hand. Emmett went down into the dirt, dizzy, his lip bleeding.

"No more of that crazy talk. It's time you grow up," said his father, leading the horses away toward the barn.

The bike was the boy's sign that even though his father had been silent as a gravestone on the subject, he was sorry for what he'd done. That was enough for Emmett, that and the bike, which was finally a means of getting out into the world, beyond the limits of walking. The last book he'd borrowed from the little library Mr. Peasi, the barber, kept in the corner of his shop in Threadwell was Washington Irving's *Tales of the Alhambra*. In daylight Emmett was also a wanderer in both mind and body, a naturalist of the creek bed, a decoder of clouds. While the sun shone, he longed for the world to reveal its mysteries, but at night, without the tea, he'd wake screaming in the clutches of those mysteries within.

The night terrors started the year Emmett was five. For years following, his parents often wondered what had ignited them. They couldn't remember a single remarkable event from that time, traumatic or otherwise. The demons bloomed in a scream one night in the middle of January. It was brutally cold even with both the stove and fireplace roaring. Emmett lay between his parents on a makeshift bed of comforters close to the fire. His sudden bellow, a croaking cry from somewhere deep within, made the blizzard outside seem something out of summer. The boy was never able to give any substantial details about what dreams had plagued him.

Happy to be free of school for the summer and free of his chores for the day, he rode along at a good clip, barely noticing the heat. Pastor Holst's wife passed in her white Studebaker, smiled at the boy in his overalls, no shirt or shoes, and hit the horn, but Emmett was so preoccupied he barely thought to wave until she disappeared ahead in a cloud of dust. He'd been picturing the Addison place, abandoned since five summers earlier—a farmhouse and outbuildings left just as they were, beds made, belongings still in the dressers and closets. The family had fallen on hard times and had left to live with

Mrs. Addison's folks in Indiana. Mr. Addison was supposed to return for some of their things, but once they were gone, they never came back. Emmett's father would say, "I understand Mr. Addison liked his whiskey."

A mile from home, he came to the drive of the abandoned farm, stopped pedaling, and turned to look around. There wasn't a soul in sight. The air, of course, was still, and the sun-burned weedy jumble that was the front lawn of the place was alive with the buzz of insects overheating. Other than that, the day was silent, not even a dog barking in the distance. He rode down the drive and into the open barn, where he dismounted and leaned the bike against the low wall of an empty horse stall.

Last he'd been to the Addisons' two weeks earlier, the mysteries of the main house were plumbed—a broken mirror, which made him wonder if it had been the beginning of their bad luck, women's undergarments in a dresser drawer turned to lace by the swarm of white moths that flew out when he opened it. The place had smelled of mildew and mice, and he decided not to disturb it again, but to investigate the outer buildings, the various sheds, the silo, the icehouse. In his day-dream, he opened the door to the last, and there, still unmelted, were shimmering blocks of frozen freshwater cut from Ziegler's pond, east of Mount Victory, back during the winter he was nine. "Eternal ice," he said to himself as he walked across the burned brown field.

He headed for the icehouse, which sat beneath a giant white oak. On the way, he noticed a well that lay right on the border of the barnyard and the growing fields—a turret of limestone blocks, a wooden support each at north and south to hold the windlass, but the windlass and rope and bucket were missing.

Emmett leaned over the turret's opening and peered down into the cylinder of shadow. He called hello to hear the echo and tossed a stone in to listen for a splash. No splash sounded but he could hear the stone hitting rock at the bottom, and from the sound, the bottom didn't seem all that deep. He backed away from the edge a little and moved a few degrees to the side. The sun directly overhead shone down into the dark, revealing something that made Emmett squint. He stared for a long while and then pushed off the edge of the limestone and ran back to his bike.

He raced down the dirt road, a wake of dust trailing, feeling sick with both excitement and fear. When he was back in the yard of his own home, he jumped off the bike and let it fall in the dirt. "Pa," he yelled. His father called to him, "In the barn." The old man, his shirt drenched, his hat in hand, was sitting on a milking stool, back against the workbench.

Emmett stopped before him and leaned over to catch his breath.

"Well?" said his father.

"Pa, there's a dead person in the well at the Addisons' place." In the instant he'd spoken, he suddenly realized how much trouble he'd be in for having been over there.

His father sat forward and put the hat on. "What were you doing at the Addisons'?"

The boy was silent. Finally he said, "Exploring."

The man shook his head in disappointment. "A dead person?"

"At the bottom of the well."

"You sure the well is dry and you weren't seeing your reflection?" he said and stood up.

"I threw a rock in, there was no splash, and I saw a skull looking up at me."

Dusk gathered in the barnyard of the Addison place and had filled the well to the brim with shadow. Emmett's father said to him, "There better be something down there." Fritz Dibble, a Threadwell Fire Department volunteer, lowered a glowing lantern on a rope into the murky depths. Chief of Police Benton, smoking a roll-up cigarette, hat cocked back, followed the path of light in its descent. He wiped his arm across his forehead and said, "Whew. It's hotter than the widow Alston out here." Dibble smiled, but Emmett's father didn't. Emmett said, "I'm pretty sure I saw a skull," and the chief said, "We'll see about that."

Just as the boy had predicted, the skull was slowly revealed. The attached skeleton still wore tattered clothing. Emmett felt his father's hand lightly touch him on the top of the head. "The lantern?" asked Dibble. The chief said, "Leave it down there," and then called over his shoulder to his young officer, "Johnson, let's get you ready." A new rope was used for Johnson, tied around the tops of his legs and then crisscrossed behind him so that he would sit upright in his descent. When he and the chief thought his rigging was secure, he crawled up onto the edge of the well. Emmett's father sent the boy to the buckboard to fetch their horse, Shadrak. A harness was placed on the animal. "We could use the Model T, but I think the horse'll be gentler," said Benton.

"Just make sure that limestone edge don't cut my rope," said Johnson, who took off his hat and handed it to Dibble. Once his rope was attached to the metal rings of the horse's harness, he lowered his legs over the side and sat on the edge of the well. Emmett's father took the horse by the reins and moved Shadrak forward till the rope connecting Johnson to the animal was taut. "Okay, here we go," said the chief. Johnson leaned forward and inched off the edge of the well. Emmett looked over the side as the horse stepped backward and the officer sank one jerky increment at a time into the orange lantern glow.

"Smells like death," Johnson called up, and the voice echoed.

"Send him down the hook," said the chief, and Dibble set another line over the side tied to the end of a rusty hand scythe he'd found in the Addison barn. "Coming down to your right," Dibble called to Johnson. By then the officer was nearing the bottom of the well. He picked up the lantern by its rope and held it nearer the skeleton. "About a half ton of mouse shit down here," came the echo. Then they heard him gagging. "I think I know who this is," Johnson yelled.

"Who?" asked the chief.

"Jimmy Tooth."

Benton nodded, and after a vacant moment, said, "That actually makes sense," in a voice too low for Johnson to hear. He yelled, "You got him hooked?"

"Yeah."

"Okay, Mr. Wallace," said the chief. "Bring him up."

Emmett's father took the horse by the reins and started forward, again one labored step at a time.

"Jimmy Tooth," said Dibble. "If that's him, he's been down there for about three years."

"That's about right," said Benton.

"Do you think he was drunk and fell in?"

Emmett looked away from the well opening and realized it was twilight. He saw the moon coming up out across the fallow field and had a memory of Jimmy Tooth—a handsome young man with dark eyes, a wave of dark hair, and always a vague grin. He'd heard his mother describe Jimmy as "simple." Tooth worked as an assistant to Avery Cross, the blacksmith, and lived in the back of the shop. Whenever Emmett had been there with his father, he'd never noticed Jimmy say a word that wasn't a repetition of what Cross had just told him. Once every few months, he would spend his pay on a bottle of Old Overholt and rampage through the town, openly leering at women and screaming nonsense.

"Why you say it's Jimmy?" asked the chief.

"The skeleton's wearing the same religious medallion Jimmy used to wear," said Johnson. "Every time we arrested him, and I'd have to remove his belt and belongings, I'd have to take it from around his neck. I remember what it looks like. Saint Benedict."

"Jimmy was a good kid, but a bad drunk," added Dibble.

Emmett's father joined the men at the well and said, "Cross told me Jimmy said that one day he'd take off to Kenton and become a conductor on the railroad to Chicago. When he vanished, that's where we thought he'd gone."

"Threadwell didn't exactly miss him," said the chief.

Night fell, and the empty sockets of the skull peered above the rim of the well.

"Whew, what a stink," said Dibble.

The three men on the rope gave it a long pull to get the corpse to clear the opening, and though it did, falling in a clatter on the ground next to the well, the left leg hit the limestone turret the wrong way and kicked up into the air. It came down right on its heel, and the bony foot cracked off and fell back into the pit.

"Chief," said Johnson, "I ain't going back in after that foot. You want it, you're going to have to go down there."

Benton laughed. "In that case it stays where it is."

Emmett's father retrieved the lantern from the well and held it up high. The chief stood over the corpse. "Looks like someone knocked Jimmy Tooth's teeth out," he said, pointing with the toe of his boot at the one incisor that remained on the upper jaw. "That's irony."

"He could have lost them in the fall," said Johnson. "Or maybe they came out while he lay there rotting. The mice could have took them."

"Did you notice the crack in the back of the skull?" asked Benton.

"Head could have got bashed in the fall," said Johnson.

"I heard you can see the stars during the day from the bottom of a well," said Dibble.

Chief Benton took the feet and Johnson took the shoulders, and they hoisted the remains into the air. Blue flannel shreds, once a shirt, hung down, and the medallion clattered within the rib cage. The jeans, but for small holes, were still intact, the belt fastened around the hip and pelvic bones. Emmett followed them to Dibble's truck, wondering what had happened to the shoes and socks.

"I want a raise," said Johnson, and he and the chief laughed as they loaded the corpse onto the flatbed.

It was past ten when they entered, by the back door, the oven that was their home. Emmett began to sweat the instant they stepped into the kitchen. His father said, "Christ," in a mournful sigh. They moved through the house into the parlor, lit by a single candle. All of the windows were open and the beetles and moths outside bounced and fluttered against the screens. Emmett's mother, dressed in her white cotton shift, lay back in the cushioned chair, mouth open, arms folded, feet up on the hassock, lightly snoring. Her hair was down, draping over her shoulders, and a fly circled her head. On her lap, folded in half, were a few pages of last week's newspaper.

The boy took a step toward her, but his father grabbed him by the shoulder and said, "It's a gift to fall asleep in this weather. Don't wake her."

Emmett stared at the unmoving flame of the candle on the table next to her and forced himself not to mention his tea. His father's hand stayed on his shoulder till the boy turned around and headed for his room.

"Good night, son," said a voice in the dark.

Emmett stripped to his underwear and got into bed. He used the corner of the cover to wipe his forehead and neck before pushing it into a pile at his feet. There was no cool side to the pillow, just one less warm. He lay down in the dark on his back, and before he'd settled his head, he was thinking of Jimmy Tooth. Bits of gristle on the ribs, mouse turds dotting the blood-smeared shreds of blue shirt, cavern openings where the eyes belonged, pencil-sharp fingertips, and that rattling medal. Without the thyme tea, he knew his dreams were sure to be full of demons. He breathed deeply as his mother had taught him when he'd wake screaming from one of the nightmares. "Think logical," she'd repeat, "think logical," and so he tried to.

It didn't make sense that the blacksmith's assistant would be drunk and all the way out at the Addison place when he lived near the center of town. It was a couple miles or more. And with drink in him, he'd be less likely to stray from Main Street, where Emmett knew Jimmy liked to spout lewd sayings and songs in the presence of ladies. Emmett traveled in his mind from farm to farm and house to house throughout town, thinking of each neighbor and what his or her chances were of having committed murder. This had the same effect as counting sheep, and before he was half through the Threadwell of his imagination he fell into a sweat-drenched sleep.

The demons that hunted him in dreams were shadows with teeth. At times they surrounded him, but he never got a clear look at one, only aspects of their silhouettes—a horn, a wing, a mane, a darting serpent tongue. As insubstantial as they seemed, he felt every bite and scratch, every kick and head butt. He was on his bike, pedaling hard, but the road had turned from packed dirt to deep sand. They swept down out of the sky crying like roosters for dawn and snatched him up into the night. For the first time in weeks, he felt the wind in his face. The next he knew, they were flying over the Addison place beneath the stars. They cleared the barn, and, not slowing in the descent, they plunged into the well with Emmett in tow. The pitch-black hole had lost its bottom, and he knew he was headed for that distant place Pastor Holst referred to as perdition.

He woke thrashing and screaming. Before he opened his eyes, he felt a pair of arms around him instead of the clutches of the demons, and he heard, "Shhhhh." With that assurance, he caught his breath and stopped writhing. A moment later, he opened his eyes, and though he expected it to be his mother next to him in the bed in the dark, he slowly came to realize it was his father. "It's all right, I'm here."

A moment later, candlelight seeped into the room and a globe of it encircled his mother as she entered, her white shift glowing. As she spoke, she wiped the sleep out of her eyes. "I hate to start the stove up, but I guess I should brew him a cup of thyme."

"No," said his father. "I'll stay with him. Go on to bed."

Emmett watched, in his mother's expression, her weighing of his words. She lifted her hand holding the candle and wiped the sweat from her brow with the back of her wrist. Finally, she nodded. "It'd be better not to light the stove." She turned and left, darkness reclaiming the room. The boy wanted to reach for her, but he didn't. Instead his father placed an open hand on his chest and gently pushed him back onto the pillow. "Lay still," came the voice. "I'll be here." Emmett closed his eyes. Once sleep rose up around him like water, and once he felt himself on the verge of falling into it. With both instances, he reached for his father and both times he was there.

The demons didn't slip into his ears again till dawn, but when they did, Emmett came screeching out of sleep from the pressure in his head. His heart pounded, and he gasped for breath. With the faint light seeping in the windows, he saw that his father had gone off to bed and left him. Even after waking and regaining composure, his head still spun with the circular motion, thinking, and torment of his phantasms. A memory of Jimmy Tooth in skeletal form farming three hundred burning acres in hell kept flickering behind his eyes. Instead of wheat, his crop was flames, and at harvest, he took them to market to sell to the devil.

He got out of bed and slipped on his overalls. Tiptoeing through the kitchen, he avoided the spots where the floorboards squeaked. Quietly opening the back door, he stepped out into the early light. It was so humid, he felt as if he were at the bottom of the pond. Nothing moved. The birds were too hot to sing, and the creepers must have turned to dust. He made his way to the kitchen garden, knelt down and grabbed a handful of thyme, and tore it out by the roots. Part of the jumble was still green but part had burned in the glare of the sun. He brought it to his mouth, but then heard his father and mother up in the house. Emmett took off and ran around behind the barn. With his back to the wall, listening to the noise of his mother heading out to the well pump to fetch coffee water, he stared into the field, waiting for her to be done.

At the boundary where the rows of corn met the yard there was a disturbance in the air. It wasn't a breeze, as the corn stood stock-still. At first he thought it was some large insect, hovering—a moon moth late in fleeing the sun. But no, the very air seemed to pucker there and grow a vertical seam. When two bony hands clawed through the fabric of the air, Emmett shoved the handful of thyme from the kitchen garden into his mouth and chewed, his teeth sparking off grains of dirt, the green peppery taste of the herb mixing with his saliva.

Sharp skeleton fingers pried an opening through which the boy saw fire and heard distant voices crying for mercy. The corpse of Jimmy Tooth stepped through that hole into the day, left foot missing, still dressed in the shreds of shirt and jeans. It moved toward Emmett unevenly from foot to tibia end and back, lurching forward with clear intent. The boy chewed faster as it approached and faster still. After two more steps, the grim skeleton evaporated, leaving no sign that it had come for him. He sighed, and when he did he noticed the corn ripple slightly in a breeze.

He wore a starched white shirt and a tie, his short hair pushed up and stuck in place with Bear Wax. The ride from home in the buckboard—his mother and father up front and him in the back watching the wake of dust trail behind them—was glorious. The early evening fields swayed with the motion of the newborn wind and brought him smells of the creek, wildflowers, and honeysuckle. The tiny chorus frogs had found their old rhythmic thrum and two saw-whet owls perched in the dead tree next to the bridge that crossed a shallow gully just before town.

The church seemed stuffy in comparison with the coolness of the evening outside. The coffin, made of simple pine, rested on a pair of sawhorses draped with a red cloth and flanked at head and foot by tall candle stands each holding three lit tapers. It was a closed casket, of course. Mrs. Williams, the local carpenter, who'd taken on the business when her husband had passed away, could be overheard to say she'd worked on the box half through the night. As a special touch in honor of Jimmy, she'd chiseled out the likeness of a locomotive on the lid. "Well, he can finally be a conductor," Avery Cross said and smiled. Mrs. Williams patted the blacksmith on the shoulder. Mayor Fense was present and Chief Benton, Officer Johnson, Mr. Dibble, and all the neighbors, men and women and girls and boys. Mothers and wives brought food, and once the pastor had said his piece for the unfortunate young man, the mourners would convene at tables on the lawn and feast in the miraculous breeze. As Emmett looked around the church, he noticed no one was crying, and no one was standing near the coffin. There were pockets of people milling in the aisles and sitting side by side in the pews, but the conversations looked so casual and offhand that it was obvious they were discussing the weather. Miss Billie Maufin, the schoolteacher, said to Emmett's parents that the windless weeks reminded her of a poem wherein a ship was becalmed upon the sea. "'The Ancient Mariner,'" said his father, and Miss Maufin nodded. "Like a painted ship upon a painted ocean," she said. "That's what we were."

Mayor Fense, holding his bowler under his arm and frequently stroking his beard, told anyone who would listen to him about his theory of where the wind had gone. In his no-hurry drawl, he said, "Down in Kentucky, on July the seventh they had a biblical windstorm that flattened buildings, killed dozens, and tossed the trains from the tracks in Cincinnati. They said they never saw the like of it. But don't you know, that's where our wind went to. It got used up in that storm and we had to wait some weeks for another crop."

"Poor Jimmy Tooth," said Mr. Peasi, the barber. "Last I cut his hair—he had strong hair—he told me that he was soon gonna run off and get married to a secret sweetheart. Daft, but a likeable fellow nonetheless."

"I recall him being gentle with the horses," said the pastor.

When all the gossiping and talk of the wind diminished into silence, Pastor Holst put on his hat—a broad-brimmed affair with a black satin handkerchief stitched to the front of the inner brim so that the material hung down, covering his face to midchin. He'd taken to wearing it for funerals, baptisms, and marriages, after having read a story about a preacher who wore one in a book he got from the barber's library. When wearing it, he assumed a stiff posture and intoned his words in a voice from the distant past. "Ridiculous," whispered Emmett's mother.

"Jimmy Tooth, you were one of us," said Holst, the satin lifting slightly with every word. "We thank you for sharing your days with us. We thank you for your hard work at the anvil. We forgive your indiscretions and offer prayers to carry you to your just reward." The pastor stepped away from the coffin, and his wife stepped forward. She carried a basket at her side. With her free hand, she reached into the basket and brought out a fistful of dried thyme to place in a small pile at the head of the coffin. This she did three times so there was a sizeable mound of the green powder. "Go forth in peace," she said, as she always did at wakes. The words and the ritual had been passed down from the grandmothers of grandmothers. The herb that brought peace in sleep also offered courage in death.

There was an amen from the pastor that echoed through the church, and a feeble response. Then the doors were thrown open and the neighbors of Threadwell filed out. Emmett was slow to get up, thinking about, as Holst had put it, Jimmy Tooth's just reward—a fire farm in hell. "Em," his mother called to him from the center aisle, and he looked up. She waved her hand for him to follow, and he did. With the doors open before them, the wind swept in and down the aisles of the church to snuff the candles.

There were three long tables set with white tablecloths and napkins held down against the breeze by utensils and plates. These along with eighteen long benches were set up on the lawn of the church. The sun was going down, and the pastor's wife was lighting candles in glass globes. Kids were running in circles on the dry lawns. The trees at the boundary of the churchyard shook their leaves in the wind. People chose seats along the three tables, and the potato salad, chicken, coleslaw, and biscuits were passed. Chief Benton leaned against the giant wooden cross in the center of the lawn, smoking a cigarette, and Dr. Summerhill smoked his pipe. Emmett told his mother he was going to go run with the other kids for a few minutes and she said, "Fine." He left her side and bolted across the lawn, where kids from his school were chasing lightning bugs. On his way toward them, though, he was stopped cold. His body registered it before he was even sure what had frightened him. There, sitting at the end of the third long table, the one farthest from the church door, was Jimmy Tooth, not a ghost but his gnawed skeleton as it had been dragged from the well. Mr. Dibble sat next to the corpse but didn't seem to notice it was there. Across from the specter sat Miss Billie Maufin. She buttered a biscuit and smiled and listened to Mr. Peasi, who was next to Dibble.

Emmett dropped to his knees on the dry grass. He was already trembling and was having trouble catching his breath. He watched, trying to croak out the word *help*, as Jimmy Tooth's skull swiveled around, taking in the crowd. Thinking that if he averted his eyes, he wouldn't be seen, the boy turned his face to the ground. The realization came to him then that no one else could see the skeleton in jeans and blue tatters. He looked back to check if his nightmare had vanished. At that moment, Tooth's empty eye sockets seemed to take him in. The skeleton stood awkwardly up from the table, holding on with one bony hand and righting its imbalance. Once the figure was stable, it started in Emmett's direction, limping along on foot and tibia stub.

Suddenly at his side was a girl from school, Gretel Lawler, who sometimes sat quietly next to him and read, as he did, on the bench beneath the oak during recess. "Are you all right, Emmett?" she said.

He looked up into her face, stunned with fear. At any other time he'd not have minded her being so close, but it was almost as if he was afraid that she'd see the reflection of Jimmy Tooth in his eyes.

"I'll get your ma," said Gretel.

Emmett shook his head. "I'm fine," he managed. He felt her hand on his shoulder, and he looked up at her. She was smiling down at him, and her green eyes and dimples and freckles diverted his fear for an instant. He was about to say thanks, when from behind her sweet face, Jimmy Tooth's skull descended into view and his jaw squealed open. A burst of adrenaline went off in the boy's chest like a half stick of dynamite, and he scrabbled up off the grass and ran, his heart pounding, a ringing in his ears.

The gathering shadows of twilight covered his retreat, and everyone was preoccupied with the dinner and conversation. Emmett didn't look back to see if the corpse was following him. Opening the oak door of the church, he slipped inside and let it swing shut behind him. Someone had relit one of the tapers in the candelabra at the foot of the coffin, and that meager flame was the sole light he had to navigate his way to the altar.

When he reached the coffin, he heard the church door open behind him. He didn't turn but reached up onto the top of the pine box and with his right hand swept the top half of the pile of dried thyme to the edge of the planks. Cupping his left hand he caught the dark green powder and then brought it directly to his mouth. He chewed on it like he was chewing on dust. It stuck in his dry throat, and he momentarily choked. Thyme sprayed out onto the altar at his feet. Still he didn't turn, but swept the remainder off the coffin. Swallowing hard with little spit, he poured the second handful into his mouth and resumed chewing.

He sat down on the altar step to catch his breath as he worked the second load of thyme down his throat. And now he looked to see if Jimmy Tooth was coming up the aisle for him. Instead he saw, standing a few paces behind him, a figure in black without a face, wearing a broad-brimmed hat.

"What are you doing?" asked Pastor Holst in his most austere voice.

Emmett stammered, thyme spewing from his mouth. He eventually managed to get out that he needed the herb to keep the demons away from him.

"I see," said Holst, removing his hat. He squatted down next to the boy and told him, "You're safe now. We'll keep this to ourselves." As it turned out, everyone in Threadwell knew by the end of that week. When at the close of July, after having been spotted raiding the kitchen gardens and herb gardens of neighboring farms by dark of night, Emmett was found one morning in his underwear, lying filthy and unconscious in the garden of the widow Alston. His cheek was puffed out like a pouch to hold the cud of thyme he chewed even in sleep. In his left hand his fingers clutched another shock of the green, ripped out by its roots. It was the widow herself who first used the words *thyme fiend*, but the name caught on and it spread like fire through the community.

The harvest was blighted by the heat of July, a full quarter of the crop gone brown and desiccated. A day in late October after the last yield was taken, Threadwell and the surrounding area were inundated with a plague of ash-colored moths that appeared by the millions overnight. A day later they vanished, but not before Pastor Holst could use them from the pulpit in reference to the burning city of Gomorrah. He'd taken to wearing the hat and black handkerchief now also for Sunday mass, and he bellowed that sin was afoot. "Strange customs have been allowed to flourish," he said, turning his face in the direction of Emmett and his mother and father in the third row of pews.

"Strange customs my eye," said Emmett's mother as they rode in the buckboard back to the farm. "Like him wearing that fool hat and mask." Emmett's father nodded, and that's all that was said on the journey. The boy sat in the back of the rig, staring off across the fields where the leaves of the windbreaks had gone yellow and orange. He hadn't had a full night's sleep for three days. The insomnia came with his realization that there was no more thyme in Threadwell. He'd decimated every garden, even snuck into the church the nights of two wakes and consumed every grain of dust that made up the ritual piles atop the coffins. There'd be no relief till spring. Emmett shifted his gaze from the distant trees to the bony remains of Jimmy Tooth, sitting across from him in the back of the buckboard.

The phantasm had not come to harm Emmett but to follow him, and when the last of the herb had been swallowed and its effects dissipated, that's what it did. It appeared first in his room, in the dark, standing at the window in the moonlight peering out across the fields. The boy was too terrified to scream and lay trembling. Occasionally, Jimmy would turn his skull, that stringy patch of hair barely hanging on, and move his bottom jaw up and down as if talking. No words came forth, only a subtle squeaking noise of the dry joint. Although the eye sockets were hollow, the corpse had a way of staring, and more than once seemed to focus those portals on Emmett. Even after the birds sang, the rooster crowed, and sunlight filled the room, Jimmy Tooth remained, sitting at the end of the bed while Emmett got dressed for school.

After only a week, his mother and father noticed his feeble condition—weary and yet fidgeting with nerves, a pale complexion, a drawn expression. They ambushed him in the barn one afternoon when he was stowing his bike after school. His mother was sitting on an overturned bale of hay, his father on the workbench. They had a chair ready for him. Jimmy sat up above in the hayloft, his foot and stump dangling above Mrs. Wallace's head. The boy took the seat they pointed to and looked up. The bone architecture was lit by the beams of sunlight slipping through tiny holes in the roof. His arms were raised, and he was wiggling the sharp white fingers of both hands.

"Emmett, you're not well," said his father.

"Do the children torment you at school?" his mother asked.

Emmett nodded. "The whole town thinks I'm touched."

"What can we do?" asked his father.

"It's the thyme," said his mother. "You need it, don't you?"

"I need it," he said. "Without it I see something bad all day and night."

"Well, I put an order in at Stamp's Grocery for a five-pound satchel of it, dried. Should be here in a couple days," said his father.

The boy got up and went to his mother and hugged her, then his father, who patted him lightly on the top of the head.

"Now," said his mother, "do you want to stop going to school? Maybe for a while?"

"You could help me here," said his father.

"No," he said. "I want to go."

On the day the satchel of thyme arrived, Emmett and his father and Jimmy Tooth sat at the kitchen table. Mr. Wallace instructed on how to roll a respectable cigarette. It took the destruction of a half-dozen rolling papers and a scattering of thyme before the boy caught on. When he finally had before him a tightly rolled bone of uniform width, his father handed him a box of matches. Emmett lit one, brought it to the end of the cigarette, and inhaled the way he'd seen Chief Benton do.

"Easy," said his father and the boy exploded with a choking cough.

When Emmett was done gasping and wiping his eyes, he noticed Jimmy Tooth was gone. Just that second, his mother had come in from the parlor and pulled back the chair the skeleton had been in.

"I hope you two aren't engaging in strange customs," she said.

Emmett took another drag, and laughed along with his father.

"At night you'll have the tea," said his mother.

Thyme as smoke still had the same dark green taste and subtle bite. The boy could feel it wafting in lazy cyclones through his mind, and after three drags and three long exhalations of the gray-green mist, he felt the tension leaving the muscles of his neck and back. He blew a smoke ring, and as he watched it float out over the table, where his father poked a finger through the widening circle, it came to him that his parents must think him insane or simple or both. Their insipid smiles became clear to him. Were they trying to help him or help themselves in the eyes of the community? It was all too much to decipher. Jimmy Tooth was gone, and the rest he'd worry about later.

A cup of tea at bedtime took care of the visitations through the night. One roll-up before school and one after kept the day revenant free. On a rare occasion, the doses of thyme wouldn't quite overlap and Emmett would catch sight of Jimmy, approaching across the barnyard or sitting cramped in the corner of the outhouse, watching the boy with a hollow stare as he shit. These sudden relapses were startling, but once they happened, Emmett gained control of himself, knowing there was plenty of thyme left in the satchel.

The protocol worked smoothly into November. He was doing better in school, getting sleep and feeling good. The ruckus over "the thyme fiend" died down, and no longer were people shouting at him or saying mean things. Their hot disdain had cooled into a general agreement that he was to be avoided. That change was good enough for Emmett. He didn't mind going his own way.

The break from Jimmy Tooth gave him time to get back to reading, and he finished Irving's *Tales of the Alhambra*. The next day he brought the book to school and afterward to the barbershop to return it and see if he could borrow another. When he entered the shop from the side door, he noticed that Peasi had a customer in the chair. The barber looked over and saw Emmett standing there holding the book. The scissors stopped snipping and with one hand Peasi ran a comb through the customer's hair. With the other, he motioned for the boy to stand where he was and then put his finger to his lips. Emmett nodded.

A few moments later the barber was applying a hot towel to the customer's face. Once that was securely in place, he turned to Emmett and motioned for him to come forward. He nodded toward the bookshelf and again brought his finger to his lips. The boy understood and paced softly on the sides of his shoes. Even with the precaution, he hit a creaking plank right behind the barber's chair. The customer's voice sounded, "Someone come in?" Emmett knew immediately it was Chief Benton.

"No, no," said Peasi. "Just the floorboards. They creak and pop all day and night. This place is like an old bum with arthritis."

"That makes two of us," said Benton.

Emmett placed his book on the shelf, and, not wanting to get the barber in trouble for being nice to him, just grabbed the first book to hand. He waved as he crept cautiously back toward the door. Peasi wasn't watching but was busy with his lather cup and brush. Once out in the lot next to his bike, Emmett quickly looked at the title—*Off on a Comet*, by Jules Verne. He stowed the novel in his bike bag, mounted up, and headed down the alley for the street. When he came clear of the buildings, he looked across Main at the door of the Handsome Man Tavern and knew he'd taken too long to get home from school.

There was Jimmy Tooth, standing, facing the plate glass window, showing no reflection. The corpse gave an awkward half turn, and Emmett heard the medallion bounce from across the street. Jimmy focused that cavernous gaze from over his shoulder. He lifted a thin white arm and waved to Emmett as if to follow. The shreds of blue shirt rippled with the motion, and he did it again, twice. Emmett took off down Main for the dirt road that led out toward the farms.

A half hour later, he was sitting in the hayloft, smoking a thyme roll-up and paging through the Verne book. He'd have loved to start reading it, but something bothered him about his encounter with Jimmy Tooth. The specter hadn't followed him as he fled home for his cure. He wasn't waiting in the barnyard, slouched against the white oak, wiggling his sharp fingers at the sun. He was nowhere. As Emmett smoked the rest of the cigarette, he pictured the figure waving for him to follow. In that arm motion and that hollow gaze there was a purpose.

There was still snow on the ground the following week when he left school and rode into town instead of going home. A freezing wind shrieked across the fields and made pedaling difficult. There weren't many people out, but those there were, Pastor Holst and Mr. Dibble, both in turn crossed to the other side of the street when they saw him riding toward them. Emmett noticed that the pastor had taken to wearing the hat and veil all the time now, stumbling along partially blind, grazing the poles of the gas lamps and keeping his right arm extended.

Emmett rode his bike to the edge of town where it bordered on a tract of woods. There was a bench there, down an embankment, by the edge of Wildcat Creek. It was out of the wind. He watched across the frozen creek, scattered with leaves, trying to catch the moment when the influence of that morning's thyme smoke would finally pass. He felt no change. Leaning back, he closed his eyes, sighed, and conjured a recollection of a moment he spent with Gretel Lawler after school the day before. He always stayed in the schoolhouse and waited for the other kids to clear out before going to his bike. When they were gone, he slipped out, and she was there, next to her bike, which was next to his, waiting for him.

Her hair was in a single long braid, and her red winter hat framed her face, set off her green eyes. Emmett noticed that her freckles had faded, and instead her cheeks were dotted with glitter from the day's Christmas project. "Emmett Wallace, we should go for a bike ride some day after school," she said.

He stopped walking, numb with surprise. Finally, he said, "Don't you know I'm the thyme fiend?" He forced a laugh, but it came too quiet and flat.

Gretel laughed. "What's the sin?" she said. "It's like eating grass. My old man drinks Overholt till he's blind drunk and nobody bats a lash."

"When?" asked Emmett.

"You say," she said.

"Next Wednesday."

She laughed again. "Why Wednesday?"

"That's what came to me."

She reached out and touched his shoulder, and Emmett came awake with that touch to see Jimmy Tooth standing over him, quickly withdrawing his hand. The boy gasped and reared back, pressing himself into the bench. He was startled and confused as to whether the touch he felt on his shoulder was merely the one from the daydream or if the specter could now make contact. Sunset was coming on. The corpse turned and motioned for the boy to follow across the frozen creek.

His parents would be wondering where he was. He'd miss dinner. He was frightened, but he leaped up, leaving his bike, and hobbled down the bank, slid across the ice, into the woods beyond. Jimmy Tooth was waiting for him in a small clearing. When Emmett caught up, the skeleton reached out as if to shake hands. The boy was stunned for a moment and then backed up a step. Jimmy held his posture, waiting, skull cocked to the side like a marionette at rest. A minute passed in silence, and then Emmett stepped forward. His hand passed through its skeletal partner. It wasn't merely thin air, though; he felt something like a mild turbulence when his fingers failed to grasp Jimmy's.

In that instant, the two of them turned to salt and were whisked up into the sky in an insane whirlwind. They were moving fast through the dark, and how Emmett knew he'd been turned to salt, he didn't know. He saw the lights of the town below and in the distance the last line of pink on the horizon. Then they descended and were standing in the dark, again by the creek, but somewhere different from where they'd started.

"What was that?" asked the boy, working to regain his balance.

Jimmy put a finger to his bottom jaw to signal silence and led the way.

They came out of the woods on the opposite side of town in the field behind the church. Off to the left was a stand of half a dozen horse chestnuts, and from within their cover, Emmett spotted a lighted window. Jimmy headed directly for it, and the boy had to run to catch up. In under the barren branches of the trees, drawing closer to the glow of the window, they slowed and crept to avoid breaking sticks underfoot. Each took a side and peered in—a skull in the bottom left pane and Emmett Wallace in the bottom right.

In lantern light, Mrs. Holst sat with her back to them at a vanity with a large oval mirror. Emmett could see the reflection of her face in the glass as she brushed her hair. She never appeared in public with it down, and he couldn't believe how much of it there actually was. He wondered how she stowed it on her head. She had remained kind even after the town and particularly the pastor had turned against him. There had been more than one occasion when he'd gone to the back door of the very house he now hid beside, and if her husband was out, she'd give him two pocketfuls of thyme from the supply they kept for wakes. He had a crush on her smile and the way she drove the white Studebaker, speeding along once out of town.

A heartbeat later, Jimmy Tooth was inside the room, and Emmett leaned dazed against the house. He watched as the skeleton slowly walked up behind the pastor's wife. She was brushing on the left, holding the hair back away from her ear and neck. Jimmy descended with grace, turned his skull head toward her cheek, and gave her a quick kiss. Before her brush rose to the top of her head again, he was up and away, walking back toward the window. Just as the corpse stepped through the wall of the house, Emmett again caught a glimpse of her reflection and noticed that where Jimmy had kissed her, she now bore a black spider of a scar.

So intense was his focus on the mark that he didn't notice at first the figure in a black hat and handkerchief mask enter the room. Jimmy obviously did, though. He grabbed Emmett by the wrist and pulled him back. "How?" Emmett wondered, feeling the hard bony grip on his arm. In the next moment, the pastor was at the window, peering out through the dark scrim and glass into the dark. He lifted off his hat to see better, and that's when the boy and skeleton again turned to salt and were whisked upward into the sky.

When they coalesced this time, they were standing in front of an ancient structure that Emmett, even at night, was able to identify. It was the old Threadwell icehouse, the one that had been on the farmland that the town was eventually built on. It happened to sit behind the Williams place, a hundred or so yards behind the carpentry shop. His father had brought him back to see it one time when they'd been to visit Mrs. Williams about building a dresser for Emmett's mother. Mr. Wallace had explained that there was an outer and an inner wall, separated by about a foot all around, and that space was filled with sawdust for insulation. As old as the icehouse was—built in 1887— and as hard worn, it was still intact. The big door was on its hinges, the walls stood save for splintering and wormholes, and there were no windows, so no glass to be broken.

Jimmy Tooth pointed to the door and motioned for Emmett to open it and go inside. The boy looked at him, and, thinking about how the specter had physically seized him before, he was skeptical. Tooth put his palms together in the sign of prayer and then pointed to the door again, as if begging. After seeing the mark he'd left on Mrs. Holst's cheek, Emmett wanted nothing but to be home, a roll-up in the corner of his lips, paging through Jules Verne. He'd thought he wanted to know what it all meant, but that was forgotten. Jimmy clasped his hands with a click in front of him again, and a voice came out of the night from up by the back of the carpentry shop.

"Who is that over there?" it called.

Emmett knew it was Mrs. Williams.

"Get away from there." It sounded as if she was getting closer.

The skull gazed directly at the boy, and in its empty sockets, something strange was happening. Emmett saw the colors of sunset deep inside Jimmy's head. Then he felt a cold wind, the one everyone had wished for in July, rushing around him. Mrs. Williams bellowed, "Emmett Wallace, is that you?"

"Run now," whispered Jimmy.

The boy moved his legs, up and down, up and down, and looked across the fields to the sunset. Jimmy's diminishing whisper was still on the wind. A moment later, Emmett came to the realization that he was riding his bike on the dirt path homeward from town and the sun was still an hour from setting. He'd not missed dinner. In fact, he would hardly be later than usual. The entire episode seemed a dream, and yet he was certain it had all really happened.

His conviction was borne out at Sunday mass when Mrs. Holst appeared, bearing the mark on her face. He was certain that no one else was seeing it as no one else seemed disturbed and it was perfectly disturbing—a black center with thin black cracks radiating away from it. He was sure it had grown larger. Still, he wondered why it was that he had to be there to witness Jimmy Tooth kiss the pastor's wife. And how did it involve the old icehouse? His mind wandered for a moment and he remembered that the day he'd discovered Jimmy, he was heading for the icehouse on the Addison property. His vision of eternal ice came back to him, but none of it led anywhere, and it turned to salt on the wind.

After mass let out, the parishioners stood on the church lawn in small clusters, catching up on news and gossip. Emmett stood off by himself near the buckboard while his parents passed the time with the widow Alston. Studying the scene from afar, he closely followed the actions of Mrs. Holst. She had knelt on the cold ground to put her arms around the youngest Fenwick girl. "She's going to die," he said to himself. "That's what the mark is." He watched as she rose, her beaming smile nearly a distraction from the horror on her cheek. "No," he whispered. "Someone's going to kill her."

Emmett thought frantically about how he could warn her, but his concentration was broken by a voice close by. He looked up and saw Mrs. Williams standing a few yards off. She was dressed in a blue, man's roll-collar coat, beneath the hem of which showed the striped design of her dress. Her long frizzy hair undulated in the wind. She was wide in the shoulders and slim at the waist, and her eyes crinkled down to mere slits when she spoke.

"You know something, don't you, Thyme Fiend?"

Emmett was caught off guard. He stared at the ground and said, "Yes, ma'am."

"I know you know something," she said and then walked off to join the others.

He spent the ride home in the buckboard and the better part of the afternoon trying to figure out what she thought he knew.

On Wednesday, he left for school prepared for the afternoon, with a thyme roll-up and a box of wooden matches in his pocket. The smoke he'd had after breakfast took him through the school day and after, when he met Gretel Lawler by the bike rack. They made for town, pedaling through the golden last light of the afternoon, heads down against a fierce wind. There was a light dusting of snow on the frozen dirt road, and their bikes skidded here and there, which they pretended was hilarious. He led her to the bench in the woods at the edge of town, next to the creek, and proceeded to tell her everything.

Every few minutes out of the forty-five it took him to tell her pretty much the whole strange saga of his doings with Jimmy Tooth, he asked her a question. "You following this?" "You scared?" "You think I'm crazy?" To all of these, she answered by shaking her head. He could tell she was getting it, and better yet, could picture it, by the gleam in her eyes. The relief of being able to share all of his fear and confusion nearly brought tears. She didn't laugh or act stupid about it. She listened so intently, at one point he wondered if she was crazy.

When he finished speaking, relating to her his flight above the town with Jimmy Tooth and the peeping tom visits to the pastor's wife and Mrs. Williams, there was a brief silence before she said, "So you must be wanting to go see what's in that old icehouse."

"That's what I want to do," he said.

"Okay."

In his plans for Gretel Lawler, he never imagined it would be so easy.

They left the bikes and headed across the creek into the woods. The carpentry shop wasn't far at all from that end of town. They could circle around behind it through the trees, cross the creek again, and come out in ten minutes a few feet from the icehouse. He led the way, bent slightly and whispering because they were on a secret mission. "That pastor is mighty strange, eh?" she said. "My pa says they'll be sending him off to the loony bin before long."

"You think he could have killed Jimmy Tooth and thrown his body in the Addisons' well?"

"I can't see it," she said. "He seems kind of useless, like it would be too much for him. Best he can do is put on that hand-kerchief hat."

"I know what you mean," said Emmett.

"Mrs. Williams, though," said Gretel, "why's she so worried about what you know?"

"She always seemed nice to me, but when she said what she said to me out on the church lawn, it gave me a shiver. I got the feeling she could be as mean as she wanted."

"What about the spider kiss the skeleton gave Mrs. Holst?" asked Gretel.

"I have a feeling somebody is gonna kill her."

"Like Jimmy Tooth knows the future? Or like Jimmy Tooth put a curse on her?" she asked.

Emmett had no answer and shook his head. They got down on their hands and knees and crawled to the edge of the treeline. From where they squatted, behind the bole of a long-ago fallen oak, they could see the icehouse, clear as day, no more than twenty-five yards into the open field behind the carpentry shop. From up in the shop they heard the sound of a hammer pounding cut nails. Emmett turned to Gretel and looked at her. He couldn't believe he had a friend after not having one since July. She smiled at him, and he said, "Let's go."

They crouched as they made their way to the structure, using it to block any view of them from the carpentry shop. When they stood against its western wall, Emmett inched forward and looked around the corner to see if Mrs. Williams was in sight. Eventually he waved over his shoulder for Gretel to follow him. He got his hand on the door and pulled back, expecting it to be locked. Instead it swept open with little more than a grumble from the hinges. They slipped inside, and he said for her to hold it open just a sliver so he could see. There was an old oil lantern hanging from a hook just inside the door. He reached into his pocket and took out the box of wooden matches. There was still oil in the rusted old lamp and the wick was damp with it. He removed its glass globe, thumbnail lit a match, and brought light to the shadows. The sight of the flame reminded him he hadn't smoked his afternoon roll-up yet.

The inside of the place, lined with cedar wood, was much smaller that the outside. The walls were in the shape of an octagon. They were standing on a huge trapdoor, and Gretel said, "They must keep the ice down there." With the exception of a couple of wooden shelves lining each wall, and the remainder of the floor not covered by the hatch being poured concrete, there was nothing much to see.

"Looks like Jimmy Tooth sent you on a wild-goose chase," said Gretel.

"Maybe he meant we have to go down there," he said, pointing to the trapdoor. He leaned over and tried the handle. It didn't budge and he tried it with two hands. Gretel walked over when he was done and gave it a tug.

"Well," he said, and they stood there close together in silence for a long while.

"Hey, what's that in the corner?"

He lifted the lantern off the hook and followed her. She knelt next to the wall opposite the door they'd come in. Emmett tried to see what she was looking at over her shoulder. She slowly turned toward him, her palm up and her brow furrowed.

"Is that chips of ice?" he asked and brought the lantern closer to her hand.

"No, teeth."

A moment passed and then Emmett said, "You gotta know what I'm thinking."

Gretel nodded. "Jimmy Tooth's teeth."

"The rest must have got cleaned up, but they missed these."

"I'll bet."

She handed him the three teeth, each cracked off at the root, and he stowed them deep in his pocket.

"Let's get out," he said, and with that, the icehouse door slammed shut and they heard a key turning in its lock.

"Wait!" he yelled. "We're in here."

"Hey," called Gretel, whose voice was higher and louder than his.

In the silence that followed, as if from a great distance, they heard a woman's voice. At first they couldn't make out what she was saying, but slowly her words came clear. "You've gobbled your last thyme patch, Emmett Wallace."

"Please," he yelled back. "We won't tell anyone."

"Is she going to bash our teeth out with a hammer?" asked Gretel.

The friends stood perfectly still, taking shallow breaths in order to better hear their captor. Emmett was sure it was Mrs. Williams. Even in her muffled voice he could detect that chilling thread of nastiness. The time passed, but they were afraid to move. When after a long while, they heard nothing, they went to work on the door by which they'd entered, kicking it and ramming their shoulders into it. It didn't move an inch.

"If she comes in with her hammer, we'll both rush her at the same time," said Gretel.

Emmett swallowed hard and agreed, unsure if he'd be able to.

They wore themselves out pounding and screaming and eventually slumped down together onto the trapdoor at the center of the eight-sided room. She put her arm around him, put her head on his shoulder, and neither of them spoke. The oil lamp flickered now and then, and Emmett wondered how much longer it would be before they were swamped by total darkness.

An hour later, they heard knocking noises from outside. Emmett crawled forward to the door and put his ear to the thin slit between its bottom and the floor. He barely heard Mrs. Williams's voice. "We'll be done with this little peckerwood," she said. Then another voice answered her. "A blight of a child," said a man.

"What about Miss Angel Cake?"

"I fixed the brakes, and I'm sending her on an errand to Mount Victory," he said.

"More kerosene around the base," she commanded. "That dry old sawdust'll go up in a blink."

Emmett felt a hand on his shoulder. "What's she doing?" whispered Gretel.

Jeffrey Ford

"The pastor is with her," said Emmett, moving back away from the door as the smell of kerosene sifted in beneath it. He didn't have the heart to tell her the rest.

A few minutes later, the cedar room grew hotter, smoke issuing in from beneath the door and between the wall slats.

"I want to go home," cried Gretel. She screamed for help and lunged at the door, pounding and kicking. Emmett was paralyzed with fear, unable to move off the concrete. That's when the lamp went out and they heard the crackling of the fire all around them. She found him in the dark, and they put their arms around each other. They were gasping. Their hearts were pounding.

Just as the flames began poking through the inner wall, bringing back the light and casting jittery shadows, there was a loud bang. The trapdoor flew open and slammed back on the concrete only inches from them. Jimmy Tooth slowly ascended from the ice hold below. His skull and ribs glowed in the firelight, and the tattered shirt smoldered where embers had landed. Emmett saw him emerge through the smoke, that near-toothless open mouth either screaming or laughing. There were tiny fires burning in the hollows of his eyes. With sharp, cold hands, the phantasm grabbed both the boy and girl by the wrists, and they were off.

Emmett felt himself dropping, felt the heat increasing. He finally mustered the courage to open one eye. They were drifting down through the darkness, into a vast cavern. Everywhere, stretching out to the horizon of the cave as big as Ohio, there were fields of fire, the flames growing individually in rows like corn. Their orange stalks, their sharp white tips bowed and rippled in a strong sweltering breeze. Directly below there was a clearing of black rock where the boy spotted Jimmy Tooth's farmhouse as he'd seen it in his daydream.

There was an instant of forgetting and then Gretel and Emmett were standing beside Jimmy Tooth at the edge of the field of fire. The skeleton was sweeping his arm out to indicate his infernal crop. "I got a thousand acres of torment here," he said, speaking in the voice of the Jimmy Emmett remembered from life. Words came forth from the empty skull in a weak echo. "For every acre's worth I bring to Satan, he reduces my own anguish a half a dust mote's worth."

The boy had the sense that they'd been on a tour of the farm for a while before he'd come to. "Are we dead?" he asked.

"You ain't dead," said Jimmy.

"What about me?" asked Gretel.

"You're neither dead nor alive. We've gotta see."

She asked, "What do you mean?" but the skeleton turned away and walked back toward the red barn. On the way they passed a massive creature with six legs and the scaly head of a dragon, chewing flame like hay out of a bale that wriggled with bright intensity.

"My trusty plough horse, Sacload," said Jimmy. "You could pet him if you like." Emmett and Gretel declined. They moved on a few more yards across the adamantine surface before the skeleton announced, "And lookee here. I got a well." A stone well like the one at the Addisons' appeared before them where there'd been none a second before. "Maybe someday I'll find myself at the bottom of it," he said. His jaw opened wide and laughter, like a trumpet, issued forth.

"Why are we here?" asked Emmett.

"You kids make yourselves at home for a spell. I've got some pressing business up in the house."

"Wait," said Gretel, more than a hint of desperation in her voice, but before the word fully sounded, Jimmy had vanished. She began crying, and the only thing preventing Emmett from doing the same was his fear. He drew close to her and said, "Come on. I'm going to tell him to take us back home." He put his arm around her and moved her slowly toward the house. He looked up at their destination—a gray, three-story structure, listing forward, with broken windows and a round cupola on either side of the patchy roof. Green mist curled from the chimney and reminded Emmett of thyme smoke.

On their way to the house, they passed the sagging old barn, and just as they drew even with the entrance, a man walked out of it. He was middle-aged, bald on top but with a full red beard reaching to the center of his chest. He was dressed in a work shirt and jeans and pair of farm boots. Emmett thought he recognized him from town. "Hey, mister," he said. "How do we get back to Threadwell?" The figure paid no attention to him and kept heading for the house. "Scuze me, sir," said Gretel. She shrugged off Emmett's arm and ran to catch up with the adult. "Can you help us?" she yelled to him.

The fellow just kept moving forward, not even turning his head to acknowledge their presence. "He doesn't see you," said Emmett. Gretel stopped following and watched as the man climbed the back steps to the house, opened the door, and went inside. When that door latched shut again, there came a low roar from out across the fields. Both she and Emmett turned around to see what was happening. At first it was unclear if anything in the strange setting was different, save for the fact that the wind had picked up considerably.

In an instant, it grew stronger yet, and there was a howling that echoed throughout the enormous cavern in which the farmland lay. It was Gretel who noticed it first. She pointed to the boundary of the field and shouted over the noise, "It's moving toward us." Emmett focused and realized that the crop of flames had grown higher, become more violent in its crackling and waving, and was rolling toward them now like an ocean wave. Gretel moved first, running back to grab Emmett's hand and pull him in the direction of the house. Her touch woke him from his stupor, and they ran.

By the time they made it to the steps, the back of the barn was on fire. They got through the door and slammed it behind them. For all the din of the blaze outside, it was silent in the kitchen, the only sound the slow ticking of a clock on the wall with chains and pinecone weights. Each second sounded like a drip of water. The room was lit by the light of the fire outside slipping in through two windows. The dance of the flames as they consumed the barn cast wild shadows on the walls.

"Jimmy Tooth!" Emmett yelled. He and Gretel left the kitchen, ran down a dark hallway, and stepped into a parlor. "We want to go home," he was about to call out, but the phrase never made it past his lips. The man they'd seen exit the barn was on his knees, his fingers on Jimmy Tooth's wrists, trying to pry the grip from around his neck. His face was blue, his eyes popping, and foam and drool dripped from his lips. Jimmy's eyes widened, and the empty mouth was a grimace of exertion.

The gurgling noise coming up out of the victim filled the room, and his body jerked and writhed with its last pulses of life. When the figure eventually went limp, Jimmy released his grip and the corpse fell to the floor with a thud. Emmett just then realized that the house was on fire around them, flames coming up through the floorboards, piercing the lathing of the walls. Jimmy turned toward the children, arms outstretched. The skull snarled viciously. He lunged for them.

Emmett felt a hand grasp his ankle and he came to, cocooned in heat and thick smoke. He felt himself being dragged, and a moment later a pair of hands under his arms lifted him up. "I've got him," yelled a voice. Emmett's eyes opened, the lids fluttered, and he caught a glimpse of Officer Johnson before dropping into darkness again. The next thing, sunlight. He opened his eyes and found himself lying on a cot in the police station.

Benton made him drink a cup of black coffee. Emmett sat, wrapped in a blanket, across the desk from the chief, who smoked a roll-up.

"Your folks'll be here soon to get you. I told them to let you stay here for the night. Doc Summerhill looked you over and gave you the okay."

Emmett nodded.

The lawman took a last toke on his butt and then stubbed it out. He sat back in his chair and said, "Your dad showed up here last evening and said you hadn't come home. He had the wagon and was looking for you. Me and Officer Johnson weren't doing anything so we took the Model T out and helped search. We just happened to be passing the carpentry shop and saw the flames out back. We carried water from the creek, maybe two dozen times. And I'm too old to be hauling water. You're a lucky cuss. Johnson heard you screaming in there or we'd have let it just turn to cinders, which in the long run it mostly did anyway. Now, suppose you tell me why we had to pull you free of that burning icehouse last night."

"Gretel," said Emmett. "Is she okay?"

"Gretel who?" asked Benton.

"Lawler."

"When we put the fire out, all we found was you."

"She was with me."

"Maybe she slipped out. The back wall had collapsed by the time we got there. You're lucky you're not barbecue, son. Where's this girl live?"

"Gretel Lawler. She lives out on the Chowdry Road."

The chief leaned forward, lifted a pencil from the desk, and made a note. "Okay, now, what were you up to?"

Emmett sat for quite a while, willing to talk but not knowing where to begin. There was almost too much to tell. Every time he picked a launching point, he thought of some other thread that needed tending if he was to get it all right. His mind was still bleary from the smoke, but while he sat and thought, he drank the coffee and that cleared things a bit with every sip. Benton rocked slightly in his chair, the spring beneath him quietly squealing, and seemed to study something on the ceiling.

Finally, Emmett said, "It started back when I found Jimmy Tooth in the bottom of the Addisons' old well."

"Good lord," said the chief.

It was late morning by the time the boy stopped talking.

Benton shook his head, and said, "That's one hell of a tale, Mr. Wallace. Jimmy Tooth come back from the dead to get justice? Ha. I like it, but it's lunatic. You're saying that Mrs. Williams killed Jimmy Tooth and because she knew you knew something, she trapped you in the icehouse and tried to cook you? And that's not even the most absurd part."

"Jimmy wanted justice," said Emmett, "but I think to also confess. It never struck me to wonder why Jimmy Tooth had a farm in hell. He wanted me to know that he choked a man to death."

"Oh, right," said Benton. "Who?"

"I've seen him before, but I can't place him. A man with a red beard down to here." He moved the side of his hand across his chest. "Bald head."

Benton squinted and leaned on the desk. He smiled with only the left side of his mouth. "You know who you're describing?" he asked.

Emmett shook his head.

"Mr. Williams."

"Oh, that's right. I barely remember him."

"That's interesting," said the chief. "You know, when he died, I don't remember being called to the carpentry shop. I can't remember if the doctor took a look at him. I just heard he had a heart attack and then there was a wake. Mrs. Williams made his coffin and chose a closed lid. We knew her so well, and she was in such grief no one asked any questions."

"I think she got Jimmy to kill her husband, and then she killed Jimmy. Oh, and I almost forgot, the pastor was part of it. He was outside the icehouse and helped her make the fire."

"The pastor too?" said Benton.

"He did something to the brakes on his wife's car. He's gonna kill her. Jimmy put the spider kiss on her."

"All right, calm down now. This is getting crazier by the second."

"I can prove it," said Emmett. "Or at least part of it." He stood up and reached into the pocket of his jeans. His hand came out in a fist. Leaning over the desk, he opened his fingers, and three little nuggets dropped onto Benton's calendar. "I found those on the floor of the icehouse. Jimmy Tooth's teeth. I bet they'd match up to where they were busted out of his jaw."

"She killed him in the icehouse?" asked Benton.

"With a hammer, I think."

"I'll need these for evidence."

"Okay."

"All very interesting," said the chief. "Now, Mrs. Williams could have pressed charges. She claims you burned down her icehouse. Mr. Dibble did find a charred box of wooden matches among the debris. Anyway, this woman you are claiming beat a man to death with a hammer is willing to forgive your trespass and mischief and let you go scot-free. She says she understands your insane condition."

"She's in romance with the pastor, and he's guilty so he wears the hat," Emmett blurted out.

"In romance?" Benton laughed. "That's a neat little theory, but it's time for you to stop thinking, son. I want you to go home with your parents and stay there. I want you not to go near the carpentry shop or Mrs. Williams anymore. In fact, you can stay out of school till after Christmas too. I'll tell Miss Maufin I told you to. You need some rest, my friend. Peace and quiet and try to think of something other than walking skeletons and farms in hell."

Two days later, the news spread through Threadwell that Mrs. Holst, the pastor's wife, was killed in a tragic car accident on the way back from Mount Victory. She came around the curve by the Vesper Woods, lost control, and smashed into an ancient horse chestnut tree. She was flung through the windshield, and the broken glass ripped her face off. The pastor was distraught, but still he presided over her wake.

The town gathered at the church to pay their last respects to the poor woman. She had been a great favorite of nearly everyone in the community. Even Emmett attended with his parents. Neighbors, having heard of the icehouse incident, gave him a wide berth and dirty looks. Even his parents kept a few feet between themselves and him. Before leaving for the wake his father had wanted him to smoke a thyme roll-up, but he refused, saying he didn't need it anymore. The church was packed, and he sat in a separate pew, his parents in the next one over. He paid no attention to the words that rhythmically puffed out the handkerchief of the pastor, but scanned the crowd. Sitting in the back row of pews he spied Gretel Lawler, dressed in white and carrying a hymnal. When no one but Emmett was looking she winked at him, and he smiled, relieved to know she had somehow escaped the icehouse and run for it. He was amazed by her. The only other person to look Emmett's way was Chief Benton, and he stared at the boy all through the pastor's eulogy.

Emmett went through his days in Threadwell an outcast, shunned by everyone, ignored by his parents. He felt like a ghost in his own home. They gave him his dinner separately and rarely asked him to do a chore. His mother still did his wash and swept out his room now and then, but conversations were never more than a sentence. He stopped going to school and instead roamed the countryside on his bike, which still stood next to the bench by the creek when he went to recover it weeks after the icehouse night. Mr. Peasi still let him borrow books from the barbershop, and so he read when he wasn't out exploring. His only real joy was the nights he snuck out and met Gretel Lawler at the top of Chowdry Road. From there, they rode their bicycles everywhere while Threadwell slept.

On the night of the day in early July when Chief Benton ordered the exhumation of Jimmy Tooth's body and matched the three teeth to their homes on the jaw, Emmett sat with Gretel in the moonlight on the bank of Wildcat Creek where it wound through the cemetery beyond the church. It was after midnight, and a beautiful breeze blew across the fields. They leaned together and she kissed him. His hand, resting on the ground, gripped the grass, and when they pulled apart, he'd squeezed his fist so hard he pulled a clump of it up. "Do you love me?" she asked. He smelled the aroma of wild thyme and realized that's what he clutched in his fingers. The sound of water passing over stones, the light on Gretel's face, the scent of the herb, dark green and peppery, intoxicated him. "Yes," he said, and then ripped a swatch of thyme off the clump and put it to his mouth. She grabbed his wrist. "Don't," she said. He never did again, and from then on, she was always with him.

The Prelate's Commission

The new fresco that graced the inner dome of the Cathedral of St. Elovisus was a masterpiece of perspective and illusion—the fall of the rebel angels into hell. They hurtled downward through an aquamarine sky swirled with pale pink clouds, their feathers disintegrating in the descent, their features growing ever more monstrous. Some, just ejected from paradise, appeared small and vastly distant, while the progressively larger ones took on weight and velocity. The largest seemed just above the viewer, desperately clawing the sky, eyes wide with the discovery of gravity, about to slam into the marble floor, which was inlaid with a deep and spiraling scene of Hell. At the center of the inner dome above was an illuminated circle where one could glimpse, as if from the bottom of a well, the enormous, angry face of God.

The Prelate who oversaw the project for the church had watched closely the processes of the master, Codilan—the mixing of the plaster and lime, the cyphering of how much could be painted in a day, and the rendering of the marvelous figures. The look in the eyes of any who beheld it revealed its genius. Codilan had also designed the dome itself, an engineering feat of equal astonishment, but it wasn't the great artist that the Prelate gave most of his attention to. There was an assistant to the master, a very young man named Talejui, who hailed from the northern forest of the realm. The master had turned over to him the responsibility for the rendering of the figures. After the first day of painting, it was clear the young man was a prodigy. The expressions and postures of the falling angels were mesmerizing. Even the mere rendering of the hands, fingers clutching at nothing, made the Prelate sense them clutching his soul.

Word of the great work spread quickly, and in the months following its completion, throngs came to the cathedral from all corners of the realm to gaze first upward and then down into the illusion of the abyss. Sinners were brought to their knees, and quite a few converted on the spot. The Prelate, of course, took much of the credit for the fresco, but there was still a surplus to go around and the master and even Talejui were given appropriate shares. In having witnessed the creation of a masterpiece, the Prelate, over the five years it took them to paint the inner dome, slowly conceived of his own magnificent project, one no less intricate than the dome, nor less angry than God.

Codilan had already begun planning for his next work, a marble sculpture of the Holy Ghost. "The ineffable made manifest in stone" was how he put it to his patron at the house of Walsneer. He and Talejui spent days conspiring just how to render a spirit in marble. Work went along well for two weeks, and then the young man was summoned to a meeting one rainy afternoon at the Prelate's chambers. He feared he had been called in due to his recent nightly conduct of drinking and fighting. He'd felt the need for a certain wildness, a release from the concentration on the fresco. When he reached the cathedral, he stood beneath his handiwork and marveled, his neck craning back till it ached. Suddenly he felt a hand upon his shoulder and the words, spoken softly, "Don't forget what's beneath your feet."

Talejui looked down into Hell before turning to see who'd touched him. It was the Prelate.

"I have a mission for you," said his holiness.

The young man's heart sank as he knew that whatever was asked of him, he could not refuse.

"A mission from God. Follow me to my chambers and I'll explain."

The office of the Prelate was carpeted and hung in red velvet. They sat in hand-carved wooden thrones, the older man and younger on either side of an ornate desk. Each had a goblet of honeyed wine and each a lit roll of tobacco from the distant Islands of Night.

"I was much impressed by your work on the inner dome," said the Prelate.

"Thank you, your holiness, but I owe my inspiration to the master, Codilan."

"This is where you're wrong, my son. You owe it to God. Your gift is from heaven, and now you're called upon by the church to serve the almighty."

"Yes, your holiness."

"You will go on a journey."

Talejui took the tobacco from his lips and said, "But we've just begun a new commission for the Walsneers' . . ."

The old man leaned forward across his desk and fixed the artist with a withering stare. His pointy fingernail twice tapped hard wood. "The House of Walsneer is a dung pile, its members feast on shit, do you understand?"

"Yes, your holiness."

"Now I have something that will test your talents to the limit. As an artist and a man of the church, you can't refuse."

Talejui nodded.

"I want you to go forth into the world, find the devil, and paint his portrait."

The young man could not suppress a laugh.

"Your arrogance will be your undoing," said the Prelate.

"No, your holiness, I laugh with joy that you might think me capable of such a feat. How exactly am I to locate the devil?"

"Men such as you find the devil every day. He's always gracious about stopping to tempt a sinner."

"And if I do find him, how will I convince him to sit for me?"

"The church asks not for your questions but for your action. That's all."

"Why, though?"

"He is a great trickster with infinite guises. Men and women are defenseless against him. They need to be able to identify the demon, so that they know when he comes for them. I want his true portrait executed with all the art God gave you."

"Yes, your holiness. And when am I to begin my journey?"

"Immediately. We will bequeath you a donkey to carry your supplies and a bag of gold for expenses. When you complete the portrait, you will be paid handsomely for it."

Talejui never actually agreed, but he need say nothing. To refuse the Prelate would find him cooking atop a stack of logs and kindling in the town square, his flesh disintegrating into smoke like the feathers of the falling angels. He finished his tobacco while the old man offered a suggestion.

"There's a legend that he keeps house in an abandoned summer palace on an island in a lake somewhere amid the Carapace Mountains."

The artist nodded humbly, but behind his eyes he made his plan. He'd travel on the church's money for a year, and then when the mystery of the open road lost its charm, he'd simply paint a portrait of the devil from his imagination and make up a story as to how he got the demon to sit for him. The Prelate would buy it without a doubt. And still, he would be able to return to work on the master's Holy Ghost.

"The devil is sly, so stay awake."

"Yes, your holiness," he said. "I leave tonight. Please have someone from the stable bring the donkey around to my place and I will load the beast with my easel and paints."

The Prelate tossed a pouch of coins onto the desk. "Twelve pieces of gold," he said. "It should take you far."

"And what if I find the devil in the arms of a woman?"

"It's not her arms I'd worry about," said the Prelate.

"And what if I need break the law to find the devil?"

"More questions? I told you, action. You know what needs to be done. Do it. Let your faith guide you."

By the time Talejui left the cathedral, the rain had stopped and he walked through the village of thatched, stone homes, over and down the green hills on a dirt path that was said to have been trod by Adam and Eve as they fled paradise. Out at the edge of things, he came to the master's workshop. The helpers were off to the south, purchasing a block of marble for the coming sculpture. Talejui found Codalin sitting at his drafting table, his head propped by one fist under his chin, snoring. The window looking out into the meadow was flung open, and a warm breeze carried the buzz of insects, the grief of mourning doves. All was hushed in the huge workshop, motes of marble dust floating in the sunlight.

"Master," whispered Talejui. The old man stirred and slowly came back from sleep.

"Yes," said Codalin, yawning. "I wanted to tell you what I realized about the sculpture. It will all depend on light. Only through light can stone become weightless."

"I've come to tell you I must leave town."

"What's this? I'm not paying you enough?" Codalin sat straight, fully awake.

"The Prelate has given me a secret mission for the church."

"The Prelate? An imbecile."

"Yes, but burning at the stake is an inconvenience."

The master reflected and then nodded. "A worthy argument," he said.

"I intend to pretend for a year's time and then end the comedy through my art. Can you delay the Walsneer commission until then?"

"Only if you promise to finish it should I grow too old. Now what's this secret mission?"

"Forgive me, but I'm sworn to secrecy. I leave tonight."

Talejui, good to his word, set out at the propitious hour of midnight, beneath a silver moon. He wore his cape and wide-brimmed hat. The donkey, Hermes, a slow and cantankerous beast, was piled high with supplies. The journey was not a race, though, and the young man was content to follow the animal's lead. They took the path away from the village into the greater realm. Talejui whistled the simple psalm of St. Ifritia, and every hundred steps or so, Hermes made a sound like a sinner's last breath.

A beautiful day broke around the travelers, warm sun and cool breeze, and Talejui decided to sleep. He bedded down in a stand of cedar trees at the top of a tall hill. Wild flowers of white and yellow dotted the needle-strewn floor, and the sunlight through the branches fell soft upon his face. The morning swirled around him and he dreamed about the Holy Ghost in marble, like a bedsheet on a line rippling in the wind yet made of stone. It spoke to him in a hollow, holy voice that echoed in the caverns of itself. "Your mission is no less important than the work of the bees," it said.

Talejui awoke in the late afternoon to the donkey's loud braying. Only when he got to his feet did he realize there was a man standing behind him. It was the hunter Pervan. He had feathers twisted into his nest of hair and a string of rabbits over his shoulder, a pheasant tucked into his belt.

"What are you doing out here, Talejui?" he asked.

"I'm on a mission for the church, sent by the Prelate."

"You have my pity," he said.

The artist smiled. "Do you know of an island in the mountains where the devil lives?"

Pervan laughed for a long time and then dried his eyes. "The Prelate is a flagon of lunacy. To the west from here. Straight over these hills. Find a path that's marked every few leagues by a stone with a cross carved into it. These stones go back to the earliest folk. That pass winds through the mountains. Take it till you come to a barren area next to a lake. You'll see the island and the roof of the palace from the shore. Wait for the tide to go out and you can walk through shallow water to it."

"How do you know this?"

"I kill for a living. I've been there."

"How far must I go?"

"If you start now, you can make it before the weather gets cold." The hunter turned and walked away through the trees.

"Can you tell me anything about the devil?" called Talejui.

"Nothing you don't already know."

The artist and the donkey walked through the mornings of the coming days, and in late afternoon, after a bite to eat, Talejui painted small landscapes to keep his brush adept. At night, he smoked nettlemare in his long pipe and, in the fog that followed, carried on a one-way conversation with Hermes about his dreams of the Holy Ghost. The donkey stared at him with knowing eyes and expressions, gasping last breaths at the perfect moments.

There were times during the journey when Talejui would completely forget where he was going and be taken up by the beauty of the landscape and the sounds of birds that filled the forest to either side of the path. And then there were other instances when he felt a prisoner to the Prelate's demand and sorely regretted his time for creation being scattered like dust. On these bad days, he was unsure if he could last a year and began contemplating how the devil should appear in his painting. The images that came to him were fleeting and soon forgotten, as if a spell had been cast to weaken his imagination.

It had already grown cold by the time they stood on the edge of a lake the very color of the sky in the fresco at St. Elovisus. A brisk wind blew ashore from the direction of the island a half mile out. From where he stood, Talejui could see the slanted roofs of the devil's palace above the barren trunks of oak. The tide was high, so the travelers took shelter beneath a ledge of an enormous boulder sitting in the sand like an egg in a nest. The artist made a fire, ate a fish he'd caught the day before, and lit his pipe. Hermes stood close to the flames and every now and then turned to warm a different part of his body.

Strange sounds came out of the dark, growling, weeping, and a prolonged laughter that always petered into anguish. Talejui pulled his cape tighter around himself. For a solid hour, he was transfixed by what appeared to be someone walking out on the lake. Eventually it became clear that it was merely an illusion of the starlight, the water, and the wind. Hermes was agitated, braying often, his eyes wide, nostrils flaring, and the artist, himself, shivered at more than the cold. Sleep was fitful, illuminated not by the presence of the Holy Ghost but by quick glimpses, shards, of a grisly murder. Three times he woke up spitting, and twice he roused enough to hear a distinct whispering, someone out in the dark, feverishly praying. He fled back into sleep as if it were an iron cocoon that would protect him.

The morning was overcast, and ever since waking he couldn't get the taste of ashes off his tongue. After eating a strip of dried venison, and drinking the last of his wine, he walked, accompanied by Hermes, to the shore. The tide had definitely gone out, but the wind was cold and the knee-high water frigid. He pulled on the donkey's rope to bring him along, but the beast would have none of it. Cursing Hermes, he dropped the rope, and inched forward into the lake. The icy water was startling, and he momentarily lost his breath. It was at this very point that the mystery of the open road lost its charm. He slogged forward, into the wind, his cape quickly soaked by the wavelets breaking against his knees. Halfway through the crossing, a powerful gust lifted the hat from his head and carried it up toward the clouds.

It took over an hour for him to reach the shore of the island, which at times seemed to retreat as he grew nearer. He was shivering and blue as he scurried up the beach into the forest. Immediately, he set to gathering kindling and fallen branches for a fire, his desperation guiding him. By the time he took the flint from his pocket, his hands were so numb he could hardly hold it, but eventually a fire sprang to life and he felt relief from the cold. He rested for a time, letting the heat of the flames dry his clothes. In late afternoon, when the sun had partially broken through, he headed in the direction of the abandoned palace.

The limestone façade was crumbling, the stained-glass windows nearly all broken. Enormous rooms were still furnished with mildewed couches, divans, and rotting chairs. The chandeliers and their chains had turned to rust, the pendants shattered on the floor like a pile of crude salt. Pigeons were living in a wardrobe in one room, a fox growled at him from a fireplace a few rooms later, and the rooms went on and on. Some sections of the palace roof had caved in. The stairs to the second floor were splintered and too rickety to climb. He passed through an inner courtyard where weeds grew to prodigious heights, and then down a colonnade and into another labyrinth of rooms. In one he found a well-preserved mural. It was contained in an archway, a view of the sea, and a wave breaking at the opening from just outside so it appeared the water would rush into the room.

Talejui wondered about the days that were spent by those who had once lived there and about the story as to how the devil had eventually taken it over. "The devil, my ass," he finally said, and turned back in order to make it outside before sunset. In his retreat he passed through the courtyard of weeds, but when re-entering the palace must have chosen a different door for he couldn't remember traversing the rooms he now passed through. In one, he found the skeleton of a child in a rocking chair, something he was certain he'd not passed earlier on his way in. More rooms as if they were multiplying, and all the while the sun sank lower and the shadows grew more pronounced.

Then Talejui was in a hallway of peeling green paint, and at the end of it was a door. His first thought was of escape. He ran to it and opened it wide. Instead of it being an exit it revealed a set of steps leading down into the darkness of a basement. The smell that rose from that lower floor made him wince and turn away. He was shutting the door, when he heard a step of the stairway creak down below in the dark. Then there was a knock and another creak, and another. Out of the gloom from below appeared a face pointed at both the crown and the chin, hair and complexion a frosty blue. The wide eyes revealed vertical slits in yellow irises. Horns curled like a ram's jutted from bulging temples. By then the entire figure of the devil was visible. Hooves, an icy coat, and a sharp smile.

The artist backed away slowly, dumbfounded by the reality of legends. The devil reached the top, stepped into the room, and quietly shut the door behind him. "A visitor," he said. "I don't get many."

Talejui tried to compose himself and tell the devil he'd come to paint his portrait, but instead all he managed to get out was, "Why blue?"

"The color of the stillborn," said the fallen angel.

"I'm an artist. I was told you lived here and was wondering if I might paint your portrait." In a blink, the strange figure before him transformed into that of an old man dressed in fine golden attire. That icicle head had rounded and become more jolly. Tufts of white hair like innocuous summer clouds had sprouted just above the ears.

"What's your game?" asked the devil with a smile and a voice now weighted with age.

"My game?"

"I know the Prelate sent you."

Talejui was about to lie, but the old man shook his head in warning. "Yes, then, the Prelate sent me."

"You did the figures of the new fresco in the cathedral of St. Elovisus."

"I did."

"I've seen and admired them."

"Then you will allow me to paint you?"

"I might."

"It must be your true self."

"I'm not in the habit of showing my true self to the Lord's clay dolls, but I will for a price."

"What would you have?"

"If you'll kill someone of my choosing, I'll present myself to you in order that you might complete a portrait."

"Who?"

"First you must agree, and then I'll reveal my choice."

"I'm no murderer," said Talejui.

"Not yet."

"Even if I thought the payoff worth it, I'm skeptical that such a portrait would be worth anything. I'm sure you don't always appear as Jack Frost or an old man."

The devil laughed. "You artists have balls," he growled. "But I see your point. I'll make it so that anyone who casts their eyes upon the portrait will know me when I approach no matter what guise I'm in. You can't get a better deal than that at the market at Cathool."

Talejui found the devil's offer tempting, and at that moment he knew he was in danger. He took a step back and brought his hands up to cover his face. "I'll not murder anyone," he said through his fingers.

"Not just anyone, but a certain someone," said the devil.

When he awoke on the sand of the shore across the lake from the palace island, Hermes was still there. Talejui knew days had passed but could remember nothing after his encounter with the devil. Lying next to him on the beach, he found a framed blank canvas. He picked it up and added it to Hermes' load. He stretched, took in deep breaths of cold air, shook his head, grabbed the donkey's lead, and headed back toward St. Elovisus. The return road seemed longer than the way out and the night chills left morning frost in the steaming fields. Winds from the north stabbed through his cloak and hood, and sleep became the act of shivering. No matter the roaring fires he built, there remained a winter chill within. He drew so close to the flames that one night he burned his hand. The pain coursed through him and, in its wake, he remembered.

The blue devil had his arm around Talejui's shoulders as the painter suffered the coarseness of icicle hair and a bad-meat stench. "The painting is done," the devil whispered, pointing to the blank canvas on the easel. "Take it with you. Kill who I tell you to. The moment your victim's heart stops beating, the canvas will reveal the portrait of my true self to the world. All who see the painting will know me when I approach them. Now, go back to the village and await word from me as to whom I've chosen for you to take." Talejui now recalled how he'd shaken his head and said, "No," only to find a moment later that he was nodding and saying "Yes." Then they were on a balcony, and the devil was biting the head off a pigeon that had landed on the rusted railing.

Just before the snow came sweeping down from the mountains, the painter and donkey arrived back at St. Elovisus. Talejui wasted no time in going to see the Prelate, and it wasn't until he was sitting in the old man's red velvet office, smoking tobacco and drinking honeyed wine, that the chill began to leave him.

"I thought this might take longer," said the Prelate. "You mean to tell me you met the devil and convinced him to sit for his portrait and completed that painting in a few brief months? You must think me a fool."

"Hear me out, your holiness," said Talejui. "I met the devil in the palace on the island you had told me of. Over a period of days, I painted him, but I don't remember everything. While I worked, it was as if I slept. Here's the painting." Talejui lifted the framed canvas from beside his chair and handed it across the desk.

The Prelate's eyes widened when he saw it was blank. "What is this?" he said.

"The painting is there, but you can't see it. It will only be revealed on the condition that I murder someone of the dark lord's choosing. I want your permission to kill in the name of the church."

"The serpent's mind is twisted," said the Prelate. "Imagination run amok. Yes, of course, kill someone. If one person must be lost to save thousands, it shall be done. Do you have a dagger?"

"A dagger I have, but not the courage."

"When you find out who your victim will be, tell me, and I will help you."

Talejui shook his head but said, "Yes."

"I will hang the portrait here behind my chair. When you've done the deed, I'll know."

The prelate threw Talejui another bag of coins and blessed him with the sacred signs.

"Wait," said the painter. "What if he tells me to kill you?"

The Prelate sat back and lifted his hands. "Then you must."

Talejui returned to Codilan's studio and threw himself into the work on the sculpture of the Holy Ghost. The master's workers had long returned with an enormous block of the finest white marble, the perfection of which made the painter forget the devil's portrait. Freezing, snow-covered days passed with Codilan and Talejui sitting at the drawing table, a fire roaring in the hearth, discussing the Walsneers' project. "After all my research, I'm convinced no one truly knows precisely what the Holy Ghost is," said the master.

"You can't see it," said Talejui.

"And yet it has the power to impregnate."

"It's a ghost, but not of the dead."

"Here's what I propose," said Codilan. "I want to create an enormous marble globe that will rest upon a base that will give the illusion that the granite ball is floating in the air."

Talejui laughed.

"It can be done with mirrors. The base must be concave and the globe must touch it only at a single point. The illusion isn't difficult, but balancing the weight of the globe will be."

They began work on the sculpture, and the master taught his pupil the art of stone-cutting as they went along. Talejui was a quick study and enjoyed the physical nature of the work. He felt himself growing stronger from the constant weight of the hammer and chisel, and he challenged himself to cut finer and finer slivers of marble until it was as if he was shaving the stone. The day that Codilan commended him on his technique, Talejui caught a chill. It came to him that his enthusiasm and love of learning to work with stone was like a pigeon on the rusted railing of a balcony. He pictured the devil lifting it and biting off the head. "If true to his legend, he will now tell me I must kill the master," thought the painter. But the days passed, and the devil was silent as the snow.

On the shortest day of the year, the sun descending through barren trees, the Prelate appeared at the door of Codilan's shop. One of the workers, hat in hand, ushered him in. The master stopped work and went to speak to him. Eventually, he called to Talejui, who was trying to hide behind the diminished block of marble. He put down his tools and approached.

"Business of the church," the Prelate said to Codilan.

"I'm dismissed?" asked the master.

The holy man nodded.

"Thanks be to god," he said and as he walked away they heard him laughing. Soon after, the striking of hammer upon chisel echoed through the workshop. "I suppose the devil has been struck dumb?" said the Prelate.

"You know how busy they say he is," said Talejui.

"You've heard nothing?"

The young man shook his head.

"This must be clear—if the devil tells you to kill, you must without hesitation. And, might I add, without any consideration for your own safety. It's for the greater good and glory. Do you understand?" The old man reached out and grabbed Talejui's wrist. The power of his grip startled them both.

"Yes," said Talejui, "yes." He nodded nervously.

"The devil never waits to take a sinner. I expect to see his portrait upon my wall within the coming days."

Talejui told Codilan the story of his journey to the abandoned palace and how the Prelate had ordered him to kill for the devil. The master said, "He's lost his mind. I know some powerful people in the church outside our village who will hear of this. It will all be taken care of quietly."

The young man thanked the master, and went back to work. In the following weeks, the smooth sphere revealed itself from marble, and the wonder of that process forced Talejui's holy mission from his mind. He cared only about the perfection of the sculpture. To set his apprentice at ease, Codilan left the workshop one day and travelled to the city of the Holy See to speak with his acquaintances. The fathers of the church desperately wanted to commission him to build a domed basilica, and this was the weight of his influence. When he returned, he told Talejui, "The case has been made to friendly ears. But you know, it is the Holy See, where the worm turns slowly. If you can dodge the Prelate till the spring, when the Holy Ghost is finished, I'm sure the matter will be resolved." After that, Codilan posted one of his men near the door to the workshop to watch for the Prelate's carriage, and when it was sighted the young man would slip out the back, across the meadow, and into the forest. On the Prelate's third impromptu visit, he told Codilan, "You are not above four bundles of kindling and a flame."

"Interesting," said the master, "that's not what I was told at the Holy See."

The Prelate took a step back, trying to mask his shock, for only in that moment did he realize that Talejui had told his master everything. Instantly he made an amiable face and said, "Please, tell the boy he must come and see me as soon as possible."

"Of course, your holiness."

That night, the master and Talejui, by candlelight, drinking adder wine, stood before the mirrors for the sculpture that had arrived from the Floating City, and imitated the Prelate in all his jabbering buffoonery. Codalin laughed so hard he wet his pants when his apprentice told him he'd asked the holy man "What if the devil tells me to kill you?" When he learned the Prelate's response, he doubled over and fell to his knees. "No more," said the master gasping for air. Some weeks later, though, when the first buds appeared through the snow and the marble globe floated in mid-air, complete, the echo of that laughter haunted Talejui.

The night on which the Holy Ghost was to be delivered to the Walsneers', an event accompanied by a great feast, Talejui hid in the master's workshop alone. There was no doubt the Prelate would be present at the event, and as of that moment there had come no word from either the devil or the Holy See. Without the work of the chisel, all the twisted ramifications of his holy mission came back to him like a hammer blow. He tried to pass the night drawing, but every line seemed wrong, and eventually he left the workshop and headed through the ice-melted streets to the Inn of Night and Day. There, dashing off drams of aqua vitae that slurred his words, he confessed to all present a murder he would eventually commit at the behest of both the Prelate and the devil.

At the unveiling of the Holy Ghost in a torch-lit garden outside the west wing of the Walsneer's castellated palace, the devil arrived among the guests in the guise of Pervan the hunter. No one noticed him at first, although all but he wore finery. The serving of lilac liqueur followed directly the dedication of the master's new wonder. The sculpture was roundly applauded and all were enchanted by its magical illusion. It was then that the hunter broke from a crowd beside the woodwind quartet and rushed at the Holy Ghost. Codilan, taking in full draughts of praise from the extended Walsneer family, noticed Pervan run and leap, and in an instant calculated the trajectory. It was too late, though. The hunter fell upon the marble globe, tipping it off its single point and riding it down into an explosion of glass that cut him everywhere. His face flopped like bloody strips of bacon as he groaned at the bottom of the glittering mess. Before he died, the devil leaped out of him and like the ghost of a praying mantis scaled the wall of the palace to look down upon the chaos. The guests fled screaming, and the master was again on his knees, this time in tears. The evil one smiled briefly, and then a scent caught his attention.

Even before Talejui lurched out of the Day and Night, a spy for the church had slipped away from the inn and gone in search of the Prelate. The painter stumbled along the road, weaving and talking to himself. He'd decided to head toward his cottage instead of the workshop. The one thing he wanted more than even another drink was to lie upon his own bed with the blanket pulled up to his chin, and sleep. "To the devil with the devil," he said, spat, and shuffled forward with determination. Soon enough, he approached his cottage. Its shadow in the dark brought tears to his eyes. He'd not been inside since returning from his journey to find the evil one. He opened the low wooden gate at the edge of the road and stepped one foot on the path to his door. Before taking another step, though, he felt a presence in the road behind him. Turning, he saw a large darker shadow amid the darkness. From out of the night, Hermes the donkey stepped forward, his lips curling back to reveal all his teeth.

Talejui laughed upon finally recognizing the beast. He let the gate shut and walked back into the road. "What are you doing here?" he said and petted the side of Hermes' face. The donkey was restless and pulled back away. "What is it?" asked the painter.

The creature reared its head back and opened its mouth. "I'm here to tell you whom I want you to kill," it said in the devil's voice. Talejui froze, and his drunkenness evaporated in an instant. He stood with his mouth open and stared, all his limbs numb.

"Do you hear me?" asked the devil.

Talejui shook his head but said, "Yes."

"Listen well, for I want you to kill . . . ," he said, but with the next word language exploded into the braying of a donkey.

"Who?" whispered Talejui. "Who?"

"I want you to kill . . ." and then more braying. The same repeated again and again, and each time Talejui leaned forward, hoping for the name but instead heard the screech of an ass. Finally, he drew his dagger, lunged at Hermes, and with a sudden slice cut the animal's throat. Blood spilled onto the road, and still the creature managed to speak it twice more. "I want you to kill . . ." It fell while braying, a waning cry that gave way to gurgling. The carcass twitched and wheezed as the devil rose in the steam from the warm blood and floated away on the wind. The painter opened his gate and took the path to his cottage door. He retrieved the key from a chain round his neck. Inside it was cold and musty. Completely sober now and calm, he built a fire in the hearth and sat in his armchair with a blanket round him, staring at the motion of the flames.

The next morning, long after the hearth was cold, he was still there in his chair, wrapped in a profound sleep. That was how the soldiers found him, who broke down his door and ripped him from the chair and a dream of the Holy Ghost. They shoved him along through the village to the cathedral, where a pyre of kindling and logs and a crowd had already been gathered. His neighbors drew away when he passed among them. He was roughly ushered up onto the kindling, and the soldiers tied him by the wrists and feet to a pole. The cathedral workers moved quickly, painting the larger wooden logs below with pig fat to make them burn more fiercely. When all was prepared, and the captain of the cathedral guard held a lit taper, the charges were read by the Monk in Good Standing. "For consorting with the devil, the painter, Talejui, is condemned to burn at the stake until death."

Talejui was paralyzed with fear, his chest heaving for every breath, his heart pounding in his ears. He thought nothing, and though he tried to cry out, not a word found its way. Among the crowd, he saw Codilan and his workers being held at bay by guards with pikes and drawn swords. The master screamed, demanding his apprentice's release. The captain of the guard looked up to the Prelate's office window, where the holy man stood dressed in golden robes and triangular hat, the ritual vestments for immolation. The prelate made the sacred signs with his left hand, and the crowd was astonished by the graceful manner with which he moved his wrist and fingers as if an afterthought. The pyre was lit, and the smoke rose. Talejui cried out when his blood began to boil and his flesh bubbled up and sloughed away to become smoke. His screams made the crowd weak, and they cowered where they stood while the Prelate stared down at them from his perch. He waited until the smog obscured his view of them, and then closed the wooden shutter of the window and stepped away.

He waved his hand in front of his nose in an attempt to clear the stink of burning flesh. "Heinous," he said and tried to cough the taste out of his mouth. On his way back to his desk, he looked up and from the corner of his eye noticed that the blank canvas was no longer blank. At first he glimpsed only the golden, holy vestments, and groaned, "It can't be me." He froze in place until it became clear that he wasn't the devil, although the evil one wore the habiliments of someone of his religious station. He studied the portrait for a long time and after searching his memory was sure it was no one he knew. The gentleman in the painting was of an advanced age yet had a jolly aspect, a round face like that of a favorite fat uncle, and tufts of white hair above the ears. He wore a golden brocade jacket pinned with the Axe of Stone, a medal given by the Holy See to those who had seen combat for the church. Both a warrior and a spiritual leader.

In the days that followed, the Prelate had numerous clergy, nuns included, into his office to see if they could identify the man in the portrait. "That's the devil," he'd tell them, and they would nod and back slowly out of the door. If he wasn't mistaken, they seemed more frightened of him than of the painting. With all his attempts to discover who the man was, he managed to find out nothing.

Two weeks to the day after the painter was turned to ash, at the crack of dawn, the very man in the portrait, dressed in gold brocade, rode a white horse through the open gates of the cathedral. Riding with him were three dozen of the Holy See's finest soldiers. The strings Codilan had pulled had finally resulted in something. The soldiers took the Prelate away, and the old, rounded man with the jovial disposition, whose portrait already hung behind the Prelate's desk, became the new Prelate.

The old Prelate was thrown in a dungeon in the basement of an ancient basilica of the Holy See where dead saints were entombed. He was fed slops once a day and his cell had but one spot where the sunlight managed to send a beam through a crack in a floor above. At night, the spirits of the saints tormented him, brought him nightmares full of anguish and lunged now and then from the dark to bite him. Eventually, the guard who fed him was reassigned to the worksite where Codilan's new dome was to be built. Without sustenance, the old man starved and withered away.

As the Prelate drew his last labored breaths, the ice-blue devil appeared to him.

"The poor Prelate brought low by his own vanity," said the evil one as the temperature of the room plummeted. "You believed you would be the one to outsmart me? Your scheme, a work of genius more resplendent than any cathedral?"

The old man cowered in a dark corner, praying for death before his soul was snatched.

"It seems, your holiness, that your name has already been forgotten."

The Prelate prayed as loud as he could, which was little more than a shallow croaking, to try to block the sound of the devil's voice.

"Do you know why I'm here?"

"No," came the whispered reply.

"To grant your wish. That's what I do." With this, the devil stepped forward, leaned over, dug his icy nails into the gaunt hollow beneath the old man's stubbled chin, and with a laugh ripped upward. There was an agonizing scream that snaked up from beneath the ground and pierced the afternoon. It sounded throughout the Holy See, so that all stopped for a moment in their daily tasks and looked around. The devil held up the face of the Prelate, which hung loose as a worn leather sac in his cold hands. Pulling it taut, he stared at the mask of flesh and then vanished with it. At some point in the days that followed, that withered visage replaced the angry face of God upon the inner dome of the Cathedral of St. Elovisus.

Acknowledgments

A heartfelt thanks to all of the editors who helped to make these stories the best they could be—Ellen Datlow, Maurice Broaddus, Gordon Van Gelder, Terri Windling, Ann VanderMeer, Jonathan Strahan, Gavin J. Grant and Kelly Link.

About the Author

Jeffrey Ford was born on Long Island in New York State in 1955 and grew up in the town of West Islip. He studied fiction writing with John Gardner at S.U.N.Y Binghamton. He's been a college English teacher of writing and literature for thirty years. He is the author of eight novels, including *The Girl in the Glass,* and four short story collections. He has received multiple World Fantasy and Shirley Jackson awards as well as the Nebula and Edgar awards, among others. He lives with his wife, Lynn, in a century-old farm house in a land of slow clouds and endless fields

Publication History

"The Blameless" is published here for the first time.

"Word Doll" was first published in *The Doll Collection*, 2015.

"The Angel Seems" was first published in *Dark Faith, Invocations*, 2012.

"Mount Chary Galore" was first published in *Fearful Symmetries*, 2014.

"A Natural History of Autumn" was first published in *The Magazine of Fantasy & Science Fiction*, July/August 2012.

"Blood Drive" was first published in *After*, 2013.

"A Terror" was first published on Tor.com, July 2013.

"Rocket Ship to Hell" was first published on Tor.com, 2013.

"The Fairy Enterprise" was first published in *Queen Victoria's Book of Spells*, 2013.

"The Last Triangle" was first published in *Supernatural Noir*, 2011.

"Spirits of Salt: A Tale of the Coral Heart" was first published in *Fearsome Journeys*, 2013.

"The Thyme Fiend" was first published on Tor.com, 2015.

"The Prelate's Commission" was first published in *Subterranean Magazine*, 2014.